Praise for *New York Times* Bestselling Author

SAMANTHA YOUNG

"This is a really sexy book and I loved the heroine's journey to find herself and grow strong. Highly recommend this one."

—USAToday.com

"Will knock your socks off . . . [an] unforgettable love story."

—*RT Book Reviews*

"Humor, heartbreak, drama, and passion."   —The Reading Cafe

"Truly enjoyable . . . a really satisfying love story."   —Dear Author

"[Samantha Young's] enchanting couples and delicious romances make her books an autobuy."   —Smexy Books

"Hot, bittersweet, intense . . . sensual, with witty banter, angst, heartbreaking moments, and a love story you cannot help but embrace."   —Caffeinated Book Reviewer

"Filled with heart, passion, intensity, conflict, and emotion."

—Literary Cravings

"[Young] is a goddess when it comes to writing hot scenes."

—Once Upon a Twilight

"Ms. Young dives deep into the psyche of what makes a person tick emotionally . . . [The] one thing you can count on from Ms. Young is some of the best, steamy, sexual chemistry."   —Fiction Vixen

"Smart and sexy, Young writes stories that stay with you long after you flip that last page."   —Under the Covers

"Charismatic characters, witty dialogue, blazing-hot sex scenes, and real-life issues make this book an easy one to devour. Samantha Young is not an author you should miss out on!"   —Fresh Fiction

Every Little Thing

The Hart's Boardwalk Series

SAMANTHA YOUNG

BERKLEY SENSATION
New York

BERKLEY SENSATION
Published by Berkley
An imprint of Penguin Random House LLC
375 Hudson Street, New York, New York 10014

BERKLEY and BERKLEY SENSATION are registered trademarks and the B colophon
is a trademark of Penguin Random House LLC.

Library of Congress Cataloging-in-Publication Data

Names: Young, Samantha, author.
Title: Every little thing / Samantha Young.
Description: First edition. l New York : Berkley Sensation, 2017. l
Series: Hart's Boardwalk ; 2
Identifiers: LCCN 2016041980 (print) l LCCN 2016044735 (ebook) l
ISBN 9781101991695 (softcover) l ISBN 9781101991701
Subjects: LCSH: Man-woman relationships—Fiction. l
BISAC: FICTION / Romance / Contemporary. l FICTION / Contemporary Women. l
FICTION / Romance / General. l GSAFD: Love stories.
Classification: LCC PR6125.O943 E94 2017 (print) l LCC PR6125.O943 (ebook) l
DDC 823/.92—dc23
LC record available at https://lccn.loc.gov/2016041980

First Edition: March 2017

Printed in the United States of America
1   3   5   7   9   10   8   6   4   2

Beach at sunset © Alberto Biscaro/Masterfile/Corbis
Cover design by Alana Colucci
Book design by Laura K. Corless

For my nephew Mason.

I was writing this book when you were born,
so this one is for you.
But when you're older don't read past this dedication . . .
because that would be weird for me.
I love you.

ACKNOWLEDGMENTS

My mum was the first person to read a draft of book one in the Hart's Boardwalk series and the first thing she said after reading it was, "Are Bailey and Vaughn getting a story? Are you writing it now? When can I read it?"

I knew from the moment I introduced Bailey and Vaughn on the page that their story would be next, and I want to thank you, Mum, for making me confident in my instincts, but mostly for your honesty and for loving my books . . . even though you're Stephen King's number one fan. Not exactly my target audience. It means a lot to me that you are genuinely swept up in my worlds.

Like every writer I get writer's block but it usually passes within a few days. Just as I was starting to write EVERY LITTLE THING I got hit by the worst case of writer's block I've ever had. It lasted *weeks*. Perhaps it was because I turned thirty years old during the writing of it, who knows! All I know is that it took my friends, my family, my agent, and the two very insistent voices of Bailey and Vaughn to pull me through it. A massive thanks to the aforementioned non-fictional people for your unwavering support while I was a frantic, frustrated artist.

On that note, as always, a massive thank-you to my agent, Lauren Abramo, who provides me with a never-ending well of support and advice; and is an exceptional brainstorming partner.

As is my wonderful editor at Berkley, Kerry Donovan. Thank you for working so hard on this book with me, Kerry. It truly is the best possible version of itself because of your amazing insight. You get me! I love being part of your team.

Moreover, thank you to the fantastic team at Berkley, including my publicist, Jessica Brock; and the art team for creating another stunning cover for this series.

A huge thank-you to my UK team at Piatkus, including my editor Anna Boatman, for all their support and enthusiasm for the series. It is so appreciated! And thank you, too, to the art team, for the beautiful cover for the UK edition.

Finally, the biggest thank-you of all:

To you, my reader.

ONE

||||||||||||||||||||||||||||||||||||||||||||||||

Vaughn

The early morning was dull, the waves a little rougher, a little more hurried than usual as they rushed the shore, and gulls flew above in a sky that matched the water perfectly in its melancholic gray.

Behind the floor-to-ceiling glass of his penthouse suite Vaughn stared out from his boardwalk hotel at the scene and thought how it wasn't whole without his other senses in play. The boardwalk below, the beach, the ocean, it all seemed but a moving picture. The reality of it was in the caws of the gulls he couldn't hear behind his expensive triple glazing. The reality of it was in the smells beyond the window—the salt air, the hot dogs, burgers, and the warm sweetness of cotton candy.

That's what made his boardwalk feel like home.

Home.

Hmm.

He'd come to Hartwell to escape the ugliness he'd left behind in Manhattan. Hartwell was peaceful. Although it had thousands of tourists pouring in every summer, and there was always some kind of festival or celebration going on, there was a tranquility here that crowds of people couldn't diminish.

Vaughn had needed that serenity. The plan was to soak up all that peace until the time came for him to go back to the center of his business operations in New York.

Somewhere along the way, Hartwell changed from a refuge to home.

Home is where the heart is.

His gaze wandered back outside to the stillness of the boardwalk, and to his utter frustration his heart jumped in his chest at a glimpse of bright auburn hair. He leaned forward to get a better look.

Sure enough.

It was her.

Bailey.

She strode down the boardwalk from the direction of her own establishment, Hart's Inn, her long hair blowing in the wind. Vaughn pressed closer to the glass, trying to get a better look, but it was impossible from this height.

All he could make out were the jeans she wore tucked into brown ankle boots and the green sweater that was far too thin to be worn this early in the morning.

He frowned. The woman needed to buy a goddamn jacket.

She smiled and he caught sight of her neighbor Iris approaching her. For a moment he envied Iris that smile. It was hard to resist Bailey Hartwell's smile. It had an effect on people.

On him.

Unfortunately.

Especially since he couldn't recall a time when that smile had ever been directed at him.

Bailey followed Iris out of his line of sight.

He tried to follow them and smacked his head off the glass. "Fuck." Vaughn rubbed at his forehead and turned away from the window.

His eyes were drawn to the huge bed across the room where a slender redhead whose name he couldn't remember was lying sleeping.

One immediate problem was that he saw Bailey everywhere.

He even saw her in other women despite his best efforts to channel his attention elsewhere.

Ignoring the growing ache of longing in his chest, a half-dressed Vaughn took the white shirt that had been pressed and hung up for him off the hanger and shrugged it on. Then he chose a blue silk tie from his collection. His waistcoat and jacket followed suit. Dressed for the day, he strolled over to the bed and leaned down to nudge the redhead awake. She groaned and opened her eyes and instead of clear green eyes that made his blood burn, brown ones stared up at him.

"Time to leave." He walked away without looking back.

TWO

|||||||||||||||||||||||||||||||||||||||||||

Bailey

I was on a mission.

A mission to cross the distance that suddenly stretched between my boyfriend Tom and me. Ten years we'd been dating. It was safe to conclude that we'd hit a rough patch.

But when your guy pushed you off him in bed because he was too tired to have sex then there was a problem.

I aimed to fix that problem.

First I yelled at him a lot and called him an asshole, because, seriously, *asshole* move.

Then I calmed down and I started to think. To plan. To fix the situation.

With sexy lingerie and a raincoat.

First I needed the sexy lingerie. I had a few pieces of hot under-wear in my closet but Tom had seen them. I wanted to dazzle him with something new.

Sherry's Trousseau just off Main Street was an expensive little boutique but none of the other stores or the mall near Dover sold anything as nice as Sherry's. The only issue with buying lingerie in a small town, however, was the fact that anyone in the store, includ-ing Sherry, knew I was planning on getting lucky sometime soon, and had no qualms bringing up the subject like they had a right to the details of my sex life.

"Tom will have a lot of fun taking those off." Sherry rang up the red silk bra, panties, matching garters, and sheer silk stockings. I had a pair of red stilettos I planned on wearing with them.

"Yeah," I said. "Here's hoping he'll explode all over me with excitement."

I grinned to myself as I left the store, savoring Sherry's blushing mortification.

Apparently it was okay for her to discuss my man touching my lingerie but not okay for me to discuss the consequences of such an act. Oh well. She should have been used to my inappropriate responses by now. It's how I survived small-town life. I said what I was thinking, no filter, and I beat nosy busybodies at their own game by divulging too much information.

It was fun.

I glanced back toward the shop to see if she was sharing her shock over what I'd said with Ellen Luther, the only other customer in the shop at that moment, and—

"Oof!" Pain shot up my jaw as I collided with something hard that knocked me off balance. The movement caused the paper bag with my lingerie in it to swing, and the thin handle snapped with the force, sending my new purchases scattering all over the pavement.

I stared down at it in surprise as my jaw throbbed. And then I caught sight of the shoes at the edge of the scene.

Polished to a shine.

Black leather Derby shoes.

I'd bet everything I had they were Prada.

And there was only one man in Hartwell who wore designer like it was made especially for him.

My heart sank as I lifted my gaze.

Sure enough, staring down at my new underwear like he was staring at a lamppost, or something equally mundane, was Vaughn Tremaine.

Now my whole body thrummed along with the throb in my jaw where I'd collided with one of his broad shoulders. As always he wore a tailored three-piece suit that fit him beautifully.

I watched in horror as he unbuttoned his jacket and lowered to his haunches to pick up my underwear. If it had been anyone else reaching for those items I wouldn't have cared less. But Vaughn Tremaine wasn't just anyone.

With my new bra dangling in his clutches he looked up and quirked an eyebrow my way.

Not for the first time I found myself squirming under his steel-gray gaze.

Silence stretched between us as we stared at one another and I fought the urge to abandon my stuff and run off in the opposite direction away from him. The problem was—well there were a number of problems with Vaughn Tremaine—the fact that a) he was much too attractive for his own good and b) unlike anyone else, he had the ability to make me feel insecure.

Right now, for instance, as much as I didn't want the thought in my head I couldn't help but note how unaffected he appeared at holding my sexy underwear in his hand.

I was as attractive as a limp noodle to him.

And it shouldn't bother me.

The man was a jerk.

"Looks like Tom is in for an interesting evening." Vaughn held the bra up toward me.

I snatched it from him, my cheeks blazing. Clearly karma was getting back at me for what I'd said to Sherry. As he reached for the panties and garter I snapped, "Leave it."

"But I'm already down here." He ignored my demand as he collected the broken bag and carefully placed the underwear back inside. As he stood up Vaughn handed me the bag.

In my angry embarrassment I leaned in to yank it from him, only to stumble as I did so. Vaughn moved to steady me, his strong fingers curling around my bicep. His touch panicked me and I jerked away, scowling at him.

Perhaps a year ago I wouldn't have scowled so hard at him.

I would have scowled for sure, but maybe not so emphatically.

Up until last summer our interactions had always been antagonistic because from the day we met Vaughn had made me feel I was
the uneducated provincial to his superior cosmopolitan self. He did
this by mocking me, mocking Tom, and I didn't like it. He was no
better than me.

Admittedly, however, there was a certain amount of fun in teasing and mocking him back. That is until last summer, when during
one of our many verbal battles he'd out and out said that he disliked
me in front of Jess and everyone else whose opinion I valued. And
okay, I might have deserved a harsh retaliation because I'd been
particularly bitchy to him that day because of an argument I'd had
with Tom . . . but . . . well . . .

The son of a bitch had hurt my feelings, and that was unfor-
giveable.

"As ever the gentleman, Tremaine."

"Helping you retrieve your belongings was gentlemanly, I
thought."

"No—the gentlemanly thing to do would have been to assess the
situation, realize that touching a lady's unmentionables is ungentle-
manly, ignore said unmentionables, and go merrily on your way
while I tried to inconspicuously recover the unmentionables."

The right corner of his mouth tilted up in amusement. "You've
never crossed me as the shy and retiring type, Miss Hartwell. I
wouldn't have thought my seeing your panties would get them in
such a twist."

"Ha, clever." I ignored him calling me Miss Hartwell. Or I
attempted to. I never wanted him to know how much it bugged me
that he never called me by my name. In retaliation I never referred
to him out loud as anything but Tremaine.

We really brought out the maturity in one another.

He grinned. "I do find I'm wittier around you."

"Yes, well, that happens when arming yourself in a battle of wits
against a wittier opponent."

There were moments, like now, when I thought I glimpsed a flash of respect in Vaughn's eyes. But I knew that couldn't be true. I was just looking for something I wanted to see. "We're particularly feisty today."

"Don't royal 'we' me, Tremaine. I'm not impressed by your pomposity. In fact it pisses me off."

He stepped closer into me, and I had to steel myself against stepping back. Vaughn Tremaine did not need to know his nearness made my breath catch. His eyes drifted over my face. He always did this, like he was savoring my every feature, and I knew his only purpose in doing so was to make me feel uncomfortable.

Mission accomplished.

Bastard.

"You shouldn't tell me when something pisses you off," Vaughn said. "You know it only makes me want to do it more."

If he'd been anyone else, I would have laughed in grudging respect. Instead, like always with him, I took it personally. Like I said, it didn't start out that way. Vaughn was smart. I think a large part of me actually enjoyed our battle of wits. But after he said he didn't like me, everything he said to me became an insult. Worse, at around the same time he admitted his dislike for me, I actually began to see more in him than just an arrogant, selfish businessman who thought himself superior to me.

Deep down I knew Vaughn wasn't a bad guy. I discovered that when he helped out my friends Cooper and Jessica last year. When Jess was convinced that things between her and Cooper were falling apart, Vaughn gave her a place to stay in town so that Cooper had time to win her back.

And the truth was we all felt safer with Vaughn around: there *was* the matter of Ian Devlin and his sons.

Devlin owned a lot of property in Hartwell, including the Hartwell Grand Hotel in town, and the amusement park behind the boardwalk. But he didn't own anything *on* the commercial north end of the boardwalk. And just as he'd used less than honorable means to gain properties on the popular, touristy Main Street, he'd tried underhand ways to gain property on the expensive coastline. He was desperate to add boardwalk property to his portfolio. In fact, I guessed he was desperate to one day own the entire length of the north boardwalk. He had it in his head to turn it into a five-star resort, which would decimate what made Hart's Boardwalk so charming.

When the old boardwalk hotel went up for sale, we, the close-knit community on the boardwalk, thought we were done for. Ian Devlin was the only man we knew who could afford to buy it.

But then came Vaughn. A hotelier with more money than God and a better pedigree than most Manhattanites. For whatever reason, he bought the old boardwalk hotel, knocked it down, and put up his own establishment.

The good thing though—despite the modern appeal of his hotel—was that Vaughn liked the boardwalk as it was. And even I had to admit that he seemed to genuinely like and respect Cooper. So when Devlin threatened Cooper's boardwalk bar by bribing someone on the city board to deny Cooper his liquor license renewal, Vaughn stepped up alongside us to put a stop to it.

And despite the fact that was the moment he told me he didn't like me, I saw what I hadn't wanted to see.

Vaughn Tremaine may have been a pompous, smug, wealthy, arrogant businessman who thought he was better than me, but he could also be kind of honorable when he wanted to be.

Moreover, he was our defense against Ian Devlin.

According to Cooper, Vaughn had said something that made Cooper feel confident that Vaughn would never let Devlin do anything to damage what we'd built on our boardwalk.

And Vaughn had the money and influence to back up that sentiment.

"What? Do I have something on my face?" Vaughn said.

I realized at that moment I'd just been staring into those startling gray eyes of his. No one had a right to eyes like those. He must have known what those eyes did to a woman.

To wom*en. Other* women. Not me.

"No." I stepped away from him, even if doing so did give him the upper hand.

"What? No sharp reply? You sure you're feeling alright?" He cocked his head to the side, studying me. A crease formed between his brows. "You do look a little tired."

I huffed, running a hand over my hair. I hated when he scrutinized my personal appearance. "Always so complimentary, Tremaine. It's a wonder you don't have a trail of panting ladies following after you. Oh, wait a second. It's not."

He just stared at me, which for some reason made me feel worse, because it felt like he could see right into me, and that he could see how unhappy I was and—

"No wonder you're single." I gave him a look that would have made a lesser man's balls jump back up inside him. "You're cold through and through. You haven't got anything real to offer a woman. Nothing but money. And sooner or later they'll realize not even money is worth a lifetime of nothing."

It was harsh.

It was horrible.

And it was all about me, not him.

Immediately I wanted to take the words back, but they were out there.

Me and my stupid no brain-to-mouth filter.

Like the ice I'd accused him of being, Vaughn's expression turned an arctic level of cool. "I'm single because I want to be, Miss Hartwell. Unlike you I'm strong enough to be alone rather than settle for mediocre. But then like attracts like, doesn't it."

And on that parting shot, a shot he had no idea hit dead center on target, Vaughn Tremaine sauntered away like he hadn't just had a bitter encounter with me.

I didn't touch him.

Ever.

But he always got me.

And it always hurt.

Bastard.

Pissed, I marched off in the opposite direction back to the inn, trying to will Vaughn's words out of my head, trying to shake off what he made me feel.

After all, I couldn't be angry and pissed when I showed up to "raincoat and sexy lingerie" Tom to get us back on the right track.

Vaughn

For not the first time, Vaughn fought the urge to turn back around, find Bailey, get on his knees in front of her, and beg her for forgiveness.

No one else pushed his buttons like Bailey Hartwell. He'd had people say worse things to him than Bailey did, although always in that passive aggressive, superficially polite manner he couldn't stand.

Yet, Bailey was the only person he ever lost his cool with. He retaliated. Lashed out like an immature teenager.

And he hurt her every time.

She wasn't like the women he'd grown up around. They had learned from a young age the art of masking one's emotions.

Bailey's emotions were out there for all to see.

For instance . . . he knew she was attracted to him. He also knew she hated that current of attraction because she may have been attracted to him but she didn't *like* him. Bailey hadn't liked him from the moment they'd met and that was partly why he lashed out at her, too.

But sometimes, like just then, he went too far.

He winced as the words he'd said to her reverberated around in his head. That resentful longing he felt whenever he was around her became a throbbing pang, an ache—an ugly ache of regret in his chest. Bailey Hartwell was anything but mediocre.

In truth, it had taken all of his willpower to will away his erection when that lingerie had tumbled out of her shopping bag. He'd stared up at her, imagining her in it, and the blood had shot straight to his dick.

In an effort to not get aroused in public he'd turned his thoughts to Tom Sutton and let his angry frustration take over. It was absurd that an idiot like Tom Sutton got to enjoy the honor, the unadulterated pleasure, of seeing Bailey in skimpy lingerie. It was a sin that he got to hold her at night, to walk by her side in the daytime, to be one of the people she cast her light over. So much light. He'd never met a woman like her. Every thought, every feeling she had she put out there—brave, upfront, outspoken. It was refreshing coming from a world where women rarely spoke their mind, where they played subtle games, to a world where someone like Bailey Hartwell existed.

And she cared so much.

Too much.

Sometimes he wanted her to stop caring so much because he was terrified she was going to get hurt beyond repair.

He'd heard about how much she had cared when Dahlia McGuire moved to Hartwell to run the gift store she'd bought from her great-aunt. There were rumors that Dahlia had taken herself for a midnight swim just after she'd moved to town and she'd almost drowned. Bailey apparently saved her life. They were best friends now.

And he'd witnessed firsthand how Bailey cared when Jessica Huntington came to Hartwell. Bailey had latched on to that woman from the moment they met, like she knew Jessica was harboring a secret, like she knew Jessica needed a friend. Bailey befriended her, no questions asked.

Vaughn had watched how Bailey cared about her town and the people in it—how she felt like he was a threat to all that and tried to make his life as difficult as possible until she realized he wasn't out to hurt her beloved town.

But she would have fought against him if he had been. Bailey, with her little inn, and nothing but friends to back her up.

She would have gone up against him. Vaughn with all his money and power.

No fear.

Just fire.

Fuck, he admired her fire.

And Tom Sutton didn't seem to realize he was in bed with fire. He had no clue he had something extraordinary in Bailey Hartwell.

She was loyal to the bone.

Vaughn admired all of that. He wanted all of that. He wanted her. He wanted her in his bed. Every night.

However, it wasn't just Bailey's dislike and the existence of her boyfriend that stood between him having her. It was partly his ability to hurt her. Like he'd hurt her only moments ago. But mostly it was his aversion to relationships. Vaughn had sworn off relationships entirely and not even Bailey Hartwell could change his mind when it was made up.

So yes, it was strange hating a man like Tom for having something he wanted, knowing that Tom didn't deserve Bailey, because as much as he hated the man, he was glad Tom existed.

There never would be a Vaughn and Bailey.

But that lingerie . . .

Tom needed Bailey to wear sexy lingerie to get turned on?

Yes. The lingerie was nice.

And picturing her in it was more than nice.

However, it was pointless to him. It covered what he wanted to see more than anything.

Bailey Hartwell. Naked. On his bed. Fire in her eyes but a submissive body. She was so fucking antagonistic and battle ready all the time . . . nothing turned him on more than the idea of winning a battle with her, of her letting him tie her to his bed—

"Fuck," he muttered, his skin feeling flushed with arousal.

He was getting turned on walking down the goddamn street.

Thankfully his cell vibrated inside his suit pocket, distracting him. He pulled it out and saw "Dad Calling" on the screen.

Grateful for the interruption to his wayward thoughts, Vaughn answered it.

"I thought you might have seen the news about Caroline in the paper," William Tremaine said without preamble.

"I did."

"Are you okay?"

This, right then, this call was one of the reasons he should go back to New York.

After his mother died of a heart condition she'd had from birth that no one knew about until it just gave out one day, Vaughn's dad had been there. He was only five when he lost his mother, and his father was a successful construction giant in New York. He didn't exactly have the time for a five-year-old son.

But he made time.

Yes, there were nannies, but Vaughn had never felt unwanted or unloved, and as he grew older he realized how rare that was in the rarified world he'd been born into. He had no doubt that his friends were loved but that love was often crushed under the weight of expectation that was thrust upon them.

William reared him to work hard, but he never pushed his own agenda on Vaughn. Not like his friends' parents. His father was his best friend. A man he admired and respected more than anyone else.

And he should go to New York for him.

He just couldn't make his feet move in that direction.

"I'm fine, Dad," Vaughn reassured him.

"I'm sure you are, just thought I'd check. You know . . . I was thinking I could stop in Delaware tomorrow. I have a business trip to London in a few days. I thought I'd make a pit stop."

Vaughn grinned. "I'm really okay."

"I'd like to see that for myself."

"Then you know you're more than welcome."

By the time he got off the phone, his brain was whirling with thoughts of his father's upcoming visit and his earlier encounter with Bailey Hartwell. He stopped in the middle of the street and realized he'd passed the sandwich shop he'd been on his way to, to pick up lunch.

The hurt in Bailey's eyes flashed before his own.

He should have let one of the hotel staff get the damn sandwich for him after all but no . . . he'd wanted a stroll.

He could promise himself that it was the last stroll he'd take for a while but he knew he'd go nuts if he stayed confined to the hotel while he was in town.

Moreover . . . as torturous as it was seeing Bailey, it was the sweet kind of torture he'd become addicted to.

THREE

‖‖

Bailey

There was something exciting, adventurous, and more than a little risqué about getting in my car wearing nothing but sexy underwear beneath a raincoat. I was positive if anyone saw me, they'd know what I was up to, and so I'd made a mad dash to my car, almost going over on my ankle in my red stilettos.

I'd laughed at myself as I pulled out of my driveway, and I'd giggled at the excited butterflies in my belly.

It felt good to be doing something out of the norm.

However, as I pulled up to Tom's apartment, the butterflies took on a different flutter. The excitement was tempered by the reminder of my partner pushing me away the night before.

I stared up at his place, saw the light burning in the window, and I froze for a moment before giving myself a pep talk.

"You're wearing a raincoat. And lingerie." There was no way a guy could turn that down.

Taking a deep breath, I let that knowledge revive my confidence and I got out of the car. That turned out to be the hardest part. As I let myself into the building with my key, I couldn't help but move quickly with anticipation. I bounced lightly up the stairs on my toes so the clacking of heels wouldn't alert him to my arrival.

I should have clacked.

I should have clacked like hell.

Perhaps if Tom had been alerted to my arrival, I wouldn't have had to witness his naked ass moving up and down as he thrust into the woman who was laid underneath him on the couch.

Shock froze me to the spot as I entered the open-plan apartment and tried to process the scene in the living space and what it meant.

They were facing away from me so they had no idea I was there, and Tom's body was blocking the woman so all I could see were her purple-polished fingernails clawing his ass in an attempt to pull him deeper inside her.

"Oh, God, yes," she panted in a high-pitched voice.

A voice I didn't recognize.

"Erin," he grunted. "Fuck."

Erin?

My gaze drifted over them, landing on Tom's feet. He was still wearing his socks and the soles were dirty. He was wearing dirty socks while he screwed someone named Erin on his couch.

I stared down at my raincoat, feeling foolish. Humiliated.

All this time I'd been worried about how to get our relationship on track and he was fucking someone else.

What an idiot.

My head snapped up on a surge of sudden fury, and I was surprised fire bolts didn't shoot at them from my eyes. *I* wasn't the idiot. *I* wasn't foolish! The fuckwad cheating on me was the goddamn idiot!

Ten *fucking* years!

Enraged, I slipped off my heels, letting my bare feet take me into the kitchen. I glanced over at the couch and noted they still were so busy getting it on that they hadn't noticed me. I yanked open the fridge and grabbed the jug of ice water he kept in there.

"What the—" Tom, alerted to the noise of the fridge door closing, looked up just as I made it to the couch. His eyes widened with horror as I upended the ice-cold water all over him and his fuck buddy.

Erin screamed as Tom cursed, jumping off of her like she was covered in fire ants.

While they scrambled off the couch in search of clothes and warmth, yelling the entire time, I spotted Erin's purse and marched over to it.

"Bailey, I can explain." Tom's voice was high with panic.

I glanced over at him as I rummaged through the stranger's purse. He was hurrying into his jeans, tripping over his feet, glancing from me to Erin with wild eyes.

As for Erin she was standing with a blanket I kept thrown over the couch, a blanket I curled up with when watching movies, wrapped around her. She was too busy looking shame-faced at her bare feet to realize I had her phone in my hand.

"Erin and I—"

"Are cheating scum!" I interrupted.

My voice brought Erin's head up and the blood that I didn't think could get any hotter in my veins hit boiling point. I recognized her after all. She was the girlfriend of one of Tom's colleagues, Rex McFarlane. His very likeable, handsome, twenty-four-year-old colleague. And Erin . . . Erin was twenty-three!

I'd been screwed over for a girl barely out of college.

Here I was, walking along thinking I could fix things, content with the idea of fixing things, my path clear and sunny with determination, when all of a sudden this giant brick wall of hate, disgust, disappointment, betrayal, hurt pride, and fury appeared out of nowhere and smashed right the fuck into me!

And I wanted Tom and his little Erin to feel everything I was feeling.

Rage was pretty much running my show.

Erin's phone didn't have a password to get into it. She might want to rethink that in the future.

"What are you doing?" Her high, girlish voice trembled.

I scrolled through her contact list.

REX.

I hit call.

"No, Tom, what is she doing?" Erin squealed.

The sound must have made the dog in the apartment below us wince but I didn't even flinch. I was too focused on destruction.

A deep masculine voice I recognized picked up after the third ring. "Hey, baby, you still at work?"

If I'd been thinking more clearly the affection in his voice would have stopped me from saying anything. But as I later realized, I wasn't running this show in my right mind. "Rex?"

"Who is this?" He sounded confused, his tone a little sharp, protective.

"This is Bailey Hartwell, Tom Sutton's girlfriend."

"Tom, stop her!" Erin cried.

"Bailey, for fuck's sake." Tom strode toward me, pleading with his dark eyes.

I whirled away from him and started walking around furniture out of his reach.

"Is that Erin I hear? What's going on?" Rex demanded.

"I just caught Tom fucking Erin on our couch. I'm guessing since Tom came home last night and showered before getting into bed and then shoved me off him when I tried to have sex with him that this isn't the first time Tom and Erin have been together."

"What?" His voice was hoarse, sounding far away.

"We got cheated on, Rex. Just thought you should know." I hung up and threw Erin's phone on the nearby chair.

She stood clinging to the throw, her shoulders shuddering as she sobbed.

Her obvious pain made me feel nothing.

Numbness had settled over me. I turned to stare at the man I'd spent ten years of my life with. "I thought we deserved each other. But I deserve better. I can't believe I wasted ten years on you. In case that wasn't clear enough: it's over, Tom."

I slipped the stilettos back on and strode out, shrugging off his hand as he tried to stop me, ignoring him as he hurried down the stairs at my back, his voice, his presence, like an annoying fly I'd gotten used to hovering over me.

Nothing he said penetrated my fog. I couldn't feel his touch or what I later remembered as his pleading, his apologies.

Instead I got in my car and pulled away so fast I almost clipped him, vaguely aware of him cursing and jumping out of my way as I drove off.

"I am going to kill that son of a bitch!" Jessica, my best friend, yelled, pacing back and forth in front of me in her living room. Louis the pup followed her every move, so now and then they tripped over one another mid-pacing.

I hadn't known where I was driving until I'd pulled up outside Jess and Cooper's place. Cooper was working at the bar but Jess was home.

Somehow I'd found the words to tell her what had just happened and her reaction broke through the numbness that had settled over me.

Nausea was the thing I was feeling most at the moment. Nausea caused by uncertainty, by fear, because suddenly—

"I'm thirty-four, Jess." I interrupted her pacing. She stopped to stare down at me, her eyes bright with hurt for me. My own eyes filled with tears. "How do I start over?"

"Oh, Bailey." She sat next to me on her couch, and wrapped her arm around me. Louis laid his chin on her knee and stared at me in what looked like doggy sympathy. "You'll find someone else. You just need to let your heart mend."

But that wasn't what I was afraid of. And I had to wonder if the anger I'd felt in Tom's apartment was only for him and Erin, or if a big part of it was directed at myself.

"I knew, Jess," I whispered, letting my tears fall, knowing she was the one person who wouldn't judge me for what I was about to confess. "I've known for a while."

"That Tom was cheating?"

"No, not that." I shook my head. "I knew . . . I knew he wasn't the one." I stared up at her, her face a blur through my tears. "I thought he was a safe bet. I chose him because I thought he was a safe bet. And it turns out he wasn't even that."

Jess was quiet awhile, holding me as I cried.

And then, "I don't think I understand."

Wiping at my tears, I pulled away and let out a shuddering sigh. "I should be heartbroken. Grief-stricken. Right?"

She nodded.

"But I'm not. I'm hurt. My pride is hurt considering I'm currently wearing red silk lingerie and a raincoat." I gave her a wry, sad smile that she returned. "And I'm mortified. Humiliated even. But heartbroken . . . no. I'm—" I sucked in a breath, like I'd just been skewered in the stomach.

"You're what?"

"Relieved," I admitted. "Terrified but relieved. Oh, God." I rested my head in my hands, looking down at the stilettos pinching my feet.

I slipped them off. "Ten years. God, ten years I've wasted on a man I knew I would never be madly in love with. I just wanted . . . I wanted a man who made me feel safe and Tom gave me that when we met. I was happy just to feel safe with him, to know that he would give me the things I wanted: marriage and kids. When my parents moved away, leaving me the last remaining Hartwell in town, I'd missed them so much that I'd felt this overwhelming need to start my own family. Tom knew about it. He knew how much kids, *family*, meant to me. I thought he loved me enough to eventually get around to making me happy. But he couldn't give me that, and I'd held on, giving him my best years, and the piece of shit cheated on me.

"How do I start over at thirty-four?" I could feel the panic rising, my breath hitching as I struggled to draw in air.

Jess grabbed my hands. "Deep breaths, Bailey." She inhaled and exhaled, gesturing at me to mimic her.

I nearly broke her fingers I squeezed them so hard as I forced through my panic to mimic her, concentrating on my breathing.

After a while I felt muscles I didn't even know had tensed relax. Slumping against her couch, I let more tears fall. "I'm scared."

Tears glistened in Jess's eyes. "I know. I've been there. But starting over can be done, no matter what age you are." She reached for my hand. "You have me, and you have Cooper and everybody. This town loves you, Bailey. We'll get you through this."

"What if I end up alone?"

"Not possible." She frowned at me. "You're not considering taking that asshole back just so you won't be alone?"

"No," I bit out. "You know, he pushed me away last night. I tried to make love to him and he pushed me away. Of course he was cheating on me! What an idiot I was for not seeing it." I laughed humorlessly. "I was so convinced he knew we couldn't do better than each other that it never crossed my mind he'd cheat."

"What do you mean 'knew we couldn't do better than each other'?" Jess crossed her arms over her chest.

I tensed again. I didn't want to admit to Jess my theory of how Tom and I made sense because of our mutual averageness. "I just mean . . . we were equals, you know."

Her eyes narrowed, like she didn't believe me. "For your information every single one of your friends thinks you deserve better than Tom Sutton and the fact that he cheated on you makes him Asshole of the Year. No, scratch that: Ultimate Asshole of the Year."

Swallowing back a smile I nodded. "Definitely Ultimate Asshole of the Year."

Jess harrumphed.

"Jess."

"Yeah?"

"You know I love you, right?"

In answer she squeezed my hands. "We'll get you through this, Bailey. And you know what? Today, tomorrow feels terrifying. But I'll bet everything I own that tomorrow, this fresh start will feel exciting."

"I hope so."

She shimmied closer to me on the couch and wrapped her arm around me again.

"Oh, God." I broke our moment of quiet as guilt and horror filled me. "Oh, God, Jess. What I did to Rex?" I looked at her, tears falling again, these ones a product of shame. "That was awful. Horrible. I'm a selfish bitch."

"Don't call yourself that. You weren't thinking clearly. And you know what, you did the guy a favor if you ask me. He needed to know his girlfriend was cheating on him."

"But not like that. I forced him into the humiliation with me. I'll have to apologize."

"Apologize if you want. Not tonight, though, okay? Tonight you'll stay here and watch stupid movies and eat junk food with me."

"No, I don't want to be a bother."

"I won't even acknowledge that comment." She got to her feet. "I'll go get you something to change into."

I gave my friend a tremulous, grateful smile. As soon as she disappeared upstairs, Louis bounding up after her and taking his comforting doggy sympathy with him, I started to cry again, harder this time. Starting tomorrow I had to begin the awful task of telling everyone close to me that Tom and I were over. I'd have to call my mom and dad, my brother, Charlie . . . I'd have to tell Dahlia and Emery. Iris and Ira.

Oh, God, the speculation.

The pity.

And Vaughn Tremaine.

It would be harder to fight his mockery of my life. I'd just have to remind myself that even though I'd lost certainty of what was to come, I hadn't lost my beloved boardwalk or the people connected to it that made up my family. They still made my life extraordinary and Tom's disloyalty or Vaughn's opinion of his disloyalty was not going to change that. I wouldn't let it.

It was easier to think that than feel it, I realized, as the fear gripped me tight. I wrapped my arms around myself and cried harder, letting the hard lump that had tightened my throat loosen with my sobs.

Not too long later I felt Jess's familiar arms surround me and she moved me closer, resting my head on her shoulder. I curled into her, muffling my sobs in her sweater as Louis nuzzled my hand in another gesture of puppy solace.

FOUR

Bailey

Around four thirty in the morning I woke up on Jess and Coop's couch and found myself wide awake unable to return to sleep.

Only a few hours ago I'd woken, confused, staring at the back of their couch, wondering where I was. It wasn't until I heard Louis's low bark and Cooper's voice that I remembered sitting watching movies with Jess. I must have fallen asleep and she'd left me on the couch rather than wake me.

"Yeah, I can see Bailey is on our couch, but I'm asking why?" I'd heard Cooper's hushed voice and the concern in his tone. "Down, Louis."

"She found Tom screwing another woman," Jess whispered back, her own voice filled with a mixture of anger, hurt, and worry.

"What?" Cooper yelled.

Louis gave another low bark.

"Shh! Both of you."

"What?" he whisper-shouted, fury evident in that one word.

I had lain tense. Once upon a time when I was a naive kid I'd crushed hard on Cooper and chased the heck out of him. As I grew older Coop somehow morphed into a big brother, a great friend. He was also incredibly protective.

"I'll fucking kill him."

I had heard the door open and was about to sit up to stop him when Jess had said, "No, you won't." The door had closed. "Bailey doesn't need that. She just needs us to be there for her."

"I'm pretty sure putting my fist through that asshole's face counts as being there for her."

Affection for Coop had filled me, sparking fresh tears.

"Maybe so," Jess had whispered. "But let's postpone that. Come upstairs so we don't wake Bailey."

Cooper hadn't spoken after that. Instead I heard the creak of the stairs as they and Louis climbed them. Exhaustion had taken me and the next thing I knew I was awake and my watch said it was four thirty. As I lay there I thought about the events of two nights ago that had led me to showing up at Tom's apartment in that stupid red lingerie.

Confusion.

That's what I had mostly been feeling as I lay in bed on my side, staring at the wall in the dark that night. I'd been confused because I didn't understand why I pretended to sleep as I'd listened to Tom enter my house, rummage around in the kitchen for fifteen minutes, before coming down the hall to my room to use the shower. I'd pretended even as he'd gotten into bed with me.

We didn't share a home. I lived in my little one-bedroom house and Tom had his own apartment. Not by my choice. For years the fact that Tom refused to commit to buying a place together had pissed me off. And yet that night as I'd pretended to sleep as he got into bed, I'd wondered why the hell he hadn't just gone home. What was the point in coming to me on a night he'd worked so late?

And then I'd wondered why the hell I hadn't turned around and kissed him hello. How many times over the years, especially these last few, had he waited up for me because of the long hours I worked at the inn?

I'd turned onto my other side, leaned on my elbow, rested my head in the palm of my hand, and I'd stared at my sleeping boyfriend.

An unfamiliar tight, horrible melancholy had gripped my chest.

Because confusion *wasn't* what I'd been feeling most.

It had been fear.

Perhaps it sounds strange but I'd always liked the feeling of missing people. It's not the actual missing them part. That part is horrible, of course. But the part when you get to see them again after a separation . . . that's the part I love. Because in that moment all the messy, complicated emotions we feel for an individual are burned, turning the bitter fragments to ashes, leaving only the sweetness: the love. All I feel in a reunion is the sweet longing of loving them, and the joy of having them in my arms again.

I liked missing my parents—my parents who sold their holdings in the town our ancestors founded, everything but Hart's Inn, which they left to me and my siblings. My brother, who had no use for the inn, my brother, whom I loved missing. My sister, who also had no use for the inn, my sister, whom I liked missing until I spent five minutes in her company.

However . . . I hadn't liked missing Tom. The horrible part of missing someone? That's all I'd felt when I'd looked at him.

I'd studied his face as he slept, remembering the contentment I'd felt once upon a time when I lay watching him sleep back when we were first starting out. If I were honest with myself, Tom had never made me feel giddy or nervously excited with uncontrollable butterflies. That's what attracted me to him. I felt safe with him. I felt in control of my emotions.

Lately I didn't feel that way.

I was thirty-four years old. I wanted to be married. I wanted babies.

And the man I'd spent ten years with, the man I thought I'd have all those things with had lain next to me . . . and he may as well have been eight thousand miles away.

Five years ago I would have reached across the distance between us and woken him up with my lovemaking. Tom said that was one of the things he loved most about me—my impulse control. Or lack thereof. I said and did whatever I wanted. Everyone around me knew whatever I was feeling in any given moment. He always said it was a miracle I was so good at my job as an innkeeper. But my mother had trained me in hospitality from the moment I could talk and I became a different person at the inn. I was professional, controlled.

In fact I think maybe I was so mouthy outside of work because I had to be the Disney version of myself *at* work—congenial, cheery, good-natured—no matter what shit a guest was giving me.

Tom wasn't always a big fan of my lack of brain-to-mouth filter, but typical guy that he was, he was a big fan of my free spirit and confidence in the bedroom.

What he didn't know was that I was only like that with him.

When we met *I* had felt average. Before I met Tom someone had stomped on me so badly I felt stupid for thinking I might be a little extraordinary. I'd grown up as a descendant of the town's founding family, people liked me, I was popular. I felt special. That guy took that away from me. However, he'd never been able to take away how much I loved my life in Hartwell. He may have made *me* feel average, but I still felt like my life on the boardwalk was extraordinary because I lived in a beautiful place surrounded by a community of people I loved.

And as long as life around me was extraordinary it was okay feeling average with Tom. We were equals. We were good enough for each other.

So I had no hang-ups in life or in our bed.

I could reach for him anytime I wanted and know that he would reach back. Or so I'd thought.

Sex between us had always been good. It wasn't the best I'd ever had but it was good. Tom seemed happy. Or I'd thought so anyway. I was more adventurous than he was so it could have been better, but it was good. It was good enough.

Lately it became nonexistent.

For the last two years I'd been working my ass off at the inn because my manager left, and I hadn't replaced him yet. In what I felt was part retaliation, Tom had started working long hours.

We barely spoke, let alone had sex.

Studying his familiar face, a face almost as familiar as my own, that horrible longing had clawed at me. My hand had slid further down his stomach as I'd moved into him, pushing the duvet off him as I'd pushed my fears aside. He'd mumbled and shifted in his sleep as I'd slid over him until I straddled him. Eyes following my fingertips as they trailed lightly over his skin, I'd let the ten years between us build my courage. His body had changed as had mine. He'd been athletically wiry when we'd first met. Now there was softness to his chest and torso when there hadn't been before. But I didn't care. That softness was a part of him growing older with me.

There were the scars on his lower belly from his appendectomy four years ago. I'd rushed him to the hospital for that. A little one at the top ridge of his belly button, another little one near his left lower pelvis, and a bigger vertical one under his belly button. They were faded now, but I could still trace them with my fingers and remember how worried I'd been about him as I waited for him to get out of surgery.

Tom had shifted under my weight and I'd felt him grow semi-hard beneath me. Tingles of anticipation had flared to life between my legs and I'd leaned over to pepper kisses over his belly. Just as my boobs no longer sat as perky as they did ten years ago, Tom's stomach wasn't flat and rock-hard anymore. It didn't matter to me, like I hoped my no longer twenty-four-year-old boobs didn't matter to him.

Huh.

What a joke, I thought.

But two nights ago I'd believed that he didn't care about that stuff. So I'd pushed my confusion and fear further away, and my lips had trailed up his body to his neck as my fingernails had dragged gently down his stomach.

He'd groaned and shifted again.

"Tom," I'd whispered in his ear before nibbling on his lobe. He'd tasted clean and fresh all over from his shower.

"Mm, Bails?" he'd groaned and I'd lifted my head to watch as his eyes flickered open. He'd stared at me with sleepy confusion. I'd known when he'd stopped feeling disoriented because his eyes had narrowed and his whole body had tensed under me.

An ugly feeling had tightened in my stomach.

"What are you doing?" he'd grumbled.

I'd smiled through my fear. "What do you think I'm doing?"

He'd rubbed his eyes and lifted his head off the pillow to stare at the alarm clock. "Shit, Bailey, I have to get up in four hours." He'd clamped his hands on my hips and shoved me off him.

I'd fallen on my side, staring at him in shock.

"Go back to sleep." He'd turned on his side, giving me his back.

Hot tears had flooded my eyes.

He had done what I'd feared.

I'd reached for him and he hadn't reached back.

Worse . . . he'd pushed me away.

Anger had flooded me. "Fuck you!" I'd thrown myself out of bed.

"Bailey," he'd groaned.

I hadn't looked at him. Like a hurricane I'd blown through the bedroom, hauling clean underwear out of the dresser, grabbing my jeans off my chair, rummaging through my closet for a clean shirt.

"Bails, I'm sorry, okay. I'm just tired. Come back to bed."

I'd heard his voice getting closer but I was already downstairs and out of the house.

My hands had shaken as I'd reached for my car door.

But Tom was faster than I thought because it had been slammed shut again and he was there standing next to me, half-naked in his boxers and bare feet. Under the light of the street lamps I'd seen remorse in his dark eyes.

"I'm sorry, babe." His hands had gripped my biceps tight. "What I did was shitty. I was half-asleep. I'm a grumpy asshole."

I'd fought the urge to cry. Tom had never made me cry and I wasn't about to start letting him make me cry now. "You *are* an asshole."

"I'm an asshole," he'd repeated. "Now will you come back to bed?"

"You can't just say you're an asshole and think that makes it okay."

"I know," he'd whispered. "But I don't want to argue about it out here in the middle of the night where we might wake up your neighbors."

I'd wanted to scream, "Fuck the neighbors!" Instead I'd nodded reluctantly and followed him inside.

He'd tried to lead me by the hand but I hadn't wanted him to touch me.

Even back in bed, when he'd spooned me and rested his chin on my shoulder, I'd stared at my wall, listening to his breathing change, feeling his body relax before his snoring kicked in.

Anger had filled me, mingling with fear.

Not just because Tom had pushed me away . . . but because . . . of how it had made me feel.

I should have been burning with hurt. Deep, anguished hurt.

Any normal woman whose lover pushed her away would feel deep, anguished hurt.

Mostly my pride had been hurt.

Mostly I felt pissed off.

And that's how I felt now, lying on Jess and Cooper's couch. I'd known that night that Tom and I were over. I just didn't want to believe that I'd spent ten important years with a man who wasn't right for me.

The fear, that fear of starting over crept upon me again, and my chest tightened in panic. Sucking in a lungful of air I sat up. Even though it was only four forty-five in the morning, I decided I might as well get on with my day. I left a note for Jess and Coop, promising them I'd see them later and thanking Jess for being there for me. And then I got in my car and drove home.

Although I was awake I also felt like I had a hangover even though I hadn't had any alcohol. I felt that empty nausea/hunger in my belly, the faded energy in my limbs; something I hated since on normal days I found myself blessed with a boundless amount of energy.

I wasn't in the mood to deal with anyone today, but no matter what, I had a business to run. My intention was to go home, shower, eat, and get to the inn.

It was not my intention to have to deal with Tom.

Unrealistically, I had expected him to just slink away and accept my pronouncement that we were over. But his car was parked in my driveway and since he had a key I knew he was waiting inside my small house for me.

That made me angry on many levels, but mostly because I'd made my mind up—no matter how scary it was—that I was starting over without Tom Sutton in my life. Right away. Immediately. Which meant I wanted him gone immediately. I didn't want him in my small house, taking up too much room, touching my things.

Yet, I knew that was unrealistic. I had to get out of my car and deal with him.

I felt that horrible nausea rise up toward my chest and took in a shuddering breath.

My front door led straight into my sitting room. Tom sat on my corner sofa, chalk white, dark circles under his eyes. He stared at me, pained, haggard.

It soothed my pride that hurting me at least caused him pain.

"You'll need to give me back my key," I said.

His gaze turned pleading. "Babe, please, let's not do anything rash."

The fact that he thought I could forgive him for his disloyalty renewed my anger. After ten years he didn't know me well enough to know that I considered loyalty of the utmost importance in any relationship?

"Speaking of 'rash' . . ." I put my hands on my hips, glaring at him. "I'm guessing I'll need to be tested for STDs since you were fucking someone else while you were fucking me because I know last night wasn't just one mistake and that you've probably been fucking her for a while and how many others were you fucking?" I rambled, something I tended to do when I was either excited or enraged.

I also didn't think I'd ever used the word "fucking" so many times in one sentence. But I think I could be forgiven on this occasion.

Tom stared at me wide-eyed. "It *was* a mistake."

That didn't answer my question. "Having an affair with a twenty-two-year-old. Yes, definitely a mistake."

"She's twenty-three."

"Oh, that makes it all okay then!" I yelled, wondering if he'd hit his head on the way over here.

Tom flinched. "I'm sorry, babe. But please believe me when I say it was a mistake. It was stupid. I don't even know what we were thinking. She loves Rex. I love you. It was so stupid!"

"How many times have you made this stupid, stupid mistake?"

His expression turned wary at my dry question.

"It had definitely happened two nights ago when you pushed me away, right?"

Guilt flooded his eyes.

And in that moment I hated him. I never thought I could feel that toward Tom but I hated him for doing that to me. For being able to do that to me. I could never hurt someone like that. No matter how attracted to someone else I was, I could never betray someone. I didn't have it in me.

And I hated him for his cavalier treatment of my affection and loyalty.

"Get out," I said, exhausted. Done. "Just get out. I don't want you anymore."

"Ten years, Bailey." Tom strode toward me and I stood my ground this time, frozen as he clutched my hands and squeezed. "You're not going to throw away ten years."

I stared at him in disbelief. "*I* didn't. *You* did."

"It was a *mistake*."

I wrenched my hands from his grip. "If I hear that one more time! It wasn't a mistake, Tom. A mistake is a onetime error. This was calculated. This was disloyalty. And I just can't look at you the same way." I shook my head and admitted, "And it's not just your fault. It was mine, too. For sticking it out this long, for giving you the best years of my life, waiting for you to commit, stuck in limbo with you . . . when the truth is I knew all along we weren't right for each other."

"I don't believe that."

I scoffed.

"Bails, you're right, I admit it. I've found it scary to commit but I'm more scared of losing you. I'll do it all. I promise. A house. Marriage. Kids."

"Why?"

"Because I love you."

"Why?"

"What do you mean why?"

"Why do you love me?"

"Because . . ." He stared at me confused. "I do."

I stared at him, saddened by his response. "Do you know why I loved you, Tom?" He winced at my use of past tense. "Because you made me feel safe. I don't feel safe anymore."

Anguish filled Tom's expression. "Bailey," he whispered.

I strode to the door and opened it. "I'll send you your stuff. I'd appreciate it if you returned the favor."

For a moment I thought he wasn't going to move, he stood and stared at me so long. However, to my relief, he walked over to me, pulled my key out of his pocket, and lifted my hand to place the key into my palm. He curled my fingers around it and then lifted my fist to his mouth. I let him place a kiss on my knuckles, tears of disappointment and regret pooling in my eyes.

"You deserved better." The words were thick with emotion. "I'm sorry."

It was only when the door had closed behind him and I'd heard his car pull out of my drive that I let myself cry.

The sobs that racked my body surprised me. The grief surprised me. In all the thoughts and fears and hurts that had whirled inside me since last night, it never occurred to me that in ending my relationship with Tom, in wanting to be done with him so I could start over, I would ultimately be losing one of my oldest friends.

Vaughn

Vaughn knew what he was going to look like when he was sixty-one years old because everyone told him he was his father's spitting image. From his dark hair to his steel-gray eyes to his height and physique.

William Vaughn Tremaine was still a powerful and well-respected man. Age hadn't changed that—in fact the amount of people who respected him had only increased over the years. And he was still a good-looking son of a bitch to boot. He stood, staring out of the window in Vaughn's penthouse suite, his hands in the pockets of his dark blue suit.

When the construction on Paradise Sands had completed, William had stood in that exact spot and said, "I can see why you chose this place."

Now he turned to Vaughn, eyes smiling. "I bet that view doesn't get old."

"No, it does not."

"Is that why you're living in a penthouse suite rather than in the house you bought down the coast?"

"It's more convenient to stay at the hotel." Vaughn shrugged.

His father narrowed his eyes on him. "Or you just don't like being alone in that big house."

There was no point answering since his dad was right. Like always.

"You know how I cured my loneliness? I got a lady friend."

Vaughn grinned at his dad's choice of words. "How does Diane feel about being referred to as your 'lady friend' after twelve years together?"

William shot him a look. "At my age it's inappropriate to call her my girlfriend."

Laughing, he nodded. "I suppose so. What about at *her* age?"

"She's fifteen years younger than me. That's nothing."

"I know, Dad. But it doesn't explain why you're referring to her as your lady friend instead of say . . . your wife?" It wasn't the first time he'd questioned why his dad hadn't married Diane already. Vaughn liked her. She was widowed at thirty-four, had no children, and while many of her peers spent their days volunteering on boards for charities, Diane was passionate about her charity work. She was kind and she was unpretentious. And Vaughn knew his dad loved her. But anytime he mentioned marriage, William closed up and changed the subject.

To his surprise, his dad turned to face him, looking somewhat sad. "I had a wife. She's gone."

Pain hit Vaughn in the chest. "Dad . . ."

"Diane had a husband and he's gone. We care about each other. We do. But neither of us can replace what we've lost and we don't want to. My wife is dead. I'll never have that back. So Diane is my companion and we're both happy to continue on in that way."

Surprised by his father's sudden openness, he treaded carefully. "People marry again, Dad. It doesn't take away what you had with my mother."

"But it will never be the same. With anyone. I know other people marry again all the time. However, that is not going to work for me. Your mother was the love of my life."

Emotion choked Vaughn and he looked down at the glass of water in his hand, hiding it from his father.

"I'm not built to love someone else the way I loved her," his dad continued. "And I suspect my son will take after me in that respect, too. But that Dunaway girl—" The hardness in his voice brought Vaughn's head up, steel meeting steel as their eyes locked. "You didn't love her, Vaughn. And I need you to stop acting like your soul mate died and get on with your life."

A sudden surge of defensiveness burned the lump of emotion in his throat to ashes and he shot up to his feet. Having his father towering over him, admonishing him, made him feel all of ten years old again. "I'm not acting like that."

"Then why are you going through women like they're going out of fashion? And why are you staying at your hotel in Delaware of all places? Last time I checked my successful son owns hotels all over the world. Of all the places he owns a hotel he chooses Delaware to set up home?"

He rolled his eyes at the sarcasm in his father's voice. "One, before that Dunaway girl, as you refer to her, I was never into monogamy. I experimented with commitment, the experiment failed, and now I've returned to what works for me. Two, I'm making sure this hotel gets off the ground. I stayed at all my hotels when they first opened."

"For about six months to a year. You've been living here for three years. You're hiding out here."

"I'm not hiding out here." He ran a frustrated hand through his hair. "Really, Dad, you came to see me to attack me?"

"I'm not attacking you. I'm concerned for you."

"And I'm telling you there is no need to be concerned." He pulled his suit jacket off the chair he'd draped it over and shrugged into it.

"Where are you going?"

"*We* are going out. For drinks."

William raised an eyebrow. "It's a little early, don't you think?"

"Normally I'd say yes, but I want you to meet the proprietor of the bar next door. Cooper Lawson."

His father followed him out of the suite. "Is he a friend?"

Vaughn hesitated over the word. A year ago he might have used the word "acquaintance" instead but during the past few months he'd grown to trust Cooper. He'd confided in the man. "Yes, he's a friend."

"Then I look forward to meeting him."

iiiiiiiiiiiiiiiiiiiiiiiiiiiiiiii

Cooper's wasn't open yet, but the owner was used to Vaughn dropping by before opening for a drink when he needed a moment of peace from the chaos of his life. Between traveling from hotel to hotel, and managing them all from Hartwell, Vaughn didn't have time for many moments of peace. It was a luxury to have somewhere quiet to go to where no one could get at him, where no one knew where he was.

And sure enough as he waited outside the locked bar with his dad after rapping on the door, it swung open to reveal an unsurprised-to-see-him Cooper.

Cooper stood before them in jeans, boots, a T-shirt, and a red flannel shirt. He was the salt of the earth type—hardworking, unpretentious, and loyal. Most people in Hartwell admired and respected him, and Vaughn had no doubt that he was the kind of man William Tremaine would respect, too.

"This is my father, William. May we come in for a drink?"

Cooper stepped aside to let them pass. His dad stopped and held out his hand to the bar owner. "You can call me Liam."

Grinning, Cooper shook his hand. "Call me Cooper."

With his eyes drinking everything in about the place, his father relaxed, a soft smile playing around his mouth as he unbuttoned his suit jacket and slid onto a stool beside Vaughn at the bar.

Cooper walked behind the counter, eyeing them with amused speculation. "Anyone ever tell you, you two look exactly alike?"

"All the time." William grinned and clapped Vaughn on the shoulder. "I passed on good genes."

Vaughn caught Cooper's grin and grunted.

Laughing, William turned back to Cooper. "You've got a nice place here. Real nice. Reminds me of my local bar back home in Augusta."

"You're from Maine?"

"Yes. Born and raised and the family goes back a couple of

generations in Augusta. My dad was a postal worker from a long line of postal workers."

Cooper raised his eyebrows.

Vaughn was proud of what his father had accomplished. "Dad started with nothing. Put himself through college on scholarship, made smart investments, worked his ass off, and is now one of the biggest real estate and construction giants in New York."

"I knew the real estate giant part, but I just assumed you were a blue blood," Cooper said. "That's impressive."

Like always William Tremaine shrugged off the praise. "I worked hard and got some good breaks."

"Still impressive. I know how hard it is just to run a bar, never mind an empire."

"On that note, we'll have two scotch on the rocks," Vaughn said.

"Vaughn told me on the way over how you turned this place around," his dad said as Cooper got them their whiskey. "It's not easy to do. Bar and restaurant statistics for failure in the first years are grim."

"Like you said . . . it's all about hard work."

"And you have a wife? Kids?"

Cooper grinned, a full, smug, big grin. "Girlfriend."

William chuckled at his expression. "She must be something special."

Dr. Jessica Huntington was definitely something special. Cooper was a lucky man. Unlike Tom Sutton, Cooper knew it.

"She's the one," Cooper admitted with ease. Most men he knew back in Manhattan would never dream of sharing those kinds of feelings. His longtime friend Oliver Spence would balk at the entire concept of thinking of a woman as "the one." Oliver had been engaged more times than Vaughn could count and Vaughn suspected he'd cheated on every single one of those women. No. Oliver and his crowd were unable to say shit like "she's the one." And Vaughn had to admit he admired Cooper for his ability to be so honest.

William scrutinized Cooper, and Vaughn could tell his father liked what he saw. "It's a rare thing to find. 'The one.' Hold on tight."

Cooper shot Vaughn a look, having heard the story of his mother's death during one of those times he'd trusted the man enough to confide elements of his personal life to him.

"Okay, I'm done listening to you two wax poetic." Vaughn took a sip of his scotch. "What else is new, Lawson?"

And just like that the grin was wiped off Cooper's face. "You'll hear it sooner or later . . . Tom cheated on Bailey. She walked in on them last night. Apparently, she wasn't quiet about confronting them at his place, so it'll be all over town by the end of the day."

Vaughn almost choked on his second sip of scotch. His body locked up on him, and despite the burn of the whiskey in his chest, he felt strangely cold all over.

"Say that again."

"That asshole cheated on Bailey with some twenty-three-year-old girlfriend of a colleague. She walked in on the two of them fucking on his goddamn couch last night."

His heart started to pound hard in his chest and he had to fight down the urge to get off his stool and hunt that asinine little prick down.

What kind of moron cheated on Bailey?

Bailey.

Christ.

She and Tom had been together a long time. How the hell would she cope? He didn't like the thought of Bailey falling apart. As strong and outspoken as she was Vaughn knew she hid her vulnerabilities.

Then a thought occurred to him and his blood turned hot. "She isn't going to stay with the idiot, is she?"

The idea that she might stick with Tom ignited a need to throw his glass of scotch at something or someone. And yet at the same time he wanted Cooper to say, "Yes. They're going to work through it." He hated the thought of Bailey giving the bastard another shot because she had to know she deserved better than that, but at the same time he hated the idea that Tom Sutton no longer existed as a barrier between "Vaughn and Bailey."

"Vaughn and Bailey" would only lead to a hurt Bailey and a fucking messed-up Vaughn.

"No. This is Bailey we're talking about. That woman practically invented the concept of loyalty. She's finished with him. I say good riddance."

Relief and fear mingled as he looked at the ice melting in his glass. "Is . . . How is Bailey coping?"

He could feel his father's curious eyes on his face.

"She'll be fine. The girls will take care of her."

"And you?"

Cooper frowned at him. "What?"

"You'll take care of her, too?" It would ease his mind to know Cooper had her back. "In case Tom gives her any problems."

As always the bar owner saw too much, and he gave Vaughn a knowing smile. "Sure thing, Tremaine." And then . . . "I guess Jess was right after all. Not that I'll tell her that. Damn woman thinks she's right about everything."

"What are you talking about?"

Cooper laughed and walked down the bar to clean up an imaginary spillage.

Vaughn stared after him, in that moment wishing he'd never let his guard down with the man or his too-smart-for-her-own-good doctor girlfriend.

"So . . ." his father drawled at his side. "Who's Bailey?"

"I find it strange that you don't want to tell me anything about this woman," William said as they walked out of Cooper's twenty minutes later.

If his father had been pestering him about any other woman he would have laughed. It was like he was fifteen all over again. His dad had walked in on him getting to second base with Jillian Grace, a girl in the class above him at their prep school, and he'd amused himself by peppering Vaughn with annoying and embarrassing questions all night.

"There's not a lot to tell." Vaughn tried not to sound exasperated. "And I thought you might want a coffee to wash down the scotch."

"Yes, it was a bit early for that." William buttoned his suit jacket as he followed Vaughn toward Emery's.

"This place does great cappuccinos. Be warned, the owner is very socially awkward," Vaughn said. "Beautiful woman. Independently wealthy. Atrocious at talking to men—crippled by inexplicable shyness. It's a shame."

"Because otherwise you would have added her to your repertoire of bedmates?"

He smirked, just to be annoying. "Probably."

"Obviously you've not had this Bailey Hartwell in your bed. I'm guessing by her name she's a member of the founding famil—wait a minute. Is this the woman that tried to postpone your plans for building the hotel?" William stopped just outside Emery's.

"Yes. When she saw the architect's drawings she campaigned with the new mayor to have the plans relooked at. But they'd already been passed by the planning council under the last mayor's purview so there was nothing they could do. Except stir up animosity from the locals. Which was fun for me." He remembered the trouble Bailey had caused. Once the hotel was up and time had passed, that animosity had waned, but no thanks to the mouthy redhead who fired up his blood beyond reasoning.

"I remember." William nodded. "She sounds spirited."

"That's not the word I would use," Vaughn muttered, pushing open the door to the coffeehouse.

He came to an abrupt halt at the sight of Bailey leaning across the counter, laughing with Emery.

One, he was surprised to see her. Two, he was surprised to see her laughing considering she'd just been betrayed by the man she loved.

His dad bumped into him. "Jesus, Vaughn, what—" His father peered past him to the two women at the counter. "Oh. Well, yes, those two are definitely stop-you-in-your-tracks-worthy."

Ignoring that comment Vaughn moved cautiously toward the counter. All of a sudden he didn't know how to act around Bailey. She straightened up at his approach, watching him with a narrowed green-gold gaze filled with the usual suspicion she felt toward him. There were dark circles under her eyes, but that was the only sign that something might be amiss. In fact she looked remarkably well for a woman whose ten-year relationship had just come to an end.

"Miss Hartwell. Miss Saunders."

Emery gave him a flustered half smile, half nod.

"This is my father, William Tremaine. Dad, this is Bailey Hartwell; she owns Hart's Inn at the end of the boards, and Emery Saunders owns this establishment."

His dad held out his hand first to Bailey and then Emery. Bailey raised an eyebrow (Vaughn assumed at his father's congeniality) but she shook his hand. Emery flushed bright red as she shook his father's hand and refused to meet his eyes as she murmured, "Hello."

William grinned harder at her shyness. "You have a lovely property, Miss Saunders." He glanced around at the feminine, cozy bookstore and coffeehouse. The coffeehouse and its shy owner had a way of making a man fully aware of his masculinity. Vaughn always felt too large, too alien in the pretty store. To some men, like Cooper who had expressed his discomfort around Emery, that was off-putting. Not to Vaughn, and he imagined not to some others. In a way both Emery and her place were altogether alluring in their utter femininity and mystery. If he were a different man who wasn't encumbered with a debilitating fear of commitment or an annoying infatuation with a certain redhead, Vaughn might have tried to draw Emery Saunders out of her shell.

And he had no doubt there were other men who would feel that compulsion. Vaughn just hoped when the time came it wasn't a man who would use her to get to the considerable wealth she'd inherited from her grandmother—information that was for now only known among the trusted community of the owners of boardwalk businesses. Unfortunately, it was also known by the Devlin family, which had researched Emery when she inherited the property on the boardwalk, property that was part of a number of investments her grandmother had made over the years.

Ian Devlin and his sons hadn't tried playing mind games or using underhand tactics in order to gain her property as they had done with Cooper and Bailey in the past. In fact Emery wasn't even aware the Devlins had looked into her when she took over the place. But Vaughn was aware, and he was keeping an eye on the situation.

Emery Saunders was vulnerable.

And he didn't like that she had no family watching her back.

"Thank you." Emery's quiet reply was a vast improvement considering it involved actual words, and Vaughn wondered if Bailey was partly responsible for helping Emery gain some social confidence.

William smiled at Bailey. "So, Miss Hartwell. I hear you're keeping my son on his toes while I'm not around to do it."

Bailey's eyes widened in surprise as Vaughn inwardly groaned.

"I don't know about keeping him on his toes but I certainly try to deflate his ego when I can." She smiled.

Bailey Hartwell had the most stunning smile of any woman he'd ever met. It was full and glamorous and completely spellbinding.

Vaughn felt a spike of envy toward his dad and shook his head in disbelief.

William laughed. "Glad to hear it. I saw your inn when I took a walk on the boards early this morning. It's beautiful."

One tiny compliment and Bailey blossomed, preening under the praise. "Thank you. That's very kind of you." Her eyes narrowed as she looked between father and son. "If you two didn't look so damn alike I would question the relation."

While his dad laughed, Vaughn squirmed, fighting the urge to respond in turn. He had to remember she was going through something traumatic and he had to be extra careful of her feelings.

Bailey seemed surprised by his lack of response. "Are you on your best behavior in front of your father or is something else going on?"

"Excuse me?" He feigned polite ignorance.

Her features tightened, her pretty lips pressing into thin, hard lines. When she did that it made him want to kiss them to soft and full again. He jerked his gaze from her mouth only to meet his father's stare. A stare that was bright with curiosity and speculation.

"Someone told you, didn't they? About my breakup with Tom. Was it Cooper? Well, he probably realized that it would be all over town by the end of the night anyway. So yes. I broke up with Tom because I found him in nothing but dirty socks, rutting with a twenty-three-year-old."

And that was just like Bailey to ignore social decorum and put the upsetting business of her breakup, and the circumstances of it, out there. Vaughn's dad was hiding a smile, apparently amused by her candidness.

Vaughn cleared his throat, not knowing whether to laugh, strangle her, or pull her into his arms. "I'm sorry to hear that."

Bailey raised an eyebrow as if to indicate, *Yeah, right.*

"Breakups are difficult," his dad said. "I'm sorry to hear you're going through that, Miss Hartwell."

Like most women who met William Tremaine, Bailey melted under the blast of his warm charisma. "Thank you. And please call me Bailey."

"Then call me Liam," he returned.

Kill me now, Vaughn thought. As much as he didn't want any kind of congenial relationship with Bailey he had to admit it stung more than a little that upon meeting him she took an instant dislike to him, but upon meeting his father she treated him with the same friendly warmth she did everyone else.

"Liam it is then."

"I hope you're doing okay," his dad continued.

Since Vaughn wanted to know the answer to that he didn't interrupt and demand two coffees to go from Emery like he probably should have.

"I am, thank you." She slumped against the counter. The seriousness of the new subject seemed to drain her. "The change is hard. We were together ten years. But . . . we weren't right for one another." She gave his dad a sad smile that Vaughn felt deep in his chest. "It's kind of a relief actually."

Not for the first time Vaughn marveled at Bailey's ability to wear her emotions on her sleeve for all to see. He admired and feared it.

He was also amazed by how calm she was about her breakup with Tom. There was no way she could really be that calm. Perhaps she was in denial. The hysterics would come later.

He winced thinking of what he'd gone through with Camille.

"It's still fresh. That relief will change to loss," he found himself saying. "You need to give yourself time to process it."

"Sure thing, Tremaine." She cheekily saluted him. "Of course you know how I'm feeling better than *I* do. You always know better than I do, right?"

His father stared at him in amusement.

He ignored them both. "Two grande cappuccinos to go, please, Emery."

Bailey sighed. "You're playing nice today, Tremaine. It's unsettling me."

Exasperated by her and knowing exactly how he wanted to take that exasperation out on her, Vaughn couldn't look at her for fear his father would see the lust pouring off of him. "I always play nice." He focused on the bestseller stand behind them, pretending to peruse it. "You just take everything I say the wrong way."

"Oh? And how should I take you calling me mediocre?"

Guilt tightened his throat at the tiny speck of hurt he heard buried beneath her dry question. The weight of his father's disapproval fell on him—he didn't even have to look at him to know William didn't like what he was hearing.

What was it about a parent's ability to make you feel like a child again even at thirty-six years old?

He forced himself to look Bailey in the eye. "I will remind you it was in retaliation to you calling me 'nothing.'"

Seemingly remorseful she gave him a taut nod. "You're right. And that was wrong of me."

"As was what I said. I shouldn't have. It was wrong and untrue."

Bailey was taken aback. "Apparently, Liam, you have the ability to make your son behave like a gentleman. That says good things about you."

Vaughn knew his dad well enough to read his expression. William was unsure and confused by the dynamic between Vaughn and Bailey. "I was under the impression my son always acts like the gentleman I raised him to be."

Vaughn shrugged, pretending to care much less than he did. "Sometimes I forget my manners. Especially when provoked."

"And he's back!" Bailey smirked at him, looking almost relieved. "I've had enough shocks for one week, Tremaine. Don't suddenly be nice to me. You almost gave me heart failure."

While his father laughed and talked with Bailey, Vaughn paid for the coffees and somehow managed to drag a reluctant William out of there. As soon as the door closed behind them, his dad said, "I like her a lot."

"Miss Saunders? Yes, she's sweet. And she makes a great coffee." He sipped at his cappuccino.

"You know fine well I'm talking about Bailey."

"Miss Hartwell? Really?"

"She's got fire. Your mother had fire like that."

Uncomfortable with the idea of his father approving of Bailey, Vaughn sought a subject change. "I was thinking of taking you to

Antonio's for lunch. We could eat at the hotel but I thought you might like something a little more down to earth. Iris and Ira own the place and the food is wonderful. The pizza is good. You like pizza."

He was almost rambling.

Shit.

"You like her," William said.

Vaughn didn't reply. He'd never been able to lie to his father. Instead they walked in silence until they came to the bandstand. His father stopped. The council had placed a plaque up on the boardwalk there years ago, telling the tale of Eliza Hartwell and Jonas Kellerman. It suggested that there was magic on Hart's Boardwalk, and that if you walked the boards with your true love beside you, you would stay in love together forever.

It was schmaltzy sentimental nonsense meant to charm the tourists.

"Interesting," his father murmured.

Of course William Tremaine, the world's biggest romantic, would find it interesting.

"It's ludicrous."

He raised an eyebrow at his son. "I don't know how you got so cynical."

"I don't know how you didn't."

"Perhaps because I was lucky enough to know your mother longer than you did."

That shut him up.

He stared out at the water. "I don't remember you being this sentimental."

"I think it's my age," William remarked as he stepped up beside him. "And the fact that you're getting older. I worry you'll end up alone. I don't like the idea of you being alone. And . . . there's a selfish part of me that would like a grandchild one day."

For the second time in the space of thirty minutes Vaughn felt guilt seize him. "I would do anything for you . . . but a grandchild isn't likely, Dad."

They were silent again for a while, and Vaughn was just beginning to hope the conversation was over when William said, "I didn't raise you to insult women. Did you really call Bailey 'mediocre'? Insulting *and* untrue."

"Regrettably I did. In my defense she insulted me first."

"That's not a defense."

"Dad—"

"She's got spunk, she's clearly intelligent and driven to be running that inn by herself, and strong to have retained her sense of humor the day after finding her boyfriend screwing a younger woman . . . and she's very attractive. Lovely eyes. And that smile . . . that's a great smile. Gets you right in the gut."

Vaughn huffed in amusement. "I wouldn't know. She's never smiled at me."

"Ah, well, you're doing something wrong."

He groaned. "Dad, I know you're worried about me, but I'm fine. I'm better than fine. And I'm living my life the way I want to live it. That means a parade of women through my bedroom. The Bailey Hartwells of the world are not for me, and sadly that means no grandkids for you. Can you please just accept that so we can enjoy the rest of your visit?"

"You know I've always tried to let you live your life your way."

"And it's one of the reasons I like you."

At that his dad gave a bark of laughter and slung his arm around Vaughn's shoulder. "Okay then. What do I get to see next?"

FIVE

Bailey

At times I wished I wasn't addicted to Emery's coffee. If I hadn't been, I wouldn't have bumped into Vaughn and his charming father, Liam Tremaine, today of all days. Then again as always my curiosity about Vaughn was piqued by meeting his father.

I usually grabbed a cup of Emery's coffee in the morning for Jessica and for myself, as I passed by her office on my way back to the inn. We both needed our coffee before we had to converse with too many people. Coffee made it easier for me to work in hospitality. Coffee made the memory of the horrible encounter with Tom this morning easier to handle and Emery's had slowly become one of my favorite hangout spots over these last few months. The hodgepodge of white-painted furniture and Tiffany lamps set against rich teal walls appealed to me. I liked cozy casualness and Emery did it in style. Not to mention I loved lazing a winter afternoon away by Emery's fireplace.

Before Jessica arrived in Hartwell last summer I didn't know Emery Saunders all that well. All I knew was that she was this ethereal young beauty with a bad case of shyness. Usually I was good at drawing people out of themselves but I think my somewhat brash style of doing so was too much for Emery. Jessica's soothing presence did wonders for the young woman and she'd managed to get Emery to open up. Well . . . open up to Jess, me, and our friend Dahlia.

She still couldn't put together more than a sentence around most strangers and men.

I'd grown fond of my coffee-giver and so I was more than a little curious about her. I had been since her arrival in Hartwell eight years ago. It was just that my curiosity had grown in proportion since becoming friends with her. We knew little of her life before Hartwell—she didn't talk about it and Jessica had urged me not to push Emery on the subject. So I hadn't.

All we knew was that she'd inherited her grandmother's company and that was probably how she had been able to afford to buy property on the boardwalk. We didn't know what kind of company it had been, or where she and this mysterious grandmother had hailed from. Nothing. Nada.

My friend could barely say two words to men but she seemed fascinated by my love life. And Jess and Cooper's love life.

I could understand her fascination with Jessica and Cooper. Since meeting last summer they had made this passionate, beautiful connection that even I envied.

They'd proven the legend of Hart's Boardwalk true.

The legend sprung from my family—the founding family. Back in 1909 my great-grandmother's sister, Eliza, was the darling of Hartwell. Our family had wealth and power and Eliza, being the eldest, was expected to marry well. Instead she somehow crossed paths and fell in love with a steelworker from the Straiton Railroad Company, based just outside of town. Jonas Kellerman was considered beneath Eliza and also a con artist. Her family tried to convince Eliza that he was only using her to gain her wealth.

But Eliza didn't believe her family and she and Jonas made plans to marry in secret. Her father, my great-great-grandfather, found out their plans and he threatened harm against the Kellermans if Eliza didn't marry the man he had chosen for her. To protect Jonas she agreed to marry the son of a wealthy Pennsylvania businessman. But, devastated, on the eve of her wedding Eliza snuck out and went to the beach late at night. She walked right into the ocean. By chance Jonas was up on the boardwalk with some friends, drowning his sorrows, when they saw Eliza. He rushed down to save her and his friends say they saw him reach her. But the ocean carried them away together and they were never seen again.

Over the years people have grown to believe in the legend that Jonas's sacrifice and the purity of their love created magic. Also because townies who fall in love on the boardwalk stay in love their whole lives. There's a spot on the boardwalk near the bandstand with a brass plaque for tourists about the legend. It says if they walk the boardwalk together, and they're truly in love, it will last forever. As for my great-great-grandfather, he made a few bad investments and lost a lot of his wealth. People believed the Hartwells were punished for what happened to Eliza.

When my parents decided to retire they sold what we had left of the Hartwell estate, with the exception of the inn. My father had run a small real estate and property management business while my mother and I ran the inn. They sold the property company to Ian Devlin. The inn they gave to my siblings and me. My brother, Charlie, was a financial advisor in Virginia, and my sister, Vanessa, was a restless, money-hungry little bird that flew around Europe chasing one rich man after the other.

Neither of them wanted to help me continue to run the inn so I considered Hart's Inn all mine.

I was possessive of it and of the boardwalk and the people in it. Admittedly that's why my antagonism with Vaughn came to fruition. I thought I was protecting everyone from him when he first arrived.

I knew my mistake but by now the tone of our acquaintance had already been set.

"I think I might have a crush on Tremaine's dad," I blurted, five seconds after the men had walked out of the door.

Emery laughed. "The term 'silver fox' was invented just for him."

"What happened there?" I threw my hands up in exasperation. "What do you mean?"

"Well there is no denying that he spawned Tremaine." Vaughn was an exact younger replica of his father. "But seriously? How did a man like Liam end up with a son like Vaughn?"

Amused, Emery crossed her arms over her chest. "It's not like you know his father. You spent ten minutes with him."

"And in that time I learned that he is way more down to earth and amiable than his son. You'd think he'd pass that kind of charm along to his only child."

"Vaughn is charming to me."

I tried to not let her words sting but in the end they did. "Of course he is. You come from money. You're one of his people."

"I don't think—"

"Maybe it's his mom," I mused, realizing I didn't know anything about Tremaine other than what everyone else knew—he was a hotelier from Manhattan and his father was the CEO of an international real estate and construction company. The secretive bastard wouldn't divulge anything else. And I was above Googling someone. Okay. I wasn't above Googling someone but I was above Googling a man who thought so little of me.

"Maybe what is his mom?"

"Maybe she's a cold fish."

Emery gave me a strange look. "Why are you speaking in present tense? Vaughn's mother died when he was very young."

Shock hit me right along with guilt for calling a dead woman a cold fish. "I didn't know that. God. That's horrible. How do you know that?" I tried not to feel peeved that Emery knew something about Vaughn that I didn't.

We weren't in high school after all.

Even though Vaughn made me feel like I was.

"My grandmother. She read the New York and Boston society pages religiously."

"Does everyone else know about his mom?" Or was I the only insensitive idiot who didn't?

"I don't know actually. Now that I think about it no one has ever mentioned it."

"What else do you know about him?"

"Not a lot. When my grandmother died so did the days of having to listen to her read the society pages to me. Grandmother died when Vaughn was in his early twenties and up until then he was always in the pages for being with a different woman at each event."

That wasn't a surprise, I thought, not at all bothered by the rumors that Vaughn had a different woman in his hotel suite every weekend.

Apparently, not much had changed. He was a player then and a player now.

He had to be charming to get all those women into bed. Of course, the fact that he looked like he did certainly helped, but women responded better to a combination of good looks *and* charm.

At least I did.

Not that I would respond to Vaughn if he did decide to turn the charm offense on me.

Still . . . it was a little hurtful that apparently I was the only one not worthy of seeing that side of him.

I narrowed my eyes in suspicion on my beautiful friend. "What do you mean he's charming to you?"

"I just mean he's always very congenial and polite to me."

"Do you like him?" I tried not to sound accusatory.

"In the way that you mean, no. He's a little too intimidating for my liking."

I studied her, my curiosity shifting from Vaughn back to Emery. "Anyone around here strike your fancy?"

Her pale cheeks flushed a pretty pink. "No one in particular. I'm not really looking . . . I mean . . . I'm not very good at talking to men."

No shit. I grinned and leaned across the counter. "Sweetie, men are easy. Just pretend to find everything they say fascinating."

"It's that simple?"

I eyed the tall, willowy blonde in front of me. "When a woman is as gorgeous as you, yes." A shallow truth, but a truth nonetheless.

Emery blushed harder. "Believe me, as soon as I try to talk to men they're desperate to get away."

I hid my wince because I knew she spoke the truth. Even Cooper had told me Emery's discomfort around him made him want to be anywhere else than in her presence.

"Man lessons," I decided. "Jess, Dahlia, and I will give you lessons."

"Man lessons?" Her blue eyes filled with trepidation.

I waved away her obvious concern. "Don't worry. We'll just teach you how to talk to them."

"I don't—"

"It's decided!" I backed away and turned on my heel before she could argue with me. "I'll organize it for this week sometime. Ta-ta!"

I grinned at my cheekiness as I wandered back out onto the boardwalk. I felt for Emery, I really did. I'd never been shy so I didn't know what it was like, but I could only imagine how it could cripple your social life. Emery Saunders was too sweet, kind, smart, and beautiful to have no social life. I was going to give her one even if the idea terrified her.

Tom had been pretty shy when I first met him but it was hard to be shy around someone like me. I remembered the way he'd blushed on our first date every time I said something inappropriate. He'd come a long way since then, making me laugh with his own dirty jokes.

I frowned.

He hadn't made me laugh last night.

Last night he'd made me cry. This morning he'd made me cry.

Melancholy washed over me suddenly and I began hurrying along the boards to my inn. To my solace. To the place I could just bury my feelings in work for now.

Two Weeks Later

The entire north end of Hartwell's mile-long boardwalk was considered prime commercial real estate. My inn sat at the top of the northern end and was a large version of a typical Hartwell home. It had white-painted shingle siding, a wraparound porch, blue-painted shutters on the windows, and a widow's walk at the top. It was one of the least architecturally commercial buildings on the boards, even down to my hand-painted sign in my well-manicured garden. A bright neon sign, like the ones so many of the buildings here had, would have clashed with my beautiful inn.

My best friend, Dahlia McGuire, owned the building next door, Hart's Gift Shop, a much smaller structure than the inn, but architecturally similar down to the white-painted shingles. It even had a porch, although not a wraparound.

Beside Dahlia's was a candy store, next to that an arcade, and from there the boards ran along the main thoroughfare. There was a large bandstand at the top of Main Street—our longest and widest avenue, with parking spaces in the middle to accommodate all the visitors to not only the beach and boardwalk but to the commercial buildings on the street. Trees lined Main Street, where restaurants, gift shops, clothing boutiques, retailers, fast-food joints, spas, coffeehouses, pubs, and markets were neighbors.

Back on the boardwalk were the ice cream shack, a surf shop, and then Antonio's, the Italian restaurant owned by an older couple, my good friends, Iris and Ira. Iris was currently frantic because the building next to hers, once a tourist gift store, was under renovation to be transformed into a restaurant by some fancy French chef currently living in Boston.

Just down from Antonio's was the largest building on the boards. A behemoth. Paradise Sands Hotel and Conference Center. There were no neon signs for that place, I'll tell you.

It was neighbor to the ever-so-popular bar Cooper's, and Cooper did have a neon sign because it was that kind of place. It *was* the boardwalk. And just down from Cooper's was Emery's Bookstore & Coffeehouse.

For the most part I enjoyed small-town life. I enjoyed my *place* in small-town life. People generally liked me, they saw me as an established pillar of society since I was the founder's descendant, and the majority of folks in my town were wonderful.

However, it wasn't the first time I'd had to suffer through the downside of small-town life. During the past two weeks I'd had to put up with people making trips to the inn to offer me their sympathy but also to try to find out for themselves if the rumor that I found Tom screwing a younger woman in his apartment was true. I almost called a town meeting at the bandstand to give them a step-by-step account of what happened just so the nosy bastards would leave me alone. However, Jessica talked me out of it.

It was hard enough getting over a breakup, and coming to terms with the realization that I was actually *okay* with the breakup, when there were a ton of people around to tell me I couldn't possibly be okay since I was a victim.

But I *was* okay! I was *not* a victim.

Only Jess and my boardwalk buddies seemed to believe me.

Iris had said, "You getting rid of him didn't surprise me. Just sorry it took you this long."

Thanks, Iris.

Emery *was* surprised but once I explained what had been going on she believed me when I said I was fine. Jess was glad I was moving on with my life in the hopes of meeting someone I deserved. Dahlia had always liked Tom but she was mad at him for cheating on me and understood why I didn't want to give him another shot.

How was *I* feeling other than okay?

Guilty. I felt guilty because I didn't feel as bad as I should. I missed my friend but I didn't miss my lover. And worse, I realized that things had become so complacent and distant between us that I'd actually been missing my friend for a really long time, so the missing him part wasn't as hard as I'd thought it would be.

In fact, I felt like this huge weight had been lifted off my shoulders.

Of course that weight had been replaced by the weight of crippling fear that I would end up alone, unmarried, and childless for the rest of my life.

"I'm considering online dating," I announced.

Cooper looked up from making two Long Island iced teas and a club soda but refrained from responding.

He left that to Jess and Dahlia, who had joined me for my first night out as a single woman. Unfortunately, we couldn't coax Emery to join us just yet but I was working on it. One day she'd be sitting that cute butt of hers on a stool next to me.

Jess shared a look with Cooper. "Well, if you think you're ready to start dating."

Dahlia grinned. "Of course she's ready. Internet dating is fun, FYI."

"That's not the whole story." Jess smirked. "You have told us some pretty hairy tales of your online dating life, Dahlia McGuire."

I chuckled as Dahlia shrugged, laughing. "Either you go out on a date and it's fun, or you go out on a date that is so epically horrifying it becomes an entertaining story to tell your friends. Either way it's a win-win."

I laughed along with them, but I was a little nervous about the whole thing. Not just because Dahlia really had been on dates worthy of episodes of *Sex and the City*, but because I hadn't dated in so long. Yeah, I was a pretty outgoing person and I had never suffered from shyness, but I was worried I was a little rusty.

Unlike Dahlia, I had no idea what the landscape was like out there now, and I didn't want to end up going through hundreds of men.

Dahlia didn't mind that aspect of it. In fact, she preferred it. If ever there was a woman who feared commitment more, I had yet to meet her. It surprised me because she was such a warm, protective, thoughtful, loving person. Any man would be lucky to have her, and I'd known men over the years who had tried and failed to pin her down, to make her theirs.

I didn't see any guy succeeding in the future, either.

Well maybe one particular guy, but that was a long shot.

Like Jessica when she arrived in Hartwell, I'd recognized the emptiness in Dahlia—the sad loneliness inside of her that I was amazed no one else seemed to see. I'd tried to befriend her in her first week as the owner of the gift store her great-aunt had once owned, but Dahlia had wanted nothing to do with me. Then one night I'd been putting out the trash and I saw her stumbling down the beach with a bottle of gin in her hand. To my horror I'd watched as she dove right into the water for a swim. By the time I got to her she was drowning, but I was trained in first aid and managed to resuscitate her.

That night after a trip to the emergency room she'd told me her story, and my heart had broken for her. I'd made a vow to help her start fresh in Hartwell. And she did. She'd stopped drinking, she started seeing a therapist, and she eventually started dating. However, she'd never been in a relationship and she didn't want one, to the despair of the men around us who drooled over her Marilyn Monroe figure, luscious thick dark hair, and gorgeous blue eyes.

What neither Jess nor Dahlia realized was how similar the pain they shared was. They hadn't told one another their stories yet, and it wasn't up to me to share. I was impatient for them to do so though, because I thought that maybe they could find solace in one another. A comfort that, try as I might, I was unable to give them.

"Where did you go?" Dahlia waved a hand in front of my face, yanking me from my musings. "You're not really worried about online dating, are you?"

"A little," I admitted. "I haven't dated in a while."

"Bailey." She gave a huff of laughter. "You are the most sociable, confident, outgoing woman I know. You'll be fine."

"I'll take you out," Ollie, one of Cooper's bar staff, called down the bar from where he was pouring a draft beer. He threw me a flirty smile, surprising the heck out of me. He'd worked for Cooper for a little over a year now and not once did he give the impression he found me attractive. Of course I was, more often than not, accompanied by Tom when I was in the bar.

"Excuse me?" I thought I'd misheard. Dahlia and Jess laughed beside me.

"You heard me." He grinned and winked at me. "I know how to show a girl a good time, Bailey."

If rumors were true then he wasn't lying. But I wasn't Dahlia looking for dinner and good sex. I was searching for the man I'd marry. "I have no doubt." I grinned because as much as I didn't want to have sex with Ollie, I was flattered he wanted to have sex with me. "However, I'm a *woman*, not a girl, and I'm looking for more than a tussle in the sheets. But thank you."

"Oh," he groaned, "that 'I'm a woman, not a girl' line just makes me want you more."

We laughed as Cooper rolled his eyes at his employee. "Then you'll just need to keep wanting," he called down to him and then nodded at a waiting customer. "Stick to pouring drinks for now, Casanova."

Ollie just laughed, winked at me, and returned to work.

I was smiling, my mood lifted by his flirtation, when I caught sight of Vaughn just a few stools down from us at the end of the bar. He was staring, expressionless, at Ollie. As if he felt my gaze, he flicked his to me.

It was a shock to see him in the bar. As far as I was aware he only ever went into Cooper's before opening.

"How long have you been sitting there?" I drew Jess and Dahlia's attention to him, too.

"Too long." He spoke to Cooper. "The usual, please."

"Surprised to see you here when the bar is actually open." Coop poured expensive scotch into a tumbler with ice. "Everything okay?"

I studied the two men, wondering how a friendship had developed between people who were so vastly different.

"It's been a long day."

Vaughn looked worn out and I almost felt sorry for him.

Almost.

"Coop, you going to let him sit in Old Archie's stool?" Hug, one of the regulars, shouted from across the bar.

I tensed, as did my friends.

Old Archie had been a regular at Cooper's for a long time. He was the most functional alcoholic I'd ever heard of, let alone met, but an alcoholic he was.

Until his partner, Anita, was diagnosed last year with cancer. Old Archie had pulled himself together to take care of her, and that included staying sober. Everyone was proud of him, and sorry for the hard journey he and Anita were currently sharing, and in reverence to that no one had sat in his stool since.

However, Vaughn, being unfamiliar with the tale of the stool, didn't know that.

Cooper glowered over at Hug. "My customers can sit wherever they please."

Vaughn looked over at Hug, too, saw the hostility in the big man's face, and calmly got up to sit one stool down, and closer to us. "Better?" he asked flatly.

"Whatever," Hug said.

Cooper continued to glare at the man, while he spoke to Vaughn. "You didn't have to move."

"I just want to drink in peace." Vaughn waved him off. "Not worth the hassle."

Cooper leaned into him and said something I couldn't hear. Whatever it was it made Vaughn smile. A real, honest-to-goodness smile. Not a smirk or a sneer. A smile. And it was boyish and mischievous, and it caused a great big flip low in my belly. A sensation that almost knocked me off my stool.

"He's a handsome son of a bitch, isn't he?" Dahlia murmured.

"Who? Cooper? Yes, Jess is a very lucky woman."

Jessica tutted. "Oh, you know who Dahlia meant."

"No. I don't." I refused to acknowledge who they were talking about or why they were talking about him. It was like they'd sensed my belly flip.

So Vaughn Tremaine was good-looking and he liked and respected Cooper, a man I thought of as family. That didn't erase the past three years of looking down his snotty nose at me.

"You are so full of it." Dahlia chuckled.

My lips parted in shock. *Seriously?* "How am I full of it?" I hissed, not wanting Vaughn to be aware of our conversation. "Are you trying to say I'm attracted to the wolf in Armani?"

"You are awfully hostile to him," Jess mused, taking a sip of her Long Island.

I glanced between my two friends, recognizing the devilish laughter in their eyes. "Stop trying to wind me up. Don't you know I'm in a delicate state right now?"

And as if the reference to our breakup conjured him, Tom walked into the bar.

A hush fell over the room.

This was another downside to living in a small town.

My ex visibly swallowed as he was bombarded with over two dozen glares. And then he paled when our eyes met across the bar. He gave me a taut nod and then marched across the room, ignoring Vaughn as he stood next to him at the counter. "I just came for that whiskey, Cooper."

I remembered then that Cooper had offered to get Tom a special-label whiskey for his grandfather's ninetieth birthday. Why on earth he thought it was smart to approach the bar during its busiest time I had no idea. Silly man.

Cooper shot me a look.

"It's okay," I said.

He nodded. "It's in my office. I'll be right back."

My gaze locked with Tom's. "How are you?" he asked.

"I'm good, thanks. How are you?"

"Getting there." His voice was a little hoarse on that last word and I noted how exhausted he seemed.

That sensation of guilt twisted in my chest. Tom didn't look like he was dealing well with the breakup. Not in comparison to me.

The silence was awkward and beyond uncomfortable as we waited for Cooper to return with the whiskey. When he did, Tom paid for it and thanked him, but he didn't move to leave.

Instead he stared at me as if he wanted to say something more.

I began to worry that he was going to do something that would make me have to embarrass him in public, and I'd hate that. Not for me, because I couldn't care less what people thought, but for him. I didn't want to humiliate Tom.

"Maybe you should leave. Now." Vaughn's tone was harsh and authoritative. Surprised, we all looked at the stern businessman. He continued to sip his scotch as if he hadn't said anything, but there was an air of something hard and threatening around him.

Tom seemed just as shocked by Vaughn's interference, but he took the warning and walked out of the bar.

There was a moment's continued silence and then the buzz of conversation started up again.

As for me I was staring at Vaughn like I'd never seen him before.

"Sticking up for me now, Tremaine?" I tried to bring some levity to the incident. "Will wonders never cease?"

I swore I saw amusement in his eyes. "It wasn't for your benefit, Miss Hartwell. The man reeks of bourbon. I just wanted him out of my vicinity."

"Bourbon?" Worry gripped me.

Vaughn gave me a mocking smirk. "Seems like the ex isn't dealing with your breakup nearly as well as you are."

"That's not funny," I snapped, concerned for Tom far more than I wanted to be. But as I'd discovered in the past, you couldn't just switch off caring about someone.

"I didn't say it was. I'm surprised you care . . . what with all the online dating you're planning on doing."

Forcing myself to ignore him, I opened my purse, pulled out some money, and slapped it on the counter.

"What are you doing?" Dahlia said.

"I'm going after him to make sure he's okay."

"Sweetie, that's not your job anymore." She was clearly unhappy with the idea. "That stopped being your job when he slept with someone else."

"Dahlia's right," Jess added.

"He reeks of alcohol," I insisted. "That's not okay. And I'm not the kind of person who'll just sit here and ignore that." I swung off my stool and strode through the bar, ignoring Vaughn's eyes following me, and ignoring my friends calling my name.

Vaughn

Vaughn stared at the door where Bailey had disappeared and cursed himself. Today had just been one bad decision after another. His quarterly stats were in and his hotel in New York was down in profits. Checking an online review site, he found disturbing guest reviews of the hotel. He'd blistered his management via video conferencing for over an hour, ending the meeting with a demand for monthly accounting and improvement upon the problems that were causing the bad reviews. If things didn't pick up, he'd have to go back to the city for a while to get it back to where it should be and the thought of returning to Manhattan for an extended period made his blood run cold.

And then he'd seen Bailey strolling arm in arm down the boardwalk with Dahlia and he'd surmised they were heading to Cooper's for drinks. Needing a drink himself he'd decided to follow them, refusing to acknowledge that he wanted to be near Bailey to check on her.

What he'd discovered was that Bailey Hartwell was stronger than he'd ever imagined, and that he'd made a mistake thinking she'd be anything like Camille. It only made him admire her more, and he was already unsettled enough by how much he admired the Princess of Hart's Boardwalk.

Then he'd gotten pissed overhearing her talk about being ready to date and watching as that stupid kid behind the bar flirted and drooled over her.

When Tom arrived Vaughn was already irritated and trying so very hard not to get off his stool and punch the stupidity out of the moron. Instead he'd pretty much threatened to do it and then he'd had to cover up the reason for it by telling Bailey about the smell of bourbon pouring off him.

And in doing so he'd not only been a bastard but he'd sent her running back to her ex.

Which should have pleased him.

Instead he wanted to kick the shit out of something.

It was aggravating how this woman could reduce him to acting like a hormonal, brooding teenager.

SIX

Bailey

Tom was making slow progress in front of me down the quiet board-walk, so I caught up with him just as he was passing Vaughn's hotel.

I'd tried calling out his name but he'd just ignored me, so when I finally caught up to him he pretended like I wasn't there.

A breeze blew up from the water and the scent of bourbon hit my nostrils.

Damn.

Vaughn hadn't been lying.

"Tom. Stop."

"Go home, Bailey. I wasn't thinking going in there tonight."

"I'm guessing because you're drunk."

"I'm not drunk. Do I sound drunk?"

He sounded quite in control, but he smelled like a distillery. It occurred to me he must have been drinking for a while to be in that kind of state.

"Despite what happened between us, I'm not going to ignore the fact that you stink of alcohol!"

That stopped him in his tracks and he whirled around to face me, his face contorted with pain. "Go back to Cooper's, Bailey. Let me be!"

"No. You're not okay, Tom."

"And what? You think you're the person to help?" he scoffed.

"Don't be a dick. Again."

At that he stumbled back against the boardwalk railing. He looked tired and mournful. "I got a suspension at work yesterday."

"What? Why?"

He gave me a wary look before he proceeded. "Rex stayed with Erin. They were going to try to work it out. Evidently he couldn't forgive her and they broke up. Yesterday he came into work and we got into a fight. A physical fight." He turned his face and that's when I saw the faint dark shadow of a bruise on his jaw. "I got suspended because . . ."

"You incited the fight by sleeping with your colleague's girl-friend?"

Tom winced. "Exactly."

"So you thought going on a bender would help?"

"My life is a mess, Bails," he snapped.

Suddenly I didn't feel so bad as I realized I was witnessing the self-pity of a man discovering actions had consequences. Instead of responding I stayed quiet, knowing that anything I said would be harsh and cutting.

Tom laughed because apparently my silence spoke volumes. "And I'm complaining to the woman I betrayed. Now I've really hit bottom."

I was unwilling to give energy or time to his self-pity. "How long is the suspension for?"

"Two weeks."

"That's nothing. In the grand scheme of things that's no time at all."

"It's not nothing! I've lost my credibility there. I've lost everyone's trust. I've lost you!"

My patience snapped. "What the hell did you think would hap-pen when you stuck your penis in someone else's vagina?"

A giggle behind me made my shoulders hunch up around my neck.

Great.

We had a witness.

My tension increased when I recognized the giggler. Dana Kellerman. Cooper's ex-wife. And she wasn't alone. Her arm was threaded through Stu Devlin's. Stu was Ian's eldest son and just like his father he was a pain in this town's ass.

I glowered at Dana, who was grinning at me, enjoying every minute of my distress. We had never liked one another mostly because I refused to kiss her ass like everyone else did just because she was so beautiful. Not that people kissed her ass anymore. She'd cheated on Cooper with Jack Devlin, the second youngest son. Worse still, Jack used to be the only Devlin I liked. We all thought he was a good guy. He'd grown up as Cooper's best friend, and I'd crushed on both of them when I was younger.

But one day Jack quit working construction and began working for his father when everyone knew that Jack couldn't stand his dad and his brothers. He'd only ever had time for his mother and little sister. No one could understand the decision, least of all Cooper.

And then Jack had gone and slept with Dana behind Cooper's back.

Cooper lost his wife and his best friend in one fell swoop.

Now it looked like Dana was moving on to another Devlin. That wouldn't make her very popular once word got out about it, but betraying Cooper hadn't made her very popular anyway, and this town had a long memory.

"Laughing out of solidarity, homewrecker?"

Dana narrowed her exotically tipped eyes on me.

Stu smirked at her side. All of the Devlin men were good-looking bastards, none more so than Jack. Stu wasn't as handsome as his little brother but he was tall with thick blond hair and a chiseled jaw. However, his dark eyes were empty and his well-formed lips had a cruel twist to them. "You're looking a little stressed there, Bailey. Anything I can do to help?"

"Sterilization," I quipped.

"Huh?"

"My point exactly. Good-bye." I wiggled my fingers at them, gesturing them to move along.

"Maybe you should think about moving your argument inside if you want privacy," Dana sneered.

"And maybe you should consider a vow of silence if you want people to find you attractive again."

Upon my last retort Devlin decided to lead Dana away, probably fearing we'd catfight and I'd do damage to her pretty face. And it wasn't like I wasn't tempted. I'd been tempted to scratch her eyes out since she destroyed Cooper's friendship with Jack.

Tom stared at me in affection mingled with sadness.

"Sterilization?" he said.

I grinned. "Yeah, I'm kind of proud of that one."

"God," he breathed out, like he was in pain, "I miss you, Bails."

"I miss you, too," I said. "But I only miss my *friend*. Maybe if you got yourself together . . . maybe one day I won't have to miss my friend."

Hurt flared in his eyes. "Your *friend*?"

I glanced down at my feet, unable to see that hurt gaze without feeling guilt. "Look, Tom, we both know what this town is like and you don't need their condemnation right now." I brought my focus back to his face, hoping I could help him somehow. "Go to Philly, see your grandfather and the rest of your family. Spend that two-week suspension getting your life together. If things are so bad at work, then maybe you should search for another job. Start over somewhere else."

"A new job would probably mean moving out of Hartwell."

"You don't know that yet, but if it does, maybe that's not such a bad thing."

"Bailey," he said, hurt again.

I felt awful hurting his feelings but I was trying to be realistic. To me being real with him was helping him, even if it didn't seem like it. I took his hands in mine and squeezed them. He gripped on tight. "The kindest thing I can say to you right now is please don't have hope that I'll change my mind about us. We'll never be together again. Friends one day I hope, but never more than that."

Tom huffed, and pulled his hands from mine, seeming winded by my words. "Cruel to be kind, huh?"

"My dad once told me that hope dies last of all and that it's so powerful it can save people. But he also said that hope is the mistress of limbo, and many a life has been wasted because of it. Sometimes hope hurts more than it helps. You and me, we're a case of some-times."

For a moment all he could do was stare at me, pained.

Finally, he gave me a small nod of understanding and walked away.

My chest ached for him, realizing that despite Tom cheating on me, I'd actually come out of the situation for the better while he struggled. I didn't want him to struggle, despite his betrayal.

I just wanted us both to move on.

Needing to rid myself of the ache weighing me down, I slipped off my heels and strode down off the boardwalk and onto the beach. My feet sank into the sand, the dry grains slipping over my toes until I hit the shoreline and it turned cold and squishy. I threw my purse and shoes behind me, away from the tide, and began to strip off, my clothes finding a spot with the purse and shoes.

In nothing but my underwear, I walked into the water, sucking in a harsh breath as the waves splashed around me like liquid ice. I kept going, used to the temperature from years of night swimming, and began to swim so that my muscles would warm me up.

I grew quickly accustomed to the cold water as I swam along the coastline, staying close to shore. I turned back after a while, near-ing my clothes again, and I stopped to float. Moonbeams danced on the top of the water around me. As I stared at the moon, I real-ized that like the hope holding Tom back, fear was holding me back.

I had to stop focusing on my age and what I didn't have, and focus on what I did have. I had boundless energy and great friends. And despite what I thought, I *did* have time.

The ache in my chest began to ease off.

Yes, I was determined now.

My only course was to move on and see where starting over would take me.

SEVEN

‖‖

Bailey

"Why am I getting a call to see if we've changed our minds about selling the inn?" my dad said without preamble.

It was the day after my tranquil midnight swim and decision to make a go at this whole starting-over business. In an attempt to do just that I'd decided to hell with my control freakery. If I wanted to start dating, I needed a personal life. And in order to have a personal life I needed to learn to trust someone to be my inn manager.

I was in my office, in the middle of posting the manager position ad online, when my dad called.

"What are you talking about? Did Ian Devlin call you? *I* own the inn."

"Along with your sister and brother. Something I reminded Ian."

I rolled my eyes. "Yeah. Sure. They're here every day to help out."

"You know what I mean. Technically they are also part owners with you. But that's beside the point. Devlin is concerned the inn is too much stress for you considering your recent breakup with Tom, and thought perhaps we, as good parents, were considering selling the place to ease your burden."

I heard sarcasm in my father's voice so I knew he hadn't bought that crock of crap. "Does that man have no shame? For your information, Dad, I am more than fine. In fact, I've decided to get a new manager. And not because I'm stressing over my breakup, but because if I want to move on, I need a personal life."

"I couldn't agree more!" I heard my mother shout in the background.

"Oh, by the way, you're on speakerphone."

"You know I hate it when you do that. I can't bitch about Mom when you do that."

"Funny," Mom said. "Does that mean you're considering dating?"

There was more than a hint of curiosity in the question so I gave a rather guarded, "Perhaps."

"Wonderful! Our neighbor, Kelly Hewitt, has a grandson in Dover. Can you believe that? How small is this world?"

"Oh yeah, it's small alright." I was not even surprised my mother had already lined up a date for me.

I thought I heard my father chuckle under his breath.

"His name is Hugh Hewitt. Isn't that adorable?" my mother continued.

"And he's still speaking to his parents?"

My father gave a bark of laughter.

"Oh, Bailey, hush. It's a perfectly musical name."

"That's a very diplomatic way to put it, Mom."

"Anyway, Hugh is forty years old, has a full head of hair, is an accountant, and recently divorced. I thought you'd have lots in common and I showed Kelly your picture and she thinks you're just so gorgeous. So we thought it might be nice if you two met. I can send you his Facebook profile link if you'd like so it's not a blind date. But I think he's very handsome. You needn't be concerned."

Ah, what the hell. "Sure, Mom. Send me the link."

"Now that you're done pushing Cherry into a date with an accountant who must spend most of his days fending off name-based mockery, can I talk to my daughter again?" Dad said.

I had to press my lips together to silence my laughter.

"And you wonder where she gets her smart mouth from," Mom said.

"Cherry, you there?" Dad ignored that comment.

"Right here, Dad."

"I thought your mother scared you off."

"Not yet. Give her time."

He laughed and then after a moment of silence . . . "Everything is okay back there? You don't need me to fly up to see you?"

I fiddled with the silver necklace Dahlia had made me. She designed jewelry and sold it in her gift shop. She'd made me a necklace with a silver cherry blossom tree pendant, because my dad's nickname for me was Cherry. I was kind of a daddy's girl, and I missed not seeing him every day. My parents visited every year for several weeks between Thanksgiving and Christmas, and they usually stayed a few weeks in May before the tourist season hit. They missed me and they missed Hartwell, but I knew they loved their life in Florida and hated flying. Visiting so soon after their last trip was kind but I didn't need them to do that for me. I hoped my dad heard my grateful smile in my words. "I'm really okay."

"And Ian Devlin? Has he been bothering you?"

No, but as I remembered the smug, calculating look in Stu Devlin's eyes last night I had to wonder if they'd decided to try to exploit me while I was vulnerable.

Except they'd underestimated me because I was far from vulnerable.

"Nope. And if they try, I can handle it."

My dad was stern. "You'll tell me if they try."

"Of course." Although I probably wouldn't because I really could handle myself.

"Okay. We'll let you get on. Talk soon."

"Bye, Dad. Love you."

"Love you, too, Cherry."

"Love you, sweetie!" my mom called, her voice sounding distant like she was in another room. "I'll send that link!"

I laughed. "Love you, Mom."

As soon as I hung up, the phone rang again. I sighed, wondering if I'd ever get that ad posted. "Good afternoon, Hart's Inn, Bailey speaking."

"Why is that bastard Devlin calling me about the inn?" My brother, Charlie, sounded aggravated.

I groaned and buried my head in my free hand.

The next day the clouds rolled over Hartwell and the rain descended in a deluge. Like Dahlia and Jessica, I'd risked my neck on the slippery boards to get to Emery's for lunch. She made the yummiest little sandwiches and canapés and we'd arranged the lunch last week. There was no way a little—okay, a lot of—rain was getting in our way of those canapés!

I moaned around a mouthful of one with crabmeat and shivered as the delicious heat from the roaring fire in her store warmed us. Emery had a reading nook next to the open fireplace where we were currently huddled.

She had decided to close the store for lunch, giving us guaranteed privacy to enjoy a girlie lunch break.

"I can't believe Devlin called your parents and brother." Jessica's hazel eyes darkened with concern. "It sounds like he's planning something. This is how it started when he was coming after Cooper."

As worried as she sounded, I wasn't. There was nothing Devlin could do to me but pester me with offers on the inn, and I could handle that. "It'll be fine. Emery, what are in these?"

"It's a secret." She grinned, knowing that would drive me crazy.

"You're lucky you're cute." I reached for another.

"Hey." Dahlia playfully smacked my hand away. "You've had more than your share of those."

"But I'm too skinny," I pouted. "I want a bigger ass and boobs."

Dahlia rolled her eyes, knowing I was joking. When I was younger my slender figure had bothered me a little, but the older I got the more I appreciated it. I had the kind of body most clothes looked good on, and I'd stopped worrying about my small boobs and ass a long time ago when I'd stopped worrying about my body in respect to what men found sexy.

Another reason to hate Vaughn Tremaine since he was the exception to my rule.

I hated that I cared about his opinion on anything, let alone my level of attractiveness.

Bastard.

"What's with the sudden scowl?" Dahlia pointed to my furrowed brow.

"Just thinking about Devlin and his never-ending need to be a pain in the ass," I lied.

"You should tell Vaughn," Jessica said.

"What?" I startled, wondering how she knew I'd been thinking about him. "Tell him what?"

"That Devlin is gearing up to bother you. Vaughn told Cooper that he wouldn't let Devlin cause trouble for us and I believe him. I know you have your issues with him, but this is bigger than that."

"I'm not telling Vaughn." I looked to Dahlia and Emery for backup but they were wearing *I agree with Jessica* expressions. "You're all crazy. Vaughn would rather see my place go under than do anything to help me." I knew that wasn't true but I wasn't asking that man for help.

"That's not true at all." Jessica sounded exasperated. "I wish you and he would just admit you're attracted to one another and stop acting like children at recess."

Shocked by her outburst I sat back in my seat and swallowed a bite of sandwich. "That was almost mean. And he's not attracted to me."

"Aha! But you're attracted to him?" Dahlia grinned with excitement at the prospect.

"What? No. What?"

"You just said '*he's not attracted to me*' when Jessica said you were attracted to one another. You made no mention of you not being attracted to him, just him not being attracted to you," Dahlia explained.

My heart started thudding hard against my chest. "But I meant that. That thing you just said. About us both. I am *not* attracted to Vaughn Tremaine."

"Methinks thou dost protest too much." Dahlia laughed.

"Methinks thou no longer deserves the last canapé." I swiped it from the plate, and grinned at her silent objection before I popped it into my mouth.

"I still think you should tell Vaughn," Jessica insisted.

"To have him laugh in my face? No thanks. Subject change!" I clapped my hands together. "Where will we start? Jessica and Cooper and wondering when he's going to get off his ass and get down on one knee, or Emery and man lessons?"

Emery shrank from me.

I almost felt bad.

Almost.

Dahlia wrinkled her nose. "Man lessons?"

"Yes—teaching Emery how to speak to men without wanting the ground to open up and swallow her whole."

"That *would* be nice, I suppose," Emery muttered.

"So lessons it is."

She blushed. "Maybe some other time."

"Bailey," Jess warned.

"Oh, come on." For once I ignored Jess. "You're among friends, Em. No one here wants to humiliate you. We just want to help. I don't want you to be alone forever. But if you do, then that's great, that's fine. I'll leave you alone to that decision because I just want you to be happy."

For a moment she looked from me to Dahlia to Jess and then back to me. Studying me, sensing my sincerity, Emery straightened her spine and threw back her shoulders. "Okay." She still seemed unsure despite her bold body language. "I don't want to be alone. Man lessons. But . . . not today. Later, okay?"

I grinned, happy and determined to help her. Jess and Dahlia shared a smile at my infectious excitement. "Later."

"Well," Jess mused. "If we're not doing any lessons . . . we could talk about the fact that Cooper proposed and we're planning to get married at the end of the summer."

This of course was met with a chorus of delighted shrieks.

Vaughn

"These figures aren't looking any better, Grant." Vaughn's voice was cold with disappointment as he spoke with Grant Foster, the manager at The Montgomery, Vaughn's boutique hotel in Greenwich Village. He'd named it after his mother, Lillian Montgomery. Unlike his father, Lillian *was* a blue blood; a descendant of Nicholas Montgomery, an Englishman who'd settled in New York and established himself as a huge player in the industrial revolution. The Montgomerys had their fingers in all sorts of pies, mostly in aeronautics and other transportation-shaped pies. As far as his dad told it Lillian was the darling of New York society and it had caused quite the scandal when she'd ignored her parents' wishes and married a nobody upstart from Augusta, Maine.

They disowned and disinherited her, and consequently Vaughn had nothing to do with that side of his family.

But his mother was a Montgomery and he was proud of who she was, no matter her family's attitude. He wasn't hiding from that side of his heritage, and naming his Manhattan hotel after them was a "fuck you" to his grandparents and a "love you" to his mother.

To see the monthly accounts in front of him showing further decreasing profits at that particular hotel burned more than it would with any of the others.

"Vaughn, I'm telling you it's the restaurant. The new chef just doesn't compare to Renata."

"This is the third chef we've hired since Renata moved on. Surely to Christ there is a cook out there just as good as or better than goddamn Renata."

"We just haven't found him or her yet."

"Then try harder. And Grant . . . Don't just blame it on the restaurant. The room occupancy rates are down, and the online reviews are not improving. There are complaints of inefficiency with the concierge service, rude customer service, dirty pillowcases, and unclean showers. What the hell is going on at my hotel? You have twenty-four hours to give me a detailed, concise report on the root of the problems or I'm flying out there. And if I have to fly out there to fix this, you can kiss your job good-bye, Grant." He slammed down his phone just as his secretary, Ailsa, popped her head around his door.

She winced at the sound of his phone crashing against his desk. "I'm sorry if this is a bad time, Mr. Tremaine, but Dr. Huntington is here to see you and insists that she has to see you now before her lunch break ends."

Vaughn closed his eyes as he rubbed at the throbbing pain between his eyes. What the hell could Jessica want? It wasn't like her to just show up. If it were anyone else, he'd tell Ailsa to say he was in a meeting.

"Send her in."

A few seconds later, Jessica strode in looking pretty as a picture in a silk blouse tucked into a figure-hugging navy pencil skirt. How good she looked, however, was overridden by the concern creasing her brow.

"Jessica, what brings you to the hotel?" He stood up and gestured to the seat opposite his desk. She took it as he leaned against his desk.

"I'm worried about Bailey."

Those four words made his heart rate pick up speed, but ever the consummate businessman he kept his expression bland. "How so?"

"I think Ian Devlin is gearing up to cause her trouble at the inn."

"And you think this why?" His tone belied the sudden heat in his blood. Every protective instinct inside of him wanted to demand

Jessica tell him what she knew so he could go straight to Devlin and
threaten to castrate him.

Jesus Christ. That damn redhead had turned him into a caveman.

"I just had lunch with Bailey. One of the Devlins caught her
arguing with Tom the other night and made comments about her
being stressed out. The next thing you know Bailey's dad and
brother both get calls from Ian Devlin asking if they were recon-
sidering selling in order to reduce Bailey's stress during the difficult
time of her breakup."

"You think they're going to come after her while she's vulnerable over the breakup?"

"Yes." Jessica cocked her head to the side in study of him. "Although,
just so you know, Bailey is doing fine. Better than fine. Breaking up
with Tom was the right thing to do and she knows it."

He ignored her pointed info-share. "But Devlin doesn't know
that."

Jess looked disappointed at his avoidance but repeated, "But
Devlin doesn't know that."

Processing this, Vaughn stood up and moved around to his side
of the desk. "Okay."

"What does 'okay' mean? Are you going to look into this?"

"There's not a lot to look into."

She glowered at him. "Don't play cool with me, Vaughn. Neither
of us wants Devlin bothering Bailey."

Sullen, he wondered how the hell the good doctor had worked
out he had feelings for Bailey Hartwell. He guarded his emotions
like they were precious stones. Yet somehow, somewhere he'd given
himself away in front of Jessica Huntington.

He didn't like it.

"Am I to take your intimidating silence to mean you'll look out
for her?"

"You don't trust Cooper to?"

"Cooper wouldn't let anything happen to Bailey. But he also

doesn't have the money, power, or influence to squash a bug like Devlin."

"Devlin hasn't done anything wrong yet. If he crosses the line, let me know."

Huffing, Jessica stood up to leave. She seemed to think better of it and glanced back at him. "You don't know how perfect you two are for each other. One ice, one fire, but both stubborn as hell."

He didn't respond to her rather poetic barb.

In answer she narrowed her eyes on him. "I also came here to say that Cooper and I want to get married at the end of the summer. On the boardwalk. You have the only establishment big enough to host a wedding reception."

"At the end of the summer? The conference center is almost booked out for the summer, and even if it wasn't, it's not enough time to prepare for a *wedding reception*."

She shrugged. "We don't want to drag our engagement out. I'm sure you could consider it a favor to Cooper." She smirked. "We both know you wouldn't do anything to harm that little bromance."

He rolled his eyes. Save him from these devious Hartwell women. "Good-bye, Dr. Huntington," he bit out.

"I'll take that as a yes. I'll speak to Ailsa about setting up a meeting with your events coordinator."

He watched her leave, an unwilling smile tugging at his lips.

Vaughn sat in silence for a while, knowing he should return to worrying about Grant's management skills. Instead he sat stewing over the idea of anyone trying to cause trouble for Bailey.

He knew of the rumors that Devlin used illegal means to further his success, but so far that's all they were. Rumors.

Vaughn had given Devlin space because there was no point in using his influence to bring down someone who wasn't causing any real trouble.

However . . . if Ian dared to go after Bailey and her inn, Vaughn *would* castrate him.

Metaphorically speaking . . .

Anger burned in his gut at the thought of Bailey losing what she loved, or worse, getting hurt in the crossfire of Devlin's single-minded aspirations.

Maybe physically, too.

EIGHT

Bailey

Watch over Jay Thursday because it's his first cover for Mona.

Remember to buy Twinings English Breakfast tea to put in the Yellow Room for the Goldmans' arrival on Friday.

Go to the bank to pay the electric bill. Joy.

Call Mom and tell her no way in hell am I going on a date with a guy whose Facebook cover photo is of two women mud wrestling.

Call the plumber about the gurgling noise coming from the shower in the Ocean View Suite.

Buy a pork loin for dinner with Jess, Coop, and family.

Ooh, and ask Mona to bake profiteroles, too.

Put the infamous red stilettos on eBay.

On that note, spring-clean my wardrobe to see if anything else can go on eBay.

I sighed, and rolled onto my side in bed.

It was almost impossible for me to drift immediately to sleep when I finally got myself into a bed. You'd think after the long hours I worked my exhaustion would pull me right under. Unfortunately, I had so many tasks and thoughts and worries whirring around in my brain on any given day that it took a while for my brain to shut down.

After another long day at the inn I'd crashed in the room I kept open at the back of the house. For the longest time I'd done my very best to drag myself home for Tom, but now I didn't have to worry about that and when I was tired it was nice that I could sleep at the inn. The small room had come in handy because like all the guest rooms it had its own bathroom, and when Jess was struggling last year I had let her stay there while she worked as my manager.

I reached over for my phone and groaned at the time. I'd thought I was being a good girl going to bed early at midnight. It was one o'clock now and I was still not asleep.

Come to me, goddess of sleep!

I huffed and kicked out the covers, flipping over onto my other side.

Just as I was drifting close to that heavenly oblivion of slumber I heard a creak down the hall from my room. Near my office.

I sat up and listened, wondering if one of my guests was wandering around. The click of my office door opening made my heart rate speed up.

None of my guests should be wandering into my office.

And shit, I needed to start locking it.

Out of nowhere, I was hit by the horrible feeling that the person who had opened my office door wasn't one of my guests.

The stairs in the inn were creaky. There was no way I wouldn't have heard someone coming down those.

The blood whooshed in my ears as my heart pounded against my chest. Grabbing my phone, I got out of bed as quietly as possible and tiptoed over to my door.

I winced at the slight snick of the handle turning and froze, waiting. When I was sure I hadn't been heard, I opened it, peering out into my dark hallway. There was a faint light coming from my office. A moving light.

A flashlight.

I felt sick at the violation of someone breaking into the inn.

But also extremely pissed off.

Tiptoeing down the hall, avoiding the all too familiar creaky spots in the floorboards, I got to the office and cautiously peeked my head around the door.

Uncertainty and, yes, not a little bit of fear moved through me at the sight of the tall masked man rifling through my files. My computer screen was on but it was password protected. There was the possibility he was looking for something to help him work out the password but he'd find nothing. I had memorized an anagram to remember my complicated password.

The man, dressed all in black, turned his head to the side, and even in the woolen ski mask he wore over his face I recognized him.

Stu Devlin.

I was sure of it.

It made sense. Was he searching for something that might be useful as leverage in obtaining the inn from me?

Moron.

There was no way that Ian Devlin put him up to this in his effort to amass more boardwalk real estate. Stu's father might be an asshole but he was a much sneakier asshole than his idiot son.

I dialed 911 on my phone as I stepped into the room.

He jerked at my arrival, his head snapping in my direction.

Dark, flat eyes stared at me and I knew without a doubt it was Stu.

"Nine one one, what's your emergency?"

"I have an intruder in my establishme—oof!" His body hit mine before I even had time to react to him suddenly launching himself at me.

My breath slammed out of me as I crashed to the floor, pain juddering through my head as it smacked against the floorboards. At the heavy, warm weight settling over me, my eyes flew open in panic.

Stu's cruel eyes glared down at me as he reached for the phone in my hand. I gripped it tighter, struggling to keep hold of it as his strong fingers clawed at mine. He grabbed my wrist and hammered it against the floor. Pain shot down my arm and I reflexively let go of the phone.

He threw it against the wall, grunting in satisfaction at the sound of it breaking.

Fury roared through me at the shock of him physically attacking me. With my good hand I reached for his mask, my nails scratching him as I tried to drag it off his face so I could finally have evidence to get a Devlin charged with a crime.

"I know it's you!" I screeched as his fingers bit into my hands.

We struggled as adrenaline aided me in my pissed-off quest to unmask the bastard. I wasn't thinking. I was just too angry.

He hissed as I clawed at his arm and he released me to pull his elbow back, his fist coming toward me as I stared up at him in horror.

But his fist never met my face.

Suddenly he was no longer straddling me because another body had launched itself at him, throwing him off me.

I scrambled to my feet. "Holy fuck," I breathed, stunned.

The other body belonged to the man who was currently wrestling Stu. And that man was Vaughn. A very furious Vaughn.

Stu grunted as Vaughn punched him, but then Vaughn grunted when Stu buried his fist in Vaughn's gut. It was a hard enough hit to wind him, catching him off guard, and off balance. He was quick to his feet though, lunging at Stu, grappling with him. I watched as they fought, Stu deftly avoiding becoming unmasked.

When he landed a punch on Vaughn's face, I'd had enough.

I jumped on Stu's back.

And found myself promptly thrown off and at Vaughn.

I felt his strong arms bind around my waist as he pulled me away from an inevitable collision with my desk, and cursed like a sailor at the sight of my attacker sprinting out of the office and out of our grasp.

"Are you okay?" Vaughn's hands roamed my body for injury.

I jerked away, unnerved by how much I wanted his comfort right then. "I'm fine."

"You're not fine, you're trembling."

I narrowed my eyes on his jaw, looking for injury. There was a faint redness that I knew was going to look bad in the morning if we didn't get some ice on it. "*I* didn't get hit in the face."

"Because *I* was there to stop him. What the hell were you—" His eyes darted behind me and he stiffened.

I glanced over my shoulder and my gut churned.

My guests were crowded outside my office, sleepy, disgruntled, and concerned.

"Everything alright?" one of my return visitors, Mr. Ingles, asked.

"A small mishap," I said cheerily, walking toward them as if I wasn't currently wearing a silk camisole and shorts that showed off *way* too much of my body. As if I wasn't walking through a scattered mess of files and objects that had crashed to the floor during all the violent tussling. "But it's quite alright."

"I'm calling the sheriff," Vaughn said behind me, and even though I knew it was the right thing to do I squeezed my eyes closed and groaned.

"The sheriff? What happened?"

"Oh dear. Are we safe?"

I listened to my guests voicing their fears, and wished just once that I could let them think what they wanted, let them leave if they wanted! I was shaken, shocked, hurt, and frankly pissed way the fuck off.

The last thing I wanted to do was play the ever-congenial innkeeper.

But I had to.

I opened my eyes and strode in among them. "Please, you are all safe. Nothing like this has ever happened before, but I can assure you that the intruder will not be returning and the inn will be secure. If you'd all like to return to your rooms while I deal with the sheriff—quietly, I promise. Of course I will deduct tonight's room fee from your bill and dining tomorrow is free all day for all guests. On top of that I will issue you all a fifty percent discount if you choose to return to the inn in the future."

As I hoped it would, all my discounts and freebies worked their magic and my guests trundled back up to their rooms murmuring to one another about the nuisance but also about Mona's delicious muffins and crème brûlée.

Wrapping my arms around myself I stared at the entrance to the inn. Both doors were wide open.

"Here." Vaughn appeared at my side.

I glanced at him, surprised to see he was offering me his leather jacket.

Accepting it, I slipped it over me, and got a giant, delicious whiff of his cologne as I did so. An inappropriate tingle shot through my breasts and I wrapped the too-large jacket shut so he couldn't see my pebbled nipples. "Thank you," I whispered, staring at him.

Vaughn stared back, concern in his beautiful eyes.

He'd never looked at me like that before.

I felt compelled to say, "I'm okay."

The concern melted under anger. "You're not okay," he snapped. "Do you have any idea who the intruder was?"

"I'm positive it was Stu Devlin."

He cursed under his breath, the muscle in his jaw working. And then that anger was directed at me. "Why the hell didn't you call the police instead of confronting him?"

My lips parted in surprise at his attack. "For your information I was calling the police *as* I was confronting him. I didn't think he'd throw me to the ground! I thought it was Stu being an ass. I didn't think he'd hurt me." I shivered at the thought.

"Well now he's a dead man."

I felt a rush of sudden desire between my legs at the strangely protective vibe I was getting off him. The feeling unsettled me. "How did . . . Why were *you* here?"

He glanced over at my open double doors. "I sometimes stroll down the boardwalk at night. When I was passing I saw your doors were open. He must have picked the lock." Vaughn's eyes narrowed. "I knew something was wrong so I came inside to check, and I heard the struggle coming from your office."

Thank God.

Never in my life did I think I'd be grateful for Vaughn Tremaine's presence but I was. In fact I was beyond grateful. I didn't know if it was adrenaline or shock or what . . . but I was a turned-on kind of grateful.

"Well . . . thanks," I whispered, unable to look at him.

If I looked at him, he'd know I was imagining stripping that gorgeous dark red sweater right off of him. I glanced at him out of the corner of my eyes. He'd rolled up the sleeves of the sweater, revealing tan corded forearms.

I had this thing about strong forearms and nice hands on a guy. Vaughn had both.

I bit my lip at the sight and tried to pull myself together.

What the hell!

It's the adrenaline, I assured myself.

The sound of my garden gate swinging open sent relief through me. A much-needed distraction in the form of Sheriff King entered my inn.

Jeff King had been voted into office the same year my mother's good friend Jaclyn Rose was voted into office as mayor. Jeff was rugged, competent, fair, an all around good guy and sheriff. He was also widowed. His wife had passed away of cancer eight years ago and the women of Hartwell had been sniffing around him ever since. Without much luck.

Dahlia had a fling with him a number of years ago, and I think Jeff had liked her. Unfortunately, she was the wrong woman to start over with. I'd been frustrated, a little annoyed even, when Dahlia broke things off with him—until I remembered my friend was too good at punishing herself. And also that she gave her heart away to someone else a long time ago, even if she refused to admit it.

The sight of Jeff calmed me.

It wasn't that I didn't feel safe. I felt safe with Vaughn standing beside me. But I didn't feel calm. There was nothing calming about being this attracted to a man I wasn't even sure I liked very much.

"Jeff," I said. "I mean Sheriff." I always forgot to call him that when he was on duty.

At six feet five, the tall, broad-shouldered police officer seemed to fill the entire space. And I was okay with that. I liked his power-ful presence right then more than I could say.

"Hey, Bailey." Deputy Wendy Rollins stepped into the inn, glancing around, taking everything in. Wendy had been part of our police force for twenty years, and was another good friend of my mom's.

I smiled, glad she was there, too. "Sorry to call you guys out so late."

"Don't be sorry." She frowned. "You've got nothing to be sorry for."

"Crime scene?" Jeff asked.

"Her office," Vaughn replied. "I was taking a walk, saw her doors open, thought I'd check it out. And I caught Stu Devlin attacking her in her office."

Wendy scowled, swallowing what I knew were probably a few choice words, while Jeff looked taken aback. "Stu Devlin? Positive ID?"

"No." I shook my head, furious. "He was wearing a mask."

"Then how do you know it was Stu?"

"Oh, come on, Sheriff, I've known him my whole life."

He sighed. "Show me to the office and explain everything from the start."

I did just that, and was comforted by the fact that Vaughn stayed by my side throughout the whole thing.

Thirty minutes later, Jeff and Wendy had our statements and were standing in the garden of the inn.

"I'll have one of the deputies drop by tomorrow morning to get statements from your guests at breakfast," Jeff said.

"Thank God I already offered them free food," I muttered, put out that my guests would have to be even more inconvenienced.

Vaughn's hand settled on my arm and I looked down at it, shocked by the touch, as I listened to him say to Jeff, "And Stu?"

"All I can do is bring him in for questioning but without a positive ID from anyone I don't have a lot to go on."

"That's bullshit."

"Tremaine," Jeff warned. "It's not that I don't believe you. I'll do what I can. I promise. Bailey, is there anything else I should know that might help me? Bailey?"

"Huh?" I jerked my head up from staring at Vaughn's hand. "Oh. No. Not that I can think of right now. If I do, I'll drop by the station."

"Get some sleep." Jeff nodded and turned to leave.

I waved good-bye to him and Wendy and then turned to Vaughn. I was more awake than ever, and I wasn't ashamed to admit that I didn't really want to be alone right now. "You should get back."

He scrutinized me for a moment, and it was as if he could read my mind. "I spotted a bottle of wine in your office that managed to escape destruction. Want to open it? It might calm your nerves."

I was more than a little surprised by the offer, and also touched. I was seeing the other side to Vaughn Tremaine that Jess swore was there. Maybe she was right. "Do you want to drink it on the beach? The water always soothes me."

He nodded, amiable.

Actually *amiable*.

"Sure."

I hid my shock as best as I could. "I . . . uh . . . Let me change first."

Vaughn's eyes drifted over my skimpy attire and he looked pissed off all over again. "You do that," he muttered, striding off in the direction of my office.

"Well this is going to be interesting," I murmured. I held the collar of his jacket to my nose and took a whiff. My stomach fluttered of its own volition at the smell of his cologne. *Oh, holy hell.* "Very interesting."

NINE

||||||||||||||||||||||||||||||||||||||||||||||||

Vaughn

He had offered to grab the bottle of wine from Bailey's office to help calm her nerves. But it wasn't just for her nerves. He needed to calm down, too. Adrenaline was pumping through him, and right now all Vaughn wanted to do was to work that adrenaline out with Bailey.

Don't go there.

He was furious at Stu Devlin for breaking into her inn.

Do *go there.*

The anger distracted him.

As far as Vaughn was concerned Stu was a dead man.

He was also angry with Bailey. So angry at her for putting herself in danger, and being so unapologetic about it, that he felt this animalistic urge to fuck her into submission.

So much for the anger distracting him.

The tiny camisole and shorts she was wearing didn't help matters and he felt like a bastard for thinking about sex when someone had just broken in and attacked her.

Vaughn grabbed the wine, knowing he hadn't just offered to sit and drink with her to calm her nerves. He didn't want to leave her alone just yet, and he had a feeling she didn't want to be left alone.

As he came out of the office he bumped into her in the hallway. Vaughn was grateful to see Bailey had changed into jeans and a thick sweater. She handed him his jacket and nodded to the wine. "Let me just grab some glasses from the kitchen."

When she returned she not only had glasses but a dish towel wrapped over ice. "For your jaw." She handed it to him.

Grateful, he took it, not really wanting to sport a bruise his staff and guests would see. A few seconds later they locked up the inn and were strolling out of the gardens onto the boardwalk. The silence between them wasn't exactly comfortable, but it wasn't the silence of two people who didn't know what to say to each other.

It felt like the silence of two people who were afraid of what they *might* say to each other.

Or maybe he was just projecting.

"So you were just strolling by and saw the door?" Bailey queried.

"Thankfully, yes."

But there was more to it than that. He had Jessica's warning about Devlin on his mind, and so he had Bailey on his mind during his midnight stroll.

He felt something was wrong deep in his gut when he looked up and saw the doors to the inn open. Fear, like he'd never felt before, had rushed over him as he stormed inside the inn and heard the struggle coming from the office. And when he saw Bailey underneath Devlin, when he saw Devlin pull back his fist to hit her, rage unlike anything he'd experienced crashed over Vaughn.

It was a bad idea to stick around a woman who inspired those kinds of emotions but Vaughn wasn't making the decisions right now; the hot blood pumping in his veins was.

They continued down the boards in silence until they neared his hotel. Bailey stopped where the railings gave way to a ramp that led onto the beach. She sat down at the top of it.

He followed suit, keeping a little distance between them, and opened the wine. Bailey held out the glasses and he filled them, feeling her gaze on his face.

"I'm not going to let him do this to me." She tried to hide the tremor in her voice and failed.

Vaughn renewed his vow to destroy Stu Devlin as he pressed the ice to his jaw.

He cleared his throat. "Do what?"

"Make me scared. Make me scared in my own inn."

"You could install security," he suggested, watching as she raised the glass to her lips. Her hand shook.

Definitely going to destroy the fucker.

"That's letting him win," she said before taking a sip of the wine.

"He won't come after you again. Even he's not that stupid."

Bailey grunted. "I knew the man was a moron but . . . what an idiot. There's no way his father had anything to do with this."

"I suspect you're right." Ian Devlin was a snake, but he was a smarter snake than his son.

Bailey threw back the entire glass of wine and then held out the empty to him to refill. He did so without questioning it.

"I'm glad you were there," she muttered as he refilled her glass.

Shock rippled through him and his eyes flew to her face.

Bailey was staring at the wine, refusing to meet his eyes.

Stubborn wench.

He smirked, amused by her. "I'm glad I was there, too."

Now her eyes met his, her own shock alight in them. She saw his smirk, but he guessed she saw his sincerity, too, because she gave a huff of surprised laughter and shook her head. "Vaughn Tremaine coming to my rescue. I would have lost *that* bet."

Something hard twisted in his gut. Did she think he would let anything happen to her?

What else should she think? You've been nothing but an asshole to her.

He sipped at his wine, staring out at the dark ocean. The usual serenity it brought him was lost in the storm of emotions the woman beside him incited.

"I like to think I'm good at reading people," she said. "But you are very difficult to read. To me you're like that ice in your hand. Like you don't care about anyone or anything but your hotels. But

Jessica and Cooper swear that you're a good man. And tonight, you came to my defense. Yet . . . here you are . . . back to ice."

Vaughn studied the wine in his hand, feeling the itch under his skin; the itch to lose control. He could throw back the entire bottle and blame whatever he said and did next on that.

On that thought, or temptation rather, he placed the glass out of his reach on the boards beside them. "Maybe you're not good at reading people, Miss Hartwell. Your boyfriend of ten years was having an affair behind your back after all."

As soon as the words were out of his mouth, he flinched.

There was a tense, awful silence but Vaughn could feel the heat of her gaze on his face. Bracing himself he turned to meet her accusing stare. "I'm sorry. I have a bad habit of being a bastard to you."

Bailey's eyebrows rose at his admission. And then something rueful and mischievous glinted in those beautiful eyes of hers. "Maybe that's because I have a bad habit of being a bitch to you."

He laughed before he could stop himself.

He felt her study his face as he did and when he stopped she was staring at him in wonder, like she'd never seen him before. Vaughn was uncomfortable with her obvious curiosity. "I do laugh once in a while, Miss Hartwell."

"Well you've never laughed around me. And stop calling me Miss Hartwell. Please, I beg of you."

He stirred, the heat in him rising as her words raised the ghost of a longstanding sexual fantasy he'd had about her.

Fuck.

"Why does it bother you? It's your name." His words came out more hoarse than he'd have liked, almost giving his arousal away.

"It's the way you say it." She shrugged, taking a sip of her wine. "And anyway, it makes me feel like a spinster at the moment."

"Because of Tom? Do you miss him?" Why the hell did he ask that?

She seemed just as surprised by the personal question, and for a moment or two Vaughn thought she wasn't going to answer.

But then she did.

And her answer shocked the hell out of him.

"No." Sadness dimmed her eyes. "I miss my friend. But I don't miss my boyfriend. What I miss are all the years I wasted with him . . . because it was a disservice to us both."

Vaughn studied her face as she stared out at the ocean, taking in the way the muscle in her delicate jaw twitched, like she was clenching her teeth against a surge of emotion.

He wanted to know what the hell she meant. Maybe it was because she'd been so open with him, or maybe it was just sitting in close proximity to a woman he'd wanted for so long, but Vaughn's self-control seemed to have taken a leave of absence. "What does that mean?"

She heaved a weary sigh. "Tom and I . . . we . . . we didn't have what Jess and Coop have. We've never had that. I stayed with him because he was safe. I stayed with him because he was what I thought someone like me deserved. And vice versa. We weren't right for each other and I knew it, and I didn't speak up. He cheated because I didn't speak up."

"You don't believe that." He sounded annoyed.

Bailey narrowed her eyes on him. "Yes. What would you know about it?"

He ignored her angry tone. "Tom Sutton was a man punching above his weight. He knew that. Everyone knew that. And that is why everyone thinks he's not only an asshole for cheating on you, but a fucking moron."

"I don't know whether to be flattered to have gotten a compliment out of you or pissed off. What does that even mean? Tom was less attractive than me? Isn't that a little shallow?"

"I didn't say he was less attractive than you. I wouldn't *know* if he was less attractive than you. I do know I never spent a scintillating moment in that man's company."

"You're saying he wasn't interesting enough to keep up with me?"

He just looked at her.

Bailey couldn't hide her amazement. "Huh. Really?"

Vaughn smirked, enjoying the fact that he could throw her off balance. "Just because you can be a bitch, Bailey, doesn't mean you're not an interesting one."

"I'm only a bitch to people who are assholes." She downed the rest of her wine. She didn't ask for more, however. Instead she placed the glass out of her way and leaned back on the palms of her hands.

"As always you flatter me."

"Why *are* you an asshole, Tremaine?"

"I would like to remind you that you're the one who started a campaign of hate against me."

"I was worried about the boardwalk. I thought you were going to erect this ugly, contemporary building that would compromise what we had here. The fact that you were so uncooperative did not help."

"I don't like to be questioned."

"By a woman."

"By *anyone.*"

"You were awful to me."

He sighed, hating the hurt she tried to hide but just couldn't. "Again, I'll remind you that you were awful to me first."

"I tried to be nice to you at first. You were a superior swine."

"The first thing you asked was to see my architect's drawings," he huffed. "Like you had a right to them."

"I felt I did."

"Because you're Bailey Hartwell, Princess of the Boardwalk. You're not pissed at me for being a superior swine; you're pissed at me for being the first person to say no to you."

"Oh, believe me, you're not the first man to say no to me."

He tensed at the bitterness he heard in her voice. "I said person. Not man."

"What?"

"Person, not man."

Bailey shrugged. "Whatever. Let's just agree I was a nosy bitch and you were a superior ass."

"We're using past tense?" he teased.

Their eyes met and he watched the way her lips trembled before they gave up and spread into a huge smile.

The constant ache inside his chest intensified as he felt the full force of that smile upon him. Its power flooded through him until he had to tense against the sudden urge to grab her and kiss her breathless.

Fuck.

What the hell was this woman doing to him?

Vaughn jerked his eyes toward the water, not needing the Princess of the Boardwalk to know she could undo him with her smile alone.

Bailey

Dear God, Vaughn Tremaine was just a man.

I didn't know why that surprised me so, but it did.

For the past few years I'd had my defenses up around him, but the attack, the adrenaline from the attack had shattered all of those. Without them, I could see Vaughn clearly.

He was just a man.

With extremely high defenses.

His words could still sting but I could also see the regret in his eyes as soon as he said them. And when I smiled at him . . . I saw . . .

Well . . .

Vaughn looked at me like he *wanted* me.

I knew there was power in my smile but wow.

For the first time since meeting this man I felt that shift of power.

Sitting beside him I no longer felt like the inferior country bumpkin I'd felt before. I felt like an attractive woman.

An attractive woman Vaughn didn't want to be attracted to.

All the hostility between us made absolute sense. Vaughn was right: maybe I wasn't very good at reading people, because we were two people who were attracted to each other and didn't want to be.

Of course there was going to be hostility.

And here I thought he was just a dick.

The truth was I should have been annoyed by the fact that Vaughn was attracted to me and didn't want to be. Instead I felt a thrill tremble through me.

Yesterday if I'd discovered he wanted me but didn't want to want me, I would have said it was because he still thought I was beneath him. Now, after having stared into those icy gray eyes of his, I saw something I hadn't wanted to see before.

Vulnerability.

A wound, even.

Something had happened to Vaughn Tremaine.

I'd bet anything that something was a woman.

"Have you ever been in love?" I blurted out.

For a moment he just stared at me. My wine-flushed skin turned hotter than hell. "Have you?"

I nodded.

"How many times?"

A month ago I would have said twice. But now I wasn't so sure. In fact . . . I wasn't even sure if I ever had been. "Does it count if the person doesn't love you back?"

And that's when it happened.

For the first time ever, Vaughn Tremaine's hard gaze softened, and I didn't feel quite as stupid for showing him my underbelly. "Yes, Bailey. I think you can love someone even if they don't love you back."

Maybe it was because he said my name. Or maybe it was the kindness I'd never seen or heard in him.

But I wanted to cry.

I looked down at my lap as I tried to control the impulse. "Then once. I've been *in* love once. You?"

"My father . . . he loved my mother. The way he talks about her I'm not sure I've ever . . ."

His tone drew my gaze and once more I found myself captured in his study of me. "I'm sorry about your mother. I know you lost her when you were young."

Vaughn stared back out at the ocean. I realized he did this, avoided a person's gaze, when he didn't want them to guess his thoughts. "I had my father."

"I like him. Your dad. I like him a lot."

"Most people do. He's a very charming man."

"A good dad?"

"A very good dad. A very good man."

"He's very . . . down to earth for a man of privilege."

"Well he wasn't always privileged. He's the son of a postal worker."

I was astonished. "I thought you were born a blue blood."

Vaughn gave me a wry smile. "On my mother's side. We're not exactly on speaking terms. They weren't too happy when their darling daughter married a man who'd muscled his way into society."

"What an outdated attitude."

"Not then. And lineage is still important to some people. Yeah, if you've got enough money and power, you can find your place. But there are still some of the old families who haven't realized we've come a long way since the times of arranged marriages. The Montgomerys are one of them."

"The Montgomerys. That's your mother's family?" Jesus. Vaughn's dad might not be a blue blood but Vaughn certainly was.

It was hard not to be intimidated by that kind of history. Even I knew who the Montgomerys were. They were giants in the industrial revolution, and now owned a billion-dollar corporation that had its fingers in all sorts of pies—mostly in aeronautics.

"That's my mother's family. Or it was until they disowned her for marrying my father."

The romantic in me swooned. "But she didn't care, did she?"

Whatever he heard in my voice made his eyes soften again. My belly fluttered in reaction, like a schoolgirl with her first crush. "She loved them. She just loved my father more."

The air between us felt too thick and I knew I was on the cusp of throwing myself at him. And I wasn't even drunk. "So, Vaughn Tremaine believes in love," I teased, trying to ease the tension between us. "Who would have thunk it?"

He gave me that lopsided smirk of his and I swear to God I felt that smirk from my nipples to the heat between my legs.

I hated that I was so attracted to him. Yet I didn't hate it as much as I hated it yesterday.

In fact, maybe it kind of thrilled me.

"So there was no one back in New York? Or are all the stories of your playboy ways true?"

"Have you been Googling me, Miss Hartwell?"

And we were back to Miss Hartwell. "Emery told me."

"Has she been Googling me?"

"No, you arrogant ass." I laughed. "Her grandmother used to read the society pages to her."

"Ah. How thrilling for her."

"You didn't like it? Is that why you came out here?"

"Why all the sudden questions?"

"Well, you see, when you helped me out tonight you made me hate you less."

He grinned and I triumphed. "Ah. My mistake."

"Yeah. You should have kept on walking when you saw my doors open."

Just like that his grin disappeared.

"I'm not the only one who isn't sure of you," I said. "If you're trying to make Hartwell your home, you're going about it the wrong way."

"What does that mean?"

I ignored his defensive tone, one that a lesser person might be afraid of. "You're a smart man. I'm sure you've figured out that what makes Hartwell Hartwell is the fact that it's a small town where everyone knows each other and we all play our part. We're involved in some way. Me, I get involved in events when I can, and I'm always a listening ear when someone wants to talk. Coop, he helps old ladies across the street, pisses off Uly's Garage by working on people's cars when they can't afford a mechanic, and he's the owner of their favorite watering hole. Jess, she's new to town, but she's a doctor. She diagnosed Anita last year and gave her more time with Old Archie. Dahlia helps make the costumes for the winter carnival every year, and is dragged into making costumes for the school plays a lot, too. But then there's you and Emery. Em is too shy to get involved and so the town doesn't look at her as one of them. She's still an outsider. As for you, you don't get involved, either. You have all that money and your fancy hotel, and you do nothing for the town."

"Outside of helping the town's economy thrive by bringing more tourists and business to them."

I'd annoyed him. That hadn't been my intention. "I know you do that. They know you do that. But have you ever even been to the music festival or the annual punkin chunkin' competition or the winter carnival? Have you donated to the causes these events raise money for? Or have you ever considered contacting Kell Summers, our councilman and events guy, and asking him if there's anything you can do to help with the organization of an event? You have no idea how something that simple will make people look at you differently, and start to see you as one of them."

"By helping organize an event?" He looked incredulous but I could see he was listening to what I had to say.

"Let me put it bluntly—"

"That wasn't you putting it bluntly?"

"Tremaine, everyone thinks you think that you're better than us. They think you have a giant stick up your ass. Show them you're fun and human. It will go a long way with them."

"Yes, that was definitely more blunt."

I grinned at him. "I'm just trying to help."

"By suggesting I remove the stick from up my ass?"

"Yup."

He shot me a bemused look and then stared out at the ocean.

I wondered if he was still considering my advice, but when he spoke his words weren't the ones I'd been expecting. "Despite our differences I hope you know I would never walk away from a woman in trouble. I would never have just walked on by when I saw the inn had been broken into."

At his stiff reply, I touched his knee without even thinking. "I know that."

He glanced down at my hand and I realized what I was doing.

I snatched my hand back. "You know I walked into my office, calling the police, so confident that Stu wouldn't hurt me, and I just strolled in there quite the thing and gave the asshole a chance to swipe at me, and he did. I still can't believe he did that, and now I have to hide it from Cooper and Jess so they don't, you know, try to kill him, and I just don't how I can hide anything from those two—"

I was cut off by the strong, warm hand that curled around mine.

I looked down at Vaughn's beautiful, masculine hand, holding my small one.

"You're rambling."

"I do that sometimes."

"I know. You've just never directed a ramble at me before."

"It annoyed Tom." I wondered if it annoyed Vaughn.

His answer was to squeeze my hand and then let it go.

My rambling didn't annoy Vaughn.

And just like that I was again overcome with the urge to throw myself at him.

Maybe it was the adrenaline still coursing through my veins, kicked up into gear again by the memory of Stu attacking me. Or maybe it was because I was just an idiot woman easily seduced by men like Vaughn Tremaine. Or maybe, and this was more likely, I was the kind of woman who was attracted to the wounded.

I liked to rescue people.

Not in an *aren't I a wonderful heroine, running around saving people?* kind of way. I just . . . So many people looked past other people's pain. Mostly because we had our own pain to deal with, it was too hard to deal with some stranger's.

But I had people in my life. People who loved me. Cared for me.

I was one of the lucky ones.

There were people out there, people like Jess and Dahlia and Emery, who didn't have anyone. So I gave them *me* because I didn't know any other way to face the world. I made wounded strangers my family in the hopes that it would make it easier for them to deal with their pain. And yes, it wasn't entirely altruistic. I missed my own family. In reaching out to those who needed it I was making another family closer to home.

I was still working on Emery.

I guess in a way I was still working on Dahlia, too.

I should not turn Vaughn into family.

I shouldn't.

"Stu will pay for tonight." Vaughn's hard words cut through my musings.

He looked fierce. Determined. Like a protector. An unexpected protector.

And that's when it hit me.

Maybe I didn't want to rescue Vaughn.

Maybe . . . holy hell . . .

Did I want *Vaughn* to save *me*?

I felt winded by the prospect that I could feel something emotional for Vaughn Tremaine. Was I willing to throw out all my fears and insecurities that only he brought out in me, because for one night he'd shown me the softer side of him? The kind side. The passionate side.

Did I want him? Really, truly?

I imagined myself naked beneath him, his hands pinning my wrists to the bed as I allowed him to take sexual control of me.

"Yes," I whispered.

Oh, holy hell, was I in trouble.

"What?" Vaughn frowned.

I realized then I'd spoken out loud.

My heart hammered in my chest. "I better get back to the inn . . . Will you . . . will you walk with me?"

If he was surprised by my question, by the vulnerability I allowed him to see, Vaughn didn't show it.

Instead, like the gentleman I'm sure his father raised him to be, he got to his feet and held out a hand to me.

I took it, acknowledging the rush of sparks I felt tingle through me at his touch.

Awareness.

Those sparks had existed between us since the beginning, but I'd refused to admit I could be that attracted to someone I didn't like, especially while I was supposed to be in love with Tom.

I could admit now that there was more to Vaughn Tremaine than met the eye, and yes he could be an asshole, but there was a reason for that, too. I hadn't missed the fact that he'd avoided my question about being in love. And I was Bailey Hartwell. There was no one who enjoyed a mystery more than I did. He was a mystery I very much wanted to work out.

As Vaughn's grip on me tightened as he pulled me up, as our eyes met and his flared at the brush of our bodies as I stood, that power I'd felt earlier surged through me.

Vaughn wanted me.

Thrill soared through me.

It was hard to puzzle out a mystery when you had no aces up your sleeve.

I had an ace in this situation, though.

I'd never used sex as an ace before. It was something we both wanted but could never admit to. Until now. And for me, it was the stepping stone I needed to get close enough to a man who I finally could admit intrigued me like no other.

TEN

Bailey

There were no more words between us as Vaughn walked me back to the inn.

"Do a walk-through with me?" I unlocked the front door as I spoke.

If he was surprised that I, Bailey Hartwell, needed a man to be at my side while I checked the inn was safe, he didn't say anything.

Instead we walked through the rooms, making sure it was all clear, leaving the empty wine bottle, glasses, and soaked dish towel in the kitchen, before I led him to my office.

It was still a mess from earlier.

"Do you want me to help you clean it up?" Vaughn frowned down at the spot where Stu had pinned me down.

"No. I'll get it tomorrow." I walked out, hoping he'd follow, and he did, a flicker of wariness crossing his expression when he realized we were standing outside a bedroom. "I sleep here when I work too late."

I read the moment he was going to walk away.

"I know you want me." Typical me to simply put it out there.

I just never thought I'd put it out there with Vaughn.

He cursed under his breath and moved to leave, but I stepped into him and placed my hands on his strong chest, pressed my legs against his.

He gripped my biceps as if to push me away, but as soon as he touched me, he froze, undecided.

My heart hammered against my chest at the feel of him against me, at the smell of his expensive cologne, at the thought of waking up with my sheets smelling of that expensive cologne. My nipples tightened beneath my sweater and I wished I were still wearing my camisole so he could see my body's blatant reaction to his proximity.

"I don't want to be alone tonight."

His grip on me loosened, and I feared that self-control of his was about to rear its ugly head. "Then I'll stay with you but we don't have to have sex."

"What did I just say about pulling that stick out of your ass?" I teased, pressing closer to him, enjoying the hard tension in his body. "I'm so tired of always being in control, Vaughn. I look after myself. I look after my inn. I look after this town. With Tom I looked after him in every way. I took control in our lives and in our bed. For once I don't want to." I reached up on my tiptoes and brushed my lips against his. The touch caused a rush of tingles between my legs and I gasped.

I felt him tremble.

Satisfaction roared through me. "Take me into my room, Vaughn. Take control so I don't have to. I want you to. I want you to lay me down on that bed and take what you want. You want to, right?" I looked deep into his hard eyes and shivered at the heat I found in them. "I bet you've thought about it. Fucking the hostile Princess of the Boardwalk into submission."

His eyes flared and his fingers bit into my arms.

I had a feeling I'd just hit the target dead-on.

"You have no idea." His mouth slammed down on mine, his kiss hard, punishing, almost painful.

Controlling.

And for once, just as I promised, I was okay with that.

No one had ever kissed me like Vaughn, like he'd die if he didn't.

I wrapped my arms around his waist, my fingers curling into his leather jacket as I tried to match him hungry kiss for hungry kiss.

His tongue swept against mine and I groaned as lust shot through my breasts and belly. Vaughn's hands had moved from my arms to tangle in my hair and as he kissed me I found myself being pushed through the bedroom door.

I heard it click shut behind us and then I was shoved onto the bed.

I bounced, startled out of the kiss.

Vaughn towered over me, his whole body rigid, his features hard, his eyes hot.

Angry.

And I knew that there was a part of him that was still on the cusp of walking away from me. Why? To protect himself?

Surely to God, if I could be brave and let myself go, stop hiding behind hostility and just let him have me, he could return the favor.

I reached for the hem of my sweater and pulled it up over my head. I threw it away and reached for the clasp on my plain white bra. I shimmied it off and dropped it at his feet.

I liked to think my breasts still looked good and right now they were swollen with desire, my nipples tight peaks.

I sat back on my hands, the natural arch of my back thrusting my breasts out.

Vaughn's hands curled into fists at his sides as his gaze devoured me.

The dampness between my legs grew wetter.

The thick silence in the room was broken by the creak of leather as he shrugged out of his jacket. He tore it off, his sweater quick to follow.

I was soaked as I took in the sight of him and thought of all that masculine beauty becoming mine.

Unlike Tom, Vaughn took care of himself. Tom's average physique had never bothered me. I was still attracted to him.

But I wasn't complaining about the chiseled six-pack in my face.

My eyes dropped to where Vaughn's trousers hung low on his narrow hips, the cut V of his obliques turning me on past the point of hot to volcanic.

"You can't do it." His words were thick with need. There was also anger in them.

"What?" I managed.

"Give up control." He unbuckled his belt, his heated, furious gaze never leaving me. "Even now, you're trying to control this, to control me. When I fantasized about fucking you into submission, princess, it involved me taking your clothes off. Not you taking your clothes off to seduce me into staying." He pushed his pants down, toeing his shoes off at the same time.

He stood before me in his black Calvin Kleins, more model than mogul, and if it wasn't for the erection straining toward his hard stomach, I might have felt a flash of insecurity to be with a man so beautiful.

"You're right," I whispered. Every inch of me was a live wire, tense, too hot, sensitive. I never knew it was possible to be so sexually alive, and yet so nervous. Because he *was* right. I said I wanted him to take control, but I *was* still controlling this moment.

I tried to relax, lowering my back to the bed. I stared at him from under my eyelashes as I lay prone and willing for him. It was one thing to want this in my fantasies, to be turned on by the idea of being a woman who had control over her life but handed it over to a man in the bedroom; it was a different thing altogether to make it a reality.

It was all about trust.

And if I wanted to unearth the secrets Vaughn Tremaine held close, I had to give him my trust.

It wasn't easy to do considering we'd spent ninety-nine percent of our acquaintance being antagonistic toward one another. It maybe even didn't make sense to give him my trust.

But I was tired of playing it safe.

His hooded eyes drifted down my body at my sudden pliancy. His dick swelled even more, stretching his CKs to the bursting point. My toes curled inside my flats.

"That's more like it." He stepped toward the bed.

He placed his hands on my knees, his thumbs on the inside of my legs, and he slowly coasted them upward.

My breath left me.

And then he reached the apex of my thighs but he kept going, his thumbs meeting in the middle over the seam of my jeans. I gasped as he pressed his thumbs down and rubbed the seam against my clit. My hand reached for his, wanting to take control. Vaughn brushed it aside with a, "Stop it or I'll stop."

That, even more than his touch, caused a rush of wetness between my legs, and my hips arched off the bed.

His eyes flew to mine. Understanding, surprise, desire, and satisfaction moved through his expression one after the other. Vaughn's lips parted as we stared at one another like two people who were starving.

I'd never felt a rush like it.

Patience gone, Vaughn unbuttoned my jeans and then yanked down the zip with barely leashed control. He grabbed the looser denim at the back of my thighs and then dragged them down my legs, stopping to peel off my flats, before throwing them and the jeans behind him.

Before relieving me of my underwear, he hooked his fingers into his own and pushed them down to his ankles, kicking them away.

I wet my dry lips with my tongue as he stood before me with his swollen, purple-red erection jutting out between muscular thighs. Every inch of him was beautiful.

My sex swelled and a little huff of excitement escaped me.

Hearing it, Vaughn's cock jerked and he blew out a "fuck" as he was moved to action. He put a knee to the bed and then moved his other into position, and he stared into my eyes as he smoothed his hand up my naked thigh. I trembled.

His eyes flared in satisfaction.

Then he brushed his fingers over my underwear, my very damp underwear, and his free hand curled into the sheets in reaction. "Jesus," he groaned, watching me as he rubbed the fabric against my clit.

Electric tingles moved through me and I lifted my hips into his touch.

"You are so fucking beautiful." His fingers slipped under my panties and slid into me. My inner muscles clamped around him in desperate need. Vaughn groaned even harder. "You feel beautiful, too."

"Fuck me, Vaughn." The raw plea fell easily, naturally from my lips.

He gave me an arrogant grin. "In my own time."

His fingers slid out of me, only to curl around my underwear. Slowly, torturously slowly, he pulled them down my legs. And then for an even longer, torturously slow moment he just looked at me.

"You want the truth, princess?" His voice was deep, gruff. "I've wanted you from the moment we met."

Exultation pulsed through me and I shifted restlessly on the bed.

"I've wanted you just like this. That smart mouth of yours sweet. That sexy body of yours mine to do with as I please. And I don't like wanting something I can't have."

But you can have me! I wanted to yell in frustration. *Take me already!*

But I'd promised him control.

"Be prepared to get a taste of what I've had to endure watching your fine ass walk up and down my boardwalk."

"Your boardwalk?"

Damn.

He got me.

Vaughn grinned. "You can't help yourself, can you?"

"Not your boardwalk, Tremaine," I whispered, itching to pull him toward me. "But in here, right now, this fine ass is yours for the taking."

His mood seemed to change, and I waited breathlessly as he straddled me, gently taking each of my wrists in his hands and pinning them to the mattress at either side of my head. I felt overwhelmed by him, and I had to relax against the urge to push up against him. He bent his head to mine, and that spicy, earthy scent of his rushed over me, sending a new set of tingles straight to my nipples.

"Never change, Bailey Hartwell," he murmured, and then he kissed me. His tongue pushed between my lips and slid over mine, dancing with it in a dirty, deep, wet kiss. My hips pulsed toward him at the feel of his hard cock rubbing against my belly.

And then he was gone, taking his mouth from mine as his grip on my wrists loosened. His fingers trailed teasingly down the soft skin of my inner arm, under my arms, and down the sides of my breasts as he stopped to pay attention to them.

"I've fantasized about what your tits looked like." He smiled up at me from under those long dark lashes of his. "Reality beats fantasy any day."

"What else have you fantasized about?"

His eyes narrowed, that smile turning to a sexy smirk. "Many things. Involving your gorgeous tits? Sucking them, licking those pretty nipples of yours." A dark heat entered his expression. "Coming on them."

A pulse of lust slammed through me and my lower belly rippled. "Vaughn," I gasped, my cheeks flushed with need.

He positioned his erection between my legs and pressed. His eyes squeezed shut for a moment, his teeth clenching. "You like that thought," he gritted out.

When I didn't answer he opened his eyes and thrust against me, sending a streak of want through me. "You like that?" he demanded. "You want it?"

"Yes, I want it," I huffed, frustrated, tortured!

He grinned. "My dirty little princess. Who knew?"

This time I laughed at his teasing. "Not me."

I felt the rumble of his own laughter and then I felt nothing but the heat of his mouth as he wrapped it around my left nipple and sucked.

Hard.

My body writhed, bucking off the bed, and I gripped the sheets in my hands to stop myself from reaching for him, from taking back control.

"You can touch me," he whispered across my nipple. "I want you to. Just remember I'm in charge."

As he turned his attention to my other breast I moved my hands to his shoulders, stroking his hot, smooth skin, and then I curled my fingers tightly into his soft dark hair as he tormented my nipples until they were swollen, almost painful buds. Until I was so ready to come it wasn't even funny.

"Vaughn," I begged, tugging hard on his hair.

He reached for my hands, gripped my wrists, and slammed them back above my head. "If you can't play nice . . ." he warned.

And then his lips were moving down my stomach, his tongue licking my belly button, before moving south. My lower belly rippled in a mini-orgasm as his mouth neared closer to where I wanted it the most.

My legs fell open, inviting him in, and I heard his grunt of satisfaction seconds before his tongue touched my clit.

Need slammed through me and my hips pushed into his mouth. He gripped them, pressing them back to the mattress, and then he truly began his torture.

He suckled my clit, pulling on it hard, and he listened to my body. He listened to my harsh, shallow breaths; he studied the undulations of my hips; and just when I was about to come, he stopped.

I cried out in frustration. "Please."

His grip on my hips became almost bruising.

And then his tongue was back, this time licking inside me. I writhed because it wasn't enough. Not nearly enough.

Hearing my whimpers, Vaughn returned to my clit, let go of my left hip, and gently pushed two fingers inside of me.

"Oh, God!" I bucked against him as he finger- and mouth-fucked me. "Vaughn."

And then the bastard did it again. Just as I was about to explode over the edge, he stopped.

"No!" I felt tears prick my eyes.

But that was only the beginning.

Vaughn tortured me with longing, just as promised, drawing his seduction to a halt every time I was about to orgasm.

I lay beneath him, staring up at him balefully. No man had ever made my body feel like this.

Made *me* feel like this.

I almost hated him for it.

As if Vaughn saw that in my eyes, he smiled in dark satisfaction.

"Is this what you want?" My mouth trembled with the urge to cry. I had no idea sex could do that to me.

Or unfulfilled desire, rather.

That hardness in his expression softened and he moved back up my body to cup my cheek in his hand. With a tenderness I never knew he had in him, he kissed me softly, sweetly. And when he pulled back, staring deep into my eyes he whispered, "Trust me."

Cool air blew over me as he got up off the bed. I glanced up in confusion, wondering if he was leaving me. My body relaxed when I saw he was pulling a condom out of the wallet in his pants.

Finally.

But he even made rolling on the condom an act of torture, taking his time, stroking his cock as he did so, his pleasure-filled eyes narrowed on me.

I had a sudden image of him straddling me, stroking himself, and coming all over my breasts.

I couldn't believe that idea turned me on so much, but with Vaughn it did.

"Vaughn. Please."

He moved back up onto the bed, moving over me almost predatorily, graceful, strong; so very, very masculine. "Beg me again, Bailey."

"What?"

His lips brushed mine, his teeth catching on my bottom lip, nibbling it. "Beg. Me." The words were guttural. Demanding.

And my overly heated body burst into flames.

Because I realized something that turned me on even more than being controlled by Vaughn in the bedroom. He may have been in control of my orgasms . . . but I was in control of him. He needed me.

I wanted to give him what he needed. "Fuck me, Vaughn," I whispered. "Please."

He pushed up onto one hand and curled his other around my thigh, opening me . . . and he thrust inside me. Rough. Fierce.

I gasped his name in pleasure. Our eyes held as my breath scattered, and as he moved inside me, thick, overwhelming, hot, hard, deep, I felt like he could see into my soul and that I finally could see into his.

And I saw something that lit my world up.

Vaughn Tremaine *cared* about me.

Just like that, the tension inside of me splintered, shattered apart, throwing me over a cliff edge higher than I'd ever been thrown. And the fall . . . the fall was exquisite.

"Vaughn!" I cried, my eyes fluttering closed as pure, undiluted bliss rushed through my entire body; its focus in my center. My inner muscles clamped around Vaughn's cock, the sensation so sexy, so raw, my fingernails dug into the muscles of his back as I held on for dear life.

I felt like it was never going to end, the ripples of my climax pulsing and pulsing around him. I was barely cognizant of the fact that Vaughn's hips had slammed hard against mine. Stilled. And then they were jerking, his cock throbbing inside me as he came.

He came hard but nowhere near as long as I did. That would have been impossible.

I lay stunned, limp, jellylike as Vaughn made a growling noise and then buried his face in my neck.

Our chests rose and fell against one another as we tried to catch our breaths.

And that's when I got it.

"*Trust me*," he'd said.

He hadn't tortured me to be cruel. He'd strung out foreplay to give me the longest, most devastating orgasm of my life.

Somehow I managed to move my languid arms and wrap them around him. I delighted in the feel of his heavy body over mine, and I remembered the look on his face as he came. His gritted teeth, his flushed skin, the dazed lust in his stunning pale eyes.

I pulsed around him, a little aftershock, and he groaned, lifting his head.

I didn't give him a moment to overanalyze what we'd done, to pull out of me and disappear. Instead I kissed him, sweet, deep, wet. He kissed me back, and I rolled until I was on top of him and he let me. His hands caressed my back, my hair, my ass as we kissed and I writhed against him, needing more, wanting him hard again, ready.

I touched and tasted every inch of him until he *was* ready, until we were replacing the used condom with a new one.

This time I explored *his* beauty, the hard planes of his muscles, the heat of his skin, the salt of his sweat, the taste of his pre-come.

This time I rode him. I rode him slow, the desperation of our need eased by our first time together.

Now I could take *my* time enjoying *him*.

And enjoy Vaughn I did.

Because even as I straddled him, rising up and down on his cock, the look in his eye told me he was still the one in control here, and I felt that. But I also felt my power over him.

And there was no headier aphrodisiac.

Vaughn climaxed first, and as his hips bucked beneath mine he tipped me over the edge, and we came together.

Exhausted, stunningly exhausted, I slumped over him, and buried my face in his neck.

"I never dreamed it could be like this between us," I whispered.

Never had I felt more relaxed, more connected, more at peace, more alive than I did in that moment, and for the first time in a long time I fell asleep without thinking about chores or work or anything . . . nothing but the man who was still inside me.

The man I thought I might have been waiting for my whole life.

All this time he'd been standing right in front of me, wearing a suit and a sexy-ass smirk.

ELEVEN

||||||||||||||||||||||||||||||||||||||||||||||||||||||||||

Vaughn

He could blame it on nature, say he was just a man, and no man would have been able to resist Bailey Hartwell when she got it in her head to seduce him.

But that kind of reasoning would make him more of an asshole than he already was.

She'd fallen asleep with his dick still inside of her.

He muffled the curse of arousal that hovered on his lips as he stared at her, his overeager erection straining toward her body for more. When he realized she'd dropped off into sleep he'd gently eased out of her and rolled her onto her side. She'd snuggled into him before he could get away, and damn but he wanted just a little more time to enjoy the fact that finally the redhead in his arms was the one he'd wanted there all along.

Her beautiful auburn curls spilled out on his arm, tickling his skin. So soft.

Everything about her was. Her skin, her eyes, even her heart.

He recognized the moment she'd decided to save him. The moment he became another Jessica, another Dahlia.

Sure, he went beyond that since she wanted to fuck him, too, but more than that she wanted to soothe his wounded soul.

And she thought sex would lower his defenses.

She was right.

It had.

Vaughn couldn't remember a time when he'd been so lost in a

woman. He felt this unsettling hum beneath his skin. This urgency. This desperation to claim Bailey Hartwell as his own like he really was a prehistoric caveman.

He could blame her.

He could blame the moment she'd said, *"I bet you've thought about it. Fucking the hostile Princess of the Boardwalk into submission."*

Perceptive of her. Hot as fuck.

Bailey Hartwell liked a little dirt in bed.

No lily-white princess.

Loyal. Fierce. Protective. Kind. Strong. Funny. Sassy. Sexy. And goddamn perfect for him in bed.

Vaughn stared at her beautiful face, at her swollen lips, flushed cheeks, and he wished she would open her eyes. He wanted to see those stunning green eyes look up at him, soft, loving, full of desire.

He wanted it because he knew he'd never again see that look in her eyes after this moment. Because now he knew for a fact that he was in love with Bailey.

And he was going to break her heart.

"I never dreamed it could be like this between us."

He had to stop this now.

As if she heard his thoughts, Bailey's eyes fluttered open. At first she seemed confused and then those gems drifted up his shoulders and over his face.

They softened.

They grew tender.

They filled with desire.

Vaughn memorized her expression, imprinting the most beautiful image he'd ever seen in his life on his brain, and he cursed himself for being a fucking swine whose heart was big enough to fall in love but too small to *stay* in love.

Relationships just weren't for him. He knew that. And he didn't want to lose the way he felt for her.

Not Bailey.

She'd hurt him and he'd hurt her. The last time that happened he nearly destroyed a woman. Relationships were just too fucked up, and he was thirty-six years old. He'd lived the bachelor life too long to change it now.

That's why giving in to temptation made him such a prick.

"Hey," she whispered. "How long did I drift off?"

"Not long."

At the flatness of his words, Bailey tensed beside him.

Vaughn rolled away from her and off the bed, striding into the bathroom to dispose of the condom. When he walked back into the room he kept his gaze toward his clothes strewn across the floor. He could feel Bailey watching his every move.

"Is this the part where you tell me this was a mistake?" she teased, though the words were tinged with bitterness.

"Believe me, it was." He glanced up at her and wished he hadn't.

She was sitting up, holding the sheet protectively to cover her naked breasts. All that glorious hair of hers, the color of the horizon at sunset, spilled around her shoulders.

Jesus.

Now she was turning him into a fucking *poet* caveman.

"You weren't drunk," she argued.

"No, not on alcohol." He flicked her a glance as he pulled on his underwear and pants. "It was a rough night. We got carried away on adrenaline."

"So now you're saying you were never attracted to me?"

"No. I am attracted to you. And now I've had you."

She sucked in a breath at what he didn't say. "So now you've had me, you don't want me again."

That ache, that horrible ache that had disappeared during their time together, returned with a vengeance. He stopped what he was doing and met her gaze. "I don't do relationships, Bailey. And you and me . . ." He gave her a sardonic grin, one he had to force out. "You know we wouldn't work. We don't even like each other."

"We liked each other for a while."

Her sad tone was like a twist of a knife in his gut. He clenched his teeth against the feeling, and held his body back against the urge to haul her up against him, hold her, shake her, tell her she deserved better than a bastard like him.

"We're just from different worlds. We don't fit."

She drew in a sharp breath. "I thought from everything you said about your mom and dad that you didn't buy into that class bullshit."

Realizing she'd taken his words the wrong way, Vaughn opened his mouth to explain and then stopped.

Maybe it was better to let her think he thought she wasn't good enough.

"I'm not my parents," he said. "I understand where my grandparents were coming from."

Her reaction was unexpected.

Maybe he'd thought she'd fight a little harder considering this was Bailey and she tried to save fucking everyone from themselves.

Maybe he'd thought she'd decide he was right and just let him leave.

Maybe she'd yell at him.

What he hadn't expected was the pain that flashed across her face like he'd physically punched her.

And then she just closed down.

He witnessed it.

Bailey Hartwell, the most passionate woman he'd ever met, just went blank.

Cold.

Her eyes turned flat.

And it scared him.

"You can see yourself out." Her words were toneless, her face expressionless as she shimmied off the bed. "I'm going to shower you off of me."

Vaughn stood frozen as she passed him, Bailey but not Bailey, and disappeared inside the bathroom with the soft click of the door.

As he reached for his sweater and jacket he noticed his hands were trembling. He curled them into fists to make it stop. But as he left the inn in the wee hours of the morning, he walked on legs that felt shaky, unsure.

Staring up at the inn, Vaughn knew with nauseating realization why he was so off balance:

He'd thought walking away from Bailey would mean they'd return to their usual antagonistic banter, and he could live with that. He'd look forward to it, because it meant, selfishly, he'd always have that from her. She'd always be a part of his life.

But apparently alluding to the idea she wasn't good enough for him had possibly severed their tie for good.

And to his frustration, confusion, and horror, Vaughn realized that the thought of losing even that small piece of Bailey Hartwell scared the absolute shit out of him.

Bailey

I scrubbed at my body, not wanting to smell or feel any traces of Vaughn Tremaine on my skin.

The sheets on the bed would have to be washed, too.

So much for wanting to smell his expensive cologne on them.

I didn't want the reminder. The flashes of memory from last night were bad enough. I could still hear his voice in my head, his groans in my ear, the thrust of his hips against mine.

"We're just from different worlds. We don't fit."

"I'm not my parents. I understand where my grandparents were coming from."

I squeezed my eyes shut against his voice and scrubbed harder. It was just like last time all over again, not good enough for him, never good enough!

And just like last time I'd convinced myself that Vaughn actually cared about me. What an idiot. I hadn't seen tenderness in his eyes as he moved in me. I'd seen smug satisfaction. He'd finally gotten one over on me. Bailey Hartwell was good enough for sex but not good enough for a relationship.

I wasn't his *kind* of people. He was a total asshole commitment-phobe.

And I'd just gotten rid of one of those.

So I wasn't going to fight Vaughn on this one; I wasn't going to wear him down and make him see that there could be something special between us. Vaughn made me feel bad about myself and I hated him for it.

Finally I was ready to do better by myself again. Being burned in the same way twice made me a fool. But I wouldn't be a fool again.

I had to say it and maybe if I said it, I would start to believe it.

"You deserve better than Vaughn Tremaine," I said aloud as I stared into the mirror.

The door to the inn blew open during breakfast and like a gust of gale-force wind, Jessica and Cooper stormed inside. I strode out of the dining room and into the reception area. Jessica threw her arms around me and hugged me tight.

"Vaughn called. He told us what happened!"

"He what?" I squeaked.

"I'm going to kill the fucker," Cooper snarled.

Oh, crap. Did Vaughn have a death wish? What was he thinking? "Look, it was nothing—"

"Stu Devlin breaking into your inn and attacking you is not nothing," Jessica snapped as she pulled out of my hold. "Don't pretend to be cool about this, Bailey. This was crossing the line. Again!"

Oh. Right. The break-in.

Vaughn had called Jessica and Cooper to inform them about the break-in.

I was unappreciative of the kind gesture. I didn't need any kind gestures from him.

"You're right," I agreed. "It was crossing the line. I didn't expect the asshole to attack me."

Cooper's face darkened.

"Calm down, Coop. Sheriff King is dealing with . . ." My voice trailed off as a deputy from the sheriff's department walked into the inn right at that very moment.

And not just any deputy.

Deputy Freddie Jackson.

My least favorite deputy. Deputy Jackass, as I called him. Not just because he was a sneering, superior little shit, but because he happened to have grown up best buds with Kerr, the youngest Devlin son. The two of them thought they were owed respect from the moment they were born, and they'd acted like assholes from that moment, too.

Great.

"Miss Hartwell." He bypassed Cooper and Jessica, ignoring them. "The sheriff has sent me along to take witness statements from your guests about the alleged incident last night."

I narrowed my eyes at the word "alleged." "You mean the incident that did in fact happen in reality. The incident that was witnessed by Vaughn Tremaine, an extremely reliable witness considering everyone knows he would never lie for me."

Jackson sneered. "Right, well . . . Mr. Devlin has a solid alibi for his whereabouts last night."

Unease moved through me. "Of course he does."

"Just show me to the guests, Miss Hartwell."

"They're in the dining room." I gestured behind me. "They're expecting you."

Without another word he brushed past me, walking leisurely into the dining room to begin his investigations.

"Oh, wonderful," I hissed, turning back to Cooper and Jessica. "They sent me the asshole."

"I'll make sure he's asking the right questions." Cooper marched past me before I could stop him.

I shot a pleading look at Jessica. "Please stop him from hassling Jackson. I need that little asshat to help me."

"I think we both know Jackson's going to be no help at all. He will deliberately ignore any facts that prove Stu attacked you last night."

"Yeah, well, now that Stu has an 'alibi' I think I'm screwed out of justice either way."

Jessica stared at me in concern for a long moment. I gave her a tired smile. "I'm okay. I just haven't slept very well. All that adrenaline." And the sex with Vaughn that led to my humiliation.

"I could kill Stu for this. Although Cooper might beat me to it."

"As much as I love that I inspire that kind of loyal violence, I'd really rather you didn't. I quite like not having to visit my friends in prison."

"Yeah, well, if Devlin keeps pulling crap like this, one of us is going to end up incarcerated for retribution."

"Ian Devlin didn't put Stu up to this."

"I know. Cooper and I said as much. He's smarter than his son. I wonder who Stu's alibi is."

I thought back to only a few days ago when Tom and I were confronted by that particular Devlin on the boardwalk. "Oh, I think I might know who."

"Who?" Cooper said behind us.

"I saw him with Dana the other night. They looked pretty cozy."

Cooper shook his head in disgust. "And I wouldn't put it past her to cover for him."

I wouldn't, either. Dana Kellerman didn't exactly like me very much. With a sigh, I reached up to push back hair I hadn't had time to style this morning from my face and found my wrist captured by Jessica. "You're hurt."

"What?" I pulled it away from her and stared at it. My God. It was bruised.

An ache flared down my arm, as though acknowledging I'd hurt it had finally awoken the pain. "Shit."

"Stu?" She glowered at me.

I remembered the way Vaughn had pinned me to the bed last night and I glanced at my other wrist. There wasn't a mark on it. "It must have been Stu." I flinched at the memory of him slamming it against the floor so I'd release my phone. "Yeah, it was." I prodded it and winced at the throb of pain.

How the hell had I not noticed the pain?

Adrenaline.

And all the sex would have helped distract me from it, too.

"I am definitely going to fucking kill him," Cooper vowed.

A throat cleared behind us and we turned as Deputy Jackass stepped into our little group. "Try not to threaten to kill someone in the presence of a police officer, Lawson."

Cooper tensed at his threatening tone. "Are you so deep in the Devlins' pockets that you, an *officer*, could give two shits a woman was attacked last night?"

Deputy Jackson flushed, his eyes darkening with impulsive anger that made him look like a spoiled little brat who had just been admonished in class. "Watch your mouth."

Jessica stepped in between Cooper and the deputy. "I assume you finished what was a thorough interview of the witnesses?" Sarcasm dripped from every word.

"Yeah, I'm done."

"Well as Bailey's doctor I will check over her injuries. Would you like me to take photographs for the incident file?"

"Not necessary."

My friend narrowed her pretty hazel eyes on Jackson. "I think Sheriff King will disagree, so I'll call him and ask him personally."

"I'm done here." Deputy Jackass shot them each a filthy look before walking out of my inn without another word.

Cooper watched him depart with a look of calculation. "I think I need to have a word with King about that little son of a bitch."

"The little creep is an idiot," I agreed. "He couldn't have been more obvious about where his loyalty lies. He has to be taking payments from Devlin, right?"

"Probably regularly," Jessica mused. "Maybe even passing information to him all the time."

"But that's just us drawing a conclusion based on speculation." I sighed.

"Nope, that's us drawing a conclusion by intelligent deduction based on fact," Cooper said.

My wrist throbbed and I rubbed at it, disbelieving it had taken me this long to realize how much it hurt. "Sometimes I really love this town."

Jessica eyed my wrist. "You need to get someone to watch the inn so I can wrap that up and check you over for other injuries. Why didn't King send for an ambulance last night?"

"He asked me if I wanted medical attention while we were in the office going over everything, but I thought I was fine and insisted he didn't send for one."

Jess did not look happy about it. And Cooper seemed to agree. "This whole thing has been bungled. King should know better."

"He didn't do anything wrong, Coop. Don't take Deputy Jackass out on the sheriff."

"Deputy Jackass," Jessica huffed with laughter. "That's cute."

I was glad for her moment of amusement because it defused some of Cooper's anger. Giving her a tender look, he slid an arm around her waist, drawing her into him like he just needed the weight of her against him. And I think he did, because his whole body seemed to relax as soon as he held her close.

Envy spiked through me. I couldn't believe that there had been a moment last night when I thought I could have what Coop and Jess had . . . with *Vaughn Tremaine*.

It was hard to imagine Vaughn ever reaching for me just because my presence brought him peace.

For a start I wasn't exactly the most calming person to be around. In fact, I pissed him off more than anything else.

Stop thinking about him!

"I'll . . . uh . . . get one of the girls to watch the inn while we check this out." I waved my wrist at Jess.

Something in my demeanor seemed to bother her. "Are you sure you're really okay?"

"I'm fine. Pissed as hell. But fine."

After a phone call to Sheriff King, in which he said he did want photos of my injury, and was more than a little mad now that I had refused medical attention because it harmed my case if we managed to get Devlin to court, Jess wrapped up my wrist. She also checked me over for other injuries, and except for more bruises on my arms and back, I didn't have any to write home about. Jess had a full day of appointments, so there was no time for me to linger and be subjected to the curiosity that was blazing in her eyes as she fixed me up.

She wanted to know what had happened in my own words, and I was pretty sure she wanted to know why the hell Vaughn had been at the inn to come to my rescue.

And I didn't want to talk about that.

Not. At. All.

I was just leaving the doctor's office when I got a hankering for Reese's Peanut Butter Cups. I kind of craved chocolate and candy when I was particularly stressed and right now was definitely one of those occasions. So instead of heading back to the inn, I headed to the market on Main Street.

It wasn't a good idea.

It wasn't a good idea because I binge-ate Reese's Peanut Butter

Cups and always felt sick afterward. But it also wasn't a good idea in hindsight.

Of course, I didn't know I would bump into a Devlin.

I was musing over the candy selection, wondering if I should add peanut M&M's to my stash, when I caught sight of him out of the corner of my eye. Looking up, the usual awful regret I felt in my chest flared at the sight of Jack Devlin.

Once upon a time I thought Jack Devlin hung the moon. He and Cooper were once a hot good-guy package deal and I loved them both.

I stared into Jack's dark blue-gray eyes wishing the devil weren't so handsome, wishing those eyes of his weren't fathomless with secrets. Secretive though they were, I'd always thought Jack had kind eyes. His mother's eyes.

Tall, taller even than Cooper, Jack was strong—lean but muscular. He had thick dark blond hair that he wore swept off his face, and these days his style was more Vaughn than Cooper. I missed his jeans and plaid shirts. The shirt-and-trousers look made him seem more distant. So did the whole cheating on his best friend thing and hanging out with a dad and brothers he used to look down on with contempt.

I didn't like unsolved mysteries. I didn't like the mystery of Jack's turnabout. And in my fragile state of rejection and fury, I looked into those soulful eyes of his and saw red.

Before he could pass me with his stoic nod of hello, I got in his face. His brows drew together as he stared down at me, standing mere inches from his body, but that was the only reaction he gave to my crowding his personal space.

"You and your goddamn family!" I yelled, more than likely drawing the attention of everyone else in the store. "I am done. Do you hear me, Jack Devlin? You tell Stu I don't care if he paid a dozen whores to give him an alibi last night, I know it was him who broke into my inn and attacked me in my office!" I waved my sprained, wrapped up wrist in Jack's face. "I'm not stupid! I've known the little prick my whole life and wearing a ski mask didn't hide his identity from me while he jumped me, broke my phone, and he would have broken my face if it hadn't been for Tremaine!" I screeched, barely paying attention to the fact that Jack's gaze was focused on my injured wrist. "And I don't like being rescued by Tremaine, Jack! I don't like it one little bit," I seethed. "So you tell that asshole brother of yours, and that swine you call a father, that if they want a fight, I'm ready for them, because Stu just took this one step too far. If there are no longer any lines, if the lines cease to exist, it goes both ways! Come at me, and I will sure as hell come back at you twice as hard!" My chest heaved as I tried to catch my breath.

I was pretty sure my face was scarlet red.

But Jack . . . well . . . Jack didn't even flinch. Instead he lowered the basket of food he'd been carrying, walked calmly around me, and strode right out of the grocery store.

"It was nice talking to you, too!" I yelled after him.

And that was when I became aware of the other customers staring at me. Thankfully, all of them in concern and not in a *I'm terrified of this crazy lady, get me out of here* way.

Huffing in annoyance at myself for my little outburst, I grabbed my Reese's Peanut Butter Cups.

The cashier, Annie, stared at me wide-eyed. "God, Bailey, did Stu Devlin really attack you?"

Oh, damn.

"Look, I really shouldn't have said anything."

"That family." She tutted, shaking her head. "They go too far."

And now so had I, because I'd bet everything I owned that it would be all over town that Stu Devlin had attacked Bailey Hartwell in her inn.

Sheriff King was going to kill me.

"Annie."

"Yeah?"

"Do you sell a hole in the ground?"

"Uh . . ."

"I'd really like to buy one. You know, so it can swallow me."

"Well . . . I'll have to ask Bob if we sell those."

TWELVE

Bailey

"Good afternoon, Hart's Inn. Bailey speaking."

"I think you've done enough *speaking* for one afternoon, Miss Hartwell." Jeff King's deep voice rumbled down my phone line.

He had kind of a sexy phone voice, but no matter how sexy it was I wanted to hang up on him. "Jeff—"

"I'm on duty, so it's Sheriff to you. Accusing a man of attacking you when you have no solid evidence for me isn't the smartest thing to do in this town. Bailey, what were you thinking, mouthing off in the grocery store? Do you know how many calls the station has received in the last two hours?"

Feeling like an admonished child, my hackles rose. "Whose side are you on, *Jeff*, because I'm starting to worry about this town's police force."

"What the hell does that mean?"

"It means your Deputy Jackass—sorry, Jackson—turned up at the inn this morning, took less than five minutes to interview my guests, and pretty much insinuated that I was making the whole thing up. It's funny he would take that stance considering what good friends he and Kerr Devlin are. He couldn't care less that I'd been attacked."

The good sheriff was quiet and when he eventually spoke, I got goose bumps from the warning in his voice. "I suggest you keep comments like that to yourself, Bailey, and let me run my department."

I knew Jeff. He wasn't warning me because he was an asshole, far from it. He was warning me because . . . he knew. He knew Jackson was a slimeball. Of course he did. Was he running his own investigation into him?

"Well, here is a heads-up. Cooper will probably be in touch about Jackson's attitude this morning. He and Jessica were at the inn when the deputy showed up and Coop wasn't exactly happy with what he heard."

"Got it. Now, let's get back to why I called. Are you intending to continue to publicly accuse Devlin? Because I've got an airtight alibi and no evidence. Unless you've remembered something from last night that might help me."

"No. I told you everything. And Dana Kellerman is lying by the way. She's always hated me."

"How did you know—" Jeff cursed, biting off his sentence. "Never mind."

"Look, I promise I'm not going to say anything more in public. I'm sorry about today. I saw Jack and I was upset—"

"Yeah, well, apparently so was Jack."

"What does that mean?"

"A guest at the Grand called the police. I had to send officers out because Jack knocked Stu out in the restaurant. Far as I can tell he went straight from the grocery store to the hotel to find Stu. Stu didn't want to press any charges. Or Ian didn't. Believe me, Bailey, if I could use Jack's reaction as evidence I would. But I've got nothing."

"Jack hit Stu?" I couldn't believe it. "For attacking me?"

"It looks that way. Anyway, if you've got nothing else, I don't know what else I can do. I'll look into it a little more. I'm going to interview Mr. Tremaine again. And you get in touch if you think of anything."

"Right. Thanks, Sheriff."

"Stay safe, Bailey."

We hung up and I reached for my cell, remembered it was smashed and that I needed to buy a new one, and started searching for my old phone book. I found it dusty and disused in the office, but in it was the number I was looking for. I just hoped Cat, Cooper's sister, hadn't changed it since however long ago I'd written it down.

She answered on the third ring.

"Cat, it's me."

"Hey, Bails, I heard what happened. Are you okay?"

"I'm fine. But I mouthed off to Jack Devlin today, accusing Stu, and he just stared at me like I wasn't even there. And then, get this, the sheriff called, and he told me Jack punched Stu. Just minutes after I told him what his brother did. What is that all about?"

"Have you told Jessica? Jack was the one that gave her the heads-up about Cooper's liquor license. The plot thickens."

"What is going on with him? And should I tell Cooper? That's why I called. I wondered if I should tell him?"

She was a quiet awhile and then . . . "Yeah. Before Jess . . . I probably would have said no. But Coop's in a good place. And . . . something isn't right with Jack and it still bothers me. I think deep down it bothers Cooper. He knows there's something more to what happened. So, yes, tell him. I don't know what it will do, if it will do anything, but I'd like to believe Jack is worth forgiving."

"Me, too." And I meant it. Jack punching Stu out for me was a sign of the old protective Jack. "I'll tell Cooper tonight at dinner. You and Joey are still coming, right?"

"Someone else cooking dinner? Yes, we'll be there. My poor kid doesn't eat anything nutritious unless someone other than his mother is cooking."

I laughed. "Then I'll see you tonight."

Just as I was hanging up, the inn door opened and Iris poked her head around it. "Heard what happened, gonna kill that Devlin, Ira and I are worried about you so we'll be at dinner tonight, too, to make sure you're okay, I gotta get back to the restaurant."

And then she was gone.

Warmth suffused me.

I didn't need Vaughn Tremaine to care about me.

I had a whole town that did.

Strolling into the kitchen wearing a satisfied smile on my face, I produced a suspicious look from my head chef, Mona. "Two more for dinner tonight."

She stared at me through her oversized black-framed glasses. Her bright lips were pursed in annoyance. As always she wore a patterned headscarf instead of a chef's hat over her dark hair. "It's a little late notice."

"I got attacked last night. *Some* people actually care," I teased. "They want to have dinner with me. What can I say? I'm kind of awesome."

Mona gave me a reluctant smile. "Fine. But I'm only letting you off the hook because of the whole attack thing. You can't milk it forever though."

I grinned because Mona not giving me shit for a last-minute meal change, a meal she was already cooking along with a separate dinner for guests, was her way of saying she cared about me, too.

To my disappointment Cooper didn't react the way I wanted him to regarding the whole Jack thing. I'd pulled him aside when everyone had arrived and informed him what his old friend had done.

"I heard," he'd said. "And?"

"Well don't you think it means something?"

"I think it means that Jack doesn't know who the hell he is anymore or what side he's really on. I think it means he's old enough to work that out for himself. I think it means I'm just getting on with my life and I don't need any more of his drama."

"But Coop—"

"Bailey, don't you think after what he did to me, he should be the one to come to me and not the other way around?"

And since I knew he was right, I reluctantly let the issue go.

Instead I'd settled my guests into the dining room. They weren't put out by the packed dining room. In fact, my loving, energetic group of friends added a warm ambience to the dining room that evening. While the guests were seated at their individual tables, I'd put together two to host my friends. Seated at the back of the room were Jess, Cooper, Emery, Dahlia, Cat, Joey, Iris, and Ira. And me of course.

Considering she had the dinner menu to cook for our inn guests and a different dinner for my private guests, Mona did an amazing job. With the help of Jay, her sous chef.

"Why don't we eat here all the time for Aunt Bailey's dinners?" Joey said to his mom. "It's so good."

"Are you trying to say you prefer Mona's cooking over mine, kid?"

Joey thought about this carefully. "It's just . . . different."

We roared with laughter at his answer while Cooper curled a hand around his nephew's neck and pulled him toward him so he could kiss the top of his head.

"We've got a diplomat in our midst." Ira grinned at Joey.

Smart as a whip, it wasn't a surprise to us that Joey understood the word. "Maybe I'd make a good politician."

"Oh, sweetheart," Iris groaned. "There are no good politicians."

"Iris," I admonished, "we have a good one sitting in our mayor's office."

She nodded her head, accepting that. "Okay. There are *very few* good politicians."

"I could be a good one," Joey insisted.

"With diplomacy like that, I'm sure of it." Cat looked around the table. "I don't know where he gets that from. It certainly isn't from me."

"And he hasn't learned it from me," I said.

Dahlia snorted. "That's a given, sweetie."

I kicked her playfully under the table. "Watch it, brat."

"So, any word from Tom?" Cooper said abruptly.

Silence fell over the table.

Then Jessica let out a chuckle. "Apparently, Joey doesn't get it from his Uncle Cooper, either."

We laughed while Cooper threw me a look of apology.

"It's fine." I shrugged. "Really. Tom emailed me. He's staying in Philly with family. He uh . . . well he quit his job in Dover and has decided to try to move on elsewhere."

"How do you feel about that?" Cat said. "I mean, you guys were together a long time."

"I'm okay with it. I don't want him to be unhappy. I'm kind of glad that we're starting over fresh away from one another."

"So you haven't told him about the break-in?" Emery asked.

"No. There's no point. I . . . Maybe in a while we'll be able to do the friend thing but I want time apart for now."

"God, you've had a terrible few weeks," Iris stated the obvious. "Things can only get better, Bailey."

Wanting a subject change I thought of someone else I hadn't seen in a while. "How's Ivy?" I asked after Iris and Ira's daughter. Ivy had been my best friend growing up, but she'd had aspirations of becoming a screenwriter. She'd gotten into UCLA's school of film and television, worked her way up from intern on productions to assistant manager, until she started to make it with her screenwriting. That's how she met her fiancé, big-time director Oliver Frost. Up until they met, Ivy had kept in touch with me, and had visited Hartwell every summer. I hadn't seen her in three years. I hadn't heard from her in a year.

Ira scowled. "Who knows?"

"Ira," Iris reprimanded him for his angry tone.

I was concerned. "What's going on? Is Ivy okay?"

The table quieted as we waited for Iris to answer.

"We don't know. Every time we call her to check in she gets off the phone as quickly as possible, giving us excuses about how busy she is."

"Maybe she is," Emery said.

"No." Ira shook his head. "Ivy has always been busy but she never let that Hollywood stuff go to her head. She's always had time for her mother and me. Something isn't right."

"Why don't you go out and see her?" Cooper suggested.

"I want to." Ira threw his wife a belligerent look.

Iris scowled. "Don't look at me like that, Ira Thomas Green." She turned to us to explain. "I have never been the kind of mother to mollycoddle or get in my daughter's business when she hasn't asked me to."

Cooper frowned at her. "Well maybe she *needs* you to."

"Exactly." Ira raised his glass to him.

From the expression on Iris's face I could tell she wanted to argue with them both, but was conflicted. As for me, I was worried about my old friend. "Iris . . . maybe you should."

She held my gaze for a moment before she gave a reluctant nod. "We'll try calling her again, try getting through. If not . . ." She looked at her husband. "We'll go there to see her."

In answer Ira simply reached for his wife's hand.

I looked away from them, letting them have their moment with as much privacy as possible, and my gaze fell on Emery. She stared at the older couple with such longing wistfulness I felt an answering ache in my chest.

"Hey, Em." I smiled at her. "The pork loin okay for you?"

She jerked her gaze away from Iris and Ira. "What? Oh. Yes. Thank you. Delicious."

The wistfulness was wiped clear of her expression now, and I wondered curiously about it. Oh, how I wanted to solve the mystery of Emery Saunders.

Patience, Bailey. Patience.

"I invited Vaughn to dinner," Jessica said. "But he was really preoccupied."

I scowled at the thought of Vaughn joining us for dinner and my tone was sharper than I intended when I offered, "He's busy with his hotel in New York; he doesn't have time for dinner with us."

"Well, yes, but he *was* concerned about you," Jess said. "He called Cooper pretty early this morning to tell us to check in with you."

My heart started to beat a little too hard, a little too fast, and a cold sweat prickled over my skin. I didn't want to talk about Vaughn. I'd been enjoying dinner because it was taking my mind off the bastard.

"You know what would be fun?" I forced a grin. "Photo albums. Emery and Jess haven't seen my photo albums. I have photos in there of Cooper, Cat, and me as kids. I'll go get them."

Iris seemed bemused. "But we're eating."

"We can do both." I waved off her comment and fled the dining room.

I was just walking down the hall to my office when I heard the footsteps behind me. Several footsteps. *Dear God.*

I strode into my office and turned to find Jess, Dahlia, and Emery in the doorway. I gave them a teasing smile to cover my sudden uneasiness. "I don't need a chaperone around my inn. Or chaperone*s*."

Jessica eyed me. "You seemed upset that I asked Vaughn to come tonight."

"I'm not upset." Oh, was I upset. "I just, I mean why would you do that?"

Jess made an *uh . . . duh* face. "Because he helped you out last night."

Right. I kept trying to forget that part. "Well what did he say *exactly*?"

"He was . . ." She frowned. "He was very cold. Distant. More so than usual. Extra-Vaughn-like. So . . . what did you do?"

My first instinct was to drop my jaw, stamp my foot like a teenager, and demand to know why she'd assumed that *I* had done something to *him*. However, in all my trying to force thoughts of Vaughn into the background today, I knew I'd already decided not to tell anyone that Vaughn had rejected and mortified me. That would stay between him and me.

It wasn't just a pride thing on my part. I just . . . as much as I didn't want to save Vaughn Tremaine from himself (knowing I'd get flattened in the process), I also didn't want Jessica and Cooper to stop being friends with him. In their own way, they were a balm to that infuriating man's brooding soul. I didn't want to take that from him just because he was a cowardly asshole who didn't think I was good enough to be in a real relationship with him. Good enough to fuck but not good enough to—

Okay.

Still angry with him.

"Nothing." I shrugged, proud of myself for being so nonchalant. I wasn't exactly known for being able to mask my emotions. "I was shocked that he stopped by to help."

"Yes, shocked, but thankful, right?" Dahlia frowned at me.

"Yes, *Mom.*" I rolled my eyes as I pulled open the drawer that held the old photo albums. I grabbed a couple and strolled back out of the office. "I showed gratitude to Vaughn Tremaine," I assured them.

"Oh, Bailey, dear." A guest, Ms. Schubert, strolled out of the downstairs restroom and stopped as she caught sight of us. A wicked glint of mischief glittered in her blue eyes as she came right up into my personal space. "I'm so glad that handsome man of yours was here to keep you company last night after that terrible ordeal. I must say it made me feel safer knowing he was here. Although, for future reference, my dear, my room is right above yours and I could hear everything. Of course, you were quite loud." She giggled like a little girl. "You made an old woman very envious." And with a conspiratorial chuck of my chin, Ms. Schubert strolled on upstairs to her room, leaving shocked silence in her wake.

Firm hands gripped my biceps, and I was hauled back into my office by Dahlia and Jess. Emery held the door open for them. They shoved me gently inside and then slammed the door closed.

Oh, holy hell.

I stared at them, my cheeks hot, my heart pounding. "Sound-proofing," I announced, my voice all high and squeaky. "It's next on the list of things to do."

"Showed gratitude?" Dahlia repeated my words from earlier, throwing her hands on her hips. "I thought you meant you said thank you, not that you let him screw you."

You have no idea. "I . . ."

"Well?" Jessica stared at me in concern.

I glanced from her to Emery, who was biting her lip, like she was trying not to smile, and Dahlia who looked pissed I hadn't told her.

"Fine!" I threw my hands up in embarrassed exasperation. "I fucked Vaughn."

Emery blushed beetroot at my coarse language. "Oh my."

"You wanted to know, Aurora," I huffed, planting my ass on my desk.

"Elsa," Jessica muttered.

"What?"

"She's Elsa not Aurora."

"Really?" Dahlia stared at her like she was crazy. "You want to argue which Disney character Em looks like or ask our friend how the hell she fell into bed with a man she hated two days ago?"

"Oh, I still hate him."

"Explain." Jess crossed her arms over her chest and leaned against the door. It was the universal body language of *you're going nowhere, bitch, until you tell me what I want to know.*

It was days like today I wished I had friends who didn't give a shit.

"It was a onetime thing. A mistake."

That seemed to piss Jess off. "You used him? Bailey, you know how he feels about you. No wonder he was so pissy today."

I wanted to defend myself but revealing the truth, telling them what really happened, somehow felt worse than their censure. "I got attacked last night, Jess. Forgive me, but I wasn't exactly think-ing straight with all that adrenaline coursing through my body. And yes, I was grateful toward Tremaine for being there and stopping Stu. So we had sex. Then he went home. End of story. And FYI he doesn't care about me. He wanted to screw me. He got what he wanted. Now we're done."

"That can't be the end of the story." Dahlia sounded horrified. "This is Bailey Hartwell and Vaughn Tremaine. This is epic enemies-to-lovers shit!" She eyed me, a thought flitting through her big blue eyes. "Was he not good?"

My shoes were suddenly very interesting to me. "I don't remember."

"He was good," Dahlia surmised.

"How good?" Emery said.

I jerked my head up, stunned by the curiosity in her question. Her cheeks were bright red again.

Jess grinned. "Yeah, how good?"

I huffed. Like she needed to live vicariously through me when she had Lawson jumping her bones every five seconds. "He was fine."

"Liar," Dahlia teased.

"Fine, he was good."

Jess shared a look with Dahlia. "Liar, liar."

"Alright, fine, sex with Vaughn was goddamn mind-blowing. Hate sex: who knew?"

Jess opened her mouth but I cut her off. "But it is not to be repeated. And no one outside of this room is ever going to find out. Jessica, that means no telling Coop."

She pouted but gave me a reluctant nod.

"Now . . . can we go eat dessert and embarrass Cat about her Sporty Spice phase?" I held up the photo albums.

Jessica stepped out of my way to let me open the office door.

"How many times did you uh . . . *screw*?" Emery asked as we trailed out.

I shot Emery a shocked look, ignoring Jess's and Dahlia's stifled snorts. "I am a bad influence on you."

Em's face lit up in a pretty smile. "Yeah."

I let go a bark of laughter, the sound mingling with my friends' amusement, and I threw an arm around Em's waist. "I knew I liked you."

"Yeah. But seriously . . . how many times?"

Meeting my expectant friends' curious gazes I sighed. "Twice. Alright? Hate sex. Twice. And before you ask both times were fantastic," I grumbled, ignoring the looks that they exchanged as we walked back to the dining room.

I felt like I might be in trouble because the look in Jessica's eyes in particular was that of a matchmaker. I knew that look. I'd worn that look the moment I met Jess and thought, *She'd be perfect for Cooper.*

Oh, holy hell.

THIRTEEN

Vaughn

The problem with The Montgomery was Grant Foster after all. As soon as he arrived at his hotel in New York Vaughn knew something was off. The atmosphere wasn't right. The staff was nervous and cagey, and not just because they were aware the boss was pissed off with the latest reviews.

There was something else going on. Vaughn could feel it.

His manager was acting strangely. Jittery. Jumpy.

Vaughn had his suspicions, and it took him a few days, but he managed to charm one of the waiters from the restaurant into telling him what was going on.

"Drugs," Paul said in a hushed voice, his eyes wide at the scandal of it all. "He's on coke, Mr. Tremaine."

Suspicions confirmed, Vaughn sighed. "Any idea when and why this started?"

"His wife left him. He started to see a girl who's into coke. That's when he started slacking off here."

"And why didn't anyone tell me this?"

"Because Foster has been threatening jobs left, right, and center. Total blackmail, too. Anything he thinks he has on us . . . well he's been using it to keep us quiet."

That son of a bitch.

Vaughn headed straight to Grant's office, stormed past his PA, and threw the door open without a warning.

"Mr. Tremaine." Grant shot up out of his chair. "How can— what are you doing?"

"Checking your drawers. What does it look like?"

"Mr. Tremaine?" he squeaked, panicked.

Vaughn yanked open all the drawers in Grant's desk, found nothing, and spotted his briefcase. Grant lunged for it, but Vaughn blocked his way, opened it, and turned it upside down.

The small clear packet containing white powder fell out on top of the files.

Fury burned through him as he whipped around to glare at his manager. "You're fired, Grant."

Grant's eyes glistened with pleading. "Vaughn—"

"Don't. I don't give a shit how many years you've worked for me. I don't tolerate drugs or alcohol abuse from any of my staff members. This is *my* fucking hotel, Foster, and you could give a shit that you are this close to flushing everything I worked for down the toilet."

The truth was Vaughn was angry with himself, too. If he had a tighter handle on things, if he hadn't run away, he would have known what was going on with Grant.

"Pack up your things, get out, and get some help for Christ's sake." He strode toward the door.

"You can't do this!" Foster yelled. "I've worked my ass off for you."

Vaughn stopped and turned around. "You worked hard for me until you stopped working hard for me. Now get your shit and get out . . . or I'll throw you out myself."

Seeing he meant it, Grant lowered his gaze to the desk, his cheeks flushed with humiliation.

On that note, Vaughn stormed out of the office, slamming the door shut behind him. He glared at Grant's personal assistant. The guy must have known what was going on. Vaughn's own PA, Ailsa, probably knew more about him than most people did.

"What's your name?" He was cold, calm on the outside like always, but furious on the inside.

The young man seemed to sense that and blanched. "Ryan. Ryan Upton, sir."

"You're fired, too, Ryan. When you took on a position here, you became my employee, not his." He pointed to Grant's door. "And I should have been informed of the situation from you, not one of my waiters."

"But, sir . . . he threatened me. I've tried. Really, I have but . . ."

Vaughn squeezed his eyes shut in aggravation. When he opened them Ryan stood up and swiveled his computer screen toward Vaughn.

"I've been trying to keep a handle on things, keep things running smoothly. He hired Kacey, the chef, against my advice. There was another chef far more qualified but Kacey is a friend of his girlfriend. I have the list of other chefs we interviewed here, if you'd like to see." He clicked a document up on the screen. It contained a list of chefs, their qualifications, previous employment, and Ryan's comments on their suitability. From what Vaughn was reading the young man appeared quite astute.

He looked up at him. "How old are you?"

"Twenty-six, sir."

"How did he threaten you?"

"To fire me. And I can't lose this job. I have a wife, a daughter."

This was getting more and more maudlin. "If you'd told me, I could have assured your position here."

"No offense, sir, but I don't know you, and I do know you have a longstanding history with Mr. Foster."

"You didn't know if I'd believe you," Vaughn surmised, biting off a curse.

"Exactly. Mr. Foster has stood in my way about a lot of things. The housekeepers have been slacking with no supervision. I've tried to enforce some authority but I'm just the PA."

"Fine. You're not fired, Ryan." Vaughn turned his computer back toward him. "I'm staying until I have the hotel under control again and a manager that I trust in place. You are now *my* PA while I'm here and you'll be the new manager's PA as long as I'm happy with your performance."

Relief flooded Ryan's expression. "Thank you, sir."

Vaughn nodded. "Your first job as my PA is to call security to come and remove Grant from his office. I have a feeling he's not going to leave without a little motivation."

His new PA gave him a concerned look. "And what if Mr. Foster decides to blab about why you let him go? The police might get involved. That would be terrible for the hotel."

"That would be terrible. But it won't happen. Foster won't tell anyone because that would mean telling them about his coke habit."

"Right."

"Call security, and then once Foster's out I want his office searched high and low for any drugs. Once it's clean, call Delia and tell her I want to talk with her in the Carrington Saloon."

"Delia, sir?"

"My head of housekeeping."

"She quit six months ago."

A new anger stirred in his gut. "What?"

Ryan winced. "She got a new position because she didn't like how things were going here. She asked Mr. Foster to contact you but . . ."

"He didn't. My God." Vaughn ran his hand through his hair. He'd hired Delia as a housekeeper ten years ago and she'd made her way quickly to head housekeeper. She was smart, funny, not intimidated by him, and the hardest worker he'd ever met.

No wonder things had gone to hell around here.

"Do you know where she works now?"

"No, but her niece, Lila, still works here. She'll know. And she's on shift right now."

Vaughn's eyebrows drew together. "You seem to know my staff well, Ryan."

"I pay attention, sir."

Thank God someone does.

Renewed irritation bubbled through Vaughn. First he'd let two sisters drive him out of his city, and then he'd let one tempting little redhead keep him away.

Now his hotel was in danger because of it.

Women.

"After you've dealt with Foster get Lila down here and get Delia's details from her. I'll call Delia and see if I can get her back. We'll go from there."

Ryan looked energized, determined, and it calmed Vaughn somewhat to know he apparently had someone on his side. He only hoped the young man proved to be as competent as he appeared.

Dealing with the mess at the hotel was a great thing because he had very little time to think about Bailey. He'd left Hartwell, needing that distance, and he did it knowing Cooper was there to look out for her.

He wasn't sure he could have left if he hadn't known there was someone he trusted to watch over her after the violent break-in.

After what he himself had done to her.

Every time he heard her flat voice saying, *"I'm going to shower you off of me,"* he felt a sharp pain in his chest.

The first few days at the hotel had been manic. He and Ryan had worked together to make sure the staff knew the boss was back in town and if they didn't start working their asses off, there would be firings. With the promise of a raise and a tighter supervision over the hotel, Vaughn managed to talk Delia into coming back as head housekeeper. He had no qualms firing the new head housekeeper since he wasn't doing his job.

There were a few more firings as Delia went through her roster of employees and discovered the housekeepers who weren't keeping up with her strict standards. He let her set up interviews for new staff, while he set up interviews for a new manager and chef.

Once the first few days of upheaval calmed a little, Vaughn found himself in Foster's old office at the end of the day, with a moment to think.

And he didn't like it.

Because when he had time to think he only thought of one person.

She made him feel weak.

This obsession with her . . . it made him feel weak.

He resented her a little.

Or a lot.

But he never stopped wanting her, and at night, when he fell into bed exhausted and closed his eyes, he saw her beneath him; he smelled her perfume, felt her soft skin, remembered the way it had felt to move inside her . . . and the longing would make him hard. He'd come by his own hand, climaxing in frustration like a pubescent teen.

Vaughn felt himself stirring at the memory of her gasping his name as he thrust into her for the first time. He clenched his fists, determined to think of anything but Bailey Hartwell.

His phone buzzed and he felt nothing but a deep-seated gratitude for the distraction. He reached over to switch the phone speaker on. "Yes?"

"Sir, a Mr. Oliver Spence is here to see you." Ryan's voice crackled over the line.

Not surprised by his friend's appearance, he glanced at the clock. It was seven p.m.

"Send him in. And Ryan?"

"Yes, sir."

"Go home to your wife and daughter."

"Thank you, sir."

He smirked. Ryan was never anything but professional and respectful, to the point he was almost amusing. But only because Vaughn could sense the hunger in the young man. He was ambitious. And he was smart. So smart, that if he'd had more experience and qualifications, Vaughn would have hired him as his new manager.

The office door opened and his old friend, Oliver, strode in like he owned the place. That was how Oliver entered any room. His air of superiority and entitlement groomed by a lifetime of privilege. They had been friends since they were small boys, but they'd grown into two entirely different men. Vaughn, his father's son, was plagued by the constant desire to strive for achievement and success, to build a name not off his father's accomplishments, but from his own determination. Oliver hadn't worked a day in his life, having been granted his eye-wateringly large trust fund at eighteen. He was smart enough to make good investments, however, and not to piss the money away.

In all honesty he wasn't the kind of man Vaughn respected very much, but he liked him even so. Oliver was charming and he was a loyal friend. He was the only person who had visited him in Hartwell, the only one who seemed to still give a damn now that Vaughn had apparently turned his back on the Manhattan social circle.

Plus, Oliver knew everyone. He was a useful man to be friends with because he made networking with the right people so much easier on Vaughn. In fact if it weren't for Spence, Vaughn probably wouldn't have considered buying the hotel on Hart's Boardwalk. For years the Spences had a mansion in the neighborhood where Vaughn now owned a home. They sold it a number of years ago but Oliver, who had spent a considerable number of summers as a young man in Hartwell, got wind of the sale of the boardwalk hotel and had suggested it might be a lucrative business opportunity for Vaughn. Once Vaughn had arrived in Hartwell to look into the property, that was it. Something about the town had hooked him immediately. It was the exact opposite of his life in Manhattan. It was earthy, it was vibrant yet low-key, and there was something incredibly soothing about the boardwalk atmosphere.

He had Oliver to thank for the birth of Paradise Sands. Mostly, however, he liked his friend because he didn't make issue of Vaughn's lack of interest in relationships. Where Vaughn was a serial bachelor, Oliver was a serial monogamist. He'd been engaged at least five times that Vaughn could remember, falling in love easily, and falling out just as easily.

When he was single he was a good wingman to have around.

A good distraction.

"I heard you were back. Rumors are flying about this place." Oliver grinned at him.

Vaughn gritted his teeth. One thing he didn't admire about Oliver: his enjoyment of gossip. "Oh?"

"Something about the ship on the brink of sinking until its good captain came to its rescue."

"I don't know what you're talking about."

"Of course you don't. Anyway"—he stared around the office with distaste and boredom—"*I've* come to rescue *you*."

And at that moment Vaughn was not averse to being rescued. "What did you have in mind?"

His smile was wicked. "I'm dating a ballet dancer. Vaughn . . . Fuck me, what that girl can do in bed. And she has a friend."

Something tight, ugly, gripped his chest at the thought of screwing a stranger.

Vaughn pushed through the constriction, needing something, anything, to break him from his infatuation. "What color is her hair?"

"The friend?" Oliver frowned. "Blond, I think. Why does it matter?"

"No reason," he muttered, switching his laptop off and pushing back from the desk. "Just no redheads."

"Why not?"

Ignoring his friend's curious, calculating gaze, Vaughn shrugged. "I've gone off them."

Oliver laughed, throwing his arm around his shoulders. "Fine. Wait until you meet Tatiana, Tremaine. Fucking goddess in the sack. I didn't know you could fuck a woman in that many positions and believe me I've done active research over the years . . ."

His friend continued on, regaling him with the benefits of sleeping with a world-class ballerina, but Vaughn was no longer hearing him. He couldn't over the pounding of the blood rushing in his ears.

His heart was in protest.

How could he touch another woman when he felt like this about Bailey?

You sound like a pussy.

And that was exactly why tonight he was going to lose himself inside a fucking ballerina and forget about a certain princess.

Bailey

It turned out Stu's attack kicked off a week of crap. The day after the girls found out about my "liaison" with Tremaine, Emery showed up at the inn with what I would soon discover was sympathy coffee.

What is a sympathy coffee, you may ask.

A sympathy coffee is one that is delivered with an empathetic expression and, "I wanted it to be a friend to tell you that Vaughn has left for Manhattan."

The words made me numb and while my reply had been "Oh" while I accepted said coffee, and not the sympathy, inside I was calling that man insulting names I didn't even know were in my vocabulary.

At my non-outward reaction, Emery had given me these big puppy dog eyes.

The puppy dog eyes, even on someone so cute, were annoying. "I don't care," I'd snapped.

She didn't look like she believed me. "If you need someone to talk to, just let me know."

And maybe because it was Emery and she was less demanding and intrusive than, say, me, I found myself calling out to her as she was leaving, "Is it permanent? Tremaine. Has he gone for good?"

My friend had given me a sad smile. "I don't know. But the staff at Paradise seem to think he'll be gone awhile."

I'd shrugged, nonchalant. "Okay."

Emery wasn't buying my nonchalance but like I knew she wouldn't, she didn't push me. Instead she'd left me to sip at my sympathy (I was kind of accepting it now) coffee while I pondered the idea of a Hartwell-less Tremaine.

"A heartless Tremaine, you mean," I'd huffed to myself, horrified at the sound of those words catching on my tears. The tears were forced down with my swallows of coffee but the pain, the hurt of his defection, gripped at my entire body.

I walked in on Tom having sex with another woman and I hadn't felt this kind of pain.

It was so typical of me to impulsively give a piece of myself to a man part of me didn't even like. To see something in him that was worth loving.

"You deserve better." I'd studiously returned to looking through the applications I'd received for the position of my manager.

I hadn't gotten far when the inn phone rang.

"So you didn't think your mother and father might want to know that you've been attacked in the inn?" my father's voice had snapped down the line as soon as I answered.

Shit.

I'd put off informing my parents of the attack because I didn't want to deal with the consequences. But it was wrong of me to keep it from them. "I'm sorry, Dad."

"So you should be," Mom had said. "We had to hear from Jaclyn."

The mayor. Mum's best friend. Of course. "I'm sorry, Mom."

"We're flying out," Dad had said.

"No." I loved my parents, I missed my parents, but the last thing I needed was the chaos they'd bring. It wasn't my dad. It was my mom. She loved me, she was proud of me, but she also, like me, did not have a brain-to-mouth filter. She would go around the inn criticizing it because it was so different to her taste, and then she'd try "fixing" it. I did not need that stress on top of everything else. Moreover, my father was too insightful when it came to me. He'd take one look at me and know I was hurting over something or someone.

"Don't do that," I'd insisted. "I'm really fine and we're handling it. Sheriff King is on it."

"It isn't up to you whether we come out there or not," my mom had screeched.

"Dad, take me off speakerphone."

"Don't you dare, Aaron!"

There had been a clicking noise and then my father's voice sounding softer, quieter. "I'm off speakerphone."

"Aaron, that's not fair!" I'd heard my mother yell in the background. She'd continued to yell, but it got more distant until it cut off entirely.

"I'm in my den," Dad had explained. "You can speak freely."

"I know Mom will be mad at me and you for cutting her out of this conversation but, Dad . . . you know I love her . . . but I can't deal with Mom being here right now. I'm in the middle of dealing with the police about Devlin, I'm up to my eyeballs in applications for the manager position, and I'm still trying to work through things after Tom and I . . ."

"And your mother would complain about the changes you've made to the inn and try to fix things," Dad had said on a sigh.

I'd smiled because I loved my father and I loved that he understood us all so well. "Yes. Exactly. It would be too much."

"And what am I supposed to do? Just sit here in Florida and worry about my kid?"

"I'll be fine. I have Jessica and Cooper watching out for me. I've got most of the town watching out for me. I am very lovable, you know." I'd winced as soon as I said it because apparently I wasn't so lovable to some folks.

"I wouldn't feel right not coming out to you."

"Let's compromise. Let me get everything in order here. Just give me a few weeks and then if you still want to fly out here you can. It's not that I don't miss you. You know I do."

"I know, Cherry." He'd sighed. "Fine. I'll give you a few weeks but if anything else happens that I don't like, I'm coming out there whether you can handle your mother's controlling behavior or not."

We'd soon hung up, leaving the poor man to deal with the aftermath of cutting Mom out of the conversation, then I'd concentrated on those applications again. In fact I busied myself as much as possible, not giving myself time to think about anything else but the inn.

But the day I discovered Vaughn had crossed states possibly to get away from what happened between us, Sheriff King showed up at the inn with more crappy news.

"I'm sorry, Bailey. I can't press any charges against Stu. I will keep an eye on things, however. And you let me know if the Devlins start harassing you."

There weren't enough words to describe the impotency I'd felt in that moment. The injustice. I wanted to track down Dana and Stu, slap her for being a traitor to womankind, and knee him devastatingly hard in the balls to save the world from the possibility of him reproducing.

I didn't voice this or my disappointment. "And what about Jackson?"

King narrowed his eyes on me. "You leave all that to me."

And on that rather attractively reassuring note (the man was potently masculine), the good sheriff had left me to brood.

You can imagine how I felt then, after suffering crappiness upon crappiness, when Rex strode into my inn that evening.

Rex McFarlane. As in, the Rex I'd called and humiliated by

sharing my mortifying discovery of our respective lovers having sex. I'd meant to apologize to him but with everything else going on in my life, I'd forgotten. Horrible but true.

I was convinced my week was about to get crappier.

Bolstering myself, I'd walked over from where I was dusting the fireplace mantel in the inn reception area, to where he was staring at the little bell located at the check-in counter.

"Rex?"

He turned toward me.

And he smiled. "Bailey."

Surprised by his congenial tone, I walked right up to him. "What are you doing here?"

This time his smile was sad as his dark brown eyes wandered over my face. I'd found Rex adorable when we first met because he reminded me of my teenage crush, Josh Hartnett. He was dark and tall like him, charming and cute. He was a very cute twenty-four-year-old *young* man.

"I . . . uh . . ." He stuffed his hands in his pockets, hunching over as if he were uncomfortable. "I guess I came here to talk."

"Is it about what I did? Calling you like that? Because I have been meaning to get in touch to apologize. I wasn't in my right mind; it had just happened, I had just caught them and they were, you know, and it was bad and I saw her purse and I just grabbed her phone and then I called you and it was bad and I shouldn't have—"

"Bailey." He interrupted my ramble. "It's okay. It may not have been the right way to do it, but it was the right thing to do. Telling me, I mean. So thank you."

"I'm still sorry."

"Yeah. I know. That's kind of why I'm here."

"Oh?"

He ran a hand through his shaggy hair and glanced around, as though he were checking we were alone. "Do you have some time right now . . . to talk?"

"I can take a walk," I said.

Rex seemed to deflate with relief. "Great. I just . . . Okay, you can say no, but I haven't been able to talk to anyone about Erin and . . . I need someone to talk to. You're the only person I know who gets it."

The truth was I had moved on from Tom. Yes, I still missed my friend. I missed the familiarity of him, and having this person in my life who knew me so well. But my heart was aching over someone else. Over a different kind of situation.

Yet . . . I could still sympathize with Rex. It might be nice to be distracted from my own hurt by talking about someone else's pain for a while.

And of course . . . I could never say no to the wounded.

After I let Mona know where I was going, I walked Rex out and onto the boardwalk. In silence, I led him down onto the beach where we both took off our shoes and let our feet sink in the soft sand. The summer season was in full swing now, and even after sunset the beach was busy. Still, we had privacy in our little bubble of two as we began to make our way along the shore.

"So what would you like to talk about?" I started.

"I feel a little weird now that I'm here. I mean, we barely know each other and this shit is kind of personal."

"I know this may mean nothing to you but believe me when I say you can trust me. I'm a vault."

"Tom used to say that." Rex flinched at his name. "He used to wax lyrical about you, about how much he trusted you, how you were so loyal. I think I was more shocked about him screwing you over than I was about Erin."

Maybe I wasn't quite over my ex's betrayal because Rex's words weren't exactly easy to hear.

"I guess he forgot all that when Erin's twenty-three-year-old breasts bounced by."

I immediately regretted my sardonic tone because Rex paled.

Squeezing his arm, I apologized. "I have no filter."

He gave me a weak smile. "Tom said that, too."

"Tom said a lot, huh?"

"Yeah. All of it good. I'm sorry he cheated on you, Bailey."

"I'm sorry Erin cheated on you."

When he kicked at the sand, staring despondently at his feet as he did so, he reminded me of a sad, lonely little boy. My heart hurt for him. "Rex?"

"I . . . I feel angry all the time," he admitted. "Not because . . . I . . ." He sucked in a deep breath and exhaled. More composed, he continued, and he spoke so quietly I had to lean in to hear. "I told Erin things about my life, about my family, that I haven't told anyone. I decided to trust her. She was the first woman I trusted."

"And she betrayed you."

Our eyes met. "Yeah," he whispered.

"I'm so sorry, Rex."

"Me, too. Because now . . . now I'm scared shitless that all the stuff I thought I got over, all my goddamn trust issues—" He broke off in a hollow laugh. "I can't believe I'm telling you this shit."

"You're telling me because you need someone to tell it to."

He stopped to stare out at the water. "I don't want to be that bitter guy who ends up with nothing and no one because he couldn't bring himself to trust anyone." I found myself captured in Rex's soulful gaze. "I'm not that guy, Bailey. I . . . Life has tried to make me that guy but deep down it's not in my nature. But I can feel it happening . . . and I just want to put a stop to it before it's too late."

Moved by his honesty and touched that he'd shared it with me, even if he only came to me through lack of options, I curled my hand around his wrist in comfort. "You're talking to me. And you might not believe this yet, but you'll learn that you *can* trust me. There are people out there worth trusting."

He covered my hand with his other one and closed his eyes. He stayed like that for a while and I let him, enjoying the calm surroundings with him, even as the sounds of laughter and conversation drifted toward us from the people on the beach.

Eventually Rex opened his eyes and he gave me this small, amazed little smile.

I couldn't help but smile in return. "What?"

He shook his head in disbelief. "That's the first time since you called that I've felt a modicum of peace." He nudged me with his shoulder, playful, teasing. "You've bookended this chapter in my life. Chaos and peace."

I gave a huff of laughter. "There are many people who would say that is a very apt description of me: bringer of chaos and peace."

"There are worse monikers."

We shared a grin and I was pleasantly surprised by the feeling of warmth that suffused me. There was no doubt in my mind that I'd made a connection with young Rex, and that life might just have handed me a new friend.

FOURTEEN

Bailey

One Month Later

"We're supposed to be discussing the bridesmaid dresses. Bailey. Earth to Bailey."

My head jerked up from my phone at the sound of my name. "What?"

I had a day off because I had a new manager to help take care of things at the inn.

The whole business of finding a manager had been stressful after the Devlin incident. If I'd found it hard to put my trust in someone before the attack, now I was even more wary. Thankfully, Cooper's sister Cat had come up with a suggestion that surprised me.

Aydan, her best friend, was working two jobs because her cheating scumbag husband had taken off a couple of years ago, leaving her alone to look after their teenage daughter, Angela. Aydan bartended at Germaine's, a bar off Main Street, at night and she worked as a part-time receptionist for a hair salon. Moreover, her daughter worked weekends at the fun park the Devlins owned a few blocks back from the boardwalk.

Aydan was exhausted and even working the two jobs together, she wasn't earning what she could be earning as my manager. Cat swore that her friend was hardworking and a quick learner. With her character reference I hired Aydan, despite her lack of qualifications.

My father said I was nuts, my mother used other adjectives, but I did it.

I worried about it.

But I did it.

A month later I was happy. Relaxed even. Between the Devlins backing off entirely because of Stu's stupid stunt and my new manager, I was almost stress-free.

Aydan was an angel sent from heaven. Cat wasn't lying when she said the single mother was a fast learner. And a people pleaser to boot. My guests loved her.

I loved her.

My life was finding balance again now that she was there to help out.

The faster she learned, the more free time I had, and she was willing to give me that free time because I was so flexible with her when it came to Angela. When Angela broke up with her boyfriend and was a sobbing wreck, I covered Aydan's shift so she could go be with her kid.

She appreciated that and we soon fell into that kind of give-and-take working relationship.

I felt like she'd been working for me longer than a month.

Jessica frowned at me. "Are you okay?"

"I'm fine."

"Well . . ." She pointed to my phone, as she petted the top of Louis's head.

"Oh. Sorry." We were at her and Cooper's place with Dahlia and Emery, and there was a whole bunch of wedding stuff scattered across the dining table. I was supposed to be helpful in this rushed wedding extravaganza, not distracted. "Rex just sent me a text."

"I thought you *just* had brunch on the beach with him," Dahlia said before biting into one of the donuts Jessica had laid out for us.

"I did. But it was kind of a hard conversation and, um . . . I think he's feeling vulnerable. He's still in Hartwell and wants to have dinner. Would you guys mind if I rain-checked ours tonight?"

While Emery and Jessica said, "Of course not," Dahlia eyed me in suspicion. "What is going on with you two?"

"Not that." I read her dirty mind. "He's nine years younger than me. He doesn't see me that way."

"Oh, of course not. He's just a man with a working penis and you're just a beautiful woman in your prime."

Jessica and Emery snorted.

I rolled my eyes. "It's not like that. He's lonely and he needs someone to talk to. He trusts me."

"And he wants to get into your pants. Maybe for revenge sex."

"Dahlia," I warned. "Not funny."

She winced. "Sorry. I . . . just . . . I'm worried about you."

"Why would you be worried about me?"

"Let's see. Your boyfriend of ten years cheats on you, you're surprisingly okay with that, you get attacked, you have mind-blowing sex with your enemy, he ups and disappears, and then you end up having this weird, cozy codependent relationship with the ex-boyfriend of the girl who fucked your ex-boyfriend."

I stared at her, my lips parted, but no words came out.

Silence rang out around the room.

And then I groaned, "Jesus Christ, that does sound insane."

"Uh-huh."

"It's not as insane as that in reality," I promised. "The Rex thing is just platonic. He needed someone to talk to, to find a way to trust again, and I gave him that."

"Yes, because you can't help yourself. You have to rescue people," Jessica said. "But have you stopped to work out how *you're* feeling? For a start: Vaughn. I don't believe for a second that you are okay with what happened between you two."

Not wanting to touch that subject, I pushed at a wedding magazine. "Hey, we didn't come here to psychoanalyze me. We came to talk weddings."

"Vaughn is back," Jessica said abruptly. "Cooper and I are meeting with him tomorrow to catch him up on the final preparations for the wedding."

My heart hammered in my chest at the thought of seeing him again. It felt like forever since we'd spoken. Our night together, although vivid, was like a memory from a long time ago.

It was easier with him gone.

The pain was lessened.

I knew that for a fact because the idea of seeing him again smarted.

Hiding the hurt, I shrugged. "Then I guess we'd better get a move on choosing these dresses. We only have a few weeks left."

"See, that right there"—Dahlia stabbed her half-eaten donut in my direction—"is why I'm worried about you. You're lying! And you never lie."

"She's right," Jessica agreed. "You always say what is on your mind. The fact that you're not means this is something we should be concerned about."

I could feel the panic starting to rise inside of me as they ganged up on me in loving but annoying concern.

"Guys." Emery was tentatively firm. "Leave Bailey alone. She's a grown woman, and I think she can handle herself pretty well. If she wants to talk about it, she will. But she doesn't, so I think we should back off and look at bridesmaid dresses."

Startled that my rescue had come from such a surprising source, I could only stare at Emery wide-eyed as an admonished Jess and Dahlia left me alone and got back to dress research.

Guilt consumed me.

For as long as I'd known each of these women I'd badgered my way into their lives with my determination to turn them into family. I'd been nosy. I'd been intrusive. And no matter that it had come from a place of kindness, I'd still done it.

I'd done it to Emery, too.

They'd given me their confidences (well . . . Emery would one day, once I was through with her), and they deserved that trust in return.

"I don't want you to hate him," I said. When they looked at me astonished, I met Jessica's gaze. "Vaughn is your friend."

Her eyes narrowed. "What the hell did he do?"

"Nothing. He didn't make any promises or . . . I . . . I was stupid." I looked at the table, watching my fingers knot together. "I've always been attracted to him but I didn't want to be. And it was that whole damsel-in-distress thing." I laughed hollowly. "Talk about letting my team down. I went weak at the knees as soon as a guy came to my rescue. And . . . I convinced myself that he cared about me."

"He does care about you," Jessica insisted. "I know it."

"I thought I saw that in his eyes when we were together. But when it was over he got out of my bed and he told me that it was a mistake, and I realized all I'd seen was satisfaction that he finally got one over on me."

Dahlia cursed under her breath.

"I've spent too long feeling like I don't deserve something special, and I promised myself after I left Tom that I would try to do better by myself. Vaughn made me feel second-rate. I need to avoid a man who would make me feel that way."

"You're wrong about Vaughn," Jess said. "He cares about you. He's just . . . I think he's scared of you for some reason."

"And if you're right? That means getting involved with a man who doesn't know what he wants. I'm not chasing someone with that many issues."

"But you'll happily deal with Rex's issues?" Jessica challenged.

"Rex is just a friend," I repeated. "He isn't a land mine waiting to explode. Vaughn is. My own personal land mine. You don't know . . . I don't even know . . . I just . . . I went from not liking that man very much to looking into his eyes and thinking, *Wow, I can't believe he was right in front of me this whole time.*" My eyes burned and blurred with tears. "I thought for a moment that that asshole was 'the one.' And while I was thinking it, he was just getting off. Do you know how humiliated I was? How *stupid* that made me feel?"

I brushed impatiently at the tears that slipped down my cheeks, and Emery reached for my free hand. I let her grip it hard.

Dahlia's and Jessica's faces were tight with emotion.

"Don't be mad at him, Jess. Please. You and Cooper are his friends, and he needs that from you."

"Why do you even care?"

"Because he never promised me anything," I repeated. "He tried to leave and I threw myself at him. I made him think it was just sex. Any normal hot-blooded male would have done the same. It's not his fault I thought it was something more."

"This is messed up." Dahlia huffed.

"No. It's just one of those things." I brushed the conversation aside, wishing I could do the same with my feelings. "Now, can we look at dresses?"

There was a moment of quiet from my friends.

Jess pointed to a dress in one of the magazines. "We can rule out pink. I don't want pink."

"Good." I was relieved for many reasons. "Pink clashes with my hair."

FIFTEEN

Bailey

It was official: I was an idiot.

How else did you explain the fact that I was standing in the lobby of Paradise Sands Hotel knowing full well I was being manipulated by a would-be matchmaker?

Jessica had called me that morning.

"I need you with Cooper and me today. I want your opinion on our final plans for the reception room."

Uh-huh. Yeah. I called bullshit. Except only in my head.

"Oh. Right. Well sure, of course," I'd answered.

At the time I couldn't believe the words had come out of my mouth. Only yesterday I was so sure that Vaughn's absence was a good thing for me. But I let Jess manipulate me . . . because I wanted to see him. I wanted to be able to be around him and feel okay. To be strong. To have him finally know, or at least think, that he hadn't gotten to me, that I wasn't in the least bit humiliated.

Plus, I needed the distraction. Last night I'd been hanging out with Rex when he dropped the bombshell on me that he was attracted to me. Although flattered, I was also a little freaked out. I wanted to continue our friendship but I didn't want to lead him on. So I'd told him about Vaughn and how I was still trying to work through getting over him.

In answer Rex insisted we stay friends. That he could wait for me.

He'd sounded sure.

I was not so sure.

Jessica led them through the hotel to the ballroom where the reception would be hosted. As soon as we stepped through the double doors, I envisioned how Jessica had described it would look on the day, and I knew it was going to be spectacular.

"I can't believe you've managed to pull a wedding off in three months. That shouldn't be possible."

"No, it shouldn't," a wry, familiar, sexy voice said from behind them.

As my heart began to pound a mile a minute, I turned on my heel to face Vaughn. He wore his usual tailored suit, his hair perfect, everything perfect.

My body reacted to him, memories of our night together washing over me.

God damn it!

I hated that he could make me feel that way.

It's just physical attraction. Nothing more.

His gray eyes were so hard to read. I wished I knew what was going on inside his head.

Oh yeah, sure, just physical *attraction.*

"I'm surprised Vivien managed to pull it off," he finished, interrupting my inner war with myself.

Vivien, I knew, was the hotel's main events manager and Jess's wedding coordinator.

"I thought you employed only the best," I said, mostly to make him look at me.

And then I wondered why I wanted that, because his gray eyes seared into me with carnal knowledge. *I've seen you naked*, his gaze said.

Well you did want to be able to read his mind. Be careful what you wish for.

I ignored the shiver that whispered down my spine.

"Miss Hartwell."

Back to Miss Hartwell, are we? Great. Well, I can play that game, too.

Even though I could feel it happening, and I disliked myself for it, I turned into a sullen teenager on him. "I'm surprised you came back. We all thought you'd left. Permanently."

"Wishful thinking, Miss Hartwell?"

"I don't care one way or the other, *Tremaine*."

"Too busy with the new boyfriend."

"What?"

"You mean Rex?" Jess said.

Vaughn raised an eyebrow. "His name is Rex? As in T. rex?"

Cooper coughed in an effort to swallow his laughter and I shot him a dirty look before swinging it toward Vaughn. "Rex like the Hollywood actor Rex Harrison. And he's not my boyfriend."

"Yet," Jess added. "He told her last night that he wants to be. He intends on being very persistent."

"Did we switch personalities or something? Usually, I'm the one that doesn't know when to shut up."

"Oh, so you're aware of that flaw." The jibe came from Vaughn. Surprise, surprise.

"Oh, really? You want to go down that path? Because we'd be here all day listing your flaws."

"Flaws? What flaws? I'm perfect."

"Perfect asshole, you mean."

He looked at Cooper and Jess. "All I heard was I have a perfect ass."

My friends tried to hide their smiles and failed. So he was being cute and funny. I could fight *my* smile.

"You just brought me here to torture me, didn't you?" I said to Jess as Vaughn and Cooper walked ahead of us.

"You didn't have to come."

"I know. I just . . . had to see something for myself."

"What? That all the hostility between you is masking an epic love?"

I shot her a look. "No."

"You told Rex you couldn't date him because you still had feelings for Vaughn. I'm just helping you out. I mean, you have to be around the guy to work out what you want."

"It's not about working out what I want. It's about working past it because he doesn't want me."

"Oh, please. He's like that kid at recess punching the cute girl on the arm every five minutes. He likes you. He just doesn't know what to do about it."

"If that really is the case, Jess, I'm not interested. I'm thirty-four. I'm not wasting my time waiting for him to grow up. I just need to move on."

"Just here to slow down the proceedings as usual, Miss Hartwell?" Vaughn called back to me.

Jess threw me a knowing look and then hurried to catch up with Cooper. Vaughn waited for me, and Jess and Coop seemed to deliberately wander out of earshot.

"Why is it you're such a jackass to me?" I asked.

Something flickered in his gaze. Something like guilt. "Because it keeps you at a distance," he answered with startling honesty. "And I like you at a distance."

In that moment I almost hated him.

Was Jess right? Did he actually care about me? If that was true . . . then wasn't that worse? That he could care about me but still not want to be with me because I wasn't good enough for him?

Anger swirled with passion, lust, and other devilish things inside me. I stepped into his personal space, our lips merely inches from one another, and his attention dropped to my mouth with hot focus. I ignored the impulse to kiss him. "Cowardice is such an unattractive quality in a man," I whispered, and his gaze flew to meet mine. The steel in his was much too hot. I thought I even saw sparks in them. Flints of anger.

Done tormenting him as he tormented me, I stepped away and watched his whole body relax. "You're right to keep your distance,

Tremaine. Not even your pretty face can make up for your character defects."

It was a terrible thing to say, but a woman scorned and all that.

"I hurt you," he surmised. "I didn't mean to hurt you. It was the last thing I wanted to do."

"Don't flatter yourself, Vaughn," I said, not unkindly this time. "You're not the first one-night stand I've ever had."

He studied me far too long, until I was squirming. "I was the first man you slept with after your breakup with Tom, however, wasn't I?"

The personal question made me want to spin around and walk away but I had to find some easy ground with this man. I had to control my emotions and stop acting like a defensive teenager every time he said something to me. "Yes. So thanks for that." I smirked. "Loosened me up, got me back in the game."

Oh, God. I sound like a moron.

His expression darkened. "In time for the T. rex."

And just like that we were back to sparring again. "*Rex*. He's a *friend*. His ex-girlfriend is the woman Tom slept with. We bonded over the betrayal."

"Wasn't the woman Tom slept with younger than you?"

"Yes." I knew what he was getting at. "And yes, Rex is nine years younger than me. What? Too hard to believe that a young, virile man would be interested in me?"

"Any man with a working dick would be interested in you," he said, throwaway style, as if the comment wasn't shocking. "So Jessica was telling the truth—he's pursuing you?"

I blinked, trying to get past his crude compliment. "Um . . . what? Yes. About Rex? Yes."

The muscle in his jaw popped as he ground his teeth together. I assumed it was to hold back a caustic comment. Instead he looked down at the floor, unable to meet my eyes.

He looked younger and very lost.

And damn it, he tugged at my heart. I remembered how I'd felt the night of the attack. How I wondered what it would be like to have Vaughn confide his worries to me, to understand this complicated, brooding man. I'd wanted his secrets. I'd wanted to salve his wounds. I'd just . . . wanted *him*.

It hurt that he hadn't wanted me the same way.

But Jessica's words kept haunting me, kept giving me that damn hope my dad had always warned us about. "Why do you care if Rex wants me?" I found myself saying, my words, my tone begging him to be honest, and to be brave.

He didn't look comforted by my kind tone. Instead he looked pissed off. More than that, he looked wary. Like a stray dog who hadn't seen much kindness in his life. I had to wonder where that came from. I'd met his father, and Liam Tremaine clearly adored his son.

What the hell had happened to screw up Vaughn?

I wished I didn't care.

"I haven't any interest in your love life, princess," Vaughn said kindly. "I better go find the bride and groom."

Frustrated anger held me in place as he walked away.

Ahhhhh!!! I screamed and raged in my head, so I didn't slip off my shoe and throw it at his departing head.

That was the second time now that he had reeled me in.

"Fool me twice," I muttered.

On that thought, I walked out of the ballroom, knowing Jessica would forgive me for my defection from the final preparations.

Marching down the boardwalk to my inn I really thought that Vaughn was the last person on earth I wanted to see at that moment. Hence my running away.

However, when I swung open one of the beautiful stained glass double doors to the inn, walked into the entrance, and saw a very thin young woman with fake boobs arguing with Aydan, I realized I was wrong.

There was one other person on earth I didn't want to see at that moment. A person I really didn't want to deal with because this person always invited chaos.

My little sister.

If it weren't for the fact that underneath her cosmetic surgery we were very alike physically, I would have doubted the relation.

For as long as I could remember Vanessa had been a selfish, spoiled little brat. She wasn't raised that way, either. It was just innate. Part of her nature. But she hadn't been all bad. In fact she'd been a soft-hearted kid who was forever finding wounded animals to bring home to nurse, much to my mother's annoyance. When Vanessa's impulsive actions hurt someone she felt remorse for the unintentional consequences. More often than not I was the one who felt the brunt of her choices, and afterward my little sister would spoil me with hugs and apologies and kisses.

That was our way. When we weren't fighting, we were cuddling.

To my regret that all changed as we got older. We were very different people. Whereas I loved Hartwell and the inn, Vanessa considered the seaside town and the inn not good enough for her. She'd wanted to see the world. It wasn't what I wanted but I understood why she did. I think, however, it made her start to feel like an outsider in our family. The distance between us grew greater, and finally, when she developed a crush on an older boy, an older boy I ended up dating, our relationship fell apart. I hadn't known about her crush, but that didn't stop Vanessa's resentment of me multiplying. I'd hoped she'd get over it, that it was just a phase, but I was sad to say our relationship never repaired itself.

Vanessa had eventually used her looks and seductive powers to seduce an older, wealthy tourist years ago and he'd taken her to Los Angeles. He'd bought her fake boobs, designer clothes, and nice jewelry.

In gratitude she ran off with a younger wealthy man. He was only in it for the fun, so she seduced his father. *He* bought her new lips and flew her to his home in Southern France.

And so on and so on.

She kept my parents updated with her shenanigans and travels but I hadn't seen or spoken to her in five years.

"Get out of my way," Vanessa hissed at my manager. She pushed her heavily made-up face into Aydan's, her boobs almost falling out of the skintight, low-cut, calf-length color-block dress she wore.

Red snakeskin stilettos put her at a few inches taller than Aydan, and I found myself mesmerized by the gaudy crystal buckle on the straps wrapped around her slim ankles.

Beside her, strewn across my beautiful hardwood flooring, were three Louis Vuitton suitcases, and three Louis Vuitton travel bags.

Holy hell.

"Vanessa?"

She whirled around at my voice, her red hair, lightened with blond highlights, sliding across her shoulders poker straight and silky, and in complete contrast to my auburn waves. She now wore a permanent pout. Her nose was still the same, and of course her eyes. It was her eyes that gave away our relation. We had our mother's eyes. Tip-tilted, light green eyes.

I missed how my baby sister used to look. The difference in her appearance only seemed to emphasize the idea that *this* Vanessa wasn't the Vanessa from our childhood.

"Where have you been?" my sister snapped, her perfectly manicured hands flying to her ultra-slim hips.

I frowned, not just at her greeting after our five-year separation, but over the realization that she was much thinner than she used to be. "Have you been eating? You look thin."

"Oh, you're sweet." She preened for a millisecond before snapping, "Now where have you been? I've been left here to deal with this little person who won't let me get settled into a room."

"We're fully booked, that's why."

"But I'm your sister."

"Yes, I am aware. Even though I haven't seen or spoken to you in five years. What are you doing here, Vanessa?"

She shrugged her narrow, bony shoulders. "I'm terribly bored," she said in an affected weird British accent. "I'm tired of wandering." She grinned. "I've come home to run the inn!"

Oh.

No.

Holy shit.

It took everything within me not to stomp my foot and bellow, *Like hell you are!*

Instead I shot a very worried Aydan a reassuring look before turning to my sister. "That's sweet, V, but I don't need help running the inn."

"No one calls me V anymore. And I'm not asking whether you need help. It's my inn, too."

"You hate the inn."

She shrugged. "I judged it too harshly. I'm growing up, Bailey. I'd like to take on some responsibility."

I crossed my arms over my chest. "Okay. What's your experience?"

"Excuse me?"

"Management experience."

She made a face. "Bailey, I'm tired, and I don't have time for this nonsense. I've flown from Monte Carlo to be here."

"Fleeing the mob? The cops?"

"What?" Vanessa said shrilly.

"You being here does not make sense."

"It doesn't have to make sense to you." She stepped toward me. "I'm here to get to know my inn."

I sucked in a breath at her audacity. This place had never been *her* inn. "I haven't even heard from you in five years!" I repeated.

"I've been busy."

"I hope to God managing a business because otherwise you are not getting near this one."

"Does *she* have experience?" She gestured to Aydan. "Somehow I doubt it. Look at how she's dressed. Do you honestly let her greet guests this way?"

Aydan narrowed her eyes and I knew she was about five seconds from removing the huge hoop earrings in her ears and telling Vanessa to step into a fight ring.

"Aydan is my manager and she is good at her job. For instance, she would know the impropriety of standing in the middle of reception arguing where any of the guests can hear."

"I'm not arguing." Vanessa shrugged again. "There is no argument. Legally this place is mine, too, and you're just being petty not letting me get to know it a little better."

"I'm not being petty. I'm being wary. I don't trust your motives, dearest sister."

"How horribly unkind of you." She sounded bored already. "Okay. I'm bored," she confirmed. "Show me to a room." She gestured to her bags like she expected me to carry them all.

"I don't have a room. I'm fully booked," I repeated through gritted teeth.

"Well, I'll just have to stay with you then."

I guffawed.

And then realized she was being serious.

"Oh, hell no." It slipped out before I could stop it.

Her eyes grew round and wet and her lower lip trembled. "What a dreadful welcome this has been. I know it's been a while since we were close"—a tear rolled down her cheek—"but I was at least expecting a hug."

There was nothing about her performance that I bought. From the moment she came out of the womb my little sister had perfected the art of the fake cry. She'd gotten my brother, Charlie, and me into so much trouble with that fake crying. My parents were the only idiots in the house who believed it.

To be fair, she was pretty talented.

"Don't cry," I grumbled, shuffling toward her. I wrapped my arms around her skinny body, wincing in concern at how frail she felt. "There, there."

"Don't"—she shoved me gently away—"you'll mess up my hair."

I rolled my eyes. "Fine. I'll call a cab to take you to my place. You can sleep on the couch."

"The couch?" She looked horrified.

"It's a one-bedroom house."

"Then I'll take the bed."

I stared at her, incredulous. "Baby sister, Mom and Dad aren't here. This is my playground now, and if I come home to find you in my bed, I will haul you out of it by that pretty flat-ironed hair of yours."

"You've gotten mean," she huffed.

"And you haven't changed a bit."

Five minutes later Aydan and I helped the cab driver out with the luggage while my sister shouted things like, "Watch the wheels on that suitcase. It cost more than you make in a year!" and "Don't snatch at the fabric like that. Do you know how much that bag will be worth in fifty years' time!"

By the time Aydan and I stumbled, exhausted, up the steps to the inn it was like we'd been through a war.

"So that's your sister," Aydan said blandly.

Something about the whole situation seemed stupidly hilarious in that moment and I broke out into hysterical laughter, having to stop mid-step. I slumped down onto the porch stairs and Aydan's laughter joined mine.

We cackled until our stomachs hurt and tears rolled down my cheeks.

I wiped them away, trying to catch my breath. "Oh, it's not funny but it is."

"I don't remember her. You would think I would remember her. Was she always like that?"

"Kind of. But she's worse now. She's spent the last eight years traveling all over the world, hopping from one rich man to the next. She's very good at the sugar-daddy thing. Not so much at the nice-human-being thing."

"Do you think she's serious about the inn?" Aydan sounded concerned.

The truth was I didn't know. I just knew that wherever Vanessa went destruction followed. "I don't know. I do know that until she realizes how bored she used to be living here, we're stuck with her. I don't know for how long."

"Is she going to be a problem?"

"Not if I can help it. If she comes here and starts ordering you around or trying to make changes, I want to know immediately."

"She's going to be a problem," Aydan surmised.

"I won't let her hassle you."

"Hey, boss, I've worked in some lousy places over the years, and this is not one of them. This is the best job I've ever had, and I'm not going to let some skinny wannabe socialite scare me off. No offense."

"Oh, none taken. I would have called her worse."

We laughed and I leaned into Aydan. "Thank God you're here."

"We'll get through this together."

Reassured that Vanessa wouldn't send Aydan running for the hills, I strolled back into the inn. Aydan went to check with Mona about the dinner menu that night, and I hurried into the haven of my office. I closed the door behind me and closed my eyes.

I was way less composed than I'd let on to Aydan.

Vanessa Hartwell was the last problem I needed. Knowing only one person who'd understand, I called him.

My brother picked up on the fourth ring. "Hey, Bails. What's going on?"

"Vanessa is here. At the inn. She just turned up. Says she wants to help run the place."

"What?" He sounded as shell-shocked as I felt.

"She says she's bored of the wanderlust and wants to take her responsibilities more seriously."

Charlie swore. "Get her out of there. Now."

"And how do you propose I do that?"

"Find a rich man, dangle him on a fishing pole, and wave him under her nose."

I snorted and then felt guilty. "Maybe I should give her a chance. She is our sister."

"And she's a spoiled, selfish, lazy little brat."

"Maybe she's changed."

"Did she seem like she's changed? Because last Thanksgiving she didn't seem like she'd changed."

"You saw her last Thanksgiving?"

"Yeah, she was in the States so she came to see me."

An old hurt flared. "She never came to see me, Mom, and Dad." *Little brat.* "I knew it. She has never liked me."

"Don't take it personally. I think she was avoiding Hartwell more than she was avoiding you guys."

"Well now she's not avoiding either of us." I groaned. "Charlie, what will I do?"

"I think I gave you a solution to that problem."

"Mom and Dad would tell me to give her a chance."

"Because Mom and Dad love unconditionally and cannot see her for the conniving little brat she is."

"Maybe we should stop letting her be a brat. Maybe if I let her work at the inn I could teach her to work hard, to see the value of hard work."

Charlie laughed.

"Everyone deserves a chance." I found myself arguing my way into a decision and situation that could end horribly for me.

"You've always been a better person than me, Bails. Fine. Let her try working there. But that inn is the love of your life, and that inn is the reason I can take my wife on nice vacations every year, so if Vanessa so much as puts a foot wrong, I want you to boot her ass onto the first plane out of there. Or I will fly up there and do it myself. Vanessa has always been trouble. And last I checked in with her, nothing had changed. She's not there for the reasons she said. My bet is that her string of sugar daddies has dried up. She's my sister, and deep down I will always love her, but she's a mercenary now, Bailey, and she'll do whatever it takes to make herself happy. Even if it means making you miserable."

My brother's warning rang in my ears. An uncomfortable weight sank down on my shoulders. The truth was I didn't like my sister much, and I only missed her when she was gone before she turned up again. Now that I was faced with her and our complicated relationship, I wanted nothing more than to find a corner to hide in.

First Tom.

Next Vaughn.

Then Rex.

Now Vanessa.

My beautiful life in Hartwell had gotten really messy lately.

SIXTEEN

Vaughn

Emery didn't blush at all as she made the coffee he'd ordered for himself and Cooper, although she was her usual taciturn self.

However, Vaughn sensed that her taciturnity wasn't due to shyness but to annoyance. She was annoyed with him. He could tell in the way her pretty lips were pressed thin, and how she avoided his eyes not because she was too shy to meet them but because she didn't *want* to look at him.

The few words she did use were terse.

Like, "Here," when she handed the coffees over.

Vaughn was bemused. "How much?"

"Usual," she replied.

He handed over the money, smirking to himself. In all honesty he found her anger a refreshing change to her shyness. Perhaps Bailey was rubbing off on her after all.

Ah.

Bailey.

Of course.

"She told you," he commented as he took the coffees off the counter.

Emery stared at the cash register. "Pardon?"

"Bailey told you we slept together."

Her eyes flew to his.

Ah, there it was.

The blush stained her cheeks. "Yes."

"And you're annoyed at me."

"She asked me not to be," she said. "But yes." She bit her lip as if she couldn't believe she'd uttered the words.

All Vaughn heard was, "*She asked me not to be.*" Bloody Bailey Hartwell. She'd gone from wanting to destroy his reputation when he didn't deserve it, to trying to protect it when he didn't deserve it.

"I was in the wrong. I apologized."

She gave him a tight nod. He was not forgiven then.

Sighing, Vaughn walked away. He'd just opened the door to leave when her gentle voice called out to him, "You made her cry."

The words pierced through him, painful in a way that still surprised him. Unable to say anything, knowing if he did, he'd give away his emotions to the woman, he kept walking.

Bailey was always so feisty and brave around him, sometimes he forgot there was a soft, emotional woman underneath all her barbs. He'd wrapped himself up in that side of her, but he'd let himself forget it existed because it meant returning to memories that tormented him.

Emery's reminder was a knife in his gut.

"You look like hell." Cooper opened the door to his bar and accepted his coffee. He stepped aside to let Vaughn pass.

"I feel it."

"So what brings you here? Not that I'm complaining."

Vaughn's gaze swept over the empty bar. "Are we alone?"

"Yeah, but Jessica gets kind of weird about me making out with other people."

"Funny."

Cooper grinned. "What can I do for you?"

"I want you to watch out for Bailey. I know you do anyway, but I'm specifically talking about this Rex person." He narrowed his eyes. "I don't like the sound of him, Lawson."

His friend took a slow, casual sip of his coffee and studied Vaughn until he was almost squirming.

"Well?" Vaughn snapped.

"I was just wondering."

"What?"

"If it's uncomfortable."

"If what's uncomfortable?"

"Having your head that far up your ass."

"You're a real comedian today, Lawson."

"You're making it easy for me." He leaned against his bar, his gaze direct, serious. "You want to tell me why the hell you're making it this hard for yourself? You want Bailey. We all know you want Bailey, and if you weren't such an ass about it, you could have Bailey. I don't see the problem."

Vaughn was tired of explaining the situation. "I don't do relationships."

"Why?"

"None of your fucking business."

"Well you're making it my business by coming to me and asking me to watch out for *your* woman. Not exactly saying much about you as a man."

His blood burned at the insinuation. "I'm doing what is best for Bailey by staying away from her."

"But you're not. Staying away from her I mean. You're sticking your nose into her life, and this is a small fucking town, Tremaine. Do you think she won't know if you're putting yourself into her business, even if it's indirectly? And that's just messing with her head. You're either in or you're out. Make a choice and stick to it."

Cooper's words echoed around and around in Vaughn's head as he made his way back to his hotel. His head was down, his eyes on his feet.

"You're either in or you're out. Make a choice and stick to it."

Deep down he knew Lawson was right. He had to make the decision to sever his connection to Bailey for good. The thought terrified him.

And that made him question everything.

Maybe—

"Ow!" a female screeched in his ear as he collided with a sharp elbow.

He caught the slim arm in his hand and steadied the woman it belonged to. Shock moved through him as he found himself looking into Bailey's eyes.

But this wasn't Bailey.

He let go of the woman and she tottered on the boards in her red high heels. Her reddish blond hair was straight and long, and she flipped it over her shoulders as she eyed him like he was a hunk of red meat and she was starving.

Which was appropriate since she didn't look like she'd had a meal in a while.

Her large boobs were barely concealed by the skintight dress she wore, a dress that showed off sharp hip bones and an altogether waiflike figure.

The woman eyed him with lust in her eyes but Vaughn was unaffected. She was attractive enough in an overly made-up way, but he didn't like dating women who clearly starved themselves to look good. Naturally slender, curvy, voluptuous, Vaughn had no preference; as long as a woman was confident and healthy he'd find her sexy.

This woman appeared to be neither but he found himself arrested by her face.

It was her eyes.

And her nose.

They were Bailey's.

"I beg your pardon." He apologized for barging right into her.

"Oh, don't worry." She waved him off. "I was admiring this new hotel." She gestured up at Paradise Sands. "It wasn't here the last time I was. It's surprising. It adds much-needed class to the place."

Vaughn frowned. "You don't like Hartwell?"

Her eyes raked over him. "I'm liking it more now."

He gave her a benign smile, not wanting to be rude in any way in case she was a guest. "Are you staying at the hotel?"

"No. I'm staying with my sister. You wouldn't know what the rates were here, though, would you?"

"Yes." He held out his hand as he realized who this was. "I'm Vaughn Tremaine. The owner. And you are . . . Bailey Hartwell's sister?"

Her eyes widened, and he could almost see the dollar signs replacing her irises. He knew the type. His father taught him to spot her kind from a young age. And he was sure he'd heard jokes being thrown around about Bailey's younger sister; that she was a gold digger making her way through all the rich men in Europe.

It was probably Iris who had said it. Maybe even Bailey herself.

"I am. I'm Vanessa." She kept a hold of his hand, and stepped in closer to him. "Do you know my sister well?"

Yes, she's the best sex I've ever had and she's currently ruining my life. "We're acquainted."

"Isn't she a bore?" She rolled her eyes. "I just dropped my luggage off at her dinky little house. Would you believe she wants me to sleep on the *couch*?" She said the word like it was dirty. "I thought I'd check out your hotel."

"Why don't I guide you inside and you can talk to reception?"

"Oh." She pouted. "Can't you help me out? *Personally*?" She brushed her fingers over his lapel.

Vaughn felt a rising panic, and extricated himself from her grasp. "That's a little below my pay grade."

The last thing he needed was rumors reaching Bailey's ears that he was flirting with her sister. It wouldn't be the first time he'd found himself caught between two sisters and considering how disastrously it ended last time, he really wasn't up to replaying that scenario.

A flirtatious gold digger Vanessa Hartwell may be but she was at least smart enough to read the situation. Her whole demeanor changed. The flirtatiousness vanished and she straightened. "Well,

I don't know if it will suit me anyway. I'm used to a certain class of accommodation. Perhaps the Grand would suit me better."

He smirked at her. "Yes, well, Paradise is a five-star hotel, and the Grand is a four-star, so I imagine you're right. The Grand would suit you better."

Her mouth fell open in astonishment at his insult, and Vaughn began to stroll toward his hotel laughing to himself.

And then a thought occurred to him. Hadn't Bailey said her siblings had no interest in the inn? And that she didn't have much of a relationship with Vanessa?

So what was the woman doing in Hartwell?

And how much trouble was she looking to cause Bailey?

Vaughn scowled at the thought. Bailey had been through enough this year without her sister creating problems for her.

He spun around to find Vanessa giving him the evil eye. He ignored it. "What are you doing here?"

She crossed her arms over her huge bosom and lifted her chin in haughty defiance. "Why is it any business of yours?"

"I make what happens on this boardwalk my business, that's why."

Vanessa raised an eyebrow at his warning tone. "Well then, you should know I intend to become more involved with my inn."

"You mean Bailey's inn."

Something flickered in her expression. "It's my inn, too. And frankly from what I can see Bailey is making a dreadful mess of it. The décor is horrific, and that woman she has working for her is . . . well . . . she needs to go. I'll have that place shipshape in no time. We'll give you a run for your money with your fancy *five*-star hotel."

Her insults to Hart's Inn, to the hard work Bailey put in there, rankled. "It may have been a while since you lived here, Miss Hartwell, but I'm sure you'll remember that your sister is very well liked by the people of this town."

"Oh, I remember," she sneered. "Everyone's favorite. Quite the popular little brat."

His eyes narrowed. "If you try to cause any problems for her, you'll find yourself out of here so fast you won't know what happened."

"Excuse me? Was that a threat?"

"As I said, Bailey has a lot of friends, a lot of people who care about her well-being. She's been through enough this year without you causing any more trouble."

"Wow. Nothing has changed. She still has everyone under her spell. God"—she rolled her eyes—"you're all just like her. Boring and uptight."

"You're probably right. You should leave."

Vanessa opened her mouth to argue, but Vaughn wasn't interested in a confrontation with her. Funny how he couldn't resist one with her sister. In fact he reveled in it. On that thought he walked away before Vanessa could say anything else.

He cursed himself for warning her against causing problems for Bailey. "God damn it," he bit out as he strode into his office and slumped in his chair. There he went again, expending energy on worrying about a woman that wasn't even *his* woman.

Cooper was right.

He was either in or he was out.

Burying his head in his hands, he groaned, "Make a choice, Tremaine."

SEVENTEEN

Bailey

"You really don't have to do this." I felt guilty as hell as Rex moved around my small kitchen preparing dinner for us. He'd turned up at the inn, out of the blue, with shopping bags full of food and insisted on cooking for me.

Aydan, who thought I was crazy for not giving the guy a chance, insisted I have dinner with him while she took care of the inn.

So that's what I did. Now my stomach was churning with butterflies.

"I feel like this is a date," I blurted out. "And we talked about that, right?"

Rex looked over his shoulder at me and grinned. "Yeah. We did. Don't worry. I know we're not dating."

Relieved, I exhaled. "Okay. So this is just you cooking me dinner?"

"This is just me cooking you dinner." He strolled toward where I was standing and held a freshly cut pepper to my mouth.

Instead of taking it into my mouth from his fingers—way too intimate—I plucked it with my own and then bit into it.

He shook his head in amusement and wandered back to where he was chopping up vegetables for his stir-fry. "So anything new in your life?" He gestured over his shoulder to the pile of suitcases in my small sitting room.

I made a face. "Oh. That. That would be my sister. Vanessa."

"You don't sound happy about that. She's the one who travels around at lot, right?"

"Yeah. But now she's come home. To run the inn."

Rex frowned. "She giving you shit?"

"In the only way Vanessa knows how." I smiled at his concern. "I'll be fine. I know how to handle my sister. Now that my parents are out of the way I can actually do something about it. They didn't raise her to be a brat, but they didn't curb it, either. I have no such qualms about squashing that crap."

"I bet you don't." He smiled as he threw the veggies into the wok with diced beef. "I've never met a woman who speaks her mind the way you do."

"Do you find it horrifying?"

"Would I be here if I did?"

Part of me wished he wasn't hanging out with me. Not because I didn't like hanging out with him. I did. He was funny and kind. And hot. He treated me much better than Vaughn.

But to my everlasting agony, Rex didn't set my blood on fire like Vaughn. I wanted to be there for him, I wanted to be a good friend to him, but I didn't long for his secrets and his tenderness the way I longed for Vaughn Tremaine's.

Why was I such a moron?

No. I didn't blame this on me. My head knew exactly what the landscape with Tremaine looked like. It was my freaking hormones that were the problem.

Stupid moronic hormones.

"Earth to Bailey."

"Huh?" I blinked and looked over at Rex.

"You went somewhere else for a minute."

"Oh. Just thinking about Vanessa and how to deal with her."

"If you need help . . ."

"I know, thanks. But I'll be fine."

A little while later we had just sat down at my dining table when the door blew open and Vanessa stormed in on a thick cloud of Chanel perfume wearing an irritated expression.

"How many men do you have?" she sniped as she set about unstrapping her stilettos from her feet.

"What?"

She nodded to Rex, who was staring at her in mild shock. I don't think he'd been expecting quite all that she was. "Another one."

"What do you mean another one?" I was already annoyed that she'd interrupted our dinner. I didn't want to argue with her.

"Well, him, whoever he is, and what is he, twelve?" She threw a hand in Rex's direction. "And then that other guy. That would-be-sexy-if-he-didn't-have-a-giant-stick-up-his-ass Vaughn guy."

My heart started to thud a little faster in my chest. Of course my vapid little sister had made sure to meet the wealthiest man in town on her first day back. The thought of her anywhere near Vaughn made me want to rip that pretty hair out and then hide all her damn shoes so she'd never find them ever again. "What are you talking about?" I said through gritted teeth.

"That Vaughn guy. Ugh! We're barely introduced and he jumps down my throat, warning me not to cause you any trouble. No man acts that territorial and exhausting about a woman unless he's screwed her nine ways 'til Sunday. Which brings me to . . . what happened to Ted?"

Too many emotions rose up in me. I was discombobulated. It took me a minute to figure out what the hell she was saying. "Ted?"

"Your boyfriend. Duh?"

"Does she mean Tom?" Rex queried.

"Tom!" Vanessa clicked her fingers. "Right. Yeah, what happened to Tom?"

"She caught him fucking my girlfriend. Ex-girlfriend now," Rex answered.

"Wow." Vanessa looked surprised. "I didn't know old Ted had it in him. Here I thought he was as boring as you, Bails."

I ignored that. "Go back to Vaughn. What did you say to him?"

"Nothing. Just a comment about the inn needing my magic touch."

Oh yeah, I was so sure. "Right."

"God, that guy is uptight. But hot. I'm right, aren't I? You slept with him." She wandered over to the table and reached for a taco.

I could do nothing as she scooped some of my stir-fry into one and started to eat it. Honestly, in the mess of confusion she'd just caused, I was glad she was eating something with actual calories in it.

Plus, staring at her eating my dinner was easier than acknowledging Rex and his burning gaze. It didn't take a genius to know that he wanted the answer to her question.

My anger over my sister's sudden arrival in my life returned with a vengeance. "Stop talking."

She huffed. "No bed. Now no talking. Fine. I'm hitting the hay anyway. You might want to leave, unless you want your boy here to get a look at my good stuff."

"We're eating dinner."

"And you're in my bedroom."

I looked to Rex, exasperated.

"We can pack it up," he offered. "Eat it at the inn?"

"My office." I nodded, sighing. "I'll get some Tupperware."

As I passed my sister I shot her a filthy look.

She smirked. "I want you to wake me tomorrow morning so I can go to the inn with you."

"Great."

Vanessa bristled at my tone. "You are so lucky I met a hot guy tonight and I'm in a good mood."

I stiffened. She better not be talking about Vaughn. "Hot guy?"

She laughed. "Don't worry. Not *your* hot guy. Mine is more of the suited-up earthy type. Money and class, but he knows how to work with his hands, if you know what I mean. I met him in Germaine's."

Poor guy. He had no idea what he was in for. "Good for you."

"Ugh. Whatever."

Once we had the food packed up I ushered Rex out of the house just as Vanessa started shimmying out of her dress.

We were quiet as we got in my car.

And then . . .

"So. Vaughn, huh?"

Maybe I'd switch out Vanessa's shampoo for hair-removal cream. I couldn't believe she'd put me in this position. Even though Rex and I weren't dating, I knew what he wanted, and it would be unfair of me not to explain. "He owns Paradise Sands Hotel."

"The hotelier from New York?" He sounded stunned. He looked crestfallen. "Wow. Hard to compete with that."

"It's not . . . Look, he was there for me during that whole Stu Devlin thing." I'd already explained about Devlin breaking into the inn.

"He was the 'friend' that helped you out that night."

"Yes. And well, emotions were high and all that and one thing led to another . . ."

"Yeah, you don't need to go into detail."

"But nothing is going to happen with Vaughn. I told you that. He doesn't want a relationship with anyone."

"But you want him."

I couldn't lie to Rex. "I wish I didn't. And believe me, I'm working on getting over that idiocy."

Hearing the sincerity in my voice, Rex nodded. "Okay."

It occurred to me as we set up my office as a private dining room and Rex peppered me with questions about growing up with Vanessa, that by giving him an explanation I was considering him as boyfriend material.

As I stared into his warm dark eyes, I let myself imagine the possibilities with Rex. No, he didn't fire up my blood like Vaughn. I felt toward him like I used to feel about Tom. But maybe that wasn't a bad thing after all.

Shit.

Wasn't life supposed to get less confusing in your thirties?

EIGHTEEN

Bailey

It was that time of year again. Music festival time. One of the things I loved so much about Hartwell was our town events. We had the music festival during the summer while all the tourists were around, a gay pride parade at the end of the summer, the chicken festival at the beginning of October to celebrate our state bird, the proud blue hen. Then there was the pumpkin festival at Thanksgiving, where we had our punkin chunkin' competition, and the winter carnival in mid-February with a royal court and parade floats.

The music festival was great because it was more laid-back than our other events. People from neighboring towns and cities got permits to set up stalls selling all kinds of music memorabilia and craft goods. Dahlia always had a stall.

Bands from all over the country played one after the other in the bandstand on Main Street. It was just a good vibe. A crush of people strolling lazily around, enjoying good music and good times. And we raised money for a state charity that used music to transform the lives of disadvantaged children.

The last few years I'd missed out on music festival day because I had to work at the inn but this year Aydan was covering for me so I could hang out with Rex and show him the side of Hartwell I really loved: the community vibe.

It was a hot day so the first thing on the agenda was ice cream from Iris and Ira's pop-up stall. To my delight we found Iris and Ira serving Anita and Old Archie. I hadn't seen Anita in months.

My delight was deflated by how poorly she looked. She was in a wheelchair, her shorn head covered by a pretty headscarf. While the rest of her body looked frail, her face appeared slightly bloated, sallow, and there were dark circles under her eyes.

Old Archie stood behind her wheelchair. He was once a well-functioning alcoholic, a big strapping man who loved Anita but wouldn't give up his scotch. When she was diagnosed with a spinal tumor last year, he'd kicked the addiction in a way that was almost miraculous. His strength blew me away.

Her strength made me want to buckle at the knees.

I leaned down and kissed her cheek. "How are you?"

She gave me a tired smile. "I wanted to come out today. See everyone."

"It's good to see you."

"It is that." Iris handed Anita her ice cream and she took it, clearly delighted.

She licked it and smiled up at Archie. "Better than the ice pops."

He laughed and explained, "We eat a lot of ice pops at the hospital. They hand them out more than they do drugs."

"Nothing beats Antonio's ice cream," I said.

"Shh, don't say that too loudly." Ira jerked his head behind him. "Ice Cream Shack."

I made an *Ahh* face. There was a long-standing competition between the couple and the Ice Cream Shack. Iris and Ira tried to be nice to the proprietor, a Mr. Shickle, but he took everything they said as an insult, and as rivalry.

"Who's your friend?" Anita looked past me.

Guilt suffused me for my rudeness. "Oh, God, sorry. This is Rex. Rex, this is Anita and Old Archie. And you've already met Iris and Ira."

"Hey." He grinned at them.

"Anyway, we better let these people get their ice cream," Old Archie said. "We'll no doubt see you two later on."

I smiled and nodded, my heart aching as they left. Iris met my gaze and she shook her head sadly. Swallowing the lump of emotion in my throat, I grinned with faux cheer. "I'd like a strawberry and white chocolate, please. Rex?"

"The same."

A minute later we were moving through the Main Street crowds. "This ice cream is so good," Rex moaned.

I laughed because he looked like a little boy. So freaking cute. And I laughed because I was glad he hadn't asked what the deal was with Anita. A year ago I'd thought she'd win her battle with cancer, but one battle had turned into a war, and the outcome didn't look good for her. She just wanted to enjoy her day, however, and I didn't want to dwell on it.

"Come on, I see someone I want you to meet."

Rex followed me through the crowds toward the bandstand.

"Kell!" I shouted.

The short blond spun around from speaking to some guy crazy enough to wear a leather jacket in the heat, and Kell broke out into a huge grin at the sight of me. "Bailey!" He hugged me, deftly avoiding my ice cream. "It's been a while, lovely. Since that terrible incident with Devlin."

"I know. But we've both been so busy. It can't be helped. Kell, this is my friend Rex. Rex, this is Kell Summers. He's one of the town councilors and the official events organizer around here."

"Nice to meet you." Rex held out his hand.

Kell peered up at Rex as he took it and shook it vigorously. "*Friend?*"

I laughed and leaned against Rex. "Yes. Friend."

"Who is a friend?" I turned as Kell's partner, Jake, arrived on the scene. While Kell was cute, blond, and excitable, Jake was tall, dark, and more reserved than his partner. He enveloped me in a warm hug, kissing my temple before stepping back. "I keep meaning to pop by the inn, make sure Devlin isn't causing you any more trouble."

"He's not," I promised him. "Believe me, you would already know if he was."

Jake nodded, satisfied, and then turned to Rex.

"This is her '*friend*,'" Kell air-quoted.

I rolled my eyes as Jake chuckled and held out his hand to Rex. "I'm Jake."

"Rex."

After they'd shaken hands Jake gave me that focused, soul-searing stare of his. "Are you doing okay? We heard your sister has come home."

"Yeah." I gestured around. "She's around here somewhere."

It had been a week since her arrival and so far it wasn't too bad. The first few days were hell but the last few days she'd been a little too preoccupied with her mystery man to annoy us at the inn.

"How's that going?"

"It could be better. It could be worse." I shrugged. "Family."

Kell grimaced. "I hear that."

"So you guys have done a great job again." I gestured to the bandstand and the cordoned-off area around it. It was alive with activity as the first two bands prepared for sound check.

"We have a special day planned." Kell clapped his hands together in excitement. "We have amazing bands this year. And guess what?"

"What?" I grinned. His excitement was infectious.

"Vaughn Tremaine helped me get some great bands from New York. Apparently he *knows* people."

"Vaughn Tremaine? Helped?" I was amazed.

"Oh yeah," Kell said. He looked up at Jake. "And wasn't he lovely? He was lovely."

Jake grinned. "He was lovely."

"Lovely how?"

"Oh, he's charming. I don't know why more people don't realize that. Everyone thinks he's got a giant stick up his butt, yet he was so down to earth with us."

"How much time did you spend with him?"

"He invited us to have dinner with him at the hotel and asked us how he could help with the events this year," Jake said.

Shock held me to the spot.

Vaughn had listened to my advice. Wow. "Okay then."

"Anyway, sweetie, I'd love to stay and chat but we have to get on. We'll catch up later, yes?" Kell kissed me on the cheek and then smiled mischievously at Rex. "Be sure to show this young man a good time."

I laughed as Rex and I walked away but I was still kind of in a daze.

"So, Vaughn, huh?" Rex said.

Oh no. It was music festival day and I did not want to discuss Vaughn with Rex.

"Bailey!"

I had never been more thankful for the sound of Jessica's voice. Following it, I zeroed in on Jess standing near the market stalls where Dahlia had set up her jewelry to sell. Jess stood beside Cooper with Louis at their feet, surrounded by Cat, Joey, and Emery.

Emery was at the festival.

Progress.

I rushed toward my friends and playfully nudged Emery. "You're here."

She blushed, smiling at me. "I didn't know it would be like this . . ." She gestured around. "It's quite atmospheric."

"I know, right? Guys, you all know Rex."

Everyone nodded but Joey. "I don't," the kid piped up, staring shrewdly at Rex.

"Well let me rectify that." I laughed. "Joseph Cooper Lawson, this is Rex McFarlane, my friend from Dover."

"Everyone calls me Joey. I'll let you know by the end of the day if you can, too."

Rex grinned. "I'll try my best to make that happen."

"How you doing?" Cooper held out his hand to him.

They'd already met but this was Cooper. He was reminding Rex that I had a Cooper in my life, a Cooper who would do him bodily harm if he hurt me.

I rolled my eyes at Jessica but she just snuggled deeper into Cooper's side, loving him for being protective of the people he cared about.

What wasn't to love about that?

"Forgive him." Cat ruffled her son's hair. "He's playing today at the festival and he's full of beans and smartbuttery."

"Smartbuttery?" I said.

"Mom doesn't want to use the a-s-s word around me," Joey explained.

"Ah, smartassery," I deduced. Everyone groaned in amusement as I made a face at Cat. "Oops. Sorry."

"It's not like I don't know what the word is," Joey blustered. "Mom is just being silly."

"I quite like the word 'smartbuttery.' I think I'll add it to my personal vocabulary," Em said.

Joey, who worshipped Miss Tall, Blond, Kind, and Beautiful, stared up at her. "Yeah?"

"Yeah."

"Okay. I guess it is kind of funny."

"Oh, sure," Cat said. "I say it, it's embarrassing, Elsa says it and it's kind of funny."

"Watch it, Catriona." Cooper tapped her nose. "Your envy is showing."

She grunted at her brother and turned to Em. "Do you want to come live with us? Make it a permanent thing?"

Emery rolled her eyes at her, which was a vast improvement, too. Cat could be a little intimidating and Em still wasn't too sure how to act around Joey's mom.

"When are you playing?" I said to Joey, looking forward to hearing him.

"In a couple of hours."

"Can't wait." I turned to Rex. "Joey is a pianist and somewhat of a protégé."

"Is that so?" Rex looked impressed. "Well I can't wait to hear you."

"Are you Bailey's new boyfriend?"

"No," I said so Rex wasn't left floundering in awkwardness. "Have you all had ice cream yet?"

"Vaughn!" Cooper shouted instead, staring off to our left.

I froze. Rex followed Cooper's gaze with intense focus. Jessica caught my eye and winced sympathetically. Emery surreptitiously squeezed my wrist and I gave her a grateful smile.

This all happened just before Vaughn appeared, Jessica and Cooper moving back to let him into our circle. I drank him in like a parched, parched woman.

In deference to the hot weather and the casual event Vaughn was wearing a polo shirt that showed off his great physique, and slim-leg light-colored chinos and boat shoes. Even casual he reeked of money. It had something to do with the quality of his clothes, his confident air, and the beautiful Rolex Submariner on his wrist.

The unfairness of his good looks made my heart pound fast and my stomach flutter.

Worse still was his complete lack of annoyance when Louis jumped up on him for attention. Vaughn just laughed and rubbed behind his ears, making me melt a little. Once Jess had pulled Louis back down, an awkward silence fell over the group.

"Enjoying the festival?" Vaughn eventually asked Cooper.

"Got a beautiful day for it. I was going to grab a beer. Do you want one?"

Vaughn's eyes flickered to Emery and me. "Maybe later. Miss Saunders, Miss Hartwell." He looked at Rex, and his expression blanked. "I don't believe we've met." He stuck out his hand. "Vaughn Tremaine."

For a moment I thought Rex wasn't going to accept the offer. I let go of the breath I was holding when he reached out to take

Vaughn's hand. Even I could see Rex's grip was too tight, and mortification swept over me. "Rex McFarlane. I'm a *friend* of Bailey's."

That dark smirk crept over Vaughn's lips, his gaze piercing. Whatever Rex was trying to do didn't work and I saw a flicker of frustration on his face as he let go of Vaughn's hand.

As for Vaughn he quirked an eyebrow at me as if to say, *This guy? Really?*

If looks could kill, mine would have sliced and diced him. "Getting involved, Tremaine?"

He shrugged, his stare too focused on me, too searing. "Just removing that stick from my ass."

No one else got it but I did, and I couldn't help the smile that played around my lips despite myself. "I think I still see a few splinters."

Amusement danced in his eyes and it thrilled me. I didn't want it to thrill me, obviously. But thrill me it did.

"Why Hartwell?"

We all looked at Rex upon his abrupt question. Directed at Vaughn.

"Excuse me?"

"Why choose Hartwell to settle down in? Don't you own hotels all over the world?"

Vaughn nodded, his focus still on me. Holding my gaze, giving me that smoldering, *I've seen you naked* look again. "A self-made man can choose his view. I guess I just like the view here."

I felt a familiar tingling between my legs, a tightening in my breasts, and my blood burned.

There was definitely subtext, right?

Oh, my God!

Stop, Bailey! Stop caring!

It was so much easier to tell myself that than to make myself stop caring. He was messing with my head. Warning Vanessa not to cause me trouble, looking at me like no man had ever looked at me before. There was this longing mixed in with that fiery, lusty storm in his pale gaze and, dear heaven, it tugged on all my mushy heart-strings, and teased all my erogenous zones.

A killer combination.

A throat cleared next to me.

Rex.

The sound broke through our staring contest and I looked around to see everyone shifting, not meeting my eyes, and definitely trying to hide their smiles.

My newest friend wasn't impressed, however. "Self-made? Really? Isn't your father wealthy?"

The group seemed to inhale simultaneously at the passive-aggressive comment.

But Vaughn didn't even flinch. "Yes." That was it. He didn't take time to explain himself to Rex, how he did everything off his own back, and not through his father's success.

Just like always.

Because Vaughn never explained himself to someone he didn't feel deserved an explanation. I realized then that I admired that quality in him. I respected that he couldn't give a shit what some stranger thought of him.

But at the same time . . . he never explained himself to me, either. And that was what hurt about his rejection, because I didn't want to be some stranger to him. I wanted him to think I was important enough to be owed an explanation.

He looked from Rex to me, and whatever he saw in my expression made him frown and glance away. "I should get going."

"No, stay," Jess tried to insist.

"Yeah." Joey surprised me. "I'm trying to talk Mom and Uncle Coop into taking me to the fun park. The lines won't be nearly so long as usual because everyone is here."

"I thought you were playing today," I said.

"Yeah, later. I want to go to the fun park first." He looked at Vaughn. "You should come."

Vaughn looked just as stunned by the invitation and also uncomfortable. "Oh, I'm not sure about that. I should probably stay here."

And that's when the little imp in me just couldn't hold her tongue. "Why? Don't you like the fun park?"

"I wouldn't know."

"You've never been to the fun park?"

Vaughn sighed and it was an irritated sound. "No, I have not."

"You've never been?" Joey repeated my question. "You should so totally come with us."

"Yeah, Vaughn. I think I'm starting to see a quarter inch of stick growing back out of your ass," I teased.

He glowered at me but I could see his heart wasn't really in it.

This was fun, I realized. Teasing him was fun. And I should stop. But I couldn't seem to help myself.

"Fine. Only if Miss Hartwell joins us."

Oh, shit.

Well I walked into that one.

"Please, Bailey, please," Joey begged. "If you say yes, Mom will say yes."

I looked at Cat and saw the evil glint in her eyes. "Yeah, if you say yes, Mom will say yes."

They were all against me.

I looked up at Rex, who was the only one not amused by my predicament. "How would you like to go to the fun park?"

"That's fine, I guess." He shrugged.

Clearly it was not fine.

Sighing, I avoided Vaughn's smug gaze and looked at Joey.

Why did the kid have to be so damn cute?

"Sure." I threw up my hands in surrender. "Let's all go to the fun park and miss out on music festival day."

"It's just for a few hours," Joey assured me. "To take my mind off my stage nerves."

"You got your way, kid, you can stop with the emotional manipulation." Cat smoothed a hand over his head in affection.

He grinned cheekily up at her.

"I guess we're going to the fun park." Vaughn gestured to Joey. "Lead the way."

"Are you okay about this?" I said to Rex as we followed the group down Main Street.

He wouldn't look at me. "Spending the afternoon with the guy you slept with? Not high on my list of things I wanted to do today."

"I'm sorry."

I was also sorry how awkward this felt. In my heart of hearts I thought of Rex as a friend, and as flattering as it was that he was attracted to me, I just wasn't there yet. So the whole jealous boyfriend thing did nothing for me but make me feel weird about hanging out with him.

Yet, I understood where he was coming from.

Rex had made himself clear. He liked me. He was pursuing me. Patiently. Having Vaughn around was going to be uncomfortable for him.

"I'll buy your ticket," Rex said as we approached the park gates and ticket booths. It was the first word he'd spoken in two minutes and it was said in a conciliatory tone.

"Vaughn bought the tickets!" Cat shouted back to us, and the group started moving through the gates.

"Of course he did." Rex sighed and shot me an unhappy look.

I grimaced.

We stopped in a circle just past the entrance to the park.

"Okay, kid," Cat said to her son. "You're running this show. What do you want to do first?"

Joey turned to Vaughn. "You've never been before, so you should choose."

Vaughn smiled at Joey. A boyish, gorgeous smile that kicked me in the chest. "That's kind of you, Joey." Then that cool gray gaze of his flew my way. "And I think since Miss Hartwell seems to know so much about being a big child, we should ask her."

Jessica and Cooper didn't even try to hide their laughter. I shot them an evil look before turning it on Vaughn. As we stared at one another, just like always, everything else melted away. "Do you want to go on a ride or play a carnival game?"

"Would playing a carnival game involve beating you at something?"

I snorted, loud and unladylike. "You think you could beat me at one of these carnival games? You who has never been here before and I who grew up here whooping the ass of men much manlier than you?"

"Ooh, fighting words," Cat said. "Are you going to take that, Tremaine?"

"Yeah, Tremaine." Cooper grinned at his friend. "Are you going to take that?"

In answer Vaughn crossed his arms over his chest and widened his stance.

I put my hands on my hips. "I'll take that as a no."

"So? What will it be?" Dahlia said. "The ring toss or the rifle range?"

Cooper coughed. "Rifle range." He coughed again. "Rifle range."

"I can hear you," I grumbled. "Whose side are you on?"

"Well I didn't know if Lawson's less than subtle suggestion was to aid you because you're excellent at the ring toss, or to aid me because you're bad. Now I know." Vaughn grinned wickedly. "Rifle range it is."

"Oh, damn it," I muttered under my breath as I strode through the group toward him. "This way."

Cooper Lawson and anyone who had spent any time with me at the fun park behind the boards knew that I was hopelessly inadequate at the rifle range. Weirdly brilliant at ring toss, but terrible at the rifle range. Which made no sense because didn't they involve similar skills?

I was so going to get my ass handed to me. Unless Vaughn was worse than me.

Oh, who was I kidding? No one was worse than me at the rifle range.

"Hey, welcome to the rifle range," the kid at the range said, sounding bored out of his mind. I was pretty sure he was Annie from the market's kid.

"Ben, right?" Vaughn and I each took position behind a rifle. I felt the heat of our small group of friends at our backs.

A thoroughly entertained group of friends.

I was going to kill them later.

"Yeah." Ben nodded.

"How much is it these days, Ben?" I nodded to the rifle.

He pointed behind him at two big signs. The first said, *Five Dollars—Hit Three Blue Hens* and the second, *And Win Prize of Your Choice.*

I'd never in my life hit one hen.

Vaughn handed over ten dollars.

"I would have paid for my own."

He smirked. "Oh, I'd gladly pay a thousand dollars to see this happen, Miss Hartwell. Five bucks is nothing."

"Hey, guess what? I don't think I like you stick-free after all."

Vaughn threw his head back in laughter, and I knew I'd just lied. I liked him stick-free. I liked him stick-free a whole lot.

Complaining under my breath, I picked up the rifle in front of me and took aim.

And missed.

I shot a look out of the corner of my eye and watched Vaughn lift the rifle and point it with expertise. He took aim. He fired.

One blue hen down.

Determined now, I tried again.

I missed.

Vaughn hit two more in the time it took me to miss once.

"Damn it!" I glared over my shoulder at Cooper, who was shaking with the effort to control his laughter. "Are you happy?"

He just laughed harder.

"Here."

I jumped because the word had been said right in my ear. Vaughn had put down his rifle and was standing right next to me. Right in my personal space. I could smell his cologne and see the silver striations in the iris of his eyes.

My body tingled all over at his close proximity.

"What are you doing?" I panicked as he slid in behind me, my ass grazing the top of his thighs. I tensed as he wrapped his arms around me, taking both my arms in his hands and adjusting me.

"You're holding it wrong." His voice rumbled in my ear.

I squeezed my eyes closed as I got a flashback of lying beneath him, feeling him move inside me while he whispered dirty things to me.

"Princess," he murmured. "Are you listening?"

Why are you doing this to me?

"I'm holding it wrong," I managed to wheeze out. "Okay. Show me how."

"With pleasure." His tone was filled with filth.

"The gun, Tremaine," I bit out.

He chuckled, the movement causing his body to shift against mine. "Right." He adjusted my stance for a few moments, his hands caressing me as he adjusted my hips, too. Frankly, it felt like an excuse to feel me up.

"You done?" I snapped.

He laughed again. "Sure. Try now. Follow the sight line. Yes, like that. Now wait. Hold it. You want to pull the trigger just as the tip of the hen's face comes into the sight line."

And my smartbuttery got the best of me. "I hope you don't take the same advice in the bedroom."

Vaughn leaned closer, the slight bristle of his cheek brushing mine as he whispered, "We both know for a fact that I don't."

I clenched my teeth. "Bastard."

"You walked into that one." He pulled back before I could dispute that comment. "Now follow my advice."

I waited. I concentrated. I followed his advice.

And I freaking hit the thing!

"Whoop!" I spun around, and smacked him playfully across the chest. "I did it!"

"You did. But I still won."

"I don't care." I shot Cooper a triumphant grin. "I hit the damn hen."

"Yeah, you did," he chuckled.

"It only took you twenty-nine years," Cat added.

"You, Cat Lawson, are a party pooper." I looked at Joey. "You want to play next?"

He shook his head. "I want to ride the roller coaster."

"Cool." I quirked an eyebrow at Vaughn. "What do you say, Tremaine? Want to hit the roller coaster? Or are you chicken?"

He gave me an exasperated look. "Really?"

"Well are you?"

"Roller coaster it is." He started walking away. "Lead the way again, Joey."

"You two are children," Jess admonished, stepping forward. "And it would be funny except you haven't even noticed that Rex has gone."

My stomach dropped as I realized she was right. "What? Where? When?"

"About a minute ago, when Vaughn started using that"—she gestured to the rifle range—"to cop a feel."

Guilt weighed on me. "I need to go after him."

"Are you dating him?"

"No. We're just friends. I told you that. I just . . ."

"We all know how he feels about you," she said. "I know I'm pushing you toward Vaughn but I feel bad for Rex now. He looked upset."

"Jess. Don't. I'm already guilt-ridden here. I have to go. Tell Joey I'm sorry."

"Doesn't anyone want to claim the prize?" Ben asked.

"I'll deal with it," Jess said. "Go."

Without another word I hurried away, running through the park and out of the main gates. That's when I ran into a problem because

Rex could have gone in either direction. I decided to head out the way we'd come in from Main Street. To my relief, just as I turned onto Main Street, I saw him in the crowds up ahead. Thankfully he was taller than the average guy, and he was wearing a red T-shirt with an album cover on the back of it.

"Rex! Wait up!"

But he either didn't hear me or he was ignoring me. I shoved through the crowds, apologizing to those I pushed accidentally or bumped into. Finally I caught up with him.

"Rex." I pulled on his arm, drawing him to a stop. "Where are you going?"

He stared at me, incredulous hurt in his dark brown eyes. "Really?"

"That?" I gestured behind me, indicating the moment at the park. "That was nothing. We were just needling each other. That's what we do."

"If you believe that, you're in denial."

"Rex."

"No." He cut me off. "I . . . I've asked myself what I'm doing these past few weeks. Convinced myself that you were what I wanted and that you were worth the wait. And I'm not saying you're not, but I think we both know that I would be waiting forever for you."

"I wouldn't do that to you. If I knew what I wanted, I would tell you."

"You do know what you want. You're just smart enough to realize he's an asshole, and that you should stay away from him."

"Rex."

"I hope either there is more to the guy than that smug arrogance I just saw, or if there isn't, I hope you come to your senses. What I do know is that there was more than one moment back there where everyone but you two melted away. It was like we didn't exist. And I'm standing there like an idiot trying to convince myself that I can win you from him. I can't win you from him . . ." He flung his hand out in the direction we'd come from. "I mean, fuck, he's like a movie star or something. And he's successful and rich, and so confident I want to knock his front teeth out."

That was kind of funny, and I struggled not to laugh.

Rex saw and gave an unwilling sigh of amusement.

"I'm sorry." I didn't know what else to say.

"Don't be. You've been honest with me from the beginning. I just wasn't listening."

We were quiet a moment.

Finally he sighed. "I'm going to go."

"No. Stay." I reached for his hand. "Enjoy the rest of the festival with me."

"Nah. I can't. Staying would just make me feel worse. I can't let another woman fuck with my head, unintentionally or not."

Understanding it and hating that I'd hurt him, I let go of his hand. "There's someone great out there for you, Rex."

"Someone that'll take on all my bullshit like you with Vaughn?"

"Not like me and Vaughn. The woman that falls in love with you will actually trust *you*. Because you'll love her. You won't ever think she's not good enough."

Hearing the slight crack in my voice, Rex pulled me into his arms and hugged me tight. I felt his sweet kiss on top of my head, and once more cursed my goddamn stupid heart.

"You deserve better, Bailey Hartwell," he whispered.

"I feel like you're saying good-bye." Tears welled in my eyes at the abrupt turn of events.

He let go of me, his expression telling me I wasn't going to see him anytime soon, and then as quickly as he'd come into my life, Rex McFarlane vanished out of it and into the festival crowd.

Melancholy swelled over me and I turned, despondent, looking for an escape. I moved through the bodies, not hearing or seeing anything as I got free of the masses on the boardwalk and let my feet take me somewhere isolated.

I ended up on the beach, following it around the coast until I came to a tranquil, solitary spot.

Pulling my dress tight under my thighs so I didn't burn myself on the hot sand, I sat down and stared out at the ocean, at the way the sun glinted off the water. It was a sight that usually filled me with peace.

But today I couldn't find it.

My life was too chaotic.

A shadow fell over me and I peered up through my sunglasses, my heart slamming against my rib cage at the sight of Vaughn standing over me holding two iced teas. He held one out to me and, dumbfounded, I took it, sipping it as he sat down so close beside me our elbows bumped.

We drank our iced teas in silence, both of us staring out at the water and enjoying the reprieve the sea breeze provided from the heat of the sweltering sun above us.

"Did I scare him away?" Vaughn eventually asked.

He must have followed me from the park, witnessed the scene between Rex and me, and followed me out to the beach. Why? Why would he do that?

God, I didn't know anymore. "I think *I* did. Or we did."

"We did?"

"Apparently we share a vibe, you and I," I said unhappily.

"Apparently we do," he replied just as unhappily. "I'm sorry if I crossed the line at the park."

More silence fell between us, and it reminded me of the night we'd spent on the boardwalk before the epic sex. It was comfortable between us—as comfortable as two people who were sexually aware of each other could be.

I didn't know when I'd become comfortable with him. How had that happened? Because I didn't trust him, obviously.

With your heart.

Right. I didn't trust him with my heart, but . . . he still made me feel safe. And I got a thrill out of verbal sparring with him. He excited me.

How goddamn confusing.

"You were gone for a while," I said.

"My hotel in New York. The Montgomery. Remember I said there were problems with it? Yeah, well I went up there to check it out. Turned out my manager had a coke addiction."

Somehow the magnitude of the problem he'd been facing made me feel better about the fact that he'd stayed away so long. "Did you solve the problem?"

"Yes. I have a new manager. I've fired the people who were slacking and rehired people he fired who weren't slacking. The hotel is back on track."

"And you got to spend time with your dad?"

He nodded. "He's the only thing I miss about New York now."

"You really do like it here, don't you?"

Vaughn studied my face. "What's not to like?"

Frustration welled up in me. "I wish you wouldn't do that."

"Do what?"

"Smolder at me."

He laughed. "I didn't realize I was."

"Well you are. And I want you to stop."

"I'd like to stop hearing your voice in my head saying, 'I bet you've thought about it. Fucking the hostile Princess of the Board-walk into submission,' but I can't."

I squirmed beside him, remembering my aggressive come-on. "Is that what this is about then? You sticking your nose into my business? Your obvious jealousy over Rex and what I think now was you putting it to him at the fun park with all that rifle adjustment stuff?"

"Obvious?" He scowled.

"Yes, obvious jealousy. Are you going to deny it?"

He finished his iced tea and placed the empty cup beside him. "No. I wanted to kill him for breathing the same air as you."

A sad thrill moved through me. "Is it just about the sex?"

"It was pretty spectacular."

"Vaughn."

He sighed, drawing his knees up to his chest to wrap his arms around them. "I try to stay away, I do, because I know I can't give you what you want." He looked at me with those pale, soulful eyes of his and I wanted to cry at the longing in them. Why? Why did he have to be the guy that looked at me that way? "I had the chance in New York to sleep with another woman. I couldn't. So . . . no . . . it's not just about the sex. But I'm . . ." He shrugged, seeming at a loss.

I let him off the hook, looking away so I didn't have to see his expression, the one that tore at my insides. I didn't even want to think about the idea of him sleeping with someone else, or how confusing and thrilling it was that he hadn't. I searched for a subject change. "You must miss your dad. You two seem so close."

"We are. He's my best friend."

Wow. That was nice. And surprisingly honest. "I'm glad. There are many people with parental issues these days. It's sort of depressing."

"Are you one of them?"

"No." I shook my head. "My mom is a little off the wall, but she loves me, I love her. And my dad is just the best guy ever."

Vaughn took a while to process that.

So long in fact I had to break the silence for fear I'd reach over to hold his hand, to touch him one last time before I got up the courage to sever this connection between us. "How is Liam?"

I heard his soft chuckle. "He'd love it that you call him Liam and still call me Tremaine."

"You keep calling me Miss Hartwell," I explained.

He shrugged and I felt the movement against my shoulder. Such an innocent touch, but it sent goose bumps up all over my arms. "My dad is well enough. I worry about him sometimes."

The confession stilled me. Was Vaughn actually talking to me, as in . . . sharing his feelings? "Oh?" I treaded carefully, not wanting to scare him off.

"Remember how I told you about how much my mother loved my father?"

"Yes."

"Well, if possible, my father loved her even more. When she died . . . he was a mess for a while. The only thing that stopped him from falling apart was me. I had a nanny but my dad was always there to tuck me in at night, read me a story, talk about our days. A day didn't go by that I didn't feel his presence in my life. As the years went on he dated but never anything too serious. Then about fifteen years ago he started a relationship with Diane. A very wonderful lady." I could tell from the tenderness in his voice that he was fond of this Diane person. "While I was in New York she pushed my dad to consider marriage, something he has been adamantly against. Now they've separated. And he loves her. However, he has this deep-seated belief that he shouldn't marry her because he gave that honor to my mother. He'll never love anyone the way he loved my mother, but that doesn't mean he can't love at all. I worry he's throwing away his happiness because of pure stubborn grief."

For a moment I was astounded by Vaughn's confidence in me. That he would share something so personal with me.

Yet as I sat there thinking about what he'd said, some things started to become clear. "You don't want to get married, either."

"What?" He frowned. "No, I've said as much."

"Well don't you think that's a little bit of a coincidence?"

"What do you mean?"

"Haven't you ever thought that your problem is actually your father's problem?"

"Bailey, stop talking in circles and just say whatever it is you're getting at."

"Vaughn, you pretty much hero-worship your dad, right? That's clear. So a lot of your emotions are tied up with him. And you've spent the majority of your life watching him pine and grieve for his lost love. He can't move on from her. No wonder you don't want to commit to a woman. You've seen firsthand what it might do to you if you ever lost her."

The muscle in his jaw ticked, a fairly good sign that he was pissed.

I braced myself.

Vaughn remained quiet for a while.

Then . . . "Maybe you're right," as he got to his feet.

I stared up at him, chilled by the blankness that had come over his expression.

"Or maybe you don't know me well enough to make that analysis."

"And whose fault is that?" I shot back.

With what sounded like a low rumble of frustration, Vaughn abruptly walked away, marching down the beach and out of sight around the bend. Running away. Like a little boy!

As for me I slumped back on the sand, willing the high-level hum to fade from my body. I was a furnace, and not because of the summer day.

To my utter horror the combination of Tremaine's smoldering eyes and confiding in me had turned me on.

"Holy hell," I grumbled, slinging an arm across my face so I could hide my mortified annoyance from the world.

Vaughn

He couldn't get away fast enough.

If he'd stayed, he would have kissed her, touched her, and made her hate him all over again. He'd hate himself if he did that to her.

So he walked away.

The nonsense she'd spewed about his father and how he felt about it . . . maybe it wasn't nonsense, maybe it was, but the fact was he'd seen the hope in her eyes when she drew that conclusion. As though finding the answer to his commitment issues would somehow solve everything.

This back-and-forth stuff had to stop. He was driving them both insane. But the jealousy, the possessiveness that had roared in his blood when he saw her with that *boy* controlled him. He wanted to lay a claim to her, and that's exactly what he'd done in the park.

When he'd seen Bailey go after Rex, he'd found himself following against his will. The relief he felt watching that kid leave was overwhelming.

That need to make sure she was okay, that relief he felt, made him question himself the entire way down the beach. It made him question himself as he sat beside her, their arms brushing. He was aware of every breath she took, every facial expression, every thought that flickered across her beautiful green-gold eyes.

And he knew he had to make a decision.

He loved Bailey Hartwell, and it was time to decide whether he could push past his own fears and take what he wanted, or finally let go.

Sitting with her Vaughn had hoped the answer would come to him, but she'd only confused and stirred him even more.

He needed time.

But he knew whatever he decided, one of them might end up getting hurt.

And that's why he was taking all the time in the world.

NINETEEN

Bailey

Almost two weeks later I woke up in my bed at the inn. I had kept myself busy at work, staying late every night. Aydan had more time with Angela as I buried myself in the needs of our guests to avoid matters of the heart. Like I had for the past few nights I decided to crash at my room at the inn instead of going home to my house that no longer felt like my home with Vanessa's crap strewn all over it.

It wasn't my alarm that woke me, however. It was the crashing sound coming from the front of the building.

Fear flooded me.

Another break-in.

I froze for a moment, remembering the last time. The sound of a louder scuffle had me reaching for my phone and dashing out of bed at the same time.

As soon as I opened the bedroom door I heard my sister's voice. "Be careful!"

Holy hell.

I relaxed marginally but hurried down the corridor past my office anyway. Standing in the split reception area, my stomach dropped to my feet at the sight of an obnoxiously modern reception counter sitting waiting to replace my beautiful, hand-carved walnut one.

Confronted by glass and black glossy wood I shook my head, struggling to contain my roar of frustration.

"Oh, Bailey, just in time. I ordered this new counter as a starting-off point for redecoration."

She'd brought up the idea of redecoration a number of times and I'd made my opinion on that clear. It was a big fat no. Apparently nothing I had said to her had penetrated.

"No," I hissed out. "No!"

Vanessa's eyes flared. "What do you mean, no? I have men wait-ing to install it and remove the old ugly one." She gestured to two beleaguered men who were glaring at her.

"First of all, it is six o'clock in the morning and I have guests who are trying to sleep. Second of all"—I stepped right into her space, getting in her face so she finally understood I meant business—"I said no to the redecoration."

She narrowed her eyes. "And I didn't agree with it."

Then something occurred to me. "Where did you get the money to pay for this?"

God, please say, "My own savings."

"Your credit card."

My tether ended with that. In fact my tether was a dot in the very far distance.

I pushed my sleepy face into hers so she had nowhere else to look, and her eyes flared like Bambi's when the hunter shot his mother. "Return that piece of modern catastrophe, give me back my credit card, and stay the hell out of my business, or I swear to God, V, I will make your life a living goddamn hell."

"I'm going to tell Mom and Dad," she snapped.

"Do what you want, just get that ugly counter out of my inn."

She studied me, trying to measure my resolve. Finally she got it, sniffed in upset, and turned to the delivery guys. "It appears I need to return it."

"No shit," one of the guys grunted. "Fucking fruitcakes."

"Hey." I shook a finger at him. "I have guests. Watch your lan-guage."

"Move the counter, man," the other one urged under his breath. "Don't mess with the crazy lady."

We stood in frozen silence as the men repackaged the counter and started maneuvering it out of the inn. Once their voices had faded down the garden I turned to my sister. "You haven't even been here for the last week. You've been off gallivanting, without a care in the world, and then you think you can just come back in here, ignore everything I said, and start making changes? What planet do you live on?"

"My personal life is none of your business." She narrowed her eyes.

"It is when it interferes with my life. Who the hell are you seeing anyway?"

This mystery-guy thing was starting to bug me. Usually Vanessa couldn't wait to brag about whom she was dating. But she had been very close-mouthed about the whole thing, even going so far as to avoid me, and spend all her time with whoever it was.

"Is he married?"

"No, he's not married," she snapped. "You really think a lot of me, don't you?"

"Right now you're about my least favorite person in the world," I said.

"How on earth do you run a successful inn with that smart mouth of yours?"

"Oh, so you finally acknowledge that I run a successful inn."

"Ugh!"

"You say that word one more time, I swear to God—"

"Ladies."

We turned around to find Aydan standing in the doorway. Her arms were crossed over her chest and she was tapping her foot on the floor in irritation.

"Do you want to wake our guests?"

Embarrassed at having to be scolded by my manager I shifted uncomfortably. "You should have seen what I just woke up to."

Aydan glowered at Vanessa. "I can only imagine. But, Bailey, you're in tiny pajamas that will give Mr. Sykes heart failure if he sees you, so please go get showered and changed before our guests come down for breakfast in"—she glanced at her watch—"thirty minutes. Vanessa, why don't you take the day off? Again."

"Don't talk to me that way in my own inn or I might just have to get physical." Vanessa threw her hands on her tiny hips. "I'm stronger than I look."

Aydan stepped up beside me, showing solidarity. "Yeah, well I'm willing to bet I could take you. I'm also not your sister and therefore not obliged to put up with your crap or stop myself from causing you physical harm. On that note, you have five seconds to get out of your sister's face before I put my job in jeopardy. Five. Four—"

"Ugh, I don't need this." Vanessa stormed by us. "And I'm telling Mom what kind of trash you hired to run this place."

I lunged at her and Aydan held me back.

"She's not worth it," she said as Vanessa disappeared out of the door.

"What did I do to deserve her?"

"Don't think about her. Let it go. Go get showered and I'll go check in on Mona in the kitchen. She more than likely heard all the commotion and is terrified to come out."

I knew Aydan was right. My kitchen staff hated Vanessa. *All* of my staff hated Vanessa. I was guessing it had to do with the way she talked to them like they were her servants.

"And Bailey," Aydan called to me as I wandered back down the hallway.

"Yeah?"

"No work for you today. You are way past due for your day off. Get showered and go out. Do something, anything. Just get some R&R, okay?"

I nodded, even though I dreaded the idea of being alone with my thoughts.

ıılllllllllllllllllllllllllllllllll

The day was overcast so I half expected it to downpour, but I held out hope as I wandered from boutique to boutique on Main Street, attempting to relax as Aydan suggested.

Problem was I wasn't much of a shopper. There was also the matter of my thoughts; my thoughts that kept wandering to all the crap in my life that I didn't want to deal with. I'd been so focused on keeping my mind on work that I hadn't really spoken to Jess and the girls. We'd checked in about wedding stuff but we hadn't had a long, meaningful conversation in which I revealed how close to the ledge I was so they could talk me off it.

When the heavens broke and thunder clapped in the skies tourists rushed for cover into restaurants, shops, and hotels, and I hurried down the slick boards to Emery's.

Her place was busier than I'd hoped, beachgoers having rushed inside to shelter from the weather. Emery looked a little flustered so I joined her behind the counter. "Can I help?"

She nodded gratefully, and while she dealt with coffee, I quickly got a grip on her cash register.

When the line was dealt with and everyone seemed settled in the sitting area of the bookstore Em turned to me and handed me a dish towel. "Not that I'm not glad to see you but what are you doing here?"

I dried the ends of my long hair with the towel. "Aydan made me take a day off."

"You have been working really hard lately. What's going on?"

I glanced around to make sure we had privacy. "I'm a little low right now. I just . . . sometimes I can't believe this is my life at thirty-four. I always thought I'd have it all by now, you know?"

"And Vaughn? Has he finally admitted he cares about you?"

I shook my head. Over the last few weeks, with no contact from him whatsoever, I'd started to grow angrier, more frustrated by him. Any trust that might have existed between us, however small, had been obliterated by the daily turmoil I felt over my unrequited—

No, it wasn't love. I didn't know him well enough to truly be in love with him.

But I still felt something. Something undeniable.

And very painful.

"He's too closed off, Em. I need someone who trusts me. Someone who will let his guard down with me. And he won't because . . . I'm not the kind of woman he'll ever let his guard down with. I'm not the *right* kind of woman."

"Or maybe he hasn't let his guard down with you because you haven't let your guard down with him?"

"Of course I have. I slept with him." I wrinkled my nose. "Plus, I'm Bailey Hartwell. I don't even have a guard, let alone one that's *up*."

She laughed. "In general, no, you don't. But . . . the way you're running from him isn't like you."

"What? Being smart isn't like me?"

"Well—" Whatever Emery might have said was forgotten when the bell above her door jangled and Jack Devlin walked into the store. Emery's face turned the deepest shade of scarlet I'd ever seen it turn.

Her reaction might have had something to do with the way Jack's gaze zeroed in on her as soon as he stepped inside the building.

I waited for Em to greet him but I could see her throat working, like she was struggling to get the words out.

Dear God.

Did Em have a crush on Jack Devlin?

"Hey, Jack." I saved her.

He reluctantly dragged his gaze from her to me. "Bailey."

"How's the fist?" I grinned.

To my delight I saw the corners of his mouth twitch, like he was fighting a smile. "It's fine."

"I'm glad to hear it. What can we get you?"

Jack looked back at Emery, and I had to bite my lip in girlish delight at the way his gaze raked over her features, like he was savoring every detail of her lovely face. "My usual," he said. "Times two."

Em nodded, not meeting his eyes, and turned to the coffee machine. Her hands trembled a little as she worked, and I felt a pang of sympathy. How I wished I could give her even just a drop of my confidence so she could converse easily with a man.

It must be horrible for her to be so shy.

I wanted to hug her.

Instead I didn't do anything that patronizing. I let her work. She finished making the coffee while we all stood in silence. She slid the coffee over to Jack. "Six dollars."

He handed her a ten, and I studied how she took it by the tip so she wouldn't have to touch him. I also studied the way this made a usually expressionless Jack frown in consternation.

And then when she handed him his change, he brushed his thumb deliberately over the top of her hand when he accepted it. Em's skin flushed red all over again.

He nodded at us and then was gone just as quickly as he had appeared.

"So Jack Devlin, huh?"

Emery blushed even harder. "No. No. I mean . . . no . . . I know he works for the devil. So no."

Methinks the lady doth protest too much.

"That doesn't stop him from being drop dead gorgeous."

Emery let out an embarrassed huff of laughter.

"Hey, if it makes you feel any better, Jack punched out Stu for attacking me."

Her eyes widened at the thought. "Really?"

"Yeah. I told Cooper after it happened, but he didn't do anything with it. I had hoped it might make him take a step toward approaching Jack but he thinks, and I suppose rightly so, that Jack should be the one to make the first step. I've always thought there was more to Jack's story. The whole going to work for his dad, the whole Dana thing, it never made sense. And I don't want to give up on him." I nudged her playfully. "Maybe a sweet, gorgeous woman just like you is exactly what a man like Jack Devlin needs."

"Me?" Emery was apparently shocked by the idea. "No. He doesn't even know I'm alive."

I considered the way Jack had stared at my friend like he wanted to eat her up. "I definitely don't think that's true."

"Even so." She frowned. "I . . . I like my life here now. I have you and Jessica and Dahlia. I can even hold a conversation with Cooper without blushing like an idiot. I wouldn't want to jeopardize what I have now by setting my cap for Jack Devlin. I wouldn't be able to trust him."

At her practical, heartfelt response I felt renewed admiration for her. I threw my arm around her shoulders. "Wow. I am so glad you are a much smarter woman than I am when it comes to men."

She smiled shyly. "I don't think I'm smarter. Just . . . isolated enough from them to be able to think more clearly."

"See? Smarter." I grinned at her. "And 'setting my cap'? Really?"

Em rolled her eyes, blushing again. "I said that, didn't I? That's all my grandmother. God, don't let me end up sounding like her, please."

"Oh, well, I'm going to find that hard to do when you say adorable stuff like 'setting my cap for Jack Devlin.'"

She laughed. "You're awful."

"I am. And it's fun. You should join me here in 'saying whatever is on my mind' land."

Wistfulness filled her expression. "Maybe I will someday."

Vaughn

"There's at least two thousand dollars' worth of damages, sir." Jannette, Vaughn's head housekeeper at Paradise Sands, sounded aggrieved.

Vaughn was feeling pretty aggrieved, too.

A couple had been staying in one of their smaller suites and checked out this morning. They had been asked during the previous evening to lower their noise level because they were disturbing other guests. His staff had even threatened to call the police, which seemed to have halted the situation.

The unpleasant surprise the next morning was the aftereffects of what had clearly been a domestic dispute.

"Was this a matter of domestic violence?" Vaughn was unsettled by the idea that something like that had been going on.

Jannette shook her head. "We don't know. Both seemed in fine physical condition and I've checked the room over. No blood."

Hmm. That still left them with the matter of his suite. Nearly every lamp in the room was destroyed. The television screen was cracked where something had been thrown at it. And there was a hole in the plaster work near the door.

"They must have been making some racket." Vaughn looked around. The place was a mess. There was a wine stain on the cream carpet in the sitting room; the bedclothes were tossed across the room, as were all the pillows and throw cushions. A curtain was half hanging off the rail.

What the hell had they been doing in here?

"Why wasn't I called? Why weren't the police called?"

His supervisor, Graham, stepped into the room from the hall. "We didn't realize the extent of the situation, sir, or we would have."

"Well we need to call the police now and file an incident report with them. After that's done I want a tally of everything that needs to be fixed or replaced. Is this room booked out today?"

"Yes," Graham said. "I've already looked and a sea-view upgrade of this suite is available for the guest."

"Upgrade them. As for the neighbors who complained about the noise, I want them compensated. Take last night's stay off their bill and give them a complimentary meal in the restaurant."

"Yes, sir."

"Jannette." Vaughn turned to her. "Once the police have come by, and you've worked out what needs to be done in here, talk to Ailsa. She can order whatever we need for in here. I want this room presentable as quickly as possible." It was one of his most popular rooms. "Give the information you've gathered to Graham as well. Graham, I want you to deal with the police and charging the couple for damages."

"Yes, sir."

With a curt nod, Vaughn strode past his employees and out into the hall. Rarely did he have to deal with situations like that in one of his establishments, but sometimes there came someone or *some-ones* who had no respect for other people's property.

Irritated he marched around the corner, heading for the elevators, and came to an abrupt stop. Vaughn quickly stepped back around the corner out of sight. Feeling like a schoolboy, he peeked his head around the wall to make sure he'd seen what he'd thought he'd seen.

Fumbling with a key card to get into a standard room was Vanessa Hartwell. And kissing her and making her falter in her progress was none other than Jack Devlin.

Her laughter floated down the hall toward him. "That coffee you got me made me all jittery!" she squealed when he bit her earlobe.

Vaughn couldn't hear what Jack said in response but whatever it was made Vanessa break into peals of scandalized giggles. She got the key card to work and the door swung open. She whirled around to throw herself up into Jack's arms, her legs wrapped around his waist, her fingers curled in his hair as they dirty kissed all the way into the room.

The door slammed shut in their wake and Vaughn stepped out from hiding.

Anger froze him in place for a moment as his suspicions overcame him.

It hit him immediately:

The Devlins hadn't stopped in their plans to get Bailey's inn from her. They were just being smarter about it. Of course, Jack could just be interested in Vanessa for sex but somehow Vaughn doubted it.

The sex was just a bonus.

The payoff was Bailey's inn.

"Mr. Tremaine." Graham caught up with him. "I was hoping we could discuss that promotion we talked about."

"What?" Vaughn frowned up at him, his mind on one thing and one thing only.

"The promotion. To daytime manager. I feel like I would be doing what I do already but with more authority and perhaps a salary increase. If—"

Vaughn held up his hand to cut him off. "I need to be somewhere right now. We'll sit down later to discuss the particulars of your promotion."

"So I *am* getting promoted?"

"Yes. We'll talk later," he called, hurrying toward the elevators. "I need to go out. You're in charge while I'm gone."

"Yes, sir!" Graham called back.

Five minutes later he pulled up outside Ian Devlin's office building in his dark blue Aston Martin Vanquish. The car barely slid into place behind Devlin's black Cadillac CTS-V when Vaughn swung out of it and marched on a mission into the building. He burst onto Devlin's floor, startling the pretty receptionist behind her desk.

Her eyes widened when she saw Vaughn and she jumped to her feet when he spotted the door with the plaque that had Devlin's name on it. He started to stride past her toward it and she cried, "Excuse me! You don't have an appointment!"

"I don't need an appointment." He grabbed the handle on the door and thrust it open.

Ian Devlin shot to his feet from behind his desk at the interruption. "What is the goddamn meaning of this?"

Vaughn slammed the door in the receptionist's face and stared the older man down.

Devlin, much like his own father, looked good for his age. Distinguished, well-dressed, and fit. But that was where the similarities between the two men ended. There was a chilling hardness in Ian Devlin's eyes, an oily slickness to his smile and manner.

From the moment he met Devlin, Vaughn had not trusted him. And for good reason it would seem.

This was a man who was trying to hurt Bailey; trying to take everything she'd worked so hard for away from her. He thought he was some kind of kingpin, that he was immune because he had all this power in a small town.

Well Vaughn understood power and if he had to he would squash this fucker. On that thought he slowly made his way over to Devlin's desk.

He stopped when the piece of furniture dug into his legs. "I'm onto you."

Ian smirked. "Really? You barge in here like a lunatic to deliver that cliché of a line."

"If anyone is a cliché, Devlin, it's you. It amazes me what you think you can get away with."

"And what is it you think I'm trying to get away with?"

"You have one of your little lackies fucking Vanessa Hartwell."

Nothing. No surprise. No disgust. No triumph. Nothing. Instead he shrugged. "I don't know what you're talking about."

"I'm talking about Jack using my hotel as a stage for his escort services. Because that's what it is, right? You're paying him to fuck Vanessa . . . to get to Bailey and her inn."

"My, my, you have quite the imagination."

Fury blasted through Vaughn and he slammed his fist down on the desk rather than into Devlin's face. "I let that other piece of shit son get away with breaking into Bailey's place, but I haven't forgotten, and I haven't forgiven. I swear to God"—he pushed his face into the old man's—"you come after Bailey again and I will end you. I will end the lot of you." His voice lowered with vitriol. "And don't think I can't do it. You are a big fish in a small pond. I'm a fucking shark in the ocean."

For a moment Vaughn thought he saw uncertainty flicker in Devlin's eyes, but if it was there, it was gone in an instant. Still sure he'd made his point, and sure that the message had sunk in, he turned on his heel to leave.

He'd just opened the door when Devlin's smug voice stopped him. "Not very smart."

Not wanting to give him the satisfaction but not liking the threat in his tone, Vaughn looked back at him.

Ian was grinning. "Not very smart, Mr. Tremaine, is it, to unmask your vulnerabilities to someone you so clearly see as a threat. All this time I had to wonder, what is Vaughn Tremaine's weakness? And what do you know? It's a redhead with a smart mouth."

The desire to punch him was so great, Vaughn felt his hand curling into a fist. Instead he threw him one last look of revulsion and stormed out of the building.

Back inside his car he let go of the breath he'd been holding in and slammed his hands down on his steering wheel. "Fuck!"

Exhausted and worried, Vaughn laid his head on the wheel and tried to will himself to calm down.

These past few weeks he'd been fighting with himself, knowing that he was in love with Bailey, but not knowing whether he could sacrifice his autonomy for her. But there really wasn't anything to think about.

Not after he'd acted like a lunatic based on a split-second assumption he'd made. Vaughn had great instincts and he knew he was right about Jack. But driving over to threaten Devlin, revealing his weakness . . .

Ian Devlin was right. Bailey Hartwell was his Achilles' heel.

On that thought he started the engine and pulled out of the parking spot. However, he didn't drive back to his hotel. Instead he drove down the coast, to the outskirts of town, to his beautiful house on the south side.

Inside, he wandered through the spacious house that was too lonely to call home and out onto the balcony that sat right on the water.

Then he called his dad.

"I'm just about to go into a business meeting," William said in lieu of "hello."

"I admit it. I'm in love with Bailey."

Silence greeted him on the other end and then he heard his dad say to someone quietly, "Can we move that meeting to two o'clock? Apologize to them, tell them something came up."

After a few more seconds of background noise, his dad's voice came on the line. "So what are you going to do about it?"

"I don't know. I've never put myself into a situation I wasn't ninety-nine percent sure I'd be able to control the outcome of."

William grunted in amusement. "Well let this be your first."

"What if I'm too late? I've fucked this up a lot. I've been immature. She doesn't trust me and I don't blame her. And what if she does end up saying she wants to give us a shot and it falls apart?"

"I can't tell you whether it will or not. There's no guarantee. But I'm guessing I'm getting this call because you know you can no longer put off what you feel for her."

"No." He couldn't. It was driving him crazy. The torment he was feeling had to be worse than facing his fear of commitment, right? "Every time I try to stay away or stay out of her business, I end up in it. Because I put myself in it." He grew quiet, slightly embarrassed. "I can't help but want to protect her."

"So what's the problem?"

"She wants it all. Marriage. Kids."

"And you don't."

"No, it's not that . . . I just . . . I gave up on believing I'd have those things."

"And now?"

"It would mean sacrifice, of my autonomy, some of my career . . . to give her those things."

"But you're willing to give her those things?"

Vaughn took a deep breath, saying the words that had been buried deep inside him for a long time. "I think I'd do anything to make her happy."

There was no hiding the joy in his father's voice. "Then go tell her that."

TWENTY

Vaughn

Once he made the decision to tell Bailey that he wanted to be with her—to see what was possible between them—Vaughn had to tell her. Immediately. He drove back to the boardwalk and parked the car in his spot in the lot behind the hotel, his body thrumming with impatience.

His intention was to go directly to the inn.

But it seemed providence was on his side because as soon as he stepped a foot onto the boardwalk he caught sight of a familiar redhead in his peripheral.

Bailey strolled down the boardwalk from the direction of Emery's.

Blood rushed in his ears as Vaughn stalked toward her watching her eyes grow round at the sight of him coming at her. "Tremaine, what—whoa!" She startled when he took hold of her upper arm. "What are you doing?"

"We need to talk," he said. Impatient was now an understatement. He'd never felt such a burning sense of urgency in his life.

"Okay, so let's talk." She pushed at his hand but he didn't let go. "We can talk without the manhandling."

"We need to talk in private."

"Has something happened—ah, where are we going?" she asked as he stole her off course to the inn and into his hotel instead. "Can you slow down and tell me what the hell is going on? I haven't seen you in days and the first time I do you accost me in the middle of the boardwalk, literally jerk me around, and haul me into your hotel and I'm just supposed to—"

"Bailey, usually the rambling is fucking cute, but can you just shut up this one time?" He was trying to work out in his head what it was he was going to say to her once he got her in his penthouse. They stopped at the elevators and she pulled at his hold.

"Vaughn."

What were the right words? Were there right words? There had to be right words . . .

"Vaughn." This time she moved into him, and his whole being came alive at the sensation of her soft curves pressed against his hard body.

"Your staff and guests are looking," she whispered, her gaze appeasing. "Why don't you let me go and I'll promise to come upstairs with you. And while you consider that, why don't you think about how much my having to ask you that makes you sound like a kidnapping bastard?"

Her words pierced through his single-minded determination to tell her how he felt. His grip on her eased and he found himself smirking at her teasing. "I want to kiss you," he murmured.

Bailey's lips parted in surprise, and her voice sounded a little breathy when she told him, "Maybe I shouldn't be alone with you after all."

The elevator doors opened and Vaughn placed a possessive hand on her lower back. "Or you definitely should." He led her inside, grateful for the guests who joined them. If he'd been alone in the elevator with her, he probably wouldn't have been able to keep his hands off her. And she knew it. He sensed it in her appraisal, in the way her chest rose and fell in shallow breaths, and in the flush high on her cheeks.

Attraction raged as hot as ever between them.

Vaughn needed to keep it together long enough to tell her how he felt.

When the elevator emptied they were alone. Holding on to the last measure of his control he stopped himself from reaching for her, placed his key card in the panel by the door, and pressed the button for the top floor.

Bailey jumped out as soon as the elevator doors pinged open.

Vaughn directed her down the corridor to his penthouse. He held the door open for her, watching her face as she absorbed the space. The first thing she did was walk over to the floor-to-ceiling window that looked out over the ocean.

"Wow," she said. "This is beautiful."

So are you.

As if she heard him Bailey whirled around. "What am I doing here?"

He found himself moving toward her, unable to stop, needing to touch her. It was inexplicable how *much* he was feeling now that he'd given himself permission to feel it.

"Don't." Her lips trembled invitingly.

"Don't what?" He continued toward her.

"Look at me like that. I've warned you about that smolder."

Amusement, tenderness, love . . . *need* filled him. "I can't help it when it comes to you."

"Holy hell," she muttered. "Vaughn . . ." She closed her eyes for a brief second. When she opened them they blazed with anger. "It's not fair. Why does it have to be you?"

"Why does what have to be me?" He reached up to cup her face in his hand.

"That makes me lose all sense of willpower," she whispered.

Gratification swelled inside him, as did something else, something headier, consuming . . . and not a little possessive. "Good." His fingers curled around her nape. His mouth took hers. And he poured everything he was feeling into the kiss.

Bailey whimpered, hesitating a second or two, before he felt the resistance melt right out of her.

Her tongue swept over his, and the sweet taste of her filled him as the slender curves of her body crushed against him. Her light fruity perfume filled his senses, taking all thought but the urge to have her. He groaned at her surrender, his hands roaming her body frantically, wanting to feel all of her at once.

Plucking at the buttons of her shirt he tore his mouth from hers, wanting to taste every drop of her. He brushed kisses down her chest, following the skin that was revealed with each button he undid on her shirt. At the revelation of her beautiful, peaches-and-cream skin, so smooth, so fine, the blood that wasn't currently in his dick rushed to it.

"God, Bailey," he groaned again, kissing the soft skin of her stomach as he pulled the shirt down off her arms. Vaughn dropped the fabric at their feet and tilted his head back to look up at her.

Bailey's chest heaved, her breathing ragged with arousal.

Vaughn stood to look directly into her eyes, wanting to make sure she wanted this as much as he did. Satisfaction roared through him as she stared up at him in dazed lust.

Wanting.

Needing.

Silent supplication in those beautiful green-gold eyes.

Yes.

That look shredded his control. This time his kisses were bruising. Before she had time to think Vaughn relieved her of her bra and edged her across the room toward the bed. Bailey's legs hit the frame and they fell onto it. Vaughn came down over her, and he pushed up her tight skirt to her waist so he could insinuate himself between her legs. Finally he broke their kiss to focus on her breasts.

They were beautiful. Perfect. Every inch of her was.

He captured a nipple in his mouth and sucked.

"Vaughn," she gasped, her thighs tightening around his hips while her fingers curled in his hair.

He growled with satisfaction and licked her nipple before moving on to its companion.

"Oh, my God," she whimpered, her hips undulating against him, teasing his arousal.

A haze washed over him.

He wanted inside her.

Desperately.

Usually he loved spending time tormenting a woman, building her up and up until she thought she was going to die with pleasure. He got off on the sounds of their pleasure-pain pleading, and nothing had turned him on more than the night he'd heard Bailey's pleas in his ears as he drove her to the brink of orgasm over and over. Because nothing was more fucking rewarding than watching a woman come *that* hard.

Nothing was more breathtaking than watching Bailey come that hard.

Yet right then all Vaughn could think about was getting inside her as fast as possible. The desire felt animalistic, instinctual, like he was trying to claim her.

If he wasn't so overwhelmed with need, he might have been appalled.

He stared down into her flushed face. She stared up at him beneath her lashes, pure craving in the depths of her eyes. Her beautiful hair spilled in rich red across his pillows. Her large dark pink nipples were tight buds, her creamy, perky breasts swollen with arousal as they rose and fell with her shallow, excited breaths.

Fuck, but he'd never seen anything more provocative in his life, his dick agreeing as it strained to be free, to be inside of her. Fingers slipped beneath her underwear and he found her already wet with anticipation.

It was his undoing.

Straddling her, Vaughn stripped off his jacket, pulled the condom out of his wallet first, and then he unzipped himself.

"Shirt off," she begged.

He cursed, ripping buttons off as he tried to rid himself of it and his tie as quickly as possible.

Bailey's elegant, soft hands gripped his hips as he worked the condom on, and then caressed his stomach and his chest as he lowered over her. "Why do you have to be so beautiful?" she whispered, and the words were almost mournful.

Her tone unsettled him. He wanted her to forget everything but what it felt like to be together.

Shucking his trousers down to his hips, Vaughn held her gaze. He held her gaze as he pulled her panties to her knees.

This was them.

This is us.

He didn't want her to try to escape from that.

With nothing between them now he pushed inside.

The velvet heat of her tight grip on his dick made his eyes roll toward the back of his head. He'd forgotten how fucking amazing she felt. "Bailey," he grunted, thrusting deeper. "God, princess, what you do . . . Fuck!" He grabbed her thigh, pulling it higher, tighter against his hip so he could slide in deeper.

In answer she wrapped her legs around his waist and he let go to brace his hands by her head.

Her fingers dug into his ass. "Vaughn," she breathed. "More."

He looked down at her lust-flushed face and felt his lower abdomen tighten with deep pleasure. Wanting her to come before he did, he grew rigid with control, willing his dire need down.

Holding tight to the reins of his willpower he slowed, no longer fucking her, but making love to her. That tickle of pleasure that crawled up from every corner of his body became like a voracious, mind-shattering desperation, a desperation that he wanted to stop but also wanted to go on forever.

Bailey's eyes flared, so bright, so gold, and her hips jerked. "Vaughn!" She undulated into each deep glide of his dick, chasing her orgasm.

"Take it, princess, take everything."

At the first tug of her inner muscles on his dick, Vaughn cried out in gratification. Each hard ripple jerked him toward orgasm.

A blaze of sensation, of heat, shot through him like a gunshot. He jerked against her as his release roared through him, the blood rushing his ears so hard her gasps of pleasure were muffled.

As he became fluid, relaxed, the aftermath of hot bliss still hummed in his groin. Vaughn strained to keep himself from collapsing over Bailey.

She stared up at him.

And reality slowly began to pierce his sexual haze.

Vaughn couldn't read Bailey's expression.

Usually he knew exactly what was on her mind. Usually it blazed out of those gorgeous eyes of hers.

Fuck.

Sex. They should not have had sex. Not then. He had not meant to do that. Not like that, so hurried, no finesse. He'd fucked her like an overexcited schoolboy, not even getting fully undressed.

Irritated with himself, he flopped down beside her and listened as they both tried to catch their breaths. He turned his head to crack a joke about it, to ease the sudden tension between them, but Bailey was already on the move.

Bailey

Oh, my God.

I'd done it again.

I couldn't believe I'd done it again.

Fear, anger, pain lanced across my chest, making it hard to breathe, and I knew I had to get out of there as quickly as possible.

Not looking at Vaughn, I pulled up my panties, ignored the throbbing between my legs, and hopped off the bed. I quickly pushed down my skirt and hurried over to where my shirt lay.

"What are you doing?" Vaughn asked, concern in his words.

I ignored the concern. "Getting out of here so I can self-flagellate in private for letting you do this to me again."

He sighed and I heard him get out of bed, but I refused to look at him. Looking at him only got me into trouble. My hands trembled as I grabbed up my bra and shrugged on my shirt. Behind me I heard rustling then the sound of his zipper going up. Then suddenly I felt the heat of his presence right next to me, felt the overwhelming focus of his eyes on my downturned face.

Gently, Vaughn swatted my hands away from my shirt and started to button it for me. My hands fell uselessly to my sides, limp with surprise. "I didn't bring you up here to do that. That . . . My dick apparently can't control itself around you."

I glowered up at him and the asshole had the audacity to grin at me.

"Nice," I snapped.

"But it wasn't my dick that led you up here." Finished buttoning me up, he took my face in his hands and looked at me with such tenderness I felt the war start up again within me. "Bailey." A look of vulnerability crossed his face; his breathing seemed shallow. "Bailey . . . I'm in love with you."

I froze.

Had I just heard correctly?

"I'm in love with you."

My breath got locked inside of my throat and I struggled to draw in air as I tried to process this revelation.

"I've been in love with you for a long time. I've fought it. I've hidden it. I've tried to cast them aside. But since our night together I haven't been able to hold my feelings down. And I don't want to anymore. I'm sorry for saying I didn't want you when I always have. I need you to know I'm done with that bullshit. I want to be with you. I want to see where this could go."

The silence fell thick and fast between us as he stared into my eyes with sincerity and tenderness in his expression.

It would have been so easy to let this moment with this beautiful man override every moment that had come before it.

But I couldn't let it.

I couldn't trust it.

I couldn't trust him.

Instead I was suddenly overwhelmed with fear and anger. I took his hands from my face and pushed him gently away.

"No."

The word seemed to wind him. "No?"

Tears burned my eyes as I backed away from the pain in his. "No. No! You can't do this to me!"

"Right now you're scared, I get that . . ." He tried to reach for me. "But that's because you care about me, too."

I dodged his touch. "I do. I absolutely do. But I don't trust you, Vaughn."

His jaw slackened as though I'd physically gutted him. "You don't trust me?"

"No, I don't." I shoved my feet into my shoes, glaring at him, and I gathered every memory of his ill treatment of me, his confused, hurtful behavior to me like armor against him. "You tell me you love me, but only a week ago you told me you didn't want anything to happen between us. Everyone knows you're a womanizer! So no, I don't trust you because the truth is I don't think you can trust yourself . . . You don't *know* what you want."

Anger tightened his expression. "Don't you dare tell me what I'm feeling. I fucking know what I want. Do you know how hard this was for me? If you walk out on me that's all about you, not me. I'm not the one running scared now, princess."

"I have every right to run scared. You were a confirmed bachelor until two seconds ago! You're lost, Vaughn, completely lost! And I don't need another guy like you in my life."

I thought of the man, the boy really, who was just like Vaughn. I thought of how easily I'd bought his lies, his apparent sincerity, and I knew I couldn't trust myself with someone like him again.

Vaughn needed to know that this moment wasn't part of the dance we'd been performing around each other for months. This was the *end* of the dance.

I stared at him, and suddenly I saw the boy from my past, smiling at me in that boyish way of his that had captured my young heart. "One summer a long time ago, I met a boy." The words spilled out of my lips before I could stop them. Vaughn seemed to draw closer to hear me, but I was barely cognizant of his movements. I was thrown back into the past.

"Do you love me, Hartwell?"

I laughed. "I told you yesterday that I do. Do you need to hear it every day?"

He stared sadly at me. "Yes. Because up until now no one has ever said it to me before."

Tenderness rushed over me. I clasped his face in my hands and whispered, "I love you. I love you so much. And I'll tell you every day from now on. I promise."

"I love you, too."

"Someone just like you," I whispered to Vaughn. The hurt was an old hurt, a wound that had healed over time, but I still remembered what it had felt like to be so blindsided by someone I'd loved. "He was handsome and charming and rich, and he told me that he wanted me. I thought it was real and I fell in love with him."

"What do you mean you're leaving?" I stared up at him, the flicker of agony beginning to tighten in my chest.

His expression was embarrassed, annoyed. "This was always just a summer thing."

"Not to me! You . . . you told me you loved me."

"I thought . . ." He shook his head, exasperated. "I was confused. Caught up in it. But it was a mistake. We were a mistake."

That agony was no longer a flicker but a burning, breath-stealing pain. "You're lying. Why are you saying these things?" I'd brushed impatiently at my tears, desperate to have him hold me and laugh and tell me he was joking.

But he didn't laugh. He looked away, seeming anxious to get away from me. "We're not from the same world, Hartwell. Surely you see that. I'm going back to New York and you don't fit into my world there."

"I don't understand."

"For God's sake, you're a townie," he snapped. "My family would never approve of you."

Rage mingled with my heartbreak as I tried to make sense of the boy who'd spent all summer saying he loved me with this . . . this pompous, arrogant asshole breaking me into pieces. "The same family who has never told you they love you?"

He had the audacity to wince. "We're . . . we're just too young to fall in love. You're too young." He tried to reach for me but I stumbled back.

Sighing, he dropped his hand and walked away.

Just . . . walked away.

Like it was that easy.

I blinked out of the memory, of the one that came after, the one where I sobbed in my dad's arms until tears of helplessness burned in his own.

No.

I would never be that foolish again.

I pinned Vaughn with my determined gaze. "He said he was confused, that our relationship was a mistake, that I didn't *fit* into his world. In other words I wasn't good enough. Sound familiar?"

Vaughn blanched, as he clearly remembered the words he'd said to me after our first night together. "Bailey, when I said that before . . . I just said it because I knew it would keep you at a distance. I lied. I could give a shit that you're not some elite New York princess. In fact the reason I love you is because you're not like all those other women."

"Really?" I was unconvinced. "Then why? Why did you need to keep your distance? Why were you adamant about not being in a relationship with me? And why aren't you now?"

"Because I love you!" he yelled, frustration darkening his eyes.

"You've loved me for a long time; you just said it. So you loved me then, but you didn't *want* me then." I wanted answers. I wanted an explanation for his behavior, an explanation that would make sense of everything. "Why now? Why not then?"

When he had no reply for me, bitterness filled me. He loved me, but I wasn't worthy of an explanation.

I was still just like everyone else to him.

"I'm not that asshole," he said. "Whoever that guy was who hurt you. But this will be an adjustment for me. I'm not going to lie about that. However, I've never felt like this about anyone, and I will sacrifice all the bullshit I thought was important to me, like being a law unto myself, if it means I get to lie next to you every night."

His words tried to worm their way inside me.

I cared about this man, I was more attracted to him than I'd ever been to anyone, and I wanted to believe his beautiful words. But all they were, were beautiful words.

They weren't an explanation for why he'd made this so damn hard for us.

He was hiding something.

And that scared the crap out of me.

"You didn't answer my question."

Vaughn stared at me in anguish, and I saw the war going on behind his eyes.

And then I saw the moment he decided not to trust me.

A flatness entered his expression and just like that, he closed up on me.

No.

No way could I risk myself on him.

If I fell in love with Vaughn Tremaine, he'd break me in half.

Tears spilled down my cheeks as I felt renewed disappointment. "You keep hurting me."

He had the decency to look guilty. "I don't mean to."

"Then stop," I pleaded. "Just stop. I need you . . . I need you to stay away from me."

Vaughn flinched but after a moment of contemplation he nodded. "I'd do anything to make you happy."

If that were true, he'd tell me why up until now he'd pushed me away. "Just words, Vaughn. Those are just words."

I turned away, needing to be out of his presence as quickly as possible. I could smell him on my skin, I could still feel him inside of me, and I was desperate to climb into my shower and sob this moment out of me.

As I stepped out into the hallway, about to close the door behind me, Vaughn called, "Wait!"

"Vaughn—"

"No, wait." He hurried toward me, cutting off my protestations. "There's something you need to know. It's about Vanessa."

TWENTY-ONE

Bailey

The lesson that I'd hoped to learn from my relationship with Tom, that thing I'd been trying to tell myself since that first night with Vaughn, had penetrated. Finally.

I believed I deserved to have the kind of passion that I'd found with Vaughn. But I believed I deserved to find it with a man who would trust me enough to let down his guard with me; to really let me get to know the *real* him.

One summer when I was nineteen years old I'd fallen in love with the wrong boy and he'd shattered me. However, he'd taught me a lesson I'd never forgotten: to trust actions over words. I'd gotten over that boy, but I'd never gotten over the lesson.

"I'm sorry." I sniffled and then blew my nose in one of the tissues Jessica had given me.

After leaving Vaughn I'd hurried home in tears. But to get to my car I had to pass Antonio's and Iris was out cleaning the windows. She'd tried to get me to talk to her, but I ran away like the melodramatic teenager I'd currently reverted to. Concerned, Iris had called Dahlia, who'd then called me. I told her not to come over.

She'd given me that.

For a while.

Dahlia, Jess, and Emery appeared early that evening with tissues, cake, and wine. My sister was nowhere in sight.

We'd had privacy for me to blubber about what had happened with Vaughn. Again.

Emery's brows were drawn together in consternation. "So . . . he told you he loved you but you're not willing to give him a chance?"

"Exactly."

"There has to be more to it than that," Dahlia mused.

"Of course there is," I huffed. "But let's not forget this is a man who has been hostile to me for years, had sex with me, said it was a mistake and we didn't 'fit,' and then veered between hostile and jealous for weeks—oh, after disappearing entirely—and then man-handled me into a room, jumped me, screwed me, proclaimed he loved me, but refused to tell me why the change of heart."

"I would say telling you he loved you was a step in the right direction though," Jessica said.

"Only marginally," I argued. "He won't tell me *why* he's been acting the way he has, or why it was so hard for him to admit he wanted a relationship with me. I mean, he's acting like loving me is some goddamn big sacrifice—actually used that word—but he won't even tell me why! How the hell am I supposed to have a relationship with someone who won't talk to me?"

"Bailey, this is you," Dahlia said. "You stick in there, you fight for the people you care about, you wear them down until you're their confidante. Why is Vaughn different? Why are you so scared to fight for him? Because we all know you'd wear him down eventually. The man looks at you like you're his last supper."

I stared from one friend to the next, reading the confusion, concern, and curiosity in their eyes. No one but my father and Ivy knew about the boy who broke my heart, not until I'd mentioned it to Vaughn. I'd held the memory close, hating how vulnerable it made me feel, made me seem. But I could never make them understand my fears without sharing that piece of my past.

"The summer I was nineteen this college guy whose family had spent the summer in Hartwell for years started to notice me. I was hanging out on the beach with Ivy, Iris's daughter, she was home from UCLA for the summer. And this guy was there with a friend who'd come down from Manhattan. Ivy liked the friend and I liked him. He said it was his last summer in Hartwell because his family was selling their summer home there, so he'd decided to stick around for a while since it would be the last time.

"He was different from the boys I grew up with. Different from the boys I crushed on, like Cooper and Jack." I smiled at Jess, having already confessed to her about my schoolgirl crush on her fiancé. "He was handsome but in this perfect Ralph Lauren catalogue kind of way. And he was funny and charming, and he loved to spoil me. He didn't take life too seriously, and I needed that then. I wanted to be with him and to do that I agreed to keep our relationship a secret. He told me his parents wouldn't like it if he spent too much time with one girl because they were afraid a girl would distract him from college.

"He was the first boy I slept with. We spent nights lying under the stars talking about everything. It wasn't some shallow summer romance," I tried to explain. "Not to me. He told me about the pressure he felt from his parents, how they never told him that they loved him and only gave praise when he measured up to their expectations. He was lonely. And scared. And I wanted to be the one person in his life that loved him no matter what. So I told him that and he told me that he loved me, too. And the sex was great. It was passionate. It was everything I thought love was supposed to be."

I smiled, grim. "So imagine my horror when he came to me at the end of the summer and told me that he'd gotten carried away, that he didn't love me, that it was a mistake, that we were too young. He told me that his parents would never approve because I was a townie. I wasn't good enough. He transformed in front of me into this person I didn't recognize. And then he left. I never saw him again. To make matters worse, Vanessa had a crush on him and I didn't know until it was too late. My relationship with her was already going downhill and it just fell apart after him."

Jessica took hold of my hand, anger burning in the depths of her hazel eyes. "He was a coward."

"Yes, he was. But no matter how much I tried to convince myself otherwise, he changed me. I used to think I was special. Maybe in a cocky way, maybe I was a little arrogant." I smiled ruefully. "But I was popular and loved, living in an extraordinary town, and I felt extraordinary, too. But I let him take that away from me, and I let him make me afraid of allowing myself to be that vulnerable to someone again. Meeting Tom was great because I knew I could love him without losing myself in him. I knew I was safe with him because I'd never feel that passionately about him . . . But Vaughn . . . he isn't safe."

"Oh, sweetie." Dahlia sighed. "Vaughn's a grown man. He's not some stupid kid who is afraid of his parents."

"Then why won't he tell me anything real about himself? Sure he'll talk about his mom and his dad and his freaking grand-parents, but God forbid anyone should ask him something real about *himself*."

"Why don't you make him?"

Because I'm afraid if I do, I will fall in love with him.

That was the truth. It had been bubbling up inside of me, trying to force its way to the surface ever since Vaughn's first rejection of me when we had sex.

I knew if he hadn't rejected me then, I would have given him a chance.

The girls waited patiently on an answer I was too scared to voice out loud.

When it became clear I had no answer for them, Jess spoke. "What about the other thing he told you? About Vanessa and Jack Devlin?"

Em winced at Jack's name, and I felt guilty. Had I actually tried to suggest something happen with her and Jack?

More than that, I'd been considering how to reunite Jack with all of us.

Only for the son of a bitch to turn around and stab me in the back.

"It makes no sense." Dahlia shook her head. "Why on earth would he punch Stu for attacking you and then weasel his way into Vanessa's pants to get to the inn?"

"I don't know." I rubbed at my forehead, feeling the pressure of a sickening headache. "But according to Vaughn, this is their new plan. And Jack's the willing whore."

"Cooper will be pissed." Jess sighed. "I think he wanted to believe that there's something more behind Jack's defection."

"I still think there is. But he's betraying friends right, left, and center now, and any forgiving feelings I or anyone else might have toward him need to be kept under lock and key. He can't be trusted. He's using my sister." Anger tore through me. "I know Vanessa and I don't see eye to eye, but she's still my family. And I don't want her to get hurt over this."

"Hurt over what?"

All of our heads whipped around in unison. Vanessa was standing in the sitting room staring at us. We'd been so deep in conversation that we hadn't even heard her enter the house.

She crossed her arms over her chest. "Well?"

I looked from her to Jessica, and she read my silent question in my eyes.

"I think we should give them some privacy . . ." My friend stood up, gesturing to Dahlia and Emery.

The three of them got up, hugged me, told me to call them if I needed them, and generally made me thankful for them, before they hustled out of my house, leaving me to tell Vanessa the ugly truth.

Her reaction was to burst into laughter.

I stared at her, stunned.

"What?" She gave me a bitter smile once her amusement died down. "You think a guy like Jack Devlin couldn't possibly want me for anything else but my connection to that stupid little inn?"

Her insults pricked. "Watch it."

"No, you watch it. It may be hard for you to understand this but some men like glamorous, beautiful women who know what to do in bed." She swished her hair over her shoulder with attitude. "Jack Devlin likes the way I get him off, and that's the reason he's paying attention to me. *Not* because of the inn."

"I'm sure sleeping with you is a bonus." I attempted to appease her. "But the Devlins are still using you to get to the inn."

"Is this what your life is?" She looked disgusted. "Are you so bored that you have to make up these little dramas? Is that why you lied and said Stu Devlin attacked you?"

There was really only so much a person could take in one day, and in that moment, realizing how little regard my sister had for me or the business my family had run for generations . . . I lost my shit. "Get. Out."

She raised an eyebrow. "Excuse me?"

"*Get out!*" I yelled, making her flinch. "Gather all of your crap and get out of my house!"

Gobsmacked, Vanessa could only stare at me. "And where am I supposed to go?"

"I could give a flying monkey's ass! You don't respect me, you don't respect this family, and I am done putting up with your shit." My chest heaved as I struggled to catch my breath.

My little sister's lips trembled and I could see the sheen across her eyes as she began to turn on the waterworks. In answer to that I snatched up my car keys and strode past her without looking at her. "You have two hours to get your crap and your butt out of my house. If I come home and you're still here, I'm calling the sheriff."

I'd barely arrived at the inn, still shaken from my confrontation with my sister, when the phone in my office rang.

And it was my parents on speakerphone.

"You threw your sister out?" my mother squeaked, appalled.

Vanessa certainly didn't take long tattling on me.

"Yes."

"Bailey, we don't treat family like that," Mom admonished.

I closed my eyes, searching for calm. Thankfully I sounded pretty in control when I replied, "Yes, well, we also don't disrespect one another but Vanessa has done that continually since her arrival here."

"She's a little temperamental but that doesn't qualify for eviction."

"She accused me of lying about Stu Devlin attacking me."

There was silence on the other end of the line.

"Why would she do that?" my father said.

I really didn't want to discuss their child's love life with them but . . . "Because she's sleeping with Jack Devlin. I have good reason to suspect that Jack is trying to use Vanessa to get to the inn. I was trying to make sure she didn't get hurt. Not only wouldn't she listen, she was insulting, and considering how insulting she's been for the past few weeks, that, I'm afraid, was the last straw."

"Should we come up there?" my dad asked. "Try and talk some sense into her?"

"Dad, I hate to say this because I don't want to see her get hurt . . . but I think it would be best for her if she did."

"What does that mean?" Mom asked, worried.

"Vanessa thinks that she can control people, *men*, with her looks. It's dangerous to think that for many reasons. Maybe this is a lesson we need her to learn. She'll find out soon enough Jack is using her, and hopefully it'll make her grow up and see that she isn't the center of the universe, and people will prey on her blind conceit."

"A little humbling might do her a world of good, you mean?"

"Yes."

My mom sighed. "I don't know."

"Stacy, I think Cherry is right. At least she's there for Vanessa if everything blows up in her face."

After a moment of silence my mom whispered, "Okay."

We hung up, all of us unsettled by the prospect of Vanessa getting hurt, but knowing it was a lesson my hardheaded, selfish, egotistical baby sister needed to learn.

A little fall back to earth might just knock some sense into her.

TWENTY-TWO

Vaughn

The last thing he wanted to do was attend a wedding.

However, when that wedding was the wedding of his friend and the reception was being held in his own hotel it was a little difficult to avoid attendance.

Plus, Bailey would be there. And despite how horrifically gut wrenching the experience of telling someone you loved them and not having them say it back was, Vaughn was not giving up.

He was Vaughn Tremaine. He hadn't created a hotel empire by giving up at the first or even the second or third hurdle. It was all about determination and perseverance.

There had to be a way to convince her to give him a shot without dredging up the past and things that didn't even matter anymore. His plan was to give her a little time, but not a lot, and then seduce her. He'd do this by becoming a constant in her life. He'd keep throwing himself into town life if that would help win her over, and he'd just *be* there for her. Time would prove that he wasn't going anywhere.

"How are things going in here?" Vaughn strolled into Cooper's hotel room. He'd given his friend the room free of charge since Jessica wanted a traditional start to their marriage and had asked Cooper to stay somewhere else the night before their wedding.

Cooper was dressed in his tux. He was a totally different man in a suit. Very distinguished. But he also looked like he was chafing in it. His sister, Cat, and her son, Joey, were in the room along with Cooper's reclusive chef Crosby.

Crosby seemed five million times more uncomfortable than Cooper in his suit. He sat on an armchair, chewing nervously at his nonexistent fingernails.

As for Cat she was smiling tenderly at her big brother and she looked stunning in a blue summer dress that matched her eyes. Her thick dark hair was pulled back from her face in some kind of messy bun thing, and it was the first time Vaughn really appreciated how beautiful Lawson's sister was.

"Uncle Coop doesn't like his tux. I don't like mine, either." Joey made a face.

Vaughn grinned at the little boy who was a miniature version of his uncle. Joey was Cooper's best man. "Well, you look good." He nodded at the boy's mother. "You look beautiful, Cat."

Surprise knocked the cockiness out of her smile, and there was an unexpected shyness to her response. "Thanks. You don't look so bad yourself, Tremaine."

"None of that," Cooper groaned. "First my pseudo sister, now my real sister. No, Vaughn. Just no."

He chuckled. "Apparently a man is not allowed to compliment a woman without it being construed as lascivious."

Cooper scowled at him. "When it's you, yeah."

"Well that's insulting. I'm a perfect gentleman."

"When a man has as many *friends* as you, other men start protecting their womenfolk from you."

"Womenfolk. Really?" Vaughn smirked. Then he thought about how much Jessica seemed to want him and Bailey to work things out. And whatever Jessica wanted, Cooper wanted her to have. He cleared his throat, pushing past his aversion to discussing personal matters in public. "Well, if it makes you feel any better I have every intention of only having one friend from now on. I just need to convince her of that."

"Bailey?"

He nodded.

That got him a shit-eating grin. "Good." Cooper clapped him on the shoulder. "About time."

"Yes, well, she's not exactly amenable but . . . I'm working on it."

Cat smirked at him. "I hope you have a lot of patience, Tremaine. I've known Bailey Hartwell my whole life and when she digs her heels in, man does she dig them in good and deep."

"I'm aware. She decided I was a—" He stopped, considering Joey who was listening intently. "Not a very nice person a while ago, and hasn't really changed her mind about that."

"If you can change how the people of this town see you, you can change Bailey Hartwell's mind," Cat assured him.

God, he hoped so. "I guess we'll see." He looked at Cooper. "Do you have everything you need?"

The nervous groom sucked in a huge breath and exhaled. "Yeah, think so."

"No nerves, Lawson. No reason for them. She loves you."

"Yeah, I know, I just want to get married quickly before she comes to her senses and changes her mind."

"Not going to happen. So you're set?"

"Crosby might need some new fingernails," Cat joked. The man hadn't said a word since Vaughn had entered the room.

Crosby scowled at Cat and dropped his hand from his mouth.

"I'm just going to check everything is as it should be for the reception." Vaughn strode to the door. "Ceremony is in thirty minutes, so I advise you to make your way down to the bandstand."

Ten minutes later Vaughn was assured that his staff had everything under way for the reception that afternoon. He wandered back through his hotel, politely greeting his guests, as he made to leave for the ceremony.

In that moment he took a surprising amount of joy in the idea of Cooper and Jessica finding a happy life together, and he had hope that he could turn things around with Bailey.

That hope smashed into smithereens when he walked into the foyer of his hotel and saw who was standing at reception.

"Oliver?"

Dread filled him as Oliver Spence grinned at him and spread his arms wide. He was wearing a tux. "Heard there was a wedding."

Fuck.

"Oliver, what are you doing here?" He noted the two women standing behind his old friend, and that dread worsened.

"I'm bored." Oliver strode over to him and slid an arm around his shoulders. "I was out last night at some boring society charity event and I bumped into your father. He said that your friends were getting married at your hotel here and I got curious. So I thought I'd come crash the party, and bring you a present, too." He gestured behind him to the two women and they strode over in their six-inch heels, their hips swaying in beautiful exaggeration.

"Vaughn, this is Karen." Oliver slid his arm around the gorgeous brunette's slim waist. "And that is Petra." He nodded to the striking blonde. "Karen and Petra are getting ready for New York Fashion Week."

Models. Vaughn wasn't surprised. They were both taller than him and Oliver in their six-inch heels, which put their non-heel-wearing height at about five ten, five eleven.

"We need to talk. Alone."

Frowning, Oliver followed him across the foyer. "What's wrong?"

"What are you doing here?"

"I told you."

"I don't need this right now, Spence. I don't need a Petra right now. I have a wedding to get to."

"Give me a break, Vaughn," Oliver groaned. "I need time away from New York, okay? I'm going out of my mind there. And I haven't seen this place in a while. I'm not trying to get in your way."

"You can't come to the ceremony."

"Of course not. I don't know these people. We're just here for the evening reception. You don't have a date for the reception, do you?"

"No but—"

"Great." Oliver smacked Vaughn on the back. "Petra is a sweetheart. She's Karen's best friend. Oh, and did I tell you Karen's surname is De Havilland? Not only is she a successful model but she's the granddaughter of Frederick De Havilland."

"The shipping magnate?"

"The very one. Blue blood through and through. My mother loves her, which should be a deterrent, but I'm crazy about this girl. She might be the next Mrs. Spence. For real this time."

"Happy for you, Oliver. But I'm going to be late."

"Go, go." He shooed him away. "We'll be here, waiting for the fun to start."

Knowing how stubborn his friend could be, and that he wasn't going to get rid of him anytime soon, Vaughn sighed and walked over to the concierge, gesturing to Oliver to follow him. "Alonso, this is a good friend of mine, Mr. Spence. Would you see to it that Mr. Spence and his friends are provided with a table in the bar? Add whatever they order to my tab."

"Of course, sir."

Oliver smacked him on the back. "Did I ever tell you that I love you?"

"Once." Vaughn nodded, shrugging his tux back into place. "When you were high, and you thought I was a Korean girl called Nari that you left behind on your travels in Seoul."

"Really?" His friend sounded fascinated. "I can't remember that. I can't remember the girl, either. Then again I hardly remember Seoul. God, you've got a good memory."

"You felt me up. Hard to forget."

His friend threw his head back in laughter and Vaughn couldn't help but join him. The dread he was feeling eased a little. Oliver was just here to relieve his boredom, but he'd never done anything truly embarrassing in public. He'd left those moments to private times. He'd behave himself. Vaughn was sure of it.

"I'll see you in a bit."

"We'll be waiting."

By the time Vaughn got to the bandstand the place was packed. All of the chairs that had been lined up in front of the bandstand on Main Street were full. He knew from listening to Jessica, and seeing the chosen decoration for the ballroom, that she was a minimalist. The chair covers were white with silver sashes but that was the extent of the decoration.

A small orchestra was set up at the back of the bandstand. The priest was waiting at the top of the stairs with Cooper and Joey beside him.

Vaughn fell into the crowds of people who stood behind the occupied chairs and checked his watch. It was a hot afternoon. Too hot to be stuck outside in a tux for too long. He clocked the refreshments tables that had been set up on the other side of the chairs. Waiters stood patiently with iceboxes that Vaughn knew were filled with champagne bottles, orange juice, and water. Empty wineglasses and flutes were set up on the tables. Hiding somewhere, he couldn't see where, was a catering van with canapés for the guests. He licked his dry lips, wishing he had a glass of water in his hand already.

Mutterings moved through the crowd and Vaughn turned with the rest of them to see a white limo pull up on Main Street. A chauffeur got out first and opened the back passenger door. Dahlia was helped out, appearing in a teal blue bridesmaid dress that molded to every amazing curve that woman had. She was followed by Emery, who wore the same dress, but it transformed from sultry to graceful on the fair, willowy woman. His breath held as Bailey emerged from the limo.

She was stunning.

All of the women had left their hair down in soft waves, and Bailey's auburn curls were striking against the color of the dress, a dress that was both sexy and elegant on her.

He couldn't take his eyes off her, watching as she waited while a fourth woman Vaughn didn't recognize got out.

This must have been Jessica's aunt he'd heard all about. Cooper said they'd been estranged for years and had only gotten back in contact in the last year. The woman didn't look that much older than Jessica, her blond hair swept up elegantly from her face. She wore the same color as the bridesmaids but she didn't wear a dress. Instead she'd donned a sexy waistcoat and high-waist tailored trousers. The aunt and Bailey bent down to help Jessica out of the car. Vaughn knew he was supposed to have eyes only for the bride, and she did look beautiful in her bridal gown, but he couldn't stop staring at Bailey.

He followed her with his eyes as she walked behind Jess, holding the bride's train off the ground for her. The closer she got, the more impatient Vaughn felt. He had the absurd urge to claim her right there and then in front of everyone.

Restraining himself, he made do with just staring at every beautiful inch of her.

As if she felt his hot gaze, Bailey frowned and searched the crowd as the musicians began to play. To Vaughn's surprise they weren't playing Mendelssohn's "Wedding March" but what sounded like Bob Dylan's "Make You Feel My Love."

It was a good song.

And very appropriate for the moment Bailey's gaze found his.

She seemed to hesitate for just a second, probably because he was pouring every ounce of heat and longing and determination he felt into that one look.

Her cheeks flushed a lovely pink and she jerked her gaze away, concentrating on arranging Jessica's train just so. When they were ready, the bridesmaids began walking down the aisle. Vaughn turned to follow them, to follow Bailey, and his breath caught when he saw the back of the bridesmaid gown. It was a halter strap and it was backless, the fabric meeting just an inch or so above her ass. That's when he realized all the dresses were slightly different. Dahlia's wasn't backless but had a fifties-style V-drop at the back and lower-cut cleavage.

Emery's was strapless with a pretty sweetheart neckline. It was probably the most sedate of the three.

Bailey's was the sexiest. Of course it was.

He devoured the sight of her creamy, smooth skin, remembering vividly what she felt like to touch, what she tasted like . . .

Blood hot, Vaughn cursed her inwardly. It was official: Bailey Hartwell would be his undoing.

Trying to pull together a measure of control Vaughn attempted to focus on the bride as she was walked down the aisle with her aunt. He studied the look that passed between Jessica and Cooper as her aunt took her hand and handed it to the groom in a symbol of giving her away.

The look was fierce, and not just from Cooper, but Jessica, too. Fierce love. The kind he'd only heard about when his father spoke of his mother.

But now he knew, as he turned his attention to Bailey, that he'd felt that fierceness. He just needed—God how he needed—her to return it, the way Jessica returned Cooper's.

As if she heard his thoughts Bailey glanced over at him. Uncertainty. Confusion. That's all he saw in her eyes. No fierce love.

Determined not to feel deflated, Vaughn reminded himself that he could do this. He'd had worse odds in his career and he'd turned those situations around.

It was a quick, sincere, not overly sentimental ceremony that Vaughn could get on board with. He appreciated the simplicity of the wedding. It appealed to the tortured wedding guest in him that had had to endure unbelievably lavish weddings over the years. Weddings weren't really his thing and he was grateful to the Lawsons for not dragging theirs out.

As the bride and groom made their way down the aisle, smiling in unadulterated bliss at their guests, Vaughn tracked Bailey as she followed with Cat and Joey at her side. If he wasn't mistaken, she was deliberately avoiding his gaze.

The bridal party, led by Vivien, Vaughn's events coordinator, met with the photographer, who then led them down the boardwalk.

"Ladies and gentlemen," Vivien announced, "the bride and groom would like to invite you to enjoy some music and refreshments while the photographer is with the bridal party."

Everyone began to make their way over to the tables as the band struck up. Vaughn, however, found Vivien. "I'm heading back to the hotel. Are you alright here?"

"Yes. Of course. And everything seemed fine at the hotel when I left," she said. "You could stay, enjoy a glass of champagne."

"Yes, stay!" Kell and Jake were at his side, thrusting a glass of champagne in his face.

Not wanting to be rude, especially to people he'd been making an effort to turn into friends, he accepted it with a smile.

"To the happy couple!" Kell lifted his glass in the air. Jake and Vaughn clinked theirs against his.

"Wait for us!" Mayor Jaclyn Rose and her husband, Cliff, pushed their way into the little circle.

Jaclyn Rose was a tall, statuesque woman in her late fifties. Vaughn had never seen her in anything but a power suit, heels, and red lipstick. She was a force of nature, outspoken and strong, like Bailey. Her husband, a man two inches shorter than her, with a receding hairline and kind eyes, was quiet and unassuming. He was her complete opposite.

Jaclyn was a good friend of the Hartwells, and when Bailey took umbrage against his hotel, she pit the mayor against him.

He had not had the easiest of relationships with the mayor, but apparently his growing friendship with Kell and Jake was working its magic on Mayor Rose.

Vaughn felt satisfaction as they all raised their glasses together and she shared a smile with him.

Three years ago he wouldn't have believed that he'd care about ingratiating himself with these people, but these people *were* the town of Hartwell. To be included as one of them, as a peer enjoying the celebration of one of their own, filled him with a pleasure he barely understood.

Finally Hartwell was truly becoming his home.

Now he only needed one thing to feel true contentment.

Bailey

As much as my chest swelled tight with emotion watching the photographer take photos of Jess and Coop in each other's arms on the boardwalk, I knew the pressure on my chest was born of another reason, too.

I wanted nothing more than to give all of my concentration to my best friends, to the bride, who looked beautiful in her ivory satin ballgown, looking like a starlet from the 1950s, and her groom, who looked so damn handsome it was a sin.

They were stunning together, and not just because they were good-looking people but because they were kind people so freaking in love they glowed with it.

I wanted to focus on that.

Yet, I couldn't.

Because I'd felt that damn devil's gaze burning through me from the moment I'd gotten out of the limo. He'd stared at me throughout the entire ceremony. And it wasn't just his attention. It was the nature of his attention. Vaughn Tremaine looked at me as if he wanted to ravish me, protect me, and keep me forever.

How was any woman supposed to stay strong against the kind of longing and determination in Vaughn's eyes? It was the kind of expression that gave a woman hope; that made a woman think maybe she *was* being a coward; maybe she *was* giving up on the one person that might be worth fighting for.

Damn him to hell!

I flushed under the hot sun, wishing the photographer would hurry up and finish so we could get into the shade. Cooper was starting to look a little flushed in his tux, and Joey, usually a good-natured kid, was ten seconds away from throwing a fit. Someone had gotten him a juice box to cool him down but it didn't look as if it was doing much to appease him.

Jessica turned to the photographer. "I think we're good!"

"Just a few more," he said.

"No. My husband is about to pass out and my nephew is about to strip naked and run into the ocean. We're good." She took Cooper's hand and led him past the unhappy photographer. "You'll get plenty of candid shots at the reception."

"But I wanted a few more of you on the beach."

"We got plenty." Cooper's tone was final.

The photographer shut up.

I grinned at my friends. "We love you."

Jessica winced. "Everyone's dying, huh?"

"Just a bit."

"Let's get inside."

We walked toward Paradise Sands and I felt a flip in my belly when I remembered the last time I'd been inside the building. Cat fell into step beside me, while Joey chatted up ahead with Jessica's Aunt Theresa.

Cat nudged me playfully. "So, I heard something this morning."

"What was that?"

"Tremaine basically announced to us that he was going to pursue you."

My heart flipped over in my chest, and my hot sweat turned to cool sweat as little goose bumps rose up all over my body. "He did not." I couldn't even imagine Vaughn saying anything so personal in public.

"He did so."

"You're not joking?"

"Not at all."

Well. That certainly would account for all the emotional eye-fucking

I'd received from him. "How dare he," I hissed, terrified and thrilled by the prospect.

"Oh, I know. A gorgeous, sexy, incredibly successful, rich man known for his taciturnity cares enough about you to declare his feelings in public. What an asshole."

I scowled. "He is actually."

"If you don't want him, I'll have him." She shrugged.

Even though I knew she was joking, jealousy burned through me at the thought.

Cat laughed at my expression. "If looks could kill."

"Shut up, Cat."

"Ooh"—she rubbed her hands together and quickened her pace to catch up with Joey—"this is going to be fun!"

"What is?" Joey asked her.

"The wedding, baby." She pulled her son into her side but flashed me a look over her shoulder. "There's going to be plenty of entertainment."

I flipped her the bird and she threw her head back in laughter.

"What do you think? Did you enjoy dinner?" Jessica stepped up beside me, sliding her arm around my waist.

We stared around at the ballroom. It was all silver and white with splashes of teal. It was beautiful. Classy. Elegant. Subtle. The table centerpieces were small, a collection of jarred silver and teal candles, with a bouquet of white peonies in the middle.

"Dinner was amazing. But how did you afford this place?" I'd been nosy and asked Vivien how much it was to rent the ballroom for the day.

"Discount, of course. Cooper *is* Vaughn's bestie."

I laughed at her teasing. "He's nice to those he likes, huh?"

"And he likes you very much. I heard what he said to Cooper and Cat this morning."

"Wow, news travels fast." I looked into her hopeful hazel gaze and sighed. "Don't. Jess. I . . . He confuses me enough without you lot ganging up on me."

"No one is ganging up on you. We just want you to be happy."

"I'm not in love with him," I declared.

She studied me. "I know. But he's in love with you. And I think if you gave him a chance, you'd fall for him, too."

"I know that," I agreed. "I know that one hundred percent. Which is why I don't want to give him a chance. He'd crush me, Jess."

"Or he'd love you forever the way you deserve." She kissed my cheek, emotion clogging her throat when she whispered, "You helped save my life, Bailey Hartwell. I want everything for you."

She pulled back and the tears that had filled my eyes, spilled over. "Thanks for that." I huffed, blotting my cheeks with the back of my hands. "Took me ages to do my makeup."

Jess laughed and handed me a tissue. "I have a ton."

"Go." I waved her away. "Make other people cry." She turned to leave. "I love you, Jess."

My friend grinned back at me. "And you know I love you."

I watched her stroll away, her heavy dress trailing beautifully behind her, and I felt overwhelming happiness for her as Cooper drew her into his arms before leading her over to greet more guests.

If anyone deserved that kind of happiness, it was Jessica Hunting-Lawson. Jessica Lawson.

It had a nice ring to it.

I needed a restroom so I could check my makeup, but as I started walking toward the ballroom exit my gaze snagged on an unwelcome sight.

A young, extremely tall blond woman who could have been a model she was so striking was standing close to Vaughn. She was smiling at him and he didn't look unhappy to be there. Why would he? She was a six-foot-something goddess in a dress that was so short all you could see were legs, legs, and more legs.

"Bailey, there you are." Iris appeared at my side. "Come join us instead of standing over here like a wallflower."

Forgetting about my makeup, I seethed as Iris led me over to
their table. Dinner was over, a band was playing onstage, and drink
was flowing. I'd kept my attention focused on the bride and groom
and on the speeches. I had been moved by Jess's Aunt Theresa as
she spoke of all the time she and Jess had missed together, but how
much joy she felt knowing that Jess had met someone who made up
for all that lost time, that unhappiness, and how she couldn't wait
to be a part of such a promising future.

I laughed at Joey, who gave the cutest speech on earth, and I
choked up when Cooper finished it off with a heartwarming, sexy
toast to his new wife.

All of that kept my focus where it should be and not on Vaughn.

So I had no idea he'd brought a freaking date to the wedding!

What?

That made no sense!

Maybe she wasn't a date.

"Who is that Vaughn is talking with?" Dahlia snapped.

My eyes flew across the room where he was still standing with
the blonde. Christ, in those heels of hers she was even taller than
Tremaine.

Ugly, bitter disappointment filled me.

"Oh, hell no," Cat huffed.

"I thought he said he was coming after Bailey?" Ira was confused.

"Does everyone know about that?" I glared at Cat.

She shrugged, scowling back at me. "How was I supposed to
know he had the attention span of a gnat?" Her expression softened.
"I'm sorry, Bails."

"Oh, for the love of God," Iris sighed. "The man is just talking.
That means nothing."

"With a stranger," Dahlia pointed out. "She's not from Hartwell,
which means he invited her."

Silence fell over our table as I digested this. Jealousy burned hot
and painful inside of me as I watched him nod at something the

Amazon said. I'd never felt this kind of envy before. It was thick and cloying, and it took my breath away.

Angry tears burned in my eyes.

And then as if he felt my attention, his head jerked in my direction. His fierce gaze bore into mine, making me breathless.

"I don't think so," Cat said, her tone softening. "No man looks at a woman the way he's looking at Bailey and invites another woman to a wedding."

I tore my eyes from Vaughn's magnetic stare.

"Speaking of invitations." Iris swiftly changed the subject. "Didn't Vanessa get one to the wedding?"

"Yes," I bit out, still disturbed by Vaughn. "But I haven't heard from her since I threw her out of the house. I know she's staying at the Grand, though." Annie at the grocery store had informed me.

"I can't believe she can't see Jack is playing her," Dahlia said.

"Vanessa only sees what she wants to see." I glanced back over at Vaughn and swiftly looked away when I discovered his attention was still on me.

Shifting my gaze to the dance floor my eyes caught on a pink dress I admired. A tall brunette I didn't recognize wore it. She was as tall as the blonde talking to Vaughn and model-like, too. I looked at her partner as they swayed around a little and recognition slammed into me with the force of a car.

No.

No way.

How?

Not here.

Fuck.

I shoved back from the table in an instinctual reaction to be further from him.

"Bailey?" Emery said. "Are you okay?"

No, I am not okay. I got to my feet, my chair screeching across the floor and drawing attention.

The man with the brunette looked over and our eyes met. He

gave me a small, arrogant smile, and then he frowned as I continued to stare at him.

Him.

The ghost from my past.

I spun around to leave, desperate for air.

"Bailey, I wanted to talk to you about the parade at the end of the summer." Kell was in my face, blocking my exit. "I was thinking—sweetie, are you okay? You're chalk white."

"Excuse me, please." I brushed past him, tripping over my stupid dress and cursing it.

"Oh, Bailey." Sherrie stopped in my path. "I have family who want to visit in a few weeks from New Jersey. Any chance you might have a room available? On discount? Bailey? So rude!"

I heard her call after me as I marched away, my dress gripped tight in my hands.

"Excuse me!"

No!

My heart started hammering so fast it felt like it was climbing upward into my throat with each pound. Nausea rose up right there with it.

"Excuse me." A strong hand curled around my bicep, pulling me gently to a stop.

I was swung around, face to face with my past.

He was still handsome. Still smooth and dapper. But there were lines around his eyes and mouth that didn't used to be there, and a hardness behind the constant laughter in his expression that hadn't been there when he was a young man, either.

"Oliver." The word croaked as it escaped me.

And it was that little croak that saved me in that moment.

Why was I running away from him at my friend's wedding?

I wasn't a naive nineteen-year-old anymore! And I no longer felt inferior to this man. Whoever he was now. Whoever he had been. I wasn't sure I even knew.

Throwing my shoulders back, I smoothed my expression. "What are you doing here?"

"So we have met?" He stepped into my personal space, smiling curiously.

Renewed anger burst over me.

The bastard didn't even remember me.

Okay. Take a breath and count to ten. Do not deck him and cause a scene at your best friend's wedding.

"What's going on?" Vaughn appeared, pushing Oliver out of my personal space. He stared at the man like he wanted to kill him.

The blonde stood at his back.

Well wasn't this nice and confusing?

No.

It wasn't confusing.

Determination flooded me.

This was a wake-up call.

"This is Oliver Spence." I gestured to my ex.

Vaughn stared at me, bewildered. "I know. He's a friend from New York."

Oh my, what a small world. That was a first for me, sleeping with men who were friends. And the fact that Vaughn was friends with him said everything I needed to know about this man who had tried so hard to get under my skin these last few months, and almost succeeded.

"How do you know each other?" Vaughn demanded of his friend.

Oliver studied me, and his brow cleared. "Hartwell!" He threw his arms wide and hugged me.

I extricated myself immediately.

"Oh, Hartwell . . ." Understanding passed across his face. "No hard feelings?"

"None." I shrugged. "I just don't hug strange men."

"Well, I'm hardly strange." He winked at me.

I made a face. Was he always this irreverently annoying?

Vaughn stepped between us. "Wait, what is going on? How do you know him?"

This was the moment. This was the moment when Vaughn Tremaine would finally get that I would never fall for his smoldering, longing looks again. "Oliver is the one I told you about. The asshole summer boy who told me he loved me when he didn't."

My revelation stunned Vaughn into silence, and I walked away, satisfied.

"That sounds like hard feelings to me!" Spence called after me.

I shuddered. God, what a stupid kid I'd been.

Vaughn

This whole reception had been a nightmare so far. First, he couldn't get rid of Petra. She'd clung to his side from the moment Oliver had brought the women into the ballroom for the after-dinner reception.

He'd tried, unsuccessfully, to get away from the small group, and then found himself cornered by the model.

Then the evening got worse. Much worse.

When he'd seen Oliver abandon Karen on the dance floor and move through the crowds, he'd been stunned when he realized whom he was chasing.

Possessiveness, protectiveness had taken over and he'd followed, hearing Petra's annoying, querying voice behind him as he did.

And then it had all gone to shit.

"Oliver is the one I told you about. The asshole summer boy who told me he loved me when he didn't."

Not only had she delivered information that made him want to kill someone; she'd said it in such a way he knew she was saying something else. *You'll never have me.*

Fury, hurt, hurt for her, for him, and yes, jealousy that Oliver had tasted what he believed was his, pounded in his head as he turned to face his old friend.

Too stupid to recognize the dangerous glint in Vaughn's eyes, Oliver chuckled. "Can you believe it? I almost forgot all about her."

Wrong thing to say.

"You *forgot* Bailey?"

"Not *now*. Now I remember her. I spent a summer with her. A hot summer." He grinned. "A lot of sex. I think I even loved her for most of it. But you know me, Tremaine, I get bored. And she's a *townie*."

Vaughn couldn't stop himself.

Every ounce of control he'd been raised with was obliterated as he pulled back his elbow and let his fist fly. He felt the hard, painful, satisfying connection and crack as it hit his friend's nose.

Oliver stumbled back.

Vaughn hit him again.

With a roar of fury Oliver lunged, wrapping his arms around his waist and taking him to the floor, but Vaughn was quicker, more agile, and much, much angrier.

His fist connected a few more times before he found himself dragged off of his now ex-friend.

He fought against it, his blood lust high. All he wanted was to knock every fucking word right out of Oliver's mouth. He wanted to take it all back. He didn't want it to be true.

"Tremaine, fuck, calm down." He heard Cooper's voice in his ear.

It sunk in that it was his friend, a good man, who was holding on to him and he stopped struggling.

Karen and Petra helped Oliver to his feet.

The band had stopped playing.

Shocked silence filled the ballroom.

He searched for her.

Bailey stood to his right, Jessica holding on to her, eyes round as she took in the scene. She didn't look mortified at least. Merely shocked.

Vaughn cursed.

"What the fuck was that?" Oliver spat blood on the floor of his ballroom. "I think you broke my fucking nose. For that!" He pointed in disgust at Bailey. "Over a fucking townie I screwed years ago."

He lunged at him again and not only did Cooper have to hold him back but Jeff King was there, his arm locked around Vaughn's chest.

"Calm down, Tremaine," Jeff urged quietly in his ear. "If he presses charges, there isn't anything I can do about it."

Struggling for that calm, for control, Vaughn trembled, his voice thick with emotion as he stared in revulsion at Spence. "Get the hell out of my hotel."

Oliver laughed bitterly. "This is what our friendship has come to? You've changed, Tremaine." He wiped at his bleeding lip. "And not for the better."

He sagged as his ex-friend shot him one last baleful look and let the embarrassed girls at his side lead him out. Murmurings grew louder and louder as they moved through the reception.

Vaughn stared at Bailey.

He shrugged out of Jeff and Cooper's hold. "I'm okay." He met Cooper's concerned gaze, and felt guilty for causing a scene at his wedding. "I'm sorry."

Cooper shook his head. "No problem. But if I were you, I'd go see your girl."

"I lost that battle, Lawson."

"I . . . I don't think so."

At Cooper's tone his attention jerked back to Bailey. His heart pounded even more wildly than it already was as he watched her approach him.

Cooper and Jeff seemed to melt away.

"So"—she crossed her arms over her chest defensively—"that was annoying."

"I am so sorry."

Confusion clouded her beautiful eyes. "Why?" She gestured to his hand. "Mister-I-would-never-do-anything-so-embarrassing-as-starting-a-fistfight-at-my-friend's-wedding. That's the second time you've punched a guy in the face for me."

Realizing honesty was his only recourse, he replied, "No one disrespects you, princess. No one."

Her gaze dropped to her feet. "You confuse me so much."

In that moment, seeing a spark of hope, he made a decision he should have made a long time ago. "Then let me clear a few things up for you. I'll tell you what you need to know about me."

Her eyes flew to his. "For real?"

"If I don't, I'm just going to lose my chance with you anyway, right? You think I'm just like him?" He gestured to where Oliver had departed.

"I don't know anything anymore."

"Take a walk with me?"

Bailey considered him for a moment, a moment that felt agonizingly long. Finally she exhaled and nodded.

Vaughn didn't know whether to be elated or to give in to the sudden nausea he felt.

TWENTY-THREE

Bailey

There was one thing very clear to me: Vaughn Tremaine caused me emotional whiplash. I didn't think there was a moment in my life where I'd felt so conflicted in one day. First I was determined to ignore him. Then the longing, smoldering thing that he did got under my skin. And then he was Oliver Spence's friend. I'd really wanted nothing to do with him in that moment.

Until he smacked the guy.

That was fifteen years in the making.

Wait until I told my dad that Vaughn got the chance to do something he'd wanted to do since I was nineteen: break the nose of the asshole who broke his daughter's heart.

It was funny looking at Spence now. I didn't even recognize him as the boy I'd loved. He was the man version of the boy who had told me I wasn't good enough for his world. Smarmy, oily, slick, and it freaked me out that he had deceived me so well the summer we'd spent together.

And Vaughn . . . well . . . not only had he caused a scene in public, which was so very un-Vaughn-like; he'd definitely proven that he couldn't give a crap that we came from different worlds.

That took me back to wanting to know *why then*? Why was his guard up?

So I found myself leaving my best friend's wedding reception—

Jess shoved me and Vaughn out the door, and I didn't blame her—and strolling along the boardwalk with Tremaine.

It was lit up in the dark, all the neon signs blinking brightly out at the ocean. The boardwalk was always busy this time during the summer and tonight was no different. Laughter, music, sounds of the arcade games, and conversation floated all around us. I shivered in the breeze that blew up from the water and rubbed at my arms.

Like something out of a movie, Vaughn shrugged out of his tuxedo jacket and draped it over my shoulders. A second shiver rippled down my spine as he lifted my hair out from under it and his fingers brushed the skin at the nape of my neck.

"Thank you."

"You're welcome." He stopped and glanced down the beach.

I read his thoughts. "It's quiet down there."

"What about your dress?"

"It's not like I'll be wearing it again anytime soon." I slid out of my shoes, grabbed them up in one hand while I lifted the hem with the other.

Vaughn followed my lead, unlacing his dress shoes and slipping them and his socks off. We slowly walked down the ramp onto the beach, and I relaxed at the feel of the dry, cool grain underfoot.

"Did he get you?"

"What?"

I gestured to his face. "Oliver?"

Vaughn rubbed his jaw. "He got in a lucky hit, but it wasn't too hard. I'll survive."

We didn't speak after that, not until the soundtrack of the boardwalk nightlife faded into the distance, and all we heard around us was the quiet rush of the dark ocean against the shore.

"I'll start," I said.

The right corner of his mouth tilted upward. "Of course you will."

Ignoring that, I proceeded. "I will say that I've been holding on to what Oliver did to me for way too long. Yes, he broke my heart years ago but I don't even know who that man in there was. Maybe I never really knew. It doesn't matter now. What matters is that I let him make me think less of myself. But I took that power back from him after Tom cheated. I'm not letting another man take it away again. Do you understand what I'm saying?"

He stared at me in open admiration. "Completely."

"You know, you staring at me with your emotions all there and smoldering out in the open for me is very unnerving. I've spent the last few years trying to read you and failing so, um . . . not going to lie, the open-book thing you're doing is freaking me out."

"I didn't know I was being an open book. And if I am, it's only around you."

Okay.

Then . . . it was time to be brave. "Say I believe you; say you really do care about me . . . that doesn't change anything. I'm still me. You're still you."

He watched his feet as we strolled and nodded. "True. But I'm not the man you think I am." Vaughn looked up at me. "I'm not the man I thought I was, either."

"What does that mean?"

"Remember the day at the festival when you suggested that my problem was my father and his inability to really let go of my mother?"

"Yes."

"I never thought about it before. Or maybe I didn't want to think about it. Yet, you're right. I was only five when my mother died, and my memories of her are very vague, like they happened in another life. But I remember my father in the years after she died. I remember the couple of times after he'd read me a bedtime story how I'd crept out of bed and wandered down the hall to the living room only to find him weeping into a glass of scotch.

"It was crippling." His words were hoarse, and they tugged at my heart. "To see a man like my father, who was this big powerful giant to a little kid, crying tears into a glass of whiskey. And even then I knew it was about her. As hard as he tried, the grief clung to that apartment. I was glad when we moved a few years later. I was glad as I got older I heard the rumors of my dad's womanizing ways. To me it meant he was living again, in some small way.

"However, I started to think he had the right idea—don't get serious with a woman. Keep it free and easy. I inherited the ambition bug from my father, and career has always been important to me. I concentrated on college and starting my own business. It wasn't until I was about twenty-four years old that I even went on a third date. Around the same time my dad started dating Diane monogamously." He threw me a crooked, boyish smile. "I didn't even put that together. Not so smart for a smart guy."

"You saw your dad finally taking a step toward something serious and you emulated him."

"Yes. But the girl got too serious on me too fast. After her I went back to what I was used to, and that was okay. I'm not going to lie to you, Bailey, it was who I was. I had no interest in marriage or kids . . . Until about six years ago." He exhaled, his features drawing tight as if he was remembering something unpleasant. "When I turned thirty I started to really think about those things. I had a great relationship with my dad, he had a good relationship with Diane that benefited them both professionally and personally. Marriage started to have an appeal. Especially because I wanted children. I wanted to have the same relationship with my own kids that I had with my father. And I wanted to give my dad a grandchild because I knew that was something that he wanted. I thought marriage would be convenient."

I guffawed at the idea. "Convenient."

He grinned at me. "Not so smart for a smart guy."

"Yeah."

His smile fell. "Diane introduced me to Camille Dunaway. She was very beautiful, poised, classy."

Huh. I didn't like the sound of her one bit. "She sounds lovely."

Jealousy must have seeped into my words because Vaughn threw me a smug, pleased look. "She was. But we weren't right for one another. I thought we were. Camille is . . . she's very reserved. People called her an ice princess but I never saw her like that at first. I just saw a woman who had been raised to play the society game and play it very well. I liked that about her. I liked that she never complained about my obsession with work, or the long hours I put in. She was there to support me, and to hold my arm at an event. Camille wanted what I wanted: marriage, a family, and the perfect society life as the perfect society wife and husband. I didn't love her, but I believed I'd grow to love her over the years, and I promised myself that I would be faithful to her and take care of her."

"So what happened?"

"We got engaged."

Surprise shot through me. Vaughn was once engaged. To be married? "Really?"

"So incredulous." He tutted. "Yes, really. Camille was happy. I thought I was happy. My father . . . he wasn't happy."

"Why not?"

"He saw what I didn't until it was too late: that we weren't right for each other. Camille was happy because she was engaged to the successful bachelor that all her friends had tried and failed to bring up to scratch."

"Such modesty."

He shot me that wicked grin. "I'm just telling you what these women thought."

"Oh, I believe you. You're a beautiful man." I shrugged. "I've never denied that. Okay. I've maybe denied that."

"You've definitely denied that."

"Wasn't it awful being wanted just for your looks?"

"Not just for my looks. My wealth, too. And was it any fairer than me wanting Camille because of her position in society and her old-fashioned view of marriage?"

"I guess not."

"We were a year into our engagement, the wedding was around the corner, and I was starting to have major doubts. Her composure in all things was starting to irritate me. She never got annoyed with me, even when she had a right; she never demanded more time of me, and I was starting to think if she cared, then she should. There was no passion between us, no fire, and it troubled me. I started to understand the moniker society had given her. Yet I continued to convince myself that the distance between us was a good thing; that no matter what, I got what I wanted out of it without getting hurt. Without either of us getting hurt.

"A month before the wedding Camille's younger sister Caroline came home from a year in Europe. We'd met briefly before she'd left, and we'd seen each other again at Christmas. But I knew nothing of her, and I had no interest in her. However, she started to show an interest in me."

"Oh boy."

"Yes. As soon as Camille's back was turned Caroline would flirt with me, and aggressively. One time she cornered me at a party and tried to stick her hand down my pants."

"What?" I was outraged on Camille's behalf. "What kind of sister is that?"

"You know all about crazy sisters, princess."

"True," I agreed, "but I'd hope even Vanessa wouldn't cross the line by feeling up my fiancé."

"Caroline did cross the line." Vaughn turned grim. "She turned up at our apartment one night when Camille was at a meeting for some charity board she was on. She was naked before I even blinked and acting like a lunatic trying to get me to sleep with her.

"I had to physically manhandle her out of our apartment. It was a fucking awful scene. She cursed and railed out in the hallway until one of the neighbors called for security. And of course it got back to Camille, and Caroline told her that we'd slept together and afterward I'd behaved like a bastard, throwing her naked out of the apartment."

"She did not."

"She did. And Camille believed her."

"Oh, my God," I breathed. "That's horrible. What a conniving bitch."

"You haven't heard the worst part." His smile was sad. "Camille said she forgave me, that she still wanted to marry me."

"What?" I couldn't imagine having taken Tom back after he cheated on me. "Why? If she believed you cheated?"

"Exactly what I said to her when I called off our engagement two weeks before the wedding. I told her I couldn't marry someone who didn't trust me. And I couldn't. I might not have been looking for the traditional things in a marriage but I at least expected trust and respect from my wife."

"Of course."

"To make matters worse, Caroline came to me and apologized, but told me she'd done me a favor and that I was marrying the wrong sister anyway. She said Camille was cold, and she was the opposite. She was also desperate. Both Camille and Caroline had been given a substantial trust fund on their twenty-first birthday. While Camille made smart investments and didn't spend too lavishly, Caroline blew it all in five years."

"She wanted to marry into money to keep up her lifestyle," I concluded.

"Exactly." Vaughn stopped. He stared out at the water and my heart started to beat a little faster at how gloomy he'd grown. "The night before the wedding was supposed to have taken place Camille called me. She begged me to change my mind about not marrying her. I'd never heard her like that. She was crying hysterically, telling me that she was humiliated, that she'd never be able to show her face again. She said if we didn't marry, her life would be ruined. All of her friends had stopped talking to her, her mother's friends had suggested she take some time off from her charity work, but it wasn't out of kindness. These women, all of them, assumed she was somehow defective because she hadn't been able to keep me. She said she couldn't stand their pity. And then she kept telling me she loved me over and over.

"Not once did I ever get that from her . . ." He turned, his eyes hollow with pain. "She told me she loved me when we were together but I never really believed it. I still don't know if she did or if she just loved our life together. So I let her rail at me. At first she begged, and then she yelled, and then she screamed, and then she cried.

"And then she hung up . . . and this awful feeling came over me." He looked deep into my eyes. "I have good intuition, always have, it's how I've become successful, and it's how I knew that I needed to check on her. I still had my key to our apartment.

"God, Bailey," he whispered, "I'll never get the image of her out of my head."

"Vaughn." I grabbed onto his arms, fearing the worst.

He shook his head. "She was in the bathtub. Drowned. I got her out. I did CPR, got the water out of her lungs, got her breathing again, and I called nine one one. She recovered. At least physically. But it took her a long time to get over me. She's engaged now to a neurosurgeon."

"Thank God," I breathed. "You should really have led with that."

Vaughn gave me a dry, humorless smile. "What happened to her fucked with my head a little."

"Of course it did."

"I happily went back to never wanting to be in a relationship again. Not just because of how my defection caused a woman to try to commit suicide, but because I was happier before Camille. I was more comfortable in my own skin without her."

That more than anything made me uneasy. What did that mean?

And why were we having this conversation if that was true? "Vaughn, her reaction wasn't a normal reaction. You get that, right? I imagine there have been other hearts broken by you and they didn't react that way."

"I get that. I do. But it still wasn't easy to know that people, that *we*, were capable of hurting each other that much, because it was part revenge; she did that to hurt me as much as she did it to escape. And it was an escape, and that's why Manhattan and I . . . we were over. If living that life, if needing the approval of those around her so badly caused a woman to try to take her own life, then I wanted no part in it. I wanted to run from it for as long as I could. That's when Oliver told me about the old Hart's Boardwalk Hotel."

"Ah."

"Yes. So I came here. I grew to like the quiet." He faced me. "And I met you."

"You hated me."

"No, you hated me." He reached out and curled my hair behind my ear and I felt that simple touch all over my body. "But you wanted me."

My lips parted in consternation. "And how do you know that?"

"I told you. I have great intuition."

"I didn't *want* to want you."

"I didn't want to want you, either, but I did." Vaughn stepped closer to me. "You are everything I've never known. I fell in love with you a long time ago, princess. I've tried to fight it, but I can't, and I don't want to anymore."

His words thrilled me, they did, but they also scared the shit out of me.

Vaughn thought Camille was only worried about her reputation when he left her, about her status, but as cold as she may have been, I knew . . . I knew she'd loved him. It would be impossible to spend a year in his arms and not fall in love with him. Even with his guard up. Vaughn was capable, successful, hardworking, protective, and gorgeous. There was a whole lot there to like.

And that was what I was so afraid of.

"I want those things you said you don't want anymore. I want marriage. I want kids."

Taking my hands in his, Vaughn leaned down to whisper across my lips. "I'll give you anything, Bailey Hartwell, anything you want."

The sincerity in his eyes caused tears to well in mine. "You need to want those things for you, too."

His expression turned thoughtful. "I used to want them. I told you that. I just . . . let myself let go of the fantasy of it. With you . . . God, Bailey, you've got me wanting things I gave up on believing I'd ever have."

There was a part of me, that bright, young, nineteen-year-old girl still inside of me, that wanted to throw my arms around this gorgeous, complicated, stubborn man and say, *To hell with it, let's give this a go.* But the cautious thirty-four-year-old who'd wasted too many years already on the wrong man was still taking the wheel on this one.

I thought of that moment months ago, a moment that felt years ago instead, when Tom had begged me to consider taking him back. I'd asked why he wanted me to. I'd asked him why he loved me.

He couldn't answer. He couldn't answer because we were stuck in limbo "loving" each other because it felt comfortable and safe. We were a part of something that people expected. And there was comfort in that.

But it wasn't real love.

Now I feared that Vaughn was confusing our sexual chemistry for something more than it was.

"Why?" I found myself stepping back from Vaughn's intoxicating proximity. "Why do you love me?"

For a moment, as he stared at me in mild exasperation, I felt my stomach drop as I foresaw a replay of that moment with Tom.

"Why do I love you?" he repeated.

"Yes, why?"

"You know this sharing thing isn't easy for me," he grumbled. "I'm not exactly used to all this declaration stuff and I've been doing a lot of it lately."

I tensed, ready to flee.

Vaughn sensed it and held up his hands. "Fine." He was completely exasperated now. "I can't believe you need to hear this. It should be obvious to you and to anyone why I'm so fucking in love with you I'm turning into a possessive Neanderthal who is going to ruin his reputation punching assholes in the face and trying to get into your pants in my hotel lobby.

"I love you, Bailey Hartwell, because you frustrate me, you annoy me, you bother me, you bewilder me, you make me laugh, you get under my skin, you take my breath away. I love you because I admire your strength, I admire how hard you work, how much you love the inn, this town, the people in it. I love how you care so much, too much, so much that it scares me because I worry someone will take advantage and you'll get hurt. I love your fire. I love that you stand up to me. I love how you force me to remove the stick up my ass.

"Mostly I love you because you make me want to live a better life as a better man."

And on that final, beautiful note, I gasped. An actual gasp. The breath escaped out of me because his words hurt. They caused a physical ache.

But in the most stunning way imaginable.

Slowly, I stepped into him and slid my hands up his chest and around his neck. His jacket fell off my shoulders with the movement and Vaughn's arms encircled my waist. His strong hands flattened against my bare back and I felt the pressure of his fingertips as he held me close, as close as he could get me.

We stared into each other's eyes, searching, enjoying the fact that we had the time to do that, that neither one of us was fighting this.

We could look as long and as hard at each other as we wanted because our defenses were lowered.

Finally.

"Okay," I whispered against his mouth. "Let's give this a try."

His answer was the happiest, sexiest grin I'd ever seen.

TWENTY-FOUR

Bailey

"I can't believe I let you drag me here." Vaughn stood with his arms crossed over his chest, looking less than impressed by his surroundings. "And no one told me I had to wear someone else's shoes."

I struggled to keep a straight face. "I thought you'd know that part. Everyone knows that part."

"And I told you I've never done this before."

"Which is why I 'dragged' you here."

"So everything I say I haven't done, you're going to make me do?"

Grinning, I sidled up to him with a hopefully mischievous and seductive smile. His eyes lowered to half-mast, shooting that seductiveness right back at me. I was halted when my chest pressed against his. "Am I planning to make sure that you experience all the things you missed out on because you were too busy working your ass off to get to the top? Yes. I am."

Vaughn's sexy look turned tender and amused. "And that includes bowling."

"And that includes bowling." I leaned past him, picked up a bowling ball, and shoved it at him. "Now have at it, mister."

He took it tentatively, like it was something heinous. "You want me to put my fingers in holes that a million other fingers have been in?" He sighed as I struggled and failed not to burst into laughter. "You're filthy."

"I'm not the one that just said . . . well . . . that." I laughed. "Oh, my God. Why am I the only one here when you said that?"

"Dirty girl," he said fondly.

"I could have responded with something smart-mouthed about you and prostitutes but I didn't. That's progress."

"You'll be pleased to know I've never been with a prostitute."

"With that face"—I brushed my fingertips over his cheek—"you'd never need to."

"Are we really having this conversation?"

"Nope." I stepped out of his way and gestured to our lane. "Now have at it." When he didn't step up to take a shot I sighed. "Come on, a little bacteria never hurt anyone."

"Lovely, thank you." He grimaced. "But I was considering the fact that I've never done this and I don't like to fail at things."

"You're worried you'll miss?" I grinned. "Baby, I know it's hard for you to process the idea of losing, so don't look at it like you have to win immediately. Look at it in the long term. The more you practice, the more chance you have of winning in the future. Kind of like how you got me into your bed permanently."

Vaughn flashed me a wolfish grin. "I only heard 'baby' and 'got me into your bed permanently.'"

"I bet you did."

Since agreeing to see where this thing between us might lead two weeks ago at Jess and Coop's wedding I owed Aydan. A lot. Why? Because I'd been in Vaughn's bed every night since and he had succeeded in making me late to work every morning.

We'd had so much sex I could have sworn my abs and legs had toned up.

"Okay." He stretched his neck from side to side and then shrugged back his shoulders. "I once walked in on my father while he was . . . well, during fellatio with my friend's mother. If I can recover from that, I can do anything."

Giggling, I stood back and watched him as he strode toward the lane with purpose. There were no words for how much pleasure I found watching Vaughn Tremaine do anything. I'd never met a man so masculine yet so graceful and strong. I'd also discovered that he kept his body as beautiful as his face through hard work. A lot of hard work. He woke up at five a.m. every morning and disappeared to the hotel gym. When he got back to the room he'd take a shower and then come wake me up to do a sexy workout with me. I didn't know where the man got his energy.

Vaughn studied the ten pins at the end of the lane and slowly slid his hands into the bowling ball with not even a hint of a grimace. Once he set his mind to something . . .

I felt a little drool at the corner of my mouth watching his tight ass in his black jeans as he bent to throw the ball. His form wasn't too bad actually, having a natural understanding of how to move it to get the best results.

I was not surprised when he knocked down eight of the ten pins.

He turned to me, expression serious. "I can do better."

"You knocked down eight," I disagreed. "That's awesome."

"I can do better."

I'd never met a man who was so competitive with himself. He had to do his best in everything. *It was exhausting.* "Your need to be the best at everything is exhausting."

Vaughn didn't even flinch at my honesty. Instead he walked up to me, wrapped an arm around my waist, and drew me in for a quick, sweet kiss. When he pulled back he murmured, "If I didn't need to be the best at everything, princess, you would have had a lot less orgasms this week."

My belly fluttered and I felt an answering tingle between my legs. I swear to God, this man now had more control over my body than I did. "Right. Well. I wouldn't want you to stop being who you are."

He grinned, smug. "That's what I thought."

"You're lucky I find you funny, Tremaine," I warned him. "Arrogance is usually off-putting."

"Then you're lucky I find arrogance attractive, too."

"Uh!" I pushed him away. "I am not arrogant."

He laughed. "You are so arrogant."

"I am not!"

"You think you're one of the best attractions around here, princess." He snatched me back toward him. "And you would be right. So never change."

I melted into him. "Do I really come off arrogant?"

"Only with me, but if you haven't noticed, it gets me hot."

We did this thing we'd been doing a lot this past week: falling into each other's eyes. That almost always led to sex. "We're supposed to be bowling," I whispered.

"Fine. First we bowl, then we fuck."

I smacked his arm. "We are in public."

Chuckling, he pulled reluctantly away from me and gestured to the bowling balls. "Your turn."

As I was setting myself up to bowl, I glanced over my shoulder at Vaughn and found him staring at my ass. I grinned, loving how sexy he made me feel. "Oy, Tremaine."

He dragged his gaze up to my face. He'd sat down to watch me, had his arms draped over the seats on either side of him, lounging with his legs out and his ankles crossed. Without even meaning to he gave off an air of power and superiority. He could turn any chair into a throne, even the little plastic bench chairs in a bowling alley.

I gave him a coy, curious smile. "You ever had sex on the beach?"

Vaughn quirked a brow. "What made you think of that?"

"When I mentioned we were in public"—I shrugged—"and we were talking about sex . . . I wondered if you'd ever done it somewhere public."

"When I was younger," he said. "Club restrooms."

"With girls you didn't know?"

"Yes."

I nodded and turned away because that bothered me. Not really because Vaughn had been with other women. I wasn't naive about that, and I had been with other men.

No, it was the strange girls part of the scenario. The idea of hooking up with some guy I didn't know in a bathroom stall sounded so empty.

Readying myself to let the ball fly, I was stopped by Vaughn asking, "And you?"

There was something about his tone . . . Looking over my shoulder, I found him no longer lounging. He was tense, and he wore this expression on his face that suggested that he was curious but almost afraid to know too much. I straightened and faced him. "Never. Tom wasn't very adventurous," I said, rueful. "And Ivy, Iris and Ira's daughter, she was my best friend growing up. She had sex on the beach once and said it was the worst experience of her life. Sand got in some really awkward places and it was cold and icky. Her description put me off the idea for good."

Vaughn studied me carefully. "But not the having sex in public part?"

"What?"

"It didn't put you off the idea of having sex in public?"

Excitement coursed through me at the thought of having sex somewhere risky with Vaughn. I shook my head, biting my lip to stop myself from grinning like a big kid.

His eyes darkened with heat. "Where?"

Where did I want to have dangerous risky sex with him? "Surprise me."

His answering smile was wicked with intent.

"No word from Vanessa then?" Emery said as we sipped coffee in the bookstore the next day.

"None." I tried not to sound as worried as I felt and clearly failed because Dahlia wrapped her hand over mine and squeezed.

"It'll be fine."

"The deeper she gets into it with Jack, the more possibility things will not be fine."

Emery lowered her gaze to her coffee, a slight blush tinting the crest of her cheeks. "Do you really think he'll hurt her?"

Damn. Was Emery still crushing on him? "The old Jack is not someone who would ever have been interested in anyone as shallow as my sister."

"He did sleep with Dana Kellerman," Dahlia pointed out.

"Yes, once. Did he ever go back there? No."

"Which makes him doing it and screwing over his best friend all the more confusing."

"Right? It also means I'm almost positive Vanessa is going to get hurt in all of this."

"Let's forget about Vanessa's feelings," Dahlia huffed. "And worry about how this problem affects you and your inn that you have worked your ass off to make super-duper successful."

"I'm not worried about that."

"Oh?"

I shrugged. "I don't think any of my people would ever let the Devlins do anything to hurt me or the inn. You all will crush them if they try."

My friends grinned at me. "Yeah, and Vaughn will be first in line. How is Mr. Hartwell since you took him bowling?"

"Mr. Hartwell?"

Dahlia smirked. "Well he's been getting awfully involved in town stuff since you suggested he should and he is in love with Hartwell's local princess."

"Cute, very cute. Don't call him that to his face though, okay? His masculine pride has been hurt enough in the last twenty-four hours."

"You whipped him at bowling," she surmised.

"I didn't whip him but I won. You know, for never having bowled before he did pretty well."

"I still can't believe you took Tremaine bowling."

"Every time he mentions something ordinary that he's never done my heart hurts a little." I shrugged. "I just want him to experience a normal life. Do normal things. He works so hard all the time and in the five-star hotel environment. He needs a break from all that hoity-toity, everything has to be perfect, 'I have to make a ton of money' stuff."

"But that is who he is, right?" Emery said. "Vaughn is career-focused."

"Yes. I know that. And I expect him to be busy a lot. As it is, last night was the first evening we spent real time together. We've only seen each other late at night, if you catch my meaning."

Dahlia rolled her eyes. "Okay, stop. Some of us aren't getting *it* regularly."

"But doesn't that bother you?" Emery said. "Not the getting it regularly part." She blushed. "The him working a lot part."

"We're both busy with our businesses. I, more than anyone, can understand it."

"Don't you want to spend time with him?"

"All of the time. I want to spend an obnoxious amount of time with this man." I huffed and flopped back in my seat. "I never felt this way with Tom. I actually liked the space from Tom, even in the beginning. But with Vaughn I just want to be with him all the time because every moment we spend together I find out something new about him—his quirks, his sense of humor, his cockiness, his flaws. And do you know what? I like it *all. Flaws* and all! What is that?"

Emery gave me a dreamy smile. "You're falling in love."

"No, I'm not. It's too soon. I'm just . . . I'm infatuated." I bit my lips as my worries came to the surface. "Shouldn't he want to spend all of his time with me?"

"You need to talk to him about this. Now. Before it goes any further," Dahlia said. "If Jess was here, she'd say the same."

Jess wasn't here. She was in Canada on a three-week honeymoon.

"I don't know . . ."

"Do you really want a husband and a father to your kids who is never there?"

"No." I didn't. "Fine. I'll talk to him. It'll probably scare him off but I'll talk to him."

"After what he said to you"—Emery smiled, referring to the speech he'd given me on the beach, the one that was too good not to share with my best friends—"I don't think anything you do will scare him off."

"Yeah," Dahlia agreed. "He certainly seems to get a kick out of your obnoxious honesty."

"My obnoxious honesty?" I gestured to her. "Pot." Then to myself. "Meet kettle."

She laughed. "Whatever. Just talk to him."

The bell tinkled over the bookstore door and Emery got up to greet her customers. She returned a minute later and sat down. "They're just browsing the books, so I told them to come get me if they need me. What were we saying?"

"We were discussing my possibly relationship-ending talk with Vaughn. Oh, and the fact that my sister seems to have disappeared off the face of the planet. I swear to God, if I don't find her soon, my parents are going to get on a flight out here."

"And that would be a bad thing?"

"Right now? Yes. I'd like to get to know Vaughn without my dad breathing down my neck. I love the man but he also is the only one in my family who knew about Oliver Spence. He might assume things about Vaughn, and I need to work out how I feel about Tremaine before I take into consideration anybody else's feelings about him."

"Oh, please, you know how you feel about Vaughn." Dahlia sighed.

"I'm going to smack you."

She grinned and turned her cheek to me, tapping her finger where her adorable dimple was. "Go ahead. Make my day."

Affection and amusement swamped me. "Ach, you're too damn cute for your own good."

"I know." She preened, making us laugh.

"Miss," a masculine voice called, and then a guy appeared at the bottom of the stairs. He walked up them, holding the hand of a short, pretty blonde. He looked to Emery. "We'd like to purchase a couple of books if that's okay." He smiled apologetically at me and then his gaze flicked to Dahlia, presumably to offer her the same.

Yet his smile froze, replaced by shock. "Dahlia?"

Dahlia was staring at him as if he were a ghost.

And a ghost she was terrified of. "Michael."

Michael? This was Michael! No wonder she'd gone chalk white.

Michael stared at her like a man who'd been lost in the desert for weeks and had finally found a watering hole. Having apparently forgotten anyone else existed he took a step toward her and stopped when the woman at his side tugged on his hand.

She scowled up at him.

Michael seemed too stunned to care about the blonde's glowering.

His beautiful brown eyes returned to Dahlia. "What are you doing here?"

Dahlia tucked her trembling hands under the table where he couldn't see. "What are you doing here?" she evaded.

"We're on vacation." The blonde spoke up, curling into Michael's side. "Mike, who is this?"

The plaintive tone seemed to cut through his daze. "Uh, Kierston, this is Dahlia. She's Dermot's little sister."

"I thought she died."

I reached out for Dahlia, grasping her hand under the table at this woman's way too casual mention of a dark time in Dahlia's life.

Michael turned his sad eyes to Dahlia. "That was Dillon."

"I need to go." Dahlia stood up, jerking her hand out of mine, and refusing to meet anyone's gaze. She stormed by, moving quicker than I'd ever seen her move.

"Dahlia!" Michael yanked out of Kierston's grip and moved to follow her.

But I was quick, too, and I rounded him, putting my hands up between us. "You're going to let her go."

He glared at me. "Move."

I wasn't going to lie, he was kind of scary, but I held my ground. "Nope."

"Mike . . ." his girl whined. "What is going on?"

The bell tinkled, signaling Dahlia's departure.

Frustrated, he ran a hand through his thick hair. His T-shirt sleeve rose, and his bicep bulged as he moved. He wasn't the tallest guy, but he was tall enough at about five ten, five eleven. He was very broad-shouldered and built. I studied him, seeing the appeal. Although not the most handsome guy I'd ever met, he had beautiful eyes and what I tended to call Indiana Jones lips. Very kissable lips. A short, scruffy beard currently surrounded those lips and I had to say the beard was hot.

I could *definitely* see the appeal in Michael Sullivan. Yes, I knew his full name. I knew a lot about this guy. Which was exactly why I wasn't letting him anywhere near Dahlia if she didn't want him near her.

"What is Dahlia doing here?" he demanded.

"She's on vacation," I lied. "Just like you. Small world, huh? But she leaves tomorrow."

"Where is she staying?"

"None of your business and I think your girlfriend"—I nodded to Kierston—"would agree."

"Wife," she corrected. "His wife."

My heart plummeted for Dahlia. Seriously just took a dive off a cliff. I remembered the night I'd saved her from drowning and all that she'd told me. It was hard to hear then, but even harder to remember it now that I loved Dahlia McGuire like she was my blood.

I narrowed my eyes on Mr. Michael Sullivan and his pretty wife. "So when does your vacation in Hartwell end?"

"That's none of your concern," he returned, clearly annoyed with my interference. "Now are you going to get out of my way?"

I considered how long it would take Dahlia to get to her car. I knew there was no way in hell she was going back to the gift store for fear she'd bump into the past there, too. "Not yet." I smiled prettily. "How about some coffee?"

The hardass in front of me seemed to deflate. Worry softened his eyes. "I just want to know how she is. It's been a long time."

"I know," I told him pointedly.

"Ah." He got me. "I see."

I flicked a look at his wife, who appeared ten seconds away from blowing a gasket. "She's doing really well."

"Are you on vacation with her?"

"Something like that."

"And she's really okay?"

"She's terrific," I lied. "Couldn't be happier."

"Good," he said.

I glanced over at Emery, who was watching all of this with concern and confusion. "Coffee to go?"

She started to walk by us when Michael shook his head. "We're okay. Really."

Considering the timing and the fact that Dahlia probably ran to her car, I stepped aside. "You are free to go then."

"Usually that's my line," he muttered, reaching back for his wife's hand.

"Huh?"

"I'm a cop. A detective."

I did not know *that*. "In Boston?"

"Yeah." He looked back at his wife, who was staring at his hand like it was a slug. "Kierston?"

Reluctantly she took it.

Michael turned back to me. "Give her my regards."

"I'll do that."

Emery and I watched as they left and I grimaced for Michael when I heard his wife hiss, "What the fuck aren't you telling me, Michael Sullivan?"

I never heard his reply because the door slammed shut behind them.

"I'm guessing you know something I don't," Emery said.

"Yes." I gave her a regretful smile. "Dahlia told me a story a long time ago, a story she has not repeated since, a story no one else knows. Maybe one day she'll tell it."

"He isn't over her."

Surprise shot through me at her supposition. "Why do you say that? How do you know they were even . . . a thing?"

She shrugged. "The way he looked at her. Like he hated and loved her all at once."

Sadness fell over me, ruining any buzz I'd had from the morning sex I'd had with Vaughn. "I'm going to go check on Dahlia."

"Give her a hug from me."

I squeezed Em's hand in answer before heading out of the store to find my best friend.

TWENTY-FIVE

Vaughn

It was unheard of for Vaughn to take two evenings off work.

Until now.

He wasn't going to lie to himself—he was a little antsy about his decision to give his night manager, Freya, and his new daytime manager, Graham, extra responsibilities so he could spend more time with Bailey.

Yet . . . he also couldn't seem to help himself. He wanted to spend an obnoxious amount of time with the woman.

He looked over at her sitting in the passenger seat of his car, unable to shift the unease he felt. When he'd picked her up from her place ten minutes ago he'd known right away just from her kiss that she was preoccupied. Usually Bailey gave her all to a kiss, just like she did with everything in life.

Something was bothering her. And Vaughn was worried *that something* was their very new relationship.

"Is it because I asked you to wear a skirt tonight?"

"What?" Bailey frowned.

"You're quiet."

"Oh." She shook her head. "No. Although why a skirt?" She pointed to the high-waist flared green skirt that came to her knee. She had a cream silk camisole tucked into it and was wearing a matching sweater. The skirt was as perfect as if he'd chosen it himself.

"I wanted to see your legs." He shrugged, nonchalant.

He felt her stare and turned to give her a quick grin before concentrating back on the road.

"You wanted to see my legs?"

"You have great legs and you've worn jeans every day this week. I've seen you wearing a dress all summer. I missed them," he teased. "And I thought you weren't offended by the request because you wore a skirt but . . . ?"

"I'm not offended. I kind of found it sexy."

He was pleased but still confused. "Then what's going on?"

Bailey sighed. "I'm a little worried about Dahlia. She had a bad day. I won't go into it. And I'm worried about Vanessa and the fact that I haven't seen her since I kicked her out. And I'm worried that you might be a workaholic who doesn't care if we don't see each other a lot and I care if we don't see each other a lot because I work a lot, too, and you work a lot and I just think that we should talk about it because I am more than willing to make time for you and I need to know if you will make time for me and this is way too soon to mention it."

God, he loved when she rambled at him.

It was unbelievably adorable.

What she had to say, though, still concerned him. "Okay. Number one on that list: Dahlia. Is there anything I can do?"

"What?"

"Is there anything I can do?"

When she didn't reply, Vaughn shot her a look. She was staring at him, openmouthed. It was his turn to ask, "What?"

"You!" She gestured to him in exasperation. "You're being perfect right now and you have to stop."

Laughter filled his voice. "Why would I stop?"

"Because it makes me want to have sex with you all the time. Like *all* the time. And my vagina might eventually break!"

Vaughn threw his head back laughing so hard he almost swerved. No woman in his acquaintance had ever used the word "vagina" in a sentence, let alone worried about how too much sex with him would break it. God, he loved this crazy, cute, sexy woman.

She smacked his arm, laughing. "Stop it!"

"*You're* laughing," he argued.

"But I'm being serious."

"Bailey, your vagina is not going to break from overuse. It might get a little sore . . ." He grinned, taking a perverse kind of pleasure in the idea of "overusing" her.

"Oh, you'd love that, wouldn't you?"

He had a flash memory of the night before and how hard she'd come while he fucked her with her hands tied to the bedposts. "Yes."

She didn't respond to that. "You can't help with Dahlia but thank you for offering."

"You're welcome. As for two: Vanessa is still staying at the Grand and partying at Germaine's. That seems to be the extent of her social life at the moment."

"How do you know that?"

"I've been keeping an eye on things." He reached over to squeeze her knee and instantly regretted it because all he wanted to do was slide his hand up her skirt. Seriously, the woman had him hornier than a schoolboy.

Patience.

He withdrew his hand. "I told you I wouldn't let anything happen to you or the inn."

"I know. Thank you for that, too."

"Again you're welcome. Now. About three." He shot her a look and saw her tense. "I'm glad you feel that way," he admitted, marveling at how much easier it got daily to be honest with her about his feelings. "I feel that way, too. I'm not saying that I'm going to change overnight, because I've spent my whole life working too hard and I imagine it's not going to be an easy habit to break. But I want to see you." He shot her another look and found her smiling at him. "A lot. You know, I've never taken two evenings in a row off work before."

"Never?"

"Never."

"That's a good sign."

"A very good sign. We just need to take each day as it comes; try and work this thing out."

"But now at least I know we're on the same page," Bailey said. "We both want to see each other more."

Vaughn's chest swelled with deepening emotion at the giddy, glamorous smile on her face. It felt like he'd waited forever to be the man she smiled at that way.

"So." She wiggled in her seat and brushed her hand over the dash of his Aston Martin. "Where are you taking me in this beautiful car?"

"The movies."

She was quiet a moment. "Um . . . the movies are back that way. You know . . . in town."

He smirked, enjoying the little game he was playing. "The movies in Hartwell are back that way. We're not going to the movies in Hartwell."

"Why not?"

"Because the movies at the mall are better."

"But farther away."

He grinned at her growing confusion. "This is a nice night for a drive."

"And a nice car," she conceded. "A very nice car."

"Do you want one?"

"What?" Bailey squeaked.

Vaughn swallowed his laughter. "Only joking." *Kind of.*

"Don't do that. You gave me heart failure." He felt her sudden scrutiny. "You know I'm not after your money, right?"

"Yes. I think it was the constant hostility for three years that gave you away."

She chuckled. "I like this you."

Contentment coursed through him. "I'm glad to hear it."

A half hour later, after discovering they had similar taste in music, they pulled up to the mall outside Johnstown.

"It's busy tonight." She unbuckled her seat belt.

"I got you." He got out of the car and hurried around to her side to open the door. She gave him that huge, beautiful smile as he held out his hand to help her out of the low-sitting supercar. "What?"

"You're such a gentleman." She moved into him, drawing circles on his chest with her fingertips and sending blood rushing straight to his dick. "It's very hot, Mr. Tremaine."

All in good time, he reminded himself. Vaughn captured her wrists and gave her a tight smile. "Not here."

Disappointment clouded her expression and he had to remind himself that she wouldn't be disappointed in ten minutes' time.

Taking her hand he led her into the mall. There were still a lot of people milling around, especially teenagers, and when they arrived at the movie theater it was no different.

Vaughn searched the movie listing.

"What are we going to see?"

He deduced that Bailey would know more about today's teens than he did. "What film would you least want to see if you were fifteen?"

She frowned at the question but turned to study the listings anyway. A few seconds later she pronounced, "The French one with subtitles."

"The French one with subtitles it is then."

"What?"

They were next in line and Vaughn bought two tickets for the foreign movie.

"Why are we going to see this?" Bailey hissed.

"It sounds interesting," he lied. He wasn't a foreign movie kind of guy. In all honesty he wasn't a movie kind of guy, period. But he wasn't here for the actual film.

Holding her hand, he led her down the hall past the theaters that were showing movies Bailey might enjoy seeing. "Here we are."

"So do you like foreign movies then?" she whispered as he pulled open the door to their screening.

"Nope."

"Then why are we here?"

Instead of answering he led her to the back row and sat her down. The movie had already started and there were a dozen people in the rows in front of them.

There were five rows between them and the person closest to them.

Bailey stared up at the screen where an Audrey Hepburn–type girl was riding her bike through the streets of some French town. Subtitles popped up on the screen as the girl apparently narrated the story. "Oh, God." Bailey grimaced.

Vaughn hid a smile and leaned down to whisper in her ear, "You're too far away."

"I'm right next to you," she whispered back.

"Sit on my lap."

"What?" She reared back in confusion.

And that's when he let his intentions blaze in his eyes. "Sit on my lap, princess," he whispered.

Her chest started to rise and fall as she tried to catch her breath. "You don't . . . ?"

Taking her hand, he guided his dazed woman off her seat and onto his lap so she was facing the screen. He wrapped his arms around her waist and she cuddled back into him. His dick delighted in the feel of her small, beautiful ass and strained to get closer to it.

His heart started to beat hard and fast.

To the outside observer it appeared as if they were just cuddling in to watch the movie.

After what felt like much too long listening to Bailey attempt to control her excited breathing, he whispered in her ear, "You cannot make a noise."

She swallowed and nodded slowly. Vaughn pressed a kiss against her throat, finding her pulse and smiling at the discovery hers was racing, too.

"Watch the movie."

She nodded again.

His dick got even harder in anticipation of what was about to happen.

Smoothing his hand down her thigh, he slipped it under the hem of her skirt and back up the inside of her leg.

Bailey reached to push her skirt back down, covering his wayward hand so no one could see should they walk by.

Her breath stuttered as his fingertips grazed her inner thigh and faltered at the feel of her underwear.

French dialogue became buzzing background noise as the theater melted away until it was just the two of them. All he could hear was her soft, shallow breaths, all he could feel was *her*, and all he could smell was the fruity scent of her hair.

"Vaughn," she whispered.

"Shh," he warned, "or I'll stop."

He knew her well enough to know the sudden rigid line of her back meant she was annoyed, and she was probably biting her lip so she didn't call him a bastard. Holding back his amusement, he slid his hand upward over her panties and then under them. Vaughn had to bite back his groan as his index and middle finger found her already wet. Hitting target on her clit, he circled it lightly, torturing her a little.

Bailey gently undulated on his lap, her little gasp sounding far too loud to his ears. He stopped fondling her, and she turned her head to glare at him.

In answer he kissed her, deep and wet, his tongue mimicking what his dick would like to be doing right that second. When he pulled back he muttered against her mouth, "Keep quiet or I stop."

She nodded, her breath ragged against his lips.

"Watch the movie, princess."

He waited for her to turn back to stare at the screen and then he started circling her clit with his fingers again, the pressure light, and not nearly enough.

She told him this in the way she impatiently moved on his lap, her ass pressing hard on his erection, stroking it with each tiny undulation until he was desperate to sink into her. He held his own needs at bay and slid his fingers down inside her. The angle didn't provide deep penetration, it was more torment than anything for her, and he made it worse by brushing his lips against her ear. "I wonder if any of them suspect that there's a man finger-fucking his woman in the back row."

Bailey whimpered and bit her lip harder, and he rewarded her by moving his thumb to her clit with more pressure this time. The hand still at her waist crept upward and he started to massage her breast, squeezing it the way she liked it, as he continued to stimulate her.

Vaughn's chest started to pump harder as he felt how soaked she was, how fucking excited she was by this, and he marveled at his good luck to fall in love with a woman so sexually in tune with him.

"Vaughn." Her soft gasp warned him, as did the tightening of her body. She turned toward him and he pressed her head to his throat, muffling her moan against his skin as she shuddered through her climax.

The man in the row nearest to them turned around and in the light of the screen Vaughn saw the stranger's suspicion.

"I think we better go," he whispered, trying not to laugh.

Bailey lifted her head. "Why?"

"We might have been foiled."

Her eyes widened and she whipped around to stare. She tensed against him. "Oh. Yeah, let's go." She reached for her bag and slowly stood up, leaving Vaughn pondering his problem:

The very noticeable erection in his lap.

Bailey frowned at him. "What?" she whispered.

He gestured to his lap.

"Oh. Right." She giggled, which earned them a "shh" from Mr. Suspicious five rows ahead. "Walk behind me."

Vaughn rolled his eyes at her suggestion but got up. When she reached for his hand, he muttered, "Princess, you touching me will get in the way of me trying to get rid of this thing."

"Okay." Her laughter bubbled in the word.

He ignored it because even her amusement turned him on.

Fuck.

Letting her go ahead, Vaughn attempted to walk behind her, and as he did he tried to think of things to cool him down. Just as the image of Ira Green naked started to work its charm, he lifted his hand to run it through his hair and got a whiff of the smell of Bailey's sex on his fingers.

"Move." He put his hands to her hips and started ushering her quickly through the mall.

"Vaughn," she complained as she stumbled on those far too sexy sandals she was wearing.

"No time to argue."

He had her back at the car in record timing.

The Aston Martin's tires squealed against the lot, drawing stares as he blew the hell out of there.

"Are you okay?" Bailey teased.

"Do I look okay?"

"No. You look like you're about to burst out of those jeans."

"Yes, well, the plan was to get you off, and then get me off."

"But we got caught."

He looked over at her and her eyes were glittering. "You liked that, too."

The desire that flushed her face did his hard dick no favors. "I liked every part of it. Thank you." She reached over and slid her hand up his leg. "I *loved* that surprise."

He groaned as she rubbed her hand over his hard-on. "Princess," he groaned again. "I'd do anything to make you happy."

"I'm getting that." She shifted closer to him. "Pull over at the next lay-by."

"We could get caught."

"Let's try and see if our luck holds out."

She didn't need to tell him twice.

"Wait," she complained as they passed the next lay-by. "You missed it."

Vaughn shook his head. "I know somewhere we're less likely to be interrupted."

Five minutes later he pulled off the road and into a public park they'd passed on the way in. The lot was empty as it was too dark for children to be there running around, and too late for parents to be enjoying eating out in the sun at the picnic benches.

"I've never had sex in a car." Bailey's words were thick with excitement as she set about unzipping his jeans.

"That makes two of us." He grinned at her as he lifted his ass up off the driver's seat to push his jeans and underwear down. Settling back down he released the seat from its position and pushed back, giving her more room to climb on top of him.

Bailey eyed him with a dark hunger that made him swell to almost painful.

"Come on, princess," he demanded.

In answer she reached under her skirt and slipped down her underwear. As she began to climb over him, he said, "Wait. I need a condom."

"I'm on the pill." She brushed her lips against his. "Do you trust me?"

"You know I do." *I love you.* "Fuck," he breathed, beyond desperate to get inside her now that he knew there would be nothing between them. But first, "Take off your top."

She didn't even hesitate. Her sweater, camisole, and strapless bra were off in seconds.

"God, I need inside you." He cursed under his breath as she straddled him, her perky tits bouncing with the movement.

As she took him in hand and guided him to her, Vaughn's breath stuttered at the first clutch of her around him. She began to lower herself slowly down over him, a satisfied, smug smile of power on her beautiful face.

We'll just see about that.

Bailey

I didn't think there had ever been a time in my life where I was more turned on. I didn't know if it was the risky foreplay in the movie theater, or how close Vaughn seemed to losing control, or how amazing it was that he'd done this for me. All I knew was that I'd never been more desperate to have a man inside me as I was to have *this* man inside me.

And right now he felt un-freaking-believable inside of me.

I moaned, leaning in to kiss him, a deep, languid, lusty kiss that made my sex pulse around his cock. Shifting upward, I was surprised when Vaughn gripped my hips and slammed me back down. Sensation blew through us and I made to ride him, but his grip tightened, keeping me still.

"What are you doing?"

He stared deep into my eyes. "I thought you liked me taking control."

I shivered, because I *loved* him taking control during sex. I'd never felt more feminine, sexy, and powerful in my life than I did when I was having sex with Vaughn Tremaine. "You know I do but I thought the purpose of me riding you was to be in control."

"Not necessarily." He grinned, and then ground up against me.

I gasped into his mouth at the sensation coursing through me.

I sighed in pleasure, dreamy, goddamn, car-spinning pleasure, as he thumbed my clit and sucked my nipple at the same time. Desperately wanting to ride him, I whimpered as he held me still with his other hand. If I had wanted to, I could have taken back the control, but his version of events felt damn good, too.

As he licked, teased, and tormented my breasts, I arched my back into his play, shifting my hips slightly into his thumb on my clit.

Higher and higher he pushed me toward the cliff edge that would take me up and over into heaven, and just as I was nearing the top he pressed his face to my breasts and gritted out, "I can't wait."

I didn't need to ask what that meant. I eased his head back, cupped his face in my hands, and rose up. We moaned into each other's mouths at the feel of his thick cock moving inside of me.

And then I began to ride him, so close to coming I lost control, riding him hard, needing the delicious satisfaction I only ever found with him.

"Fuck!" he bit out, his hands squeezing my breasts as I went wild on him.

And then I hit the top, stiffened on the cliff edge, and launched over, crying out his name. I shuddered and pulsed around his cock and his thumbs dragged over my nipples as he tensed beneath me. Seconds later his cock swelled and throbbed inside me, and as I came down from my own orgasm I felt the wet of his release.

Holy hell.

I collapsed against him, completely ruined in the best way possible.

Almost purring, I snuggled into him as he held me close, caressing my back in this soothing, tender way that, combined with the aftershocks of that outrageous orgasm, made me want to cry.

"Was it everything you hoped it would be?" Vaughn teased, sounding content.

I snuggled closer to him. "More. So much more, Tremaine."

He chuckled and hugged me. "I should get you back home."

"In a minute. This feels too nice to end it just yet."

"There will be more times like this in the future."

"I know. But this is the first time. I want to be able to remember every second of it."

Vaughn was quiet a moment as he stroked my back, and then . . . "I love you."

Fear penetrated the loveliness of the moment.

I pulled back to face him. He stared up at me and, sure enough, that look in his eyes, that soulful, smoldering look, was filled with the kind of love no man had ever looked at me with.

And it terrified me.

Unable to give him the answer he wanted, I kissed him. I kissed him with everything I was willing to give and had to hope that for now it was enough.

TWENTY-SIX

Vaughn

After a night like the one he'd just had Vaughn should have been feeling relaxed, satisfied, and more than content with his lot in life. However, the next day as Graham talked at him about introducing a custom object relating to the state of Delaware to use as an eco reuse-your-linen card instead of the actual card or something . . . Vaughn had to admit he was only half listening.

Bailey still hadn't said she loved him.

He'd said it to her a number of times now and still no reciprocation.

Vaughn knew he should be patient. Although it felt like they'd been together a long time it was technically just over two weeks.

But . . . the problem was that intuition of his told him that Bailey Hartwell was falling in love with him. No woman had ever looked at him the way Bailey had last night as he dropped her off at home.

Like she loved him.

And just when he thought she was going to say it, she bit her lip and walked away.

Which meant she didn't trust him enough to tell him.

Fuck.

Patience, Tremaine, patience.

"I think it's those little details that matter. Instead of just a card that the guest can place on the bed when they don't want their linens changed, we could put like a ceramic blue hen or . . . we could have Dahlia McGuire, the silversmith at the gift shop, custom-make something that guests can put on the linens instead. What do you think, sir? Mr. Tremaine?"

Vaughn stared through Graham, forcing himself to focus and let his brain play catch-up. "I like it," he said. "Talk to Miss McGuire. Get her to draw up some designs."

Once Graham left his office, Vaughn rested his head on his chair and picked up his phone. He opened his messages to Bailey, his fingers hovering over the buttons. How much time should he give her before he had to raise this as an issue? He couldn't go through with marrying Camille because she didn't trust him.

He definitely couldn't see his relationship with Bailey going where he wanted it to go if she didn't trust him. Yet, he was itching to have her. For good.

The idea of her not believing in him, believing that he would hurt her, scared the shit out of him. It had taken him forever to start believing he loved her enough to overcome his fears; to believe in himself when it came to protecting her and making her happy.

Her distrust was fucking all that up.

They should talk.

The phone jumped in vibration in his hand, causing him to jump. *Dad Calling.*

"You scared the hell out of me," Vaughn said in lieu of hello.

"How did I manage that?" William sounded amused.

"I had the phone in my hand about to make a call."

"Let me guess. To a certain redhead?"

"Maybe."

His dad chuckled. "I was just calling to check in. It's been two weeks since you two decided to pull your heads out of your ass."

Rolling his eyes, Vaughn sighed. "You're not expecting weekly updates, are you?"

"While it's new, yes. I want to make sure you don't fuck it up."

"Nice. Thanks for the vote of confidence."

"Okay. Something's up. I can hear it in your voice."

"It's nothing."

"Vaughn."

He sighed, knowing his father would just hound him until he told him. "She . . . she hasn't said she loves me back yet. I think I know that she does but it's like she still doesn't trust me yet. Should I be worried?"

"Son, it's been a couple of weeks. Give the poor girl a chance."

For some reason his dad's matter-of-fact response soothed him. He laughed at himself. "You're right. Jesus. I don't know what's happening to me."

"You love her. That'll make a man act like a fruitcake. Speaking of . . . I . . . um . . . well . . . I was going to wait to tell you in person but I don't see you getting out here for a while now that you and Bailey . . ."

"Dad, spit it out."

"Diane left me for good. I . . . blew it."

He was disappointed for his dad, and for Diane. "I'm sorry."

"I can't change how I feel," he explained. "I've felt this way too long. I don't want to remarry. My wife is gone."

"Dad . . . you're being stubborn, and you're going to lose someone you love because of it."

"I do love Diane. And I would be with her for the rest of our lives. But she seems to think my not wanting to marry her means I don't love her and there is nothing I can do to change her mind."

"You could marry her."

"I don't want to," he said firmly. "Sometimes . . . there's just no finding that compromise."

Frustrated with his father, but hearing the resolve in his voice and knowing what that meant, he realized this was in fact the end of his father's relationship. And he was sad for him. "I'm sorry, Dad."

"Me, too. I . . ." His words grew thick with gruff emotion. "I'll miss her."

"I don't know what to say."

"Nothing to say, son."

He had a thought. "Come out here."

"What?"

"To Hartwell. Spend a few days, a week, however long you want. Take a break from New York."

"I can't right now. I'm in the middle of an important deal. But after? I would like to spend more time with this young lady of yours."

"Definitely. Dad, you're welcome here anytime."

"Good," William said. "Well, I best get going. And you . . . give the redhead some time. Be patient."

They hung up and Vaughn put his phone down on the table. He stared at it, thinking of his father's advice, and his heart began to beat a little faster. He reached into the inside pocket of his jacket and pulled out a little black velvet jewelry box.

It was light in his hand but it may as well have weighed ten tons for all it symbolized.

"Be patient," he murmured, and slipped it back into his jacket out of view.

Bailey

I stood in the doorway of Dahlia's workshop, watching as she sat on a stool, bent over a piece of jewelry. Her brows were drawn together in focus. Her total concentration and the fact she had rock music blaring loudly meant she didn't realize I was there.

Years ago she'd given me a spare key to her shop.

The store was light and bright, and it was filled with Dahlia's own jewelry creations. She was a gifted silversmith and had converted part of the storeroom in the back of the building into a workshop. As well as jewelry, Dahlia sourced unique gifts, books, toys, witty mugs, clothes, and accessories. For the past year, since George Beckwith closed down his tourist shop, Dahlia had been selling Hartwell tourist stuff—T-shirts, magnets, mugs, postcards, key rings, etc.

The air smelled heavily of the coconut diffusers she had placed around the store to mask the heavy aroma from her workshop. Although Dahlia described herself as a silversmith, she also worked with copper, bronze, and gold. She liked to oxidize metals, using a chemical called liver of sulfur to oxidize silver, and it made the place smell like rotten eggs. Hence the diffusers.

After seeing the Closed sign on her door, I'd decided to check in on her. It was Aydan's day off at the inn. Mona was watching over the place while Jay supervised in the kitchen so I could make sure my friend was okay.

Realizing Dahlia wasn't going to look up anytime soon, I crossed the room to where her phone sat in a music dock and I switched it off at the wall.

"Ah!" she cried out behind me.

Trying not to grin and failing, I spun around to face her. "Hey, there."

Dahlia glowered at me. "I nearly died."

"You do insist on listening to your music that loudly."

"What are you doing here?"

"The shop is closed."

"Yeah." She shrugged, refusing to meet my eyes. "So?"

"Considering that blast from the past yesterday and the fact that you wouldn't talk to me at all about it, I was worried. I *am* worried."

Grimacing, Dahlia got up off her stool and wandered over to me. "You don't need to be worried. I closed the shop because . . . what if he's still here?"

I braced myself to tell her what I'd discovered in my conversation with Michael yesterday. "I don't think he is. The . . . uh . . . the woman that was with him?"

"Yeah?"

I blew out air between my lips, not sure at all how my friend was going to handle this news. "That was his wife. And I'm guessing by her angry reaction to his staggered reaction to you that they're on their way home now and she's yelling at him the entire way."

"Wow." Her eyes widened before they dropped to her feet so she could hide her expression from me. "Wow. Okay. Wow. Yeah." She threw her hands up, laughing, but it was a hard, ugly sound that made me wince. "Of course he's married. Michael wanted marriage and kids and all that jazz. All the stuff you want! What normal people want, right? Not people like me. Not weirdos like me."

"Dahlia—"

"I just, uh, I didn't want to have a conversation with him, you know?" She turned away, fiddling with tools on one of her workshop tables. "All of that was in the past. I've worked hard to start over here and I don't want to dredge all that crap up. I wonder how he knew I was here."

"He didn't. He was just as surprised to see you as you were to see him. Plus, he asked me what you were doing here."

She whirled around, clearly afraid. "What did you say?"

"I told him you were here on vacation and that you were leaving today."

Her shoulders deflated and she slumped onto a nearby stool. "Thank you."

"It was weird him being here, though, right?"

"Yes." Her expression darkened. "And a little *too* coincidental."

I thought of the letters she sent to Boston once a month. "Someone pointed him in this direction?"

"Someone definitely did."

"Maybe you should talk to him then. You can't hide forever."

"Bailey, I love you, but this is one of those times where saying what's on your mind is just going to piss me off."

Duly warned, I held up my hands in surrender. "Shutting up. And leaving. But I'm right next door, and if I see the Closed sign on the shop tomorrow, I'm coming back."

"I told you to shut up," she grumbled, grabbing her purse. "Not to go away. Do you think Mona could make me one of her famous grilled cheese sandwiches? I haven't eaten since last night."

Relieved that my friend wasn't pushing me away entirely, I slung my arm around her shoulder. "Grilled cheese sounds *good*. And she made scones this morning. I hid two from the guests. Want one?"

"Uh, like you even need to ask."

Dahlia locked up behind us and we wandered toward the inn. Just as we were climbing the porch steps I got up the courage to say, "Since you don't want to talk about your problem, maybe we could talk about mine."

"Of course. What happened? You didn't end things with Vaughn, did you?"

"No." My belly fluttered at the memory of last night. "You would not believe the night I had. The things that man did to me and where."

"So what's the problem?" She pushed open the inn door.

I can't bring myself to tell him I love him and I don't know why.
"Well." I exhaled as we stepped inside, preparing myself to tell my friend about how big a coward I was, when the sight of my sister leaning against the reception counter stopped me in my tracks.

Mona stood behind the counter, her arms crossed, and her eyes narrowed behind her thick-framed glasses. "Look who decided to grace us with her presence."

Vanessa merely quirked an eyebrow at the dry comment, and that itself put me on alert because since arriving here my sister hadn't let a moment go by when she didn't admonish our employees for something. Mona's attitude would have made her blow a gasket a few weeks ago.

Now she just smirked at me. "We need to talk."

"Hello to you, too. How are you doing? How am I doing? I'm very well, thank you. As is the inn, in case you were wondering."

She ignored my sarcasm. "I don't have time for this idiocy. I leave for New York in a few days and I've got to get my things in order."

I felt a mixture of disappointment and relief. The relief I understood. The disappointment was a surprise. But I guess, underneath all my irritation with my little sister, I'd kind of hoped that being home would miraculously change her. "Found someone new to play with?"

"No. But I will." She shrugged.

"What happened to Jack? Did you finally see the light?"

"What? That Jack was using me?" She grinned and I tensed at the wickedness of it. "You always thought you were smarter than me, but, sweetie, I knew exactly what Jack Devlin and his band of merry brothers were up to. But I've had a crush on Jack Devlin since I was fourteen. I saw the chance to sleep with him and I took it."

"So you didn't get hurt?"

"No." She smiled. "I played him. He thought he had to wine and dine me and give me multiple orgasms to get what he wanted. When the truth is I would have taken less than what he and his father offered for my share in the inn."

"What?" Dahlia snapped.

Dread consumed me and my blood buzzed in my ears. "What?" I echoed Dahlia, praying we'd both heard wrong.

Vanessa explained. Happily. Gleeful in fact. "When Mom and Dad left us the inn and we agreed on signing that contract where you got a higher stake in the place, no one put anything in the contract about limitations on selling our share."

Fury overtook the dread. "Because it's our family business!"

"Now, now, rule number one, Bailey, no disturbing the customers with a family spat."

I lunged at her and Dahlia grabbed my arms, pulling me back. "What did you do?" I bit out, my nose and eyes burning with tears.

"Not what I've done but what I'm about to do in . . ." She checked the gold cocktail watch she was wearing. "Five hours. I have a business dinner with Ian, Jack, and Stu at the Grand. Our lovely lawyers will be joining us for drinks afterward. And upon signing a contract I'll have sold them my thirty percent share in the inn."

"If you do that, Devlin will find a way to take this place from me. Do you get that?"

"Do I care? They offered me way more than this place is worth. And frankly they've been far more accommodating than my own sister. They let me stay at the Grand free of charge, in an actual bed."

"Mom and Dad won't let you do this." I grasped at straws.

"There's nothing they can do to stop me. Unlike you, I don't *need* their approval."

"If you do this, none of us will forgive you."

That made her pause for a moment, her gaze lowering to the floor. "Well, maybe not for a while." She looked up at me. "They'll get over it."

"I won't."

Vanessa sneered. "Like I care if *you* love me. Let's not pretend anymore, Bails. You and I can't stand each other."

"I don't like you," I agreed. "I think you're a selfish brat and this moment only *highlights* that fact. But I do love you. And the fact that you could do this to me—"

"Oh, please. Enough with your righteous martyr act. You walk around like you're the only one who works hard. Contrary to what you think, what I've had to do to survive has been hard work."

"Yes, well, working on your back all those long hours can't be comfortable."

Mona barked with surprised laughter at my insult and Vanessa sliced her a killing look before turning it on me.

"Did you just call me a prostitute?"

"No, prostitutes are honest members of the oldest profession in the world—they provide sex as a service to men and men pay them for that service. You manipulate men who have money with sex to get to their money. I think that makes you a whore."

"Bailey," Dahlia muttered in warning.

But I was so angry I no longer cared what I said to my sister.

"If that was your idea of talking me out of this, then you're not as smart as you think you are."

Sadness overwhelmed me. "Vanessa, you have no intention of changing your mind whether I'm sweet and pleading . . . or just damn honest."

"Yes"—she twisted her face in bitterness—"but hearing you plead would have made my day."

"You little bitch!" Dahlia let me go and this time I had to hold her back. "You evil little bitch!"

"Don't," I murmured to my friend. "She's not worth it."

Dahlia whipped around to stare at me, incredulous. "But what about the inn?"

I didn't know.

But maybe my parents did, or my brother. I strode out of reception, not giving my sister another glance, and as I made toward my office I heard Dahlia say, "You've got five seconds to get your boney little ass out of here before I smack the cosmetic enhancements off your face."

As tears spilled down my cheeks, I tried to soothe the wound my sister had opened in me by reminding myself they may not be blood but my friends were the best sisters a girl could ask for.

Closing the office door behind me, I hurried to the phone.

The words spat out of me in a jumbled, frantic mess and my dad had to ask me to repeat them. His response once I did and did it slower, clearer, was a riot of curse words I didn't think I'd ever heard my dad use before.

"This can't be right," Mom whimpered over the speakerphone. "You have to be wrong."

I did not have time for my mother's blind devotion to her children. "My inn is about to be part-owned by Ian Devlin. There is no mistake in that. Now help me or let me get off the phone. Dad, your lawyer wrote the contract. Surely, there's something we can do."

"I'll call him and get right back to you," he promised.

"I'll call Vanessa," Mom said. "I'll make her change her mind."

Good luck with that.

After I got off the phone I stared at the wall in the office.

I'd underestimated just how deep my sister's resentment and dislike for me ran.

It wasn't all about her weird resentment of me; I knew Vanessa didn't *hate* me. The problem with my sister was her selfishness, and her inability to see beyond her own needs. She had no idea what the consequences of her selling her share of the inn to Devlin were because she hadn't thought about it.

She didn't *want* to think about it.

I called my brother. He didn't answer.

Shit.

I tried again.

And again.

Just when I was about to give up on him calling me back, the phone rang. I snatched it up. "Charlie."

"Bailey, what's going on?"

"I—"

My office door swung open, and affection and gratitude rushed through me at the sight of Vaughn. His features were tight, his expression dark, and I knew that he knew.

"Dahlia called. I ran right over. What can I do?" He took my free hand in both of his and raised it to his lips to kiss my knuckles.

I leaned into him. "I—"

"Bailey, are you there?" Charlie asked in my ear.

"I'm on the phone with my brother," I said to Vaughn.

"What can I do?"

"Nothing." I squeezed his hand, giving him a sad smile. "But thank you for rushing over here."

Vaughn frowned. "Surely, there's something I can do."

"Dad's calling our lawyer and I'm just about to tell Charlie about it. He and Vanessa are closer. There's a possibility he can talk her out of this."

"Out of what?" Charlie was impatient.

"I have to—" I shook my phone at Vaughn. "Sorry. I'll come right over and see you as soon as I know what's going to happen."

Not at all happy and unable to mask it, Vaughn gave me an abrupt nod, dropped my hand, and walked out. I sighed, knowing I'd have to deal with *that* later.

"Charlie?"

"I'm still here. You're the one not talking," he snapped. "What's going on?"

After I told him, he had much the same response as our dad, except he directly insulted Vanessa. "I'm going to kill her!" he ended.

"Or you could talk to her. Make her see sense. Out of all of us she likes you best, Charlie."

"Well I don't like her very much right now."

"Uh, yeah, no, me either, but that's not going to help. Talk to her. Please."

"I'll try." He sounded grim. "I'll call you after I call her."

Once we hung up I wandered, zombie-like, out into reception, where Dahlia and Mona still waited. Dahlia sat on the chesterfield with a grilled cheese sandwich Mona had obviously whipped up for her.

I blanched, wondering if any of my guests had overheard my argument with my sister.

It was as if Dahlia could read my thoughts. "There aren't any guests around."

"Thank God." I flopped down beside her and took the plate of grilled cheese from her. She let me. But even its deliciousness did not ease my current pain so I handed it back to her instead of wasting it on me.

"Vaughn left here looking a little upset," Dahlia said.

My chest tightened at the thought of being on the outs with Vaughn so soon into our relationship and so soon after our glorious night of risky sex. "He wanted to help. I didn't let him."

We were silent as I contemplated why I hadn't let him. "I don't know why I didn't let him," I murmured.

"Well," Mona piped up. "If he's any kind of *man*, that won't stop him."

TWENTY-SEVEN

Vaughn

"Sir, Miss Hartwell is not receiving visitors today." The concierge got off the phone.

Standing in Devlin's Grand Hotel, Vaughn used his famed icy cool to deal with the concierge. Outwardly he had managed to find the control he had always maintained even around Bailey, before he got a taste of her. Inside he was a riot of fury that these people would dare to hurt someone he loved; that Bailey's own sister would dare to do this to her.

He slipped the man a hundred-dollar bill. "Call her back and tell her that Mr. Tremaine would like to discuss a competitive offer."

The man called Vanessa's room again.

At first Vaughn was angry and, yes, admittedly hurt that Bailey refused his help. She hadn't done it in an ungrateful way, but in a way that suggested she didn't even *think* about asking for his help. That was almost worse.

For a moment he considered moping like a child about it, and then he got his balls back and decided he would help his woman out, even if she were too dense to see he was her best chance. After searching Vanessa's known haunts, he had concluded the woman would be hiding out until the deed was done.

However, as he started to think about it, it occurred to him that Vanessa Hartwell was smarter than he'd first realized.

There was no reason to tell Bailey about the dinner meeting with the Devlins until after the deed was done, so why give Bailey a heads-up?

Why give her time to attempt to stop the transaction?

Because *this* was what she wanted.

Vaughn, exactly where he was right then.

She wanted a counteroffer from Bailey's wealthy boyfriend.

The thought of giving in to the little conniving snake chafed at him . . . Another sister playing him, not caring if she hurt her own family to get what *she* wanted.

But this was about the inn. It was about Bailey. And he'd sacrifice his pride, his wallet, and whatever else it would take to ensure his woman's happiness.

His phone rang just as the concierge got a response from Vanessa. It was Dahlia McGuire, so he picked up. "What's going on?"

"What's going on is that I hope you have a plan B, Vaughn," Dahlia whispered down the phone. "Right now Bailey is in the office on conference call with her family trying to calm her parents and brother down because the lawyer told them there is nothing to be done, and Vanessa won't pick up her phone."

"You're to go straight up, Mr. Tremaine," the concierge informed him. "Room 228."

He gave the man a clipped nod and strode toward the elevator. "I'm dealing with Vanessa."

"What? What are you up to?"

"Plan B, Miss McGuire. Plan B." He hung up on her and called his lawyer. "I need you on hand. We're drawing up a contract today."

Vanessa Hartwell opened the door to her suite and Vaughn was pleased to find her fully dressed. In fact she was the most conservatively dressed he'd ever seen her, wearing a crew-neck T-shirt and skinny jeans. Her makeup was pared back and her hair was tied up in a knot. She looked younger, fresher, and the resemblance to her sister was more apparent.

The thought sent another rush of anger through Vaughn but he kept a tight leash on it as he walked into the sitting room. "I see the Devlins are taking good care of you."

She flashed him a mischievous smile as she sat down on the sofa. "Once I told Jack I was thinking of selling my share in the inn I found myself upgraded."

"Imagine that," he murmured, sitting opposite her.

"Yes, imagine that. So . . . what are you doing here, Mr. Tremaine? I hope you've not come to plead on my sister's behalf."

"No, I haven't. But I am here to save her inn."

She narrowed her eyes and sat forward, studying his face closely. "What is it about her? Why do you love her?"

Hearing the bitterness in her voice, seeing the jealousy buried deep in the depths of her gaze, Vaughn replied, "Why do you hate her?"

The question surprised her. Vanessa sat back against the couch. "I don't hate my sister."

"I find that surprising."

"I said I don't hate her. But I don't like her."

"Why?"

She made a face. "Do you know how many times I heard my father ask me, 'Why, V? Why can't you be more like Cherry?' She got good grades, she was involved in school events, town events, and she was always working at the inn, learning the ropes. Because I had no interest in any of those things, my father thought I was a loser."

"I'm sure he didn't."

"Well he made me feel less than her. It never bothered Charlie, but it bothered me. Daddy and his little girl."

"You're telling me this comes down to sibling rivalry?" *Jesus Christ.* This woman had never grown up.

"I couldn't care less about that," she snapped. "All I care about is making money. I tried to get involved in the inn, make it mine, and she wouldn't let me. It was boring anyway. So selling my share makes more sense."

"But you're making money from the inn."

"Yes, but I'll make it all up front this way, and more besides. It seems Devlin is desperate to get his hands on boardwalk property."

"You do realize that once he owns a share of the inn he will try to find a way to take the rest of it. I'll try to make sure he won't succeed but he's going to make Bailey's life a living hell."

"My sister's tough. And a little melodramatic. Devlin won't be able to take the inn. Charlie has a thirty percent share and Bailey has forty percent. They're the majority shareholders and Charlie won't let anything happen to the inn for Bailey's sake. My whole family adores my sister."

Studying her, Vaughn realized that Vanessa really had no idea of the ramifications of what she was doing. She underestimated Devlin entirely. "Stu Devlin attacked your sister. It doesn't concern you that you're selling your share to the people who would do that to her?"

Vanessa shifted uncomfortably. "It was never proven. Stu has an alibi."

"I was there, Vanessa. I walked into her office and found her struggling beneath him on the floor. I got to them just as he was about to put a fist through her face."

She looked away and he saw how hard she swallowed, how her fingers curled into little fists before she shook them out and turned back to him, her eyes blazing. "Look, are you going to make a counteroffer, or what?"

Bailey

It was four o'clock and I had nothing.

We had nothing.

We'd tried calling my sister but she wasn't answering her phone. We'd tried calling the Grand Hotel but she had a Do Not Disturb sign on her room.

I'd finally hung up on the conference call with my family after we realized we couldn't stop my sister from doing this. My brother and father were threatening to disown her. My mother wouldn't stop weeping.

As for me I was exhausted.

And scared.

I knew it was all too good to be true.

Having my beautiful inn and finding someone like Vaughn? Someone who got how much it meant to me, who didn't mind me working hard because he worked hard, too. Finding someone who gave me butterflies and made my heart pound, who excited me and exasperated me . . .

Being this happy?

I knew it was too good to be true.

I'd just assumed that it was the Vaughn part I'd lose.

Not my inn.

You'll be okay, I tried to tell myself.

"Bailey, can I get you anything?" Dahlia stood in the doorway to my office.

The worry in her eyes made the tears in mine spill over.

"Oh, sweetie." She rushed over and bent down to hug me tight.

I held on and lost it completely.

Moments later Dahlia pulled away and I was hauled up out of my chair. Through confusion and blurry vision I barely recognized him. His familiar cologne and his strong embrace penetrated.

I sank into Vaughn, crying into his neck as he hushed me while gently rubbing my back.

"Princess, please," he begged. "Stop. It's going to be okay."

"It's not!" I sobbed, not caring what a mess I was. "This is my home and Ian Devlin is going to come in and make my life hell and then try to take it from me and I might let him if he starts trying to change things and drive me insane and I just don't know if—"

"Stop, stop." Vaughn pushed me from him, his grip on my upper arms almost bruising. "No one is taking anything from you." He looked back at Dahlia, who stood with tears in her eyes. "Can you give us a minute?"

She nodded and left the room, closing the office door behind her.

I sensed a new tension in Vaughn. "What? What is it? What happened?"

He let go of me to pick up papers he'd settled on my desk. He handed them to me and I stared at them, still confused. The words on the paper started to make a little sense. "This is a contract. For Vanessa's share?"

"I bought it."

"What?" What the hell did that mean? "What?" I repeated.

"That was her plan all along."

"Explain from the beginning."

"When I left here after you said you didn't want my help . . ."

I winced at that. "I hurt your feelings, didn't I?"

He gave me this sardonic *I'm a man, I don't have feelings* look, but I knew. I'd unintentionally hurt his feelings.

"I'm an asshole."

Vaughn grinned. "You're not. You were just upset. While you were talking with your family I started to think, why would Vanessa warn you about the dinner tonight with the Devlins? Why give you a heads-up?"

My God, I hadn't even . . . Vaughn was right. That made no sense. Why give me time to find a way to stop her? And then, staring up at my handsome, very wealthy boyfriend, it hit me. "You."

His expression was grim. "Me. She wanted a counteroffer."

Nausea rose up inside of me. "She used me to get to you."

"Bailey—"

"Oh, God, no, Vaughn, I won't let you do this." I stood up, holding the contract out to him. "I won't let her manipulate you like this."

"It's done," he said firmly. "And I won't be talked out of it."

As he took hold of my wrist and tugged me into him, the contract crushed between us, I felt something building inside of me, something huge and overwhelming and terrifying.

"My lawyer is going to draw up another contract in the morning. I'm handing the shares back over to you."

"No." The word was out of me before I could stop it.

"No?" Vaughn cupped my face in his hands.

My legs felt like jelly, my stomach was a riot of butterflies, and I was pretty sure even my lips were quivering.

Vaughn frowned, concerned. "You're trembling."

I nodded, swallowing hard past the lump of emotion in my throat. "I want you to keep the shares."

"What? Why?"

Finally I dropped all my defenses and let everything I felt for him show. Vaughn tensed at the emotion in my eyes, and then the most beautiful sense of wonder began to fill his expression.

"I trust you," I whispered against his lips. "I need you to know that I trust you. I know that you would never hurt me, that you would never take this place from me. So keep the shares, and do it knowing that I trust you. That I love you."

I heard his sharp inhale, felt the slow exhale of it on my lips. "You love me?"

Scary, awesome, overwhelming joy filled me as I stared up at him. "I love you more than I've ever loved anyone. It scares the living daylights out of me."

He grinned. Huge. A boyish, wicked grin that made me feel like my heart might burst out of my chest. "Welcome to my world."

I laughed and pressed a quick, sweet kiss to his mouth. "I love you," I repeated.

"I love you, too." He kissed me back, this time long and deep and soulful.

When we finally came up for air I laughed again. "I didn't think today would end like this."

"It's not over." His voice was filled with sexy promise. "First, we agree that you're taking the shares back."

"Vaughn, no. How much did you even pay for those?"

At his shuttered look I felt my stomach drop.

"You overpaid," I deduced. "By a whole lot."

"Devlin was going to overpay. I had to overpay to win."

A thought occurred to me. "She could have turned it into an auction. Made a lot of money by pitting you against one another."

"No. She never wanted to sell to Devlin."

"She wouldn't have cared. She just wanted money."

"No," Vaughn assured me. "Your sister is a brat who has never grown up and yes, definitely resents you, but she doesn't hate you. She never wanted to see Devlin take this from you. This was just her very clever way of getting money out of me."

"The little brat is smarter than anyone gives her credit for." I snuggled into him, running my hands over his chest, needing the reassurance of him beside me. "I'm still sorry she did that to you. I'm ashamed of her."

"I know." He rubbed my arms in comfort. "But she's gone. She was packing as my lawyer drew up the contracts and faxed them over. When I left her room she was right behind me. I put her in a cab to the airport."

Regret washed over me. I hated that this was the state of affairs between me and a member of my family.

"I know you're hurting, but think of your sister's scheme in a positive light. She got one over on Devlin. He'll be sitting at that table in forty-five minutes waiting for the little brat to show up, wondering what the hell happened."

I tensed.

"What?"

I looked up at my boyfriend, mirth bright in my eyes, and he grinned in response, my thoughts clear to him.

"Really?" he asked.

"Come on." I grinned, making him laugh. "It'll be fun."

We left the inn after I fixed my tear-stained face and put on a nice dress. I'd given Dahlia and Mona a quick rundown of events and asked Dahlia to call my family, to explain everything was okay, and that I'd call them as soon as I'd finished my errand with Vaughn to explain all.

Although it was a mere short walk, Vaughn insisted on driving us to the Grand in his Aston Martin.

"Is it a guy thing?" I asked when he wouldn't tell me why. "A 'my dick is bigger than your dick' thing?"

He'd grinned. "Yes."

I'd laughed, so much joy and mischief inside me I was ready to burst with it.

This man, this beautiful man, had turned the shittiest day ever into the most beautiful day ever, ever, ever.

Holding my hand in his, I felt this weird sense of possessiveness I'd never felt before as we walked through the reception of the Grand. I gloried in the fact that this guy was *my* guy, and I felt a triumphant swing in my hips as women drooled over my guy and stared at me in envy. They thought he was beautiful and they envied me my beautiful. But what they didn't know was that Vaughn Tremaine's complicated soul was a million times more beautiful to me than the pretty face *they* saw.

I wasn't triumphant because my guy was hot.

I was triumphant because I'd found the kind of love that was hard to find, and I was finally brave enough to embrace it.

Mine.

All mine.

I tightened my grip on his hand and he looked back at me. "It'll be okay." He assumed I was nervous.

I just smiled. "I know."

He squeezed my hand. "You look beautiful."

"So do you. But you always do."

Vaughn just rolled his eyes at me, making me laugh, laughter that was squashed with a more subtle glee as the restaurant maître d', Arnold Rumer, stopped us.

"Our party is waiting for us," Vaughn said, and I followed his gaze.

He'd spotted Devlin. And he wasn't alone. Ian sat with his sons, Jack and Stu.

"Table, sir?"

"Mr. Devlin's."

"Ah." Arnold recognized me. "Miss Hartwell, of course. Mr. Devlin said he was expecting you."

Not the one he was expecting but technically . . . "Yes."

Struggling not to giggle like an impish child, I curled my arm around Vaughn's and he patted my hand.

"Keep it together, princess," he murmured, amused, as we followed Arnold over to Devlin's table.

Ian Devlin's face broke into a smug smirk at the sight of us. He waved Arnold away and studied us. The bastard thought he had me in the palm of his hands.

I couldn't wait to wipe that look off his face.

As for Jack, I let him see how betrayed I felt. He stared back at me, blank, apparently unmoved by my hurt.

Fine. No forgiveness or Emery Saunders for you, you jerk.

I sneered at Stu. "No ski mask tonight?"

Stu smiled, a smile that would never reach those cold eyes of his. "I don't know what you're talking about."

"Well, it's nice to see you, Miss Hartwell. And looking so well." Ian gestured to my black dress. "I see your taste in clothing doesn't translate to your taste in men, however."

"You're right. I have much better taste in men."

"You do know he's slept with every single attractive woman that's stayed at his hotel."

Vaughn's hand tensed in mine as he scowled at Devlin like he wanted to rip his face off.

"Really?" I tugged on Vaughn gently and he turned to face me. "Huh. So that's why you're so amazing in bed. Makes sense."

His lips twitched with laughter and his whole body relaxed.

I grinned as I looked back at an annoyed Devlin. "His experience speaks volumes." I even winked.

Jack coughed into his fist and I could have sworn he was trying to cover his laughter.

Hmm.

"Enough of this." Ian sighed as if he were weary. "I take it you're here to try and stop proceedings but your sister has made up her mind. However, let me put your mind at ease, Miss Hartwell. My involvement in our inn will be a good thing. I'm going to make it the most successful business on that boardwalk."

I bristled. "I wouldn't get ahead of yourself, Mr. Devlin."

"Oh? Because of the minority share? I know. But we'll work on that. Why don't we wait for Vanessa to arrive? Take a seat."

"That won't be necessary." Vaughn moved us closer to the table. "I put Vanessa in a cab a few hours ago. She's gone."

"What are you talking about?" Stu snapped.

"I'm talking about the fact that I made a counteroffer. She accepted." Vaughn put the contract on the table. "Now *I* own her share in Hart's Inn."

Fury colored Ian Devlin's face. I thought his head might explode it turned red so fast.

Vaughn took the contract off the table and handed it to me. "Tomorrow those shares get transferred back into Bailey's name." His expression changed as he turned back to them. I shivered at the sudden blast of chill from him as he let go of me to press his hands down on the table. It brought him closer to the Devlins so they could hear his quiet but very menacing caution. "I think I warned you before that if you did anything to upset Miss Hartwell, I wouldn't be too pleased. That's putting it mildly, Mr. Devlin. So . . . here's a little heads-up. One, if you come after her again, and I wouldn't if I were you, I will cripple you financially, piece by piece. And I think we both know that is not an empty threat. Two, I was on the defense before in this little war you're waging to get a piece of property on the boardwalk. But Hartwell, as it turns out, agrees with me. I'm making it my home. Permanently. That means I'm making it my business. Do you understand what I'm saying?"

Devlin just glowered at him.

Vaughn leaned closer. "I just came off defense, Devlin. You're now looking at an offense player."

"*You* are threatening *me*?" Devlin spat.

Vaughn exhaled, all cool and casual, as he straightened to stand beside me again. "Just a friendly warning." He shrugged.

Oh boy, my guy was sexy.

I took his hand and shivered at the feel of his fingers sliding through mine in response.

"Well." I gave them all a fake sweet smile. "I'm not nearly so eloquent and scary hot as Mr. Tremaine here, so I'll just say"—I leaned in to look at each one of them individually before focusing on the father—"you can kiss my ass."

Jack reached for his glass, drawing my gaze, and I knew this time I didn't miss the smile he was hiding behind his drink.

Apparently, I was never going to understand that man.

"You all have a nice evening now." I gave them a taunting finger wave as Vaughn led us out of the restaurant.

People stared, having clearly caught the vibe at Devlin's table, but I couldn't care less.

A floating cloud.

Yup.

I was on a freaking, beautiful, floating cloud.

Vaughn was quiet as we walked out of the hotel to his car, but instead of letting me go when we reached it, he pressed me up against it and started kissing me.

Really *kissing* me.

His fingers curled into my waist as his mouth moved over mine in hungry, carnal kisses that made my knees tremble. Thankfully I was holding on to Vaughn and I had the car behind me to keep me on my feet.

When he finally released my mouth I was breathless. I stared up at him wide-eyed, my cheeks flushed as I felt his erection press into my belly. "What was that for?"

Vaughn rubbed his nose over mine in this cute, tender way that was completely at odds with the lusty kiss he'd given me. "That was 'I love you and you look sexy as fuck in that dress and you getting off on getting one over on the Devlins has turned me on.'"

"I get it," I muttered against his mouth, "because you getting all menacing with Ian Devlin got me more than a little hot and bothered. How do you fancy taking me back to your place and pinning me to the bed?"

He laughed, his eyes growing dark with heat. "Considering how hard I am right now I think that's the only plan."

"You're losing control a lot in public these days, Mr. Tremaine," I teased.

"Only with you, princess." He gave me a quick, hard kiss, and then pulled back to open the car door for me. "In."

Chuckling at his demand, I got into the car as quickly as I could.

To my surprise, Vaughn didn't drive back to the hotel. Instead he drove us to the south side, on the outskirts of Hartwell where the wealthier residents lived. The large homes were mostly owned by people who summered in Hartwell—a pity as the gorgeous houses sat empty for most of the year.

I knew that Vaughn had a house right on the water because he let Jessica live there during her problems with Cooper. But I'd never seen it.

Silent, I let Vaughn take me into the house, and I drank it all in.

It was a picturesque home—white cladding, wraparound porches on the first and second floors, pretty garden—and as we walked through I was stunned to realize that the porch looked right out over the water. Amazing. Most of the houses here had large back gardens with pools, and a path that ran down to the beach and the ocean. Vaughn's home was on a private inlay on the coast. It didn't provide the same outside space at the back but I'd soon discover it had lots of land around it, and to the right side of the house was a huge pool and patio area.

Despite the beauty of the home, inside it was cold and modern. It was a bachelor's house with a large, glossy chef's kitchen with every appliance you could think of. The furniture was contemporary and everything was black, chrome, and white with some splashes of color here and there provided by artwork and sparse soft furnishings.

It was like something out of a magazine.

It wasn't a home.

I followed Vaughn out onto the back porch, and we were quiet as we watched the sun set over the water.

"Why don't you live here?"

"Because it made me feel lonely."

At his honest answer I moved into him, wrapping my arm around his waist to rest my chin on his shoulder. He kissed my forehead, sliding his arm around my waist, too. "You're not alone here now."

"I know." He studied me, brushing my hair off my face.

"You've gone all serious on me. What happened to the raging hard-on and the need to dominate me in bed?"

Vaughn gave a huff of laughter. "It's there, believe me. But I felt like sharing this place with you tonight."

There was something tentative about his words and I grew still, contemplative.

Today I'd made the decision to trust this man, to love him, and in doing so I'd made the decision to be myself around him.

Well, being Bailey Hartwell meant always speaking my mind.

"You want me to move in with you, don't you?"

His gaze flew to mine. "It's too fast."

"But you want to ask anyway," I teased, delight bubbling up inside of me.

"You don't think it's too fast?" he asked, sounding amazed.

"Vaughn." I laughed. "We've been dancing around each other for almost four years, and we've definitely been dancing around *this* for months. It feels like we've been together much longer, doesn't it?"

And then he slayed me with that smoldering, loving look of his. "It feels like I've loved you forever."

I melted into him. "Then ask me to move in with you."

"Bailey, will you move in with me?"

"Yes." I grinned, knowing people would think we were crazy and not giving a shit. "Yes, I'll move in with you."

Vaughn turned into me, and then instead of kissing me like I thought he would, he produced a small, black velvet box from inside his jacket.

The blood whooshed in my ears as my heart raced.

I stared down at the box he had pressed tight between us. And then he opened it.

A stunning white gold band with one large, simple, but beautiful diamond.

It was the perfect engagement ring for me.

My eyes flew to Vaughn's and my already ragged breath stopped at the fierce love in his gaze.

"I've been walking around with this for the past week, knowing it was soon, but needing to have it with me anyway. I wanted to have it for that moment when I finally knew you were ready. When you finally got it: that you and I are *it*. I'm usually a very patient man when I'm going after something I want, but I'm impatient to have you. I want our lives together to start. Now. So . . . Bailey Hartwell, will you marry me?"

The moment, my life in general, felt very surreal . . .

People would call us crazy.

I'd call myself crazy!

"People will call us crazy."

Vaughn smirked. "Aren't we?"

I laughed, staring into the eyes of this sexy, smart, brooding, complicated man, and not one part of me wanted to say no. Yes, I was scared, I was nervous, I was overwhelmed, but I couldn't imagine saying no. All I could imagine was waking up every morning to

Vaughn, going to work at the inn and returning home here—to a fully redecorated house—to him, and raising our kids here.

In Hartwell.

Together.

"Yes." I nodded, grinning like a lovesick teenager. "Yes, I'll marry you."

Joy lit up Vaughn's face, the kind of joy that melted away the hardness in him, until I knew I was staring at the boy in him, the boy who actually *did* believe in love and was no longer afraid to admit it.

My feelings for him consumed me and as he tried to kiss me and slide the ring on my finger at the same time, he tasted the salty tears of my happiness and he laughed.

And it was beautiful.

EPILOGUE

Bailey

"What are you doing?" Vaughn asked, the words soft. Tender.

"Staring at you."

When he'd come home early from the hotel, he had sat down on the black leather couch I was intending to get rid of as soon as I got into redecorating mode. He usually worked a little later than this—we both did—but Jess and Cooper were home from their honeymoon and we were heading over to the bar to hang out with them.

First, upon returning home, Vaughn had changed into something casual—although casual to him still consisted of a ridiculously expensive designer sweater that fit him far too well and a pair of designer dress pants that also fit him far too well. I was still getting ready, so he had wandered downstairs, where I found him sitting having a coffee on the couch. I had immediately crawled onto his lap. Just because.

"You've been staring at me awhile."

"You've been staring back."

He grinned. "It's a great view."

I smiled. "That's why I'm staring, too."

Vaughn huffed.

I'd come to realize over the last few weeks that my fiancé—yes, fiancé!—was uncomfortable with compliments. It was adorable.

"I love your eyes," I said.

"Yeah?"

"Don't lower them," I admonished, and he looked back up at

me. I spotted a hint of annoyance in them and chuckled. "I still remember the first time we met. I couldn't stop looking at your eyes. They are the most beautiful eyes I've ever seen."

"Bailey . . ."

"Do you know what I like best about them?"

He squeezed my waist again in answer.

"I like how cool they are with the majority of people. When you're talking to your staff or your guests you don't give away anything with those eyes. So focused, businesslike. And when you used to look at me, they were cold, hard, unflinching. Resentful." He opened his mouth to argue and I shushed him. "The first time I saw them change was one night at Coop's and he made you laugh. I'd never seen you laugh. And I saw then that you liked him. You respected him. It made it worse to know that you could look at someone like that, but it would never be me. Imagine my surprise then that first night we were together . . . that's the first time you looked at me and . . . You were worried about me.

"That's what made me want you." I brushed my fingers across his cheek, finding that I wanted to touch him all the time. "Your eyes. I love that I'm one of the few people in the world that gets to see how beautiful they really are when you care about someone."

"What are you trying to do to me?" he whispered, sliding his hands under my top.

"I just want you to know that as beautiful as you are—in a masculine way." I hurried to assure him at his scowl. "That's not what I love about you. It's not even what turns me on. Although it helps, not going to lie. But it's you. Just you. And how you feel about me."

He shifted his hips up, his erection pressing into my ass. "Have we got time?"

I glanced at the clock on the fireplace mantel. *Not really.* I looked back at him. "If we're really, really quick."

I squealed as he threw me onto the couch on my stomach. The heat of his body covered mine. "Quick and dirty?" he murmured in my ear as he slid his hand under my dress and caressed my ass.

Lust fluttered low in my belly. I nodded, breathless with anticipation.

"Hands and knees, princess," Vaughn demanded.

Following his instructions, my arms wobbled a little with tremors of excitement. The sound of him lowering the zip on his trousers sent white-hot arousal through me. My nipples peaked against my bra.

"Vaughn," I whispered hoarsely as he pushed my dress up to my waist and peeled my underwear down my legs to the bend in my knees.

His words were like gravel as he caressed my naked ass. "I've dreamt about this. You. On your knees. On this couch. That ring on your finger." He leaned over me, sliding his hands down and around my ribs to caress my breasts. His warm breath whispered over my ear. "Reality kicks my fantasy's ass."

Those words, mixed with his touch, excited me, and I felt that rush of excitement between my thighs. "Come inside me," I pleaded. "Just give it to me."

Understanding I was asking for the main course and no appetizer, Vaughn straightened and I felt the hot throb of him. His hands clasped my butt, his thumbs caressing the soft skin there.

"Anything you want, princess," he avowed, and then he was pushing inside of me.

The pleasurable burn shot through my limbs and I dropped my head on a gasp as I accommodated his thick length. "Yes, yes, yes."

I felt his deep answering groan in my nipples.

"Hard and fast or gentle and slow?"

"We only have time for option one," I huffed out.

"We have time for anything you want."

I smiled even though he couldn't see it. "Option one."

"Then I get to do it gentle and slow tonight."

"Not arguing with that."

Vaughn's laughter caught on a groan as he slid slowly back out. My back arched and I whimpered as he slammed back in.

He hadn't exaggerated.

It was fast and it was hard.

And all of it was fantastic.

The first thing I did when we walked into Cooper's a little while later was head straight over to Jess. She saw me coming and jumped off her bar stool to hug me hard. Her dark blond hair had been lightened by the sun, her skin was more tan than usual, and she even had little freckles across her nose.

"It's so good to see you." I squeezed her tight. "I missed you."

Jess pulled back and studied me with a knowing glint in her eye. "You just had sex," she whispered.

Surprise made me stiffen. I'd made sure before leaving the house that I was cleaned up, my hair and makeup fixed, my dress smoothed into place. "How do you know that?"

"Because Vaughn is wearing this smug, possessive look on his face right now that says 'I just got some.'"

I glanced behind me where Vaughn was hovering close to me and I laughed. She was right. He was.

"What?" He frowned.

"Nothing." Jessica withdrew to embrace Vaughn.

Vaughn was taken aback by the embrace, and a little uncomfortable. I laughed as he patted between her shoulder blades, unsure how to deal with the hug.

Jess wasn't the least bit bothered by his awkwardness, especially when he smiled at her. Her eyes widened. "You look happy."

"I am," he said. "So are you."

"I am," she agreed and shot a smile at Cooper, who was working behind the bar.

"Tremaine." Cooper held out his hand across the bar top.

Vaughn took it. "Lawson. I assume you had a good honeymoon."

He threw a heated look at his wife. "*Great* honeymoon."

"No need for details!" Dahlia said from her stool. "No one needs to know that."

"I don't know. I'd quite like to hear about it." Iris winked mischievously at Jess.

Jess rolled her eyes before focusing in on me again. "Everyone has been acting weird since we got here. They said you had something to tell us but they won't tell us what."

It hadn't been easy telling everyone about my engagement to Vaughn. I knew some people would think it was way too fast. Dahlia was a little concerned as were Iris and Ira. Emery thought it was wonderful and even Charlie sounded happy for me. My mom and dad were worried, and that was what upset me most. I just wanted them to be happy *I* was happy.

But Jessica was not a friend I worried about telling. She met and fell in love with Cooper in record time. She'd *so* get it.

"There's lots to tell you," I said as Vaughn stepped up beside me to take my right hand. "But first there's this." I lifted my left hand.

My stunning engagement ring winked in the light.

Jessica's lips parted in shock. And then she grinned. And then, "Oh. My. God!" She threw her arms around us both, making me laugh as Vaughn grumbled in discomfort.

"What?" Coop asked.

Jess let us go and grabbed my hand to turn it to him. "They're engaged!"

Cooper shook his head, grinning at Vaughn. "You move fast once you pull your head out of your ass, huh?"

On my fiancé's behalf I flipped Cooper the bird.

The laughter it caused in the bar among the regulars—who were of course watching us like we were an entertainment show, but I was used to it—died down quite abruptly. We all turned toward the door to see what had caused the room to quiet.

My parents.

Stacy and Aaron Hartwell.

Still familiar and well-loved.

And here.

Dad stood like the giant he was at six foot four, still big and broad-shouldered with a slight gut he had gained from a love of Irish lager. His handsome, ruddy face was one that the mere sight of automatically instilled in me a sense of safety and love. But right then I couldn't work out what was going on in those blue eyes of his as he took in the bar.

As for my mom, she was almost a full foot shorter than my dad, and currently tucked into his side. She looked young for her age, her auburn hair lightened with blond highlights and bouncing around her shoulders in a wavy chin-length cut that probably cost a small fortune. She was immaculate from head to foot, and it was easy to see where my sister Vanessa inherited her fixation about her appearance.

There were no people more different than Stacy and Aaron Hartwell but they loved each other so much. Kind of like Vaughn and me.

"Mom, Dad?"

They caught sight of me and moved toward us, and my eyes drifted to the man coming into the bar behind them.

"Dad?" Vaughn was shocked.

And just like that we were surrounded.

By my mom and dad.

And Liam Tremaine, my future father-in-law.

"What are you doing here?" I asked.

"All of you?" Vaughn added.

"Coincidence," Liam said. "You told me you're engaged. I had to come out and see for myself. I bumped into the Hartwells on the boardwalk."

"And you?" I said to my parents.

"All the crap with the inn was one thing, Cherry," Dad said. "But our daughter getting engaged . . . you really think we wouldn't fly out here to see if her fiancé is good enough?" He eyed Vaughn carefully. "I'm willing to give you a shot because of what you did for Cherry for the inn but it's a shot, not a free pass."

Vaughn stared at my father in perfect seriousness. "Understood."

"Oh, he's handsome, sweetie." My mom stared at Vaughn, apparently stunned. "So handsome."

Liam grinned. "Good genes."

I snorted in an attempt to hold in my hysterical laughter and Vaughn squeezed my hand. Hard. I knew without him telling me that he didn't want to laugh in front of my dad.

"So," Aaron Hartwell said loudly as he stared at my fiancé, "let's have a drink and get to know one another. Very well. Like blood type, medical history—including any and all sexually transmitted diseases—kind of well."

"Dad," I warned him.

But Vaughn looked at Cooper. "Drinks, Lawson. A lot of drinks."

Cooper was grinning, clearly enjoying Vaughn's predicament. "What is everyone having?"

As everyone ordered their drinks, regulars swarmed Mom and Dad, happy to see them again. While they were distracted catching up with the town, I snuggled against Vaughn and whispered, "I'm sorry about this."

"Don't be," he assured me. "I'm going to like your dad. I can tell."

"Really?"

"Yeah." He kissed me, a short, sweet kiss on the lips. "He's just protecting you, wants you to be happy. He and I are already on the same page."

I smiled and melted against him, still amazed that Vaughn had changed so much in the past few months.

No.

Not changed.

Just shed his fears to become the man he'd always meant to be. I'd helped him do that.

He had helped me to be brave, too.

And right then I knew I was exactly where I was supposed to be. The truth was that loving someone wasn't always as easy as the love songs made it out to be. In fact, loving someone could be the most terrifying thing a person could ever do in life. It was difficult to make yourself that vulnerable to another, to let him be the one person who got to see who you really are, flaws and all. Yeah, especially those flaws. It was scary asking someone to love those flaws.

But I'd done it. Vaughn had helped me be courageous enough to love fully with all my defenses down; to love every little thing about this man, good and bad, because I knew without fear or insecurity that Vaughn loved every little thing about me.

Don't miss how it all began in Hart's Boardwalk
in the first book in the series,

The One Real Thing

Available now. Turn the page for a special excerpt.

Jessica

One of my favorite feelings in the whole world is that moment I step inside a hot shower after having been caught outside in cold, lashing rain. The transformation from clothes-soaked-to-the-skin misery to soothing warmth is unlike any other. I love the resultant goose bumps and the way my whole body relaxes under the stream of warm water. In that pure, simple moment all accumulated worries just wash away with the rain.

The moment I met Cooper Lawson felt exactly like that hot shower after a very long, cold storm.

The day hadn't started out all sunshine and clear skies. It was a little gray outside and there were definite clouds, but I still hadn't been prepared for the sudden deluge of rain that flooded from the heavens as I was walking along the boardwalk in the seaside city of Hartwell.

My eyes darted for the closest available shelter and I dashed toward it—a closed bar that had an awning. Soaked within seconds, blinded by rain, and irritated by the icky feeling of my clothes sticking to my skin, I wasn't really paying much attention to anything else but getting to the awning. That was why I ran smack into a hard, masculine body.

If the man's arms hadn't reached out to catch me I would have bounced right onto my ass.

I pushed my soaked hair out of my eyes and looked up in apology at the person I had so rudely collided with.

Warm blue eyes met mine. Blue, blue eyes. Like the Aegean Sea that surrounded Santorini. I'd vacationed there a few years back and the water there was the bluest I'd ever seen.

Once I was able to drag my gaze from the startling color of those eyes, I took in the face they were set upon. Rugged, masculine.

My eyes drifted over his broad shoulders and my head tipped back to take in his face because the guy was well over six feet tall. The hands that were still on my biceps, steadying me, were big, long fingered, and callused against my bare skin.

Despite the cold, I felt my body flush with the heat of awareness and I stepped out of the stranger's hold.

"Sorry," I said, slicking my wet hair back, grinning apologetically. "That rain came out of nowhere."

He gave a brief nod as he pushed his wet dark hair back from his forehead. The blue flannel shirt he wore over a white T-shirt was soaked through, too, and I suddenly found myself staring at the way the T-shirt clung to his torso.

There wasn't an ounce of fat on him.

I thought I heard a chortle of laughter and my eyes flew to his face, startled—and horrified at the thought of being caught ogling. There was no smirk or smile on his lips, however, although there was definitely amusement in those magnificent eyes of his. Without saying a word he reached out for the door to the quaint building and pushed. The door swung open and he stepped inside what was an empty and decidedly closed bar.

Oh.

Okay for some, I thought, staring glumly out at the way the rain pounded the boardwalk, turning the boards slick and slippery. I wondered how long I'd be stuck there.

"You can wait out there if you want. Or not."

The deep voice brought my head back around. The blue-eyed, rugged, flannel guy was staring at me.

I peered past him at the empty bar, unsure if he was allowed to be in there. "Are you sure it's alright?"

He merely nodded, not giving me the explanation I sought for why it was alright.

I stared back at the rain and then back into the dry bar.

Stay out here shivering in the rain or step inside an empty bar with a strange man?

The stranger noted my indecision and somehow he managed to laugh at me without moving his mouth.

It was the laughter-filled eyes that decided me.

I nodded and strode past him. Water dripped onto the hardwood floors, but since there was already a puddle forming around the blue-eyed, rugged, flannel guy's feet I didn't let it bother me too much.

His boots squeaked and squished on the floor as he passed me; the momentary flare of heat from his body as he brushed by caused a delicious shiver to ripple down my spine.

"Tea? Coffee? Hot cocoa?" he called out without looking back.

He was about to disappear through a door that had *Staff Only* written on it, giving me little time to decide. "Hot cocoa," I blurted out.

I took a seat at a nearby table, grimacing at the squish of my clothes as I sat. I was definitely going to leave a butt-shaped puddle there when I stood up.

The door behind me banged open again and I turned around to see BRF (blue-eyed, rugged, flannel) Guy coming toward me with a white towel in his hand. He handed it to me without a word.

"Thanks," I said, bemused when he just nodded and headed back through the Staff Only door. "A man of few words," I murmured.

His monosyllabic nature was kind of refreshing, actually. I knew a lot of men who loved the sound of their own voice.

I wrapped the towel around the ends of my blond hair and squeezed the water out of it. Once I had wrung as much of the water from my hair as I could, I swiped the towel over my cheeks, only to gasp in horror at the black stains left on it.

Fumbling through my purse for my compact, I flushed with embarrassment when I saw my reflection. I had scary black-smeared eyes and mascara streaks down my cheeks.

No wonder BRF Guy had been laughing at me.

I used the towel to scrub off the mascara, then, completely mortified, I slammed my compact shut. I now had no makeup on, I was flushed red like a teenager, and my hair was flat and wet.

The bar guy wasn't exactly my type. Still, he was definitely attractive in his rough-around-the-edges way and, well, it was just never nice to feel like a sloppy mess in front of a man with eyes that piercing.

The door behind me banged open again and BRF Guy strode in with two steaming mugs in his hands.

As soon as he put one into mine, goose bumps rose up my arm at the delicious rush of heat against my chilled skin. "Thank you."

He nodded and slipped into the seat across from me. I studied him as he braced an ankle over his knee and sipped at his coffee. He was casual, completely relaxed, despite the fact that his clothes were wet. And like me he was wearing jeans. Wet denim felt nasty against bare skin—a man-made chafe monster.

"Do you work here?" I said after a really long few minutes of silence passed between us.

He didn't seem bothered by the silence. In fact, he seemed completely at ease in the company of a stranger.

He nodded.

"You're a bartender here?"

"I own the place."

I looked around at the bar. It was traditional décor with dark walnut everywhere—the long bar, the tables and chairs, even the floor. The lights of three large brass chandeliers broke up the darkness, while wall-mounted green library lamps along the back wall gave the booths there a cozy, almost romantic vibe. There was a small stage near the front door and just across from the booths were three stairs that led up onto a raised dais where two pool tables sat. Two huge flat-screen televisions, one above the bar and one above the pool tables, made me think it was part sports bar.

There was a large jukebox, beside the stage, that was currently silent.

"Nice place."

BRF Guy nodded.

"What's the bar called?"

"Cooper's."

"Are you Cooper?"

His eyes smiled. "Are you a detective?"

"A doctor, actually."

I was pretty sure I saw a flicker of interest. "Really?"

"Really."

"Smart lady."

"I'd hope so." I grinned.

Laughter danced in his eyes as he raised his mug for another sip.

Weirdly, I found myself settling into a comfortable silence with him. We sipped at our hot drinks as a lovely easiness fell between us. I couldn't remember the last time I'd felt that kind of calm contentedness with anyone, let alone a stranger.

A little slice of peace.

Finally, as I came to the end of my cocoa, BRF Guy / possibly Cooper spoke. "You're not from Hartwell."

"No, I'm not."

"What brings you to Hart's Boardwalk, Doc?"

I realized then how much I liked the sound of his voice. It was deep with a little huskiness in it.

I thought about his question before responding. What had brought me there was complicated.

"At the moment the rain brought me *here*," I said coyly. "I'm kind of glad it did."

He put his mug down on the table and stared at me for a long beat. I returned his perusal, my cheeks warming under the heat of his regard. Suddenly he reached across the table, offering me his hand. "Cooper Lawson."

I smiled and placed my small hand in his. "Jessica Huntington."

"Nice to meet you, Doc."